T0162655

THE ANGRY
GODS
OF AFRICA

YAO FOLI MODEY

Assoc. Professor of History

Order this book online at www.trafford.com
or email orders@trafford.com

Most Trafford titles are also available at major online book retailers.

Printed in the United States of America.

ISBN: 978-1-4669-6726-7 (sc)
ISBN: 978-1-4669-6725-0 (e)

Trafford rev. 01/04/2013

www.trafford.com

North America & international
toll-free: 1 888 232 4444 (USA & Canada)
phone: 250 383 6864 ♦ fax: 812 355 4082

In Memoriam

———∘∘∘❭❬❬∘∘∘———

Forty million vanished
in the middle of the night
And another forty million
died in the African heat
Cruelly killed in cold blood
The children were screaming
As the old died gurgling

The nations that exploited Africa
And milked the continent for labor
Also torched and burned villages
Hauling the youth out of the land
Shattering the pride of the people
Can the world forget so soon?
The mother of all tragedies

Did Africa get anything in return?
Only majestic-looking slave castles,
rusty cannons, chapels and scars
Tons of shame and humiliation
And a stigma that lingers to today
The nations that degraded Africa
It is time to erase this disgrace
You must make atonement
Contrite from the heart and seek
Forgiveness . . . love . . . reconciliation

Professor Yao Foli Modey
Cape Coast Castle, Ghana

A HISTORICAL NOVEL

————∘∘∘)✦(∘∘∘————

T HE CALAMITIES THAT BEFELL THE African people lasted for centuries. Millions were forcibly taken to the land of no return, crossing the boisterous Atlantic Ocean. It took a bloody civil war to liberate the African slaves that toiled on the plantations in the New World. Since then some progress has been made, though this did not come easily. So, we must savor every landmark and celebrate every progress.

It also took several landmark decisions to give the Africans in the Diaspora their freedom, whether it was citizenship, voting rights or integration into the social fabric where they lived.

It also took special acts of courage to integrate the schools and other institutions, but they did not come without conflict in some of the communities. These were very difficult tasks, but as the years rolled by, with the winters giving way to summers, the nation started to get adjusted to many of these changes.

It also took a special act of courage for the U. S. House of Representatives and the U. S. Senate to pass apology resolutions condemning the slavery past of this nation. Many critics think that these resolutions did not go far enough because they did not contain any kind of atonement for the victims, yet these are certainly optimistic signs on the horizon; they are movements in the right direction.

Then the election of President Barrack Obama as the first African-American president has become one of the most positive and progressive landmarks in the history of the United States. The jubilation among the African-Americans has been epochal and still continues even today. And the tears of joy and the jubilation over how far the nation has come have been phenomenal and monumental.

But was this gargantuan historic event an implicit apology for the American past of slavery? Whatever it was, it got African-Americans jubilating and feeling good about themselves. The event has made many of them optimistic about the future. Many who thought they would never see the day an African-American would take the oath of office as the president of the United States wept openly, smiled broadly and danced with tears of joy in the streets. His election also got the whole world, even the enemies of America to look at this nation differently, obviously with increased respect, cooperation and lots of admiration for what it stands for.

> "Though people do not admit it openly, we can say that the
> election of Barrack Obama as the president of the United
> States is an indirect apology for slavery!"
>
> A quote from the preface of my book
> "Tears of Mama Africa."
> Yao Foli Modey, 2009

It has been some two hundred plus years since the end of the European slave trade to Africa. And the tragedy has receded into historical memory with every passing day. The prayer of every African, and many Europeans and Americans as well, has been that this sort of iconoclastic catastrophe should never befall any group of people on any other continent.

Well, of course, Africans are happy that those dark days of suffering, excruciating agony, rivers of blood and torrential tears are over, though many of the effects of the trauma are still very much with us today.

But the irony is that two hundred years have still not healed the psychological scars that the slave trade and plantation slavery had inflicted on the African people. Whether in the East, South, North or West Africa, the picture has been the same abysmal calamity—suffering in the African land. Whether it is disease ravaging the people or civil strife tearing apart the social fabric of many nations, the lingering effects of this sordid slavery past are still largely responsible for the plight of Africa today.

The main obstacle continues to be the deep-seated inferiority complex—the most lingering legacy of the slave trade. Africans need some help from the powers that be to overcome the posttraumatic effects of the past, help to join the community of manufacturing and exporting continents as they struggle to take their place among other nations and continents.

Africans, however, need some help from the Europeans and Americans to end this forcibly imposed inferiority. The people of Africa need them to return the help that our ancestors had given them in the past so that the continent can become self-sufficient.

The time has come for the continent to rise up from the ashes of the slave trade and become prosperous once again.

PROLOGUE

THE PROFANE PAST

"THE ULTIMATE HORROR FOR THE African victims was in the dungeons below the slave castles. Inside these underground dungeons carved out of stones, long tortuous labyrinths of tunnels that led to the door of no return, the vibrant youths of the land, sobbing, down on their luck, screaming, struggling to be set free, unprepared for their twisted fate—began the journey into the unknown, hauled to "the land of no return."

"Their fate was sealed. At that point only the gods could come to their rescue. The gods could spring to action, could cause the slave boats to overturn or could help the victims to overpower the Oburoni crew usually on the high seas. The irony, however, was that during the long slave trade, the African gods went to sleep; they did not protect the people. The gods saw the soldiers fighting the invaders with everything they had and they even saw those that sacrificed their own lives for the freedom of others, but they still stood on the sideline in the long struggle between good and evil and greed and self-preservation."

He kept hearing the same voices from the dungeons anytime he visited the Cape Coast Castle on the beach. From the labyrinth of tunnels carved in stone underground, he heard the plea of the ancestors, the cry of the downtrodden. They were spirits that revealed themselves to him through the gentle breeze from the Atlantic Ocean.

They demanded atonement from the Oburoni people.

So he listened closely to the demands of the ancestors as they dictated the terms of atonement to him, their anger became visible to every member of the kingdom. The extent of their scars from the past, the death and degradation they had to endure on the plantations, the private farms where African slaves feared that tomorrow might never come for them, the place where mercy was the last thing on the owners' mind.

The victor forgets the past, but the victim never forgets the scars.

The king had told the emissaries that the stool and the elders were ready to hear their plea. They were ready to accept any reasonable terms of atonement. The reality was that King Gizenga had not given up on the Oburonis one day returning to the kingdom to finally open up and tell the African people what they truly felt in their hearts all these years and even across generational lines. Not making up excuses, not blaming the African chiefs and kings, blaming the victims for the past, but they would place before the kings and their elders what they truly felt in their hearts—apology and terms of atonement.

The ancestors would have to be a part of the deliberation, make their wishes known and accept or deny the atonement package. The king had seen the anger on the ancestors' faces, heard their voices roaring for justice and the venom in their hearts.

The continent had lost millions in the tragic encounter.

In spite of the fact that the tragedy ended more than two centuries ago, the traumatic impacts still linger on.

The king would wait patiently for the delegation to arrive, wait to welcome them and get some answers from these visitors to questions which had lingered on many minds for hundreds of years.

Thus he would decide to get the priests to pour libation, to reach the god of music and give the annual sacrifice to the gods. He would not try to defy these gods, though he did not believe the gods did what they were expected to do during the slave trade past

He was anxious to find why their ancestors did what they did to their fellow human beings, questions that still raged inside his soul and troubled his mind.

One picture clearly emerged from his search and research, and this clearly dominated his mind. The majestic and impregnable slave castles nestled along the so-called African Slave Coast, the cannons, the lighthouses, the slave chapels, the slave boats, were all meant to facilitate the Oburoni slave trade to the African continent. These castles provided impregnable strongholds for the thousands of slave traders, whether they were brokers, dealers, transporters, missionaries, government officials or adventure-seekers, the facilities were meant for their use.

The unwanted influx of these intruders ruined the African continent.

The continent was vulnerable, helpless and defenseless as it fell to the technologically superior weapons of the slave traders, the invaders and the labor-seekers.

Then the griot saw the youths fleeing from the slave traders, falling down like Harmattan leaves, brown, yellow, dry, and they fell one after the other or on top of one another, in small clusters on the grasslands and the forests. Many of them succumbed to the harsh and voracious Harmattan winds that came like hyenas from across the Atlantic Ocean.

Africa was overpowered, ran out of time, its future was doomed. Its era of glory and ascendancy had been eclipsed by the outsiders, alien forces that were fueled by greed and other deadly passions.

Contrary to what people report, though the Oburonis overwhelmed the chiefs with their weapons, the African leaders did not sit idle. They tried to protect their birthright, their children and their way of life. They tried to ambush the invaders, to hide their gold in the ground. They tried to protect the children by hiding them in small platoons of warriors inside the forests to evade the dragnet of horror.

What the Oburoni did to the land and to the leaders still lives on in ill repute in songs, proverbs and adages on the griot's tongue all across these hallowed lands. It is no surprise that it still lives on in the minds of the African people today.

The griot has to fight his anger. Whenever he remembers how the Oburonis shipped his ancestors to the land of no return, his heart explodes with thoughts of vengeance. Lately, however, his spirit of reconciliation seems to have overpowered the part of him that yearns for vengeance, for accountability . . . the time for reconciliation is on the horizon, he mused.

He wants to find out everything about the slave castles, the dungeons, the cannons, the muskets, the rum and the shackles. He can never forget the voice of his aged great grandfather admonishing him every night, standing over him like a tall mahogany tree, restless, angry and telling him how tired he was, how he needed help to cross over to the world of the ancestors, to get the eternal rest he so badly needed.

Was this a ghost or reality?

There'd been several changes over the years, after the iconoclastic slave trade, but Africa has still not healed from the chaos, from the past brutalities, and from the trauma. It has not emerged from the ashes of destruction, from the lingering effects of all the wars that the Europeans and Americans and their henchmen had waged on the African people, and on its institutions.

They wanted the simplicity of life, the naturalism, the relative peace and the burgeoning civilization that the ancestors had before the advent of these Oburoni locusts back. They regretted how the new generations would never know this relative bucolic life of peace and serenity.

This glorious past had gone up in smoke.

The continent is still combating the eternal stigma of inferiority complex that the Oburoni people, the uninvited European guests, had stamped on the African people. They had brought this old continent to its knees as a result of centuries of repeated onslaught. Africa had paid a stiff price—a civilization quickly eclipsed and a people badly crippled on their own continent, crushed inside the ashes of history.

If you think the Africans have forgotten the tragedy, then think again. In spite of the few high sounding apologies, they are still waiting for some sort of appeasement from the descendants of those whose ancestors had committed these atrocities against their people and did so with such impunity. Some sorts of appeasement must follow these genuine and hypocritical apologies.

They are particularly unhappy with the descendants of the culprits, who instead of showing remorse, decided to add insult to the tragedy by pretending that the past is gone and buried under the carpet of history. And if they recall the tragedy at all, the shame overcomes their senses and so they end up blaming these embarrassing deeds on the Africans themselves.

This has triggered anxiety and anger inside the rank and file of the African ancestors.

To the African people, the horror and the suffering are still as fresh in our collective memories as the fresh tropical lemons of today. These are wounds deeply buried in our psyches, too traumatic to conquer, and definitely too dehumanizing to continue to relegate into historical oblivion.

As for King Gizenga, he wanted to let go of the slave trade past, but how could he let his mind rest from the onslaught the Portuguese, the British, the Dutch, the Danes, the Spanish and all the other nations that looted the African continent, shed the blood of the people freely and used the sweat of the Africans for years without any accountability.

He heaved a deep sigh. "These were some sad times for our continent," the king told the audience. "Millions of youths died in the forests, lost their lives along the shorelines, perished on the savanna grasslands, fought on the mountain ranges and drowned in the rivers of blood or inside the mighty Atlantic Ocean. The chiefs were helpless. They were unable—or rather incapable—to stop the carnage, because the Oburoni people simply overwhelmed them with their technologically superior guns, especially their deadly cannon."

Why were our ancestors so clearly vulnerable?

"You don't have to wonder why the African leaders had to obey the Oburoni demands for monthly, quarterly, semi-annually or annual slave quotas. They had to comply or else they ended as slaves themselves. Even sometimes these Oburoni slave traders, demoted, replaced or even killed some of the leaders for insubordination or for opposing their slave quotas," he told them.

"Well, King Gizenga, it was horrible. Obviously, you have been very much touched by these facts. But didn't some of the African chiefs collaborate with the Oburoni traders?" the lady asked angrily, flipping through some pages of notes she brought along.

"Well, under pressure from the invaders, some of the African leaders collaborated with the slave traders to avoid becoming victims of the ongoing slave trade. They became traitors to their people, not out of choice, but because that was the only avenue of self-preservation left for them. It was suicidal to refuse to obey orders from the cannon-blazing merchants, who brandished death in their faces, and forced the leaders to exchange their people as slaves for guns and more slaves for more guns."

"To the African people it was an enterprise of shame, an abomination—it sowed the seeds of destruction. It was the pinnacle of man's inhumanity to his fellow man."

"How did the African people manage to survive the insatiable greed of the invaders, the endless and deadly onslaught and did so for centuries?" she asked. She heaved a deep sigh of sorrow, she was becoming remorseful.

"There is the African saying that the gods wipe off flies from all animals that have no tails," he told the lady. The lady lowered her head, embraced him and began to shed silent tears, after he told her that. "Sorry, you have become so overwhelmed. But the continent somehow survived, though it has been badly crippled and had continued to limp along, though miserably even to today."

For centuries there was grief in the land. The future for the inhabitants of this once very proud continent became extremely bleak in the ensuing one-sided warfare. It was their superior weapons against the impotent ones they'd supplied to the African chiefs. The rusty, defective muskets the same Europeans supplied to the chiefs could not compete with the latest imported cannons from Birmingham, England or Copenhagen, Madrid or Amsterdam.

As the Asafo soldiers wielded their impotent guns against the enemy traders, some went in ambush to mount surprise attacks. They realized that no matter how hard they fought, they could not stop the insatiable thirst of the Oburonis for the African youths.

The African leaders hated the raids into their villages at dawn. They had to defend their homes in the darkness. They had to stop the loss of several youths in the one-sided battles. The Oburoni slave traders usually captured the victims after they'd burned down the houses, flushed out the victims into the open, then caught and shackled these fleeing youths.

It was not surprising how the Oburonis drowned their conscience in barrels of rum and kegs of whiskey. They lured the African leaders with trinkets, brass pots, broadcloth—active baits—firearms and rum and forced them indirectly to commit the utmost treason—acts of betrayal against their own people.

So, saddled with guilt from their bloody raids, they would sit in the courtyard at night and drink themselves into drunken stupors, to numb their pain from the guilt and to ease their conscience. After days of slave raiding, but for the booze, how else could they sleep at night from all the atrocities they had committed?

By the time it was all over, the Oburonis had forcibly hauled out of the continent over forty to fifty million of Africa's brightest and vibrant youths, the land's toughest workforce, the pride and joy of Mama Africa. The thirteen to thirty-five-year-olds all across the Slave Coast were snatched inside the dragnets of the slave catchers, amidst gunshots that echoed across the savannas and reverberated against the long Atlantic shoreline.

The only gifts the ancestors passed down to the many generations were rivers of blood and torrential tears of sorrow along the so-called African Slave Coast. Whether it was the Volta, the Gambia, the Senegal, the Niger or the Congo Rivers, the streams of blood which flowed into them were copious. It left the next generations with chaos, endless graves of heroes, remnants of Oburoni cannon and tales about how the ancestors fought gallantly against the Oburonis, but lost every time, though they died fighting on their feet. They fought bravely and bled freely into these rivers like patriots, but fell gallantly, broken hearted, disappointed, and most of them ended up as chattel for the Oburoni slave traders.

While the slave trade was going on, the Africans had been unable to grow food on their farms and doing so to full capacity. They could not attend funerals in neighboring villages. They could not teach the youths the way to economic success. In essence, they could not proceed with their lives the way they'd done before the advent of the insatiable Oburoni Harmattan from Europe.

King Gizenga, the king of the Bakano people, reluctantly counted the marks on the palace wall. These were marks the ancestors made to record the exodus of the departed, the abducted and the stolen. However, all they could do was to let out long, deep sighs. The king took his frustration on his wives to produce dozens of children, on his mahogany tobacco pipe, and like the Oburoni traders, drowned his grief inside calabashes of palm wine.

He wondered how long the past would continue to defeat the present.

"The Oburonis destroyed the peace in the land from the day they set foot on the land. They'd let loose in our mist forces that have continued to torment and divide us even to today," the chief of Edena said in a strangled voice. "There is no hope of recovery on the horizon for us as African people."

"The brutality and the chaos were horrible. The slave trade ended long ago, and the Europeans seemed to have moved on with their lives. Some of their descendants do not even remember what their ancestors did to the African continent. Others vaguely remember how African slaves had helped their ancestors, but they simply do not care about what their ancestors did in the past," the Queen Mother of Bakano, Nana Ayesha, said angrily.

"The psychological damage the Oburonis inflicted on the people still lingers on today. It'd hindered the continent from literally getting back on its feet, it has prevented it from making any great strides in the modern global economy," the king told the audience.

"The Europeans and Americans must put some of what they'd milked out of the continent for so long in the dark past back into the land," the linguist, the official assistant to the king, declared. "The traumatic nature of the tragedy and the sheer scope and magnitude of the horrors, the scars, the humiliation, and the posttraumatic effects, the wounds of the past from the brutal trade, still linger on in ill-repute to today and will continue its notoriety till the culprits take steps to address this sordid past."

"How can we ever heal from this squalid ordeal?" the griot asked the large gathering. "The flashbacks from the slave trade have not ended. Mama Africa and her offspring are still saddled with deep sorrow, pain, frustration, as they face discrimination all over the globe."

The Queen Mother rolled her eyes as she thought about the lost youths and the traumatized institutions. "The refusal of Europeans and Americans to make atonement for the evils of the past have displeased the ancestors, but they would not allow the debt the Oburonis owe the continent to continue forever without accountability," the Queen

Mother pointed out bluntly. "Nobody should be allowed to get away with such atrocity against another group, not without accountability."

"You think they would extend a helping hand to heal the damage that their ancestors had left behind at the time the Africans extended help to them, though forcibly," the king inquired. "That would probably ease things or calm down the anger of the ancestors."

"But some of their descendants have continued to deny the past, maybe because they are embarrassed or have no guilty conscience," the griot said. "But those that realize the "sins of their ancestors" are willing to make some reasonable amends for the past."

"Well, some of their scholars and a few erudite African stooges, sad to admit, are still busy denying the primary role the European slave traders played in the destruction of the African continent, in spite of the fact that the Oburonis conceived, masterminded, orchestrated and brought the trade to the continent. Some of them, at best, have admitted that their ancestors conducted the slave trade, but have blamed the tragedy on the Africans leaders. They put the blame on the Africans by saying that the ancestors sold their own to them," Dokuwa said. "They have chosen to add insult to the injury, and ridicule to the lingering pain and suffering. Against our poorly armed soldiers, how could our ancestors prevent their canon-wielding Oburoni ancestors from catching the slaves of forcing the leaders to procure the slave cargo?"

"Maybe it is the guilt they still bear or the fear of vengeance from the descendants of the victims that continues to haunt them," the Queen Mother said. She broke a piece of kola nut into two halves, chewed one half noisily and reluctantly broke into a sad dirge—the African blues. A group of women surrounded her, in a large circle and filled the palace with sentimental dirges to comfort the departed souls—the ancestors.

"How can they forget so easily that their ancestors arrived on the African shores uninvited, and they trickled in like the white locusts? They had guns in hand, greed in their hearts and then they forced their labor needs on the African people using their cannon and muskets. Have they forgotten that when it was all over, they'd hauled away somewhere from forty to fifty million African youths like cattle, taking them beyond the ocean, and many million others were killed or maimed. An equal number had perished in the ordeal," the women sang in the dirges.

"How could they so easily forget this bitter truth, unless they are a people who have no conscience?"

"They have not forgotten, they are just too embarrassed by the level of brutality and too ashamed about the gruesome nature of the crime of their ancestors, so they pretend not to address it," the griot said. "They could never forget the tragedy, not even if they try to do so. It is just too bitter for us or too embarrassing or too shameful for them to ever forget."

"This was the time that men slept with loaded guns next to their beds. It was the time that women hesitated to go to the farm to get foodstuff to cook for their children. It was also the time that people could not visit their relatives outside their own villages," the linguist said. "These were hard and sad times in the land, and it lasted like eternity."

"The only time we would let them forget this is if the world ends or explodes into a conflagration through an accident of history?" the king told the crowd.

King Gizenga hoped that after centuries of silence, despite some feeble voices of apology, the sufferings of the continent must finally be addressed. "Those who'd violated the land can no longer escape the anger of the ancestors," he told them.

"They cannot shift the blame to the African victims anymore. The moment of atonement has finally arrived," the griot announced, anxious to let them know the wishes of the ancestors. "The ancestors are determined to avenge the dead—time for demanding answers, appeasement and reconciliation."

"From the look of things, the ancestors have run out of patience," the priest replied. "They are tired of waiting; they are on the move. They have decided to follow the path of vengeance."

"These traders had destroyed millions of mahogany and ebony trees in the land, but, as a people, we have tried to forge ahead in the modern global economy. The damage, however, had been too deep and so the progress has been very slow," the linguist said. "Africa is in dire economic need today. Africans need help to penetrate the walls of the modern global economy and join the rank and file of other new progressive, emergent nations."

"The Oburoni people must put an end to the badge of shame that their ancestors had placed on the African continent," the king said. "Just like some of the Asian nations have excelled in recent years, the Oburonis must help Africans to master the process of manufacturing, which can lift our economies out of the doldrums."

Though it ended centuries ago, the horrible past of the slave trade has been like a dark cloud over the descendants of those whose ancestors had wronged Africa. Not just a dark cloud of shame, a dark cloud of guilt and torment, but also a sordid past calling for contrition and expiation.

"Obviously, the new generation did not participate in the slave trade and plantation slavery. Some of them continue to make this point forcefully, but they have benefited from its fruits?" the griot pointed out with absolute candor.

Trent, the other activist for peace, sat in bed pondering how best to bring about peace and end the lingering conflict in the land. How could he forget the inscription on the ancient Egyptian tablet—remorse, accountability, penitence, atonement and reconciliation?

"Well, in the end, there must be reconciliation and after that, there would be no more burdens of guilt inside any heart. The final peacemaker will rise up and lead the movement to end the wrath of the ancestors," Zogan, the priest declared. "There would be no more tornadoes or hurricanes?"

Then the three activists carried the ancient tablet from the shrine of Chucalisa high above their heads and placed it at the feet of the peace maker, the chosen one the sacred tablet predicted would emerge.

Then the team turns to the falcon for answers. The bird glides on the rays of the sun to tell the people about the advent of the peacemaker, so they wouldn't give up hope and succumb to despair. This colorful bird flew higher and higher into the sky—spreading the badly needed new hope, ushering in a warm climate of reconciliation and an era of mutual coexistence.

"The moment of truth has come—different people one destiny," the falcon muttered. The king was sitting on his golden stool with his elders when news of the peacemaker broke and spread quickly all over the kingdom. Many became intoxicated with hope and happiness, as the Africans became optimistic, expecting brighter days ahead.

He hoped that the new rising sun, the groundswell of apologies and goodwill from many of the Oburoni sympathizers would lead to final reconciliation.

Africa's priority is no longer words of sympathy—nor is it vengeance for the past. It is remorse, atonement and reconciliation.

The sun rose and shone brighter all over Ifriqiya land. The farmers grew food in abundance and finally learned to preserve some of the food. The youths learned to manufacture goods and shipped them for sale in foreign lands.

The descendants of the Oburonis must get Africa back on its feet. And with several blasts, the thunder god has spoken loudly. The god of hurricane has demonstrated its anger. The tornado god twirled ominously, leveling houses, tearing down businesses, wiping out beaches and flooding several cities in the New World. Are these the final warning events?

Gazing into the rainbow, the leaders saw a continent being placed back where it used to be in the past before the European and American Oburoni slave traders arrived to unleash their evil passions.

ACKNOWLEDGEMENTS

———∘∘∘ ❧❦❧ ∘∘∘———

I OWE A DEBT OF GRATITUDE to several people who encouraged me in the project. To my colleagues Professor Mark Ridge, Dr. Alisea McLeod, Jacqueline Slater, Dr. Marco Robinson, Dr. Namdi Anosike, Dr. William D. Scott 111, Dr. Margaret Delsahmit and Dr. Paul C. Lampley, all the scholars that gave me the necessary encouragement when the facts shocked my senses and my willpower sometimes floundered.

To Dr. Charles W. Crawford, my mentor and friend, Dr. James Chumney and Dr. David Smiley all those who guided me through my graduate work in the United States. How can I forget the legendary and wonderful chair the late Dr. Aaron Boom for his help? So my deepest gratitude also goes to Deans Henry Stroupe, Percival Perry and Dr. Howell Smith for helping me transitioned to the USA.

To my family Carl, Roland, Bernard, Kweisi, Kafui, Attafe, Sitso and Mansa and Da Grace, I say thanks a lot for just being there for me. How can I forget Asiwome, Guy Su? To my children Akofa, Wovenu, Kofi and Adzoa I salute and thank you all for being what you all are? Thanks a lot.

To the staff of Cape Coast and Elmina Castles, I say thanks for making the research a rewarding experience for me and for my colleagues.

To my friend and long time researcher the late Kamkam da Costa—with whom I carried out the research and discovered lots of the facts from the Cape Coast and Elmina area, I say thank you very much and rest in peace. This novel and "Tears of Mama Africa" reflect your thoughts as well as mine.

To my friend Tom P. who made some valuable contributions to the project, I can't thank you enough.

To my students Ismael Alonso and David Justin Smith for translating the manuscript into French and Spanish my thanks.

ONE

ZOGAN THE PRIEST OF THE god of music was not very popular among the inhabitants of the kingdom. They hated him because he represented the bitter memory of a god that did not help its people in their time of need during the endless years of the slave trade. He was serving a god that stood by in the past when the Oburoni slave traders were shamelessly ravaging and pillaging the land. The slave raiders were known to have actually used this god to facilitate the rounding up of youths that ended as slave cargoes in the land of no return. It created a backlash against him for serving a god that had let his people down.

The annual festival was in full blast and thousands had come from far and near to remember the ancestors. The seven rams were ready for the sacrifice and the seven new priestesses were seated next to the hearth as the red hot charcoal continued to burn out of control. The hot blazing tropical sun lashed at the faces of the participants revealing the fears and hopes of many of them.

The sun drenched the silvery shona stone and lashed at the effigies of the god of music, which were buried in the brown loamy clay. The sun shone directly into the faces of the seven voodoo priests who stood guard at the door to the inner sanctuary of the shrine. They had short sharp spears in hand ready to defend the shrine.

These priests also guarded the seven virgins who were seated in the front row, who were directly facing the gigantic hearth. They were scared, depressed and nervous with some of them shedding silent tears as they tried to hide their stunningly beautiful faces. Except two who remained stoic throughout the festival, all the remaining five continued to shed silent tears, though they had been warned to keep their composure throughout the event. They were obviously terrified and worried about their fate.

Who would not be afraid for his or her dear life when the high priest stood over these young beautiful girls brandishing an axe as if he was an executioner ready to send them off to the land of no return, to the world of the ancestors, where they would serve the gods eternally in the afterlife?

The thousands of festival participants from all across the globe sat in the shrine and stared piercingly at a fairly large audience that looked on the proceedings with suppressed anger, with intense concern for the fate of these young virgins.

In the new African cosmology, the virgins no longer had to fear for their lives at the ancestral shrines. They could be asked to remain silent for seven years and not indulge in sexual activities, or they could be married to the old head priest who represented the god without any acts of objection or defiance from them.

These young girls sat quietly as they played the part of what they were supposed to be—the wives of the god of music—obedient, amiable, subdued and quietly resigned to their fate. Though everyone noticed their stunning beauty, nobody dared to save them. Their bosoms were protruding enticingly and they had faces that looked exquisite outwardly, though they were worried about the traditional seven years of marriage to a god that everyone hated in the land. Any wonder that their hearts were filled with churning hurricanes and twirling tornadoes.

The shrine of music where the ritual was taking place was inside the Cape Coast Castle. This castle was a majestic-looking palace, an abode fit for royalty, though this was a notorious slave castle, a place of horrendous brutality that still lives on in ill-repute. In the past, a young virgin used to be sacrificed each year to the god of music. But the last sacrifice took place more than a century ago because the present had defeated the past. So there had been no such virgins sacrificed for the last century or two for the gods.

The festival was pure mirth, an event filled with pure excitement and lots of reverence for the heroes of the past. There were boat races, fishing competitions, libations, dancing, wrestling and communicating with the past. At the height of the festival, the people would drink till they became intoxicated and then dance to the "kpalongo" music from the youths.

Then the people of Bakano and Oguaa would gather next to the lagoon to remember the souls of the people that'd departed the land centuries ago. They would play the drums and dance in remembrance of the victims of the European and American slave trade. They would remember distant family members who were forcibly hauled away in the wild orgy of greed that had engulfed the land.

Then there were reenactments of scenes from the past, recreations of slave dealers chasing the young men and women inside the forests, across the green grasslands, placing shackles on the feet of dozens of youths and leading them in rows of two toward the shore. The blistering rays of the sun blinded the women who were shedding tears for their lost loved ones.

"Don't just stand there in the open, run to the forest and take cover," King Gizenga, a monarch ordained in the Bakano tradition, thundered as he stood in front of the crowd determined to rid the land of the pests. He was tall, dark, and good-looking and he had broad shoulders. He was pensive and dignified in demeanor especially when he spoke to the audience. He wore a lot of gold jewelry, one of the attractions of the Oburonis to the kingdom, and what gave the land its name.

King Gizenga looked at the "Wall of Shame" and saw the marks on it. They were the record of the pain and suffering of his ancestors. "Who could forget how many souls had suffered at the hands of the locusts from beyond the blue ocean—the greedy Oburoni locusts who arrived secretly in the middle of the night and gorged on the youths like blood-sucking vultures in the forests and across the grasslands."

He knew that his ancestors fought gallantly to stop more marks from going up on the walls, but the weapons the Asafo soldiers had in their possession were no match for the powerful cannon of the slave traders. So the griot had to place more marks on the wall, marks that symbolized the millions of youths that were forcibly taken out of the kingdom to the "land of no return" and were never seen or heard from again.

Meanwhile, the god of rain drenched the forests, in spite of its threats to withhold the rains from the land for several years. So the river banks were swollen, pregnant with fear and anxiety. Fortunately, however, the god of thunder was silent during the events, so the festival could go on.

The fetish priestess of Oguaa was able to appease and calm down the goddess of fertility. She made it possible for those women who were anxious to bear more children to do so by getting the fertility goddess, still angry and determined to seal the womb of every woman in the land, to prevent any more children from entering the world and ending in the hands of the slave traders. She changed the mind of this goddess and allowed the women to have more children.

Yaa Fosuwa, the oldest priestess of the god of music, could never be outdone. She wore the purple topless dress and sat next to the inner sanctuary like the supreme conscience of the shrine. Her physique was like that of an Amazon that was ready to do battle on behalf of the ancestors, ready to defend the land. Her eyes were as red as fireballs and they were searching and piercing. Her face was beautiful, though rough at the edges and her arms were powerful. Her sparkling set of white teeth that were tainted from years of coffee drinking and nibbling on kola nut were visible when she started singing.

Her headgear was knotted in the middle like a hat, with a black bow in the middle sticking up like a solitary diadem that reached into the bright blue sky. At the height of the music she would jump up and down like a possessed soul waiting on the god to descend into the arena. In the end, she would drink a lot of moonshine and pass out in the inner sanctuary, intoxicated, immobilized just as the ancestors did in those distant days of the notorious slave trade.

The kings and the elders sat on their ivory, mahogany and golden stools listening to the voices of desperation of the victims from down below the infamous dungeons of despair. Why the ancestors were still roaming about and not resting in the ancestral world and why they were without the solace they needed, was not only scary but also troubling for the leaders.

Arguing loudly, the leaders expressed their displeasure as the Oburonis said that the Africans had sold their own people into slavery. The response to that charge is that this in not the whole truth and that nothing could be farther from the actual historical reality. These critics hold these views because of the guilt they still harbor within them.

The ancestors have waited in vain for years for the descendants of the slave traders to return to our shore to seek atonement, but they have finally realized that was not going to happen. So, they decided to go on the offensive to seek justice for the free slave labor that the Oburoni people had enjoyed for nearly four centuries at the expense of the African people—sweat—blood—lives . . . and not to forget "the centuries of sorrow." The ancestors have decided to hit the land with tornadoes, hurricanes and floods, evil harbingers from the gods.

The griot was very angry. He told the gathering about how African slaves had made it possible for several governments to be standing tall today economically, enjoying a lot of material prosperity. The African help they got in the past made several countries materially wealthy; some have become wealthy beyond their wildest expectations.

Throughout these years they have not shown any gratitude toward Africa for the help they'd received, the millions of slaves they had taken. The damage Africa suffered, the losses it sustained was as debilitating, more than the tornadoes in the New World and more than the hurricanes and floods had done.

"Where is the atonement for the past injustices?" the griot asked.

The resolutions of apology passed a few years ago have given the Africans on the continent and their descendants in the Diaspora a slim glimmer of hope. The volatile debates before the resolutions of apology were signs of hope, but the fear of being held liable for the horrible deeds of their ancestors have prevented the lawmakers from confronting the past headlong and doing the right thing. Instead, they chose to swallow their best intentions. They have refused to make atonement for the misery and chaos Africa had to endure for centuries in the past.

The movement did not end in those hallowed halls of erudite deliberations. What could they do to appease the victims? Though they failed to make any promises of material atonement, they'd opened the door for the victims and their ancestors to go all out to demand some accountability, and get some redemption for the past.

Those who take for granted the profound sacrifice Africa made to help several countries, the labor the African youths provided to make them successful and to thrive must think again. The time for soothing words has ended. It is time for apotheosis; a comprehensive ritual to forgive those whose ancestors masterminded the slave trade, orchestrated plantation slavery or did both.

America has enjoyed the tremendous wealth the African slaves had generated with their labor. The wealth from the help the slaves provided reaches into trillions of dollars and the victors had continued to enjoy the proceeds from this horrible enterprise of shame even today.

They seem to forget the role the unhappy and aggrieved African continent played in the prosperity of their countries. How could they forget how the slaves used to pick cotton, to tend sugarcane plantations, to grow tobacco, to harvest rice and to process indigo? They provided the necessary household help on the plantations to make the masters' lazy lifestyles of hedonism possible?

The African ancestors had sacrificed so much for these countries to rise up and shine economically. These countries are doing so impressively today. Indeed, they are like glittering stars basking on the modern economic horizon. The helpers, the African "field hands who worked from sunup to sundown" are resolved to no longer sit idle, but to go on the offensive and demand atonement for the past.

Some of the descendants of those who did the slave trade have felt the guilt in their hearts. Their ancestors once lived in a world made up of whipping, lashing, branding, intimidation, brutality and even death, an existence in which the next day or even the next moment was never promised to the African slaves.

"The god of hurricane, the god of tornado, the god of flood and the god of fire have all been on the road seeking some sort of answers, atonement," the priest told the elders. "The ancestors tried to resolve these injustices amicably. And they have exercised a lot of restraint and patience over the years. However, the ancestors simply got tired of waiting and have decided to take matters into their own hands, to exact vengeance on behalf of the millions of victims that'd suffered during the profane past."

"Have the gods not given the Oburoni people centuries of adequate notice before they sent the harbingers of justice on the road?" the griot asked, when he spoke to the crowd at the Shrine of Music.

"Well, they did," Dokuwa said. "They gave them plenty of warning."

The griot looked at the life of luxury the descendants of the slave traders, juxtaposed against the sweat and labor of the African ancestors in the past and felt angry. He looked at the lives of abject suffering of the people on the African continent and their descendants who live in the Diaspora today and compared them to the lives of the descendants of the former slave traders and concluded that most of them are better off.

The time for poetic justice has finally arrived.

"They better address the past. And good thing there has been a groundswell of support for rectifying the evils of the past in recent years," the priest said. "The time for accountability has finally come." The griot looked as if he was truly sorry that it had finally come to a state of confrontation.

Finally the high priest emerged from his meditation from the dungeons below the Cape Coast Castle. He regretted that he had to relive the despicable horrors that took place inside those dungeons of disgust centuries ago. He still kept the seven virgins and seven doves inside the inner dungeon for peace during the festival.

Many of the people said Zogan was unique, ardent and committed. This was because he stayed below the castle in the slave dungeons consulting with the ancestors for days, pouring libation and trying his best to reach and appease the angry ancestors. He tried to stop them from a string of acts of vengeance against the Oburoni people.

His role was to sooth their anger, to appease the gods. He reached into his side pocket, got out a small bell and rang it repeatedly to get the attention of the ancestors. After a few minutes of silence, he poured some drinks on the ground for the ancestors. When he heard the roar of thunder in the distance, he knew that the ancestors had received his gift of libation.

"But the time has come to address the pain and suffering of the African people as a result of the profane past," Zogan told the elders. "The time for excuses is over. It is time to rectify the past transgressions before the window of opportunity closes and the ancestors take matters into their own hands."

He secretly hoped that the sadness of the mothers and the continued suffering of the African people would force the Oburonis to do something about the profane past. But was he hoping against hope?

The priests and priestesses sat in their colorful red, purple and gold attires. They were seated according to their ranks and ages, as they waited for the muse of the shrine to get to the heart of the ritual. They sat next to the sanctuary and waited for the ritual sacrifice.

It has been more than fifty generations since the ordeal ended. Hope was beginning to fade. The mood of the high priest was grave as he sat on the high chair and pondered what to do about the past. He was looking very serious in his purple robe. He could tell the gods were ready to send another round of poetic justice, but he was not ready, so he interceded one more time.

"It is that time again at the shrine. It is another season to perform the annual ritual for the god of music," the voice reminded him. He straightened up his ceremonial adinkra cloth with an exaggerated effort as he chewed a piece of red kola nut noisily.

"Well, with all the sunshine, the deep blue sky today is such a lovely day for the ritual," the high priest told the elders. "I am glad the god of rain has no intention of drenching the land with its sweat and tears and it has not demanded a virgin for sacrifice."

"The virgin ritual ended centuries ago," the queen mother reminded him quickly. "Good thing they ended it because it was an insult to our youths and degradation to all women."

"Look at the size of the crowd this year," Zogan told the head priest. "The number has been growing steadily each year. I am not so sure that the people come here each year for the right reasons. They either come for the good times, for the food and music, or for the spiritual rendezvous many of them want with the ancestors, an opportunity the festival provides in abundance."

"So they came to the shrine from far and near, from across the Atlantic Ocean, from Europe, from the Caribbean, from Canada, from South America, from New Zealand and from almost every African country," the head priest announced to the participants.

"Many come to the Panfest mainly for spiritual reasons—many, if not most of the visitors, come just to reconnect with their roots. They want an intense soul to soul experience with the ancestors," Zogan said.

"Their ancestors had vanished into oblivion years ago, the victims of pure human greed," the linguist told the priest. "The Oburonis had forced our chiefs and their elders to sell their own to them in exchange for guns, and sometimes for trinkets, broadcloth and rum, but mainly for firearms."

They had been anxious to return to their roots, on a pilgrimage at least—they yearn very much for their beloved motherland—in spite of the fact that most of them could not endure the rigors of the African way of life.

"That was really the saddest part of it all," the Queen Mother said. "And they dared not refuse their demands too."

The queen mother sat on her ebony stool that rested on an elephant effigy. Her gold necklaces attracted the attention of several admirers as she watched the priest with a mixture of emotions. Her dazzling diamond earrings also blinded the eyes of many, and her elegant headgear bedecked with gold got her the respect of many people. She finally broke her silence and said, "Why should we continue to give the gods the spiritual appeasement that they wanted, when they had let the ancestors down in the past?" the queen mother asked the priest,

"You must go on and give them the moonshine and the best part of the ram. Maybe that would end the destruction," the linguist interjected.

"Maybe, it might . . . ," the priest responded skeptically. Then he did his favorite thing, pointed to the blue sky and spoke to the ancestors.

Zogan, the forty-year-old priest of the Shrine of Music, felt that the slave trade was long ago and must be relegated into the past. But as he stood silently on the shore of the Atlantic Ocean, head down, arms folded, looking at the ruins of the slave trade and the legacies the Oburoni slave traders had left behind, his heart swelled with anger. His eyes roamed from the decrepit remnants of what used to be a former slave boat to the rusty cannons next to the Portuguese chapel nearby. But it was the voices he heard from the dungeons, the endless lamentation from the dungeons below that caused him to break down, filled with sorrow and anger.

"I must confess it's been a miracle that our people had survived the onslaught of the slave traders. A lot of damage had been done . . . chaos, death and degradation."

For years, he gave the gods the roosters or rams, gave them frosty gourds of palm wine, presented them with several priestesses to serve them. Zogan had tried to stop the gods from their divine duty, but unlike the head priest, he felt the time of grace was over and the time for accountability for the profane past has finally arrived.

"Have it your way," he told the ancestors during his libation. "We are in your hands. We need some sort of resolution for the profane past."

As he descended the steps, which led from the courtyard into the dungeons, he saw the agony of the victims in slow motion. It was like a dream, the silence brought to him the sorrowful pleas of the victims for freedom. He knew it was weakness for the priest to shed tears publicly, but personally the scenes before him and the voices he heard from the past, created deep pangs of sadness and feelings of anger inside him. He eventually had to let the tears loose, after he heard the clanking of the shackles and the beatings and the agonizing screams of the victims from down below.

The slave trade had been over years ago, but the wounds are still as fresh as if the tragedy had ended only yesterday.

"They can't continue to get away with this crime forever," Zogan complained to the king, as he knelt down in front of the azure shona stone to continue the ritual. "I remember how my great grandfather, the high priest, disappeared in the woods on the way from his coconut farm, as the legend has it. Maybe the time has come for the gods to seek vengeance for the victims."

"No amount of tears can bring back the victims that the Oburonis had forcibly taken out of the land. Since the victims would never return, the gods must force the descendants of the culprits to return to our shores to make atonement," the king said, trying to hide his anger behind a stoic face.

When the women saw the tears streaming down Zogan's face, the priests simply lowered their heads or quickly looked away. They understood the depth of his sorrow and the reasons why he broke down and shed those tears. They knew it was the result of despair.

The longer the griot stood there in his purple-dyed adinkra robe talking about the difficult past, the more several people broke down in tears and cried in outbursts of anger and pain.

The tall dark and lanky Zogan removed his cap, after he composed himself enough to dip the leaves in the holy water. Then he sprinkled the consecrated water gently on the people. He went from place to place and from corner to corner chasing away the evil spirits that the Oburonis or the slave traders had brought and left in the land.

"The saddest part is that our ancestors did not get much from the slave trade," the priest mused. "They got nothing tangible to show for the one-sided transactions. Whatever our ancestors got from these trades were flimsy and temporary in nature," Zogan told the audience. "The slave traders simply bullied, coaxed and intimidated our ancestors with their cannon, forcing them to accept their one-sided terms of trade."

The people who came to the Panfest Festival came from far and near. Zogan saw the anger in their souls, the deep agony on their faces and the anxiety on their minds. He turned to the returnees, the African-American identity seekers and those who were looking for answers to some very difficult and critical questions, the people who were searching for answers to a past that he knew they might never find, because there were no straight forward answers.

The visitors saw the pain on the priest's face and wondered why he had a mixture of guilt and remorse on his face. "Take your time to visit with the ancestors. Talk to the gods," Santos Davi, the young man from Brazil who had a polite and reticent demeanor, said soothingly, showing respect and empathy toward the priest, though his mind was riddled with several questions. "We have come here all the way from

Sao Paulo, Brazil to pay homage to the ancestors, but we need to know the truth about what really happened during the slave trade."

"You have asked a very difficult question, my son," the linguist said to the youth from Brazil. "There are no easy explanations. The past was difficult, painful and chaotic. All I can tell you is that the powerful cannon the Europeans brought and used freely against our ancestors to get them to comply with their demands worked."

"Why is this priority for you?" the queen mother asked him pointedly. "We are glad you made the journey, but can you tell us what really brought you to our shores, to the motherland?"

"Well, your ancestors might be your people, but they remain our great grandparents as well. They gave us life. And they are still our heroes too," Santos Davi said. "They are our roots and we need them just as much as you do."

"It is a spiritual journey for me," a lady from Byhalia, Mississippi told the queen mother politely as she wiped her eyes with a soft black handkerchief. "After all the flashbacks from my past, all the dreams I have had about the motherland, I just want to see the place, view the slave castles with my own eyes, descend into the dungeons with my feet, and walk through the door of no return the way my great grandparents did in the past."

"You can experience that dream right here," the queen mother told her. "You can sit down with Mama Africa, look into her soul and mix your soul with hers. You can make that connection right now."

"I have been in the Jah Movement for some years, so I really came to see the Portuguese chapel—that notorious symbol of hypocrisy," Jim Jacob, a Rastafarian from Jamaica, said truthfully. "I don't see how they could twist the words of Jah, the fair and just Jah, to support this evil slave trade. No matter how they justified it in their books, the slave trade happened obviously because of pure human greed."

"I don't know how much more to express our sorrow to you and to the rest of the brothers and sisters across the ocean, but we are truly sorry for what happened to our ancestors in the past," the queen mother told Jim Jacobs again. She patted him on the back gently as the young man clung to his dreadlocks firmly, twisted them in his hands and started to shed some gentle tears. While his eyes still roamed from monument to monument, he received a firm, sentimental embrace from the queen mother, which brought a flash of teary smile to his face.

"Finally, we welcome you back home. Akwaba, my sons and daughters," the queen mother said. "I am hoping that you would find whatever you are looking for during your stay. You are welcome to stay for as long as you want . . . you are even welcome to stay forever."

The linguist rose to his feet, staff of office in hand, his cloth tied firmly around his torso, cleared his throat loudly and began to address the gathering in his deep baritone voice.

"This is a day set aside to pay homage to the god of music and to remember all those victims that the Europeans had tricked, got drunk, spirited away and shipped off to the land of no return from this very shrine centuries ago," the linguist told the visitors. "This is to remind the youth to never allow the Oburonis to reap where they did not sow, to take what did not belong to them or to throw dust into our eyes again."

"It is very important that we should never ever forget the departed souls of this land," King Gizenga straightened up on his stool. "And this evil, which the Europeans and Americans brought to our land, the result of greed, must never ever rear its ugly head anywhere in the world again."

When Tony, the alderman from Natchez, Mississippi, who loved the continent very much, entered the shrine minutes later, he heard a commotion in the dungeon below. He did not understand why the Africans did not fight the slave traders to the last person, so he came to seek some answers, to see the legacies of the slave trade and to personally communicate with the ancestors. "You must make them pay for what they'd done to you and to the continent," he tensed and uttered angrily. After he saw the cannons, he understood why the chiefs were so badly overpowered and so thoroughly subjugated.

Then he moved toward the far side of the castle, next to the female dungeons. He screamed when he saw the opulence and strategic location of the governor's mansion on the far side. This majestic mansion, directly overlooking the female dungeons for obvious reasons, was elegant and majestic, yet it was degrading to women. It faced the Atlantic Ocean in its glorious opulence, caressing the gentle breezes. He couldn't forgive the traders when he saw the solitary white flag on top of the office flapping furiously against the deep blue tropical sky.

And the alderman who had tried to become the first Africa-American mayor back home in Mississippi, who had cursed the white man for bringing his ancestors out of Africa to the New World heard voices from below the dungeons. He was shocked when he found out that the Cape Coast Castle was also for many years the notorious headquarters of the British slave trade, of the exodus of slaves from the African Slave Coast. The exploitation of the continent and his ancestors, the degradation and the humiliation were too much for his soul to bear.

He tried to take pictures in spite of the warning from the tour guides—to record the suffering of his ancestors, to establish a connection with his roots. But when his camera fell and broke into several small pieces and the image of the governor's mansion vanished, he knew he was in the middle of lots of spirits. "Maybe the place is still haunted," he mumbled. "I strongly believe that the spirits from the past are still alive and active here even today. They are haunting the place, there 'aint no doubt in my mind that after all these years they are still angry and restless."

"The ancestors could not protect the youths from the slave traders because of the raw greed of the slave traders," the priest, calabash in his right hand and a talisman in the other, still struggling to keep his eyes dry, told the alderman from Mississippi and the rest of the gathering.

"We will never forget the ancestors. Never, ever, for as long as we live," the queen mother shouted. "They continue to be our heroes and our gods. They will live in our hearts forever."

Zogan got the altar ready for the sacrifice, a ritual he'd performed seventeen years in a row. "These Oburonis condemned our practices, beliefs and worldview and yet they brought their faith, their churches and their priests into our land. Maybe they did so for the sole purpose of facilitating the slave trade. If this wasn't in conflict with what their God decreed, then I don't know what this was."

"They fed the African youths to their greed, simply because they wanted to join the rich folks back home," Kesha, the lady from Trinidad and Tobago, told the queen mother. "It is surprising how these religious people forgot their faith and ignored their conscience when it came to the slave trade."

"When it came to slaves they quickly forgot about their God," she rubbed her face repeatedly, lowered her head and sighed heavily. "It is hard to talk about these things, because they bring back lots of bitter memories. To them, they did these things for wealth and status back home, but for the African people, these are deeds written in blood and tears."

"How can we as African people ever overcome the lingering effects of this tragedy?" the king asked. "Our wounds are still as deep today as if they'd been inflicted on us only yesterday."

"They'd left us with nothing good from the past," Kesha told the queen mother, looking at her in the eyes. "They'd left only rusty cannons, slave castles, shackles and tons of agony."

"This is something you don't ever want to remember," the queen mother remarked, as she walked out the door. "What use are the brass pots, trinkets, broadcloth and useless guns? Are they worth anything today?"

The priest took a deep breath, planted his feet angrily but firmly on the black shona stone in front of the Shrine of Music silencing the people with the angry spirits whispering in the background. He put on an extra adinkra cloth to beat the Harmattan chill in the air. "The ocean is rough and rowdy with the gigantic waves banging intermittently against the shoreline as if the ancestors were extremely angry and poised to move into taking the final action."

"They've got to do something about the profane past," the linguist said. "The ancestors must avenge the dead and get some atonement for the victims who had been crushed under the wheels of history."

The linguist talked about what the Oburonis did during the slave trade with relative ease. But when he tried to speak about the role the African ancestors played in the ugly drama, he started to swallow his words and choked on every word. It was as if he was devastated and was at a loss for words. When he tried to explain how some of the African chiefs had no choice, but to sell some of their neighbors in exchange for guns in order to survive, in order to defend themselves, he began to lose his voice completely.

The revelations tormented his soul. He knew those who became the stooges of the Oburoni slave traders had been tricked, bribed, coaxed and cajoled to do what they did. Some just wanted to survive the chaos and the turbulent gun politics of slave trade, which the Oburonis traders had unleashed on the land—and the old rivalries they instigated or fanned among the leaders which ensued in inter-group warfare that generated thousands and millions of slave cargoes for them.

"The ancestors should have fought harder against the slave traders," Deh-Deh Black, the African American from Winston-Salem, North Carolina on the pilgrimage for the seventh time, said angrily. "Our ancestors should never have even let these white folks inside the continent in the first place. That was where they went wrong. That was a mistake that came back to haunt them."

"Well, they didn't have a choice against the cannon anyway," Davi told her.

"They knew better not to do what they did. They should have pushed them into the bottom of the ocean, rid the land of this curse."

"The past is not that simple, my blood sister," the linguist got up and told the lady calmly. "These traders had guns and cannons at the time they came to the land. They simply blasted their way inside. There was very little resistance our ancestors could offer."

"But y'all should have done everything you could to stop them," she said half jokingly. "And then y'all should have fought them harder, maybe till the last person dropped dead. You should have driven them out as soon as you caught them abducting your sons and daughters."

"It is easier said than done, my dear sister," Mankrado, the war captain said to her. "Well, we tried to move heaven and earth to get them to leave, but our efforts came to no avail."

"I am not superstitious, but why did the gods allow such a wicked trade to take place on our shores? How could they permit such a dreadful fate to overwhelm our people?" Jim Jacobs, the Jamaican born African-Rasta with dreadlocks, who was humming reggae songs repeatedly, removed the green, yellow, and red cap on top of his dreadlocks and asked, "Where were the gods? And by the way, what were they doing all that time? Were they on a long journey somewhere or were they asleep the entire time?"

"We feel your pain, because your pain is also our pain. The Oburoni people killed our ancestors because they had cannon and our ancestors did not stand a chance against their firepower," the linguist remarked quickly. "Don't make the gods angry. Their anger can be deadly, when you annoy them."

From now onwards, the invisible hands of the gods have decided to take control of the tragedy, to seek atonement and to demand accountability for the past.

"But since the gods did not do what they were supposed to do in the past, which is to protect the people, don't you think they can still fail us again?" the sister tried to lift one of the rusty canons from the floor, but she did not succeed in doing so.

"Well, we have to give the best sacrifice to the gods each year; that's all we can do. And we expect them to protect us from harm from now onwards," the priest said. "If anything at all, we don't want these gods to become angry with us."

"No telling what else these gods might do to our people next," the lady from Mississippi said sarcastically. "Just leave these gods alone. They have done enough damage and destruction to the people already."

"After what the god of music in particular has done or not done, why should we continue to pay homage to this god every year?" the queen mother, always questioning the ways of the gods, asked pointedly. "This god in particular has betrayed his people when it stood by and watched the Oburonis abducted, captured and shipped off the sons and daughters of the land as if these youths were cattle. And it all happened right under its very nose and from this very shrine. Tell me why we should still honor this god and not trample it down?"

Zogan looked at her and shook his head briskly. "Please, do not disrespect the god of music," the priest cut in sharply. "A queen mother should not say the sort of thing that you have said about the god." He got a calabash of palm wine from a young man to cool down his anger and poured some of the foamy dredge on the ground to appease the god.

"Don't waste your drink. Was this god for us or for the white Oburoni traders since it worked against our people and did so for such a long time," the queen mother insisted.

"Hmm. You think you have a point, but we still have to honor these gods regardless of what we think they did to us in the past, good or bad," the priest warned the queen mother again. "Their wrath is relentless, so do not try to make them angry. They see in the dark, hear conversations whispered behind closed doors. They require consequences from culprits."

The priest stood next to the sacred shona stone. He allowed the fifteen year old new priestess at the shrine, obviously a virgin, to sing a dirge, a sentimental and captivating solo to the ancestors. As her voice rose to the heavens, the audience hummed along. They could hear her high soprano voice ricocheting against the walls of the Cape Coast Castle echoing across the sprawling savanna grassland with the sorrows of the past coded in every note.

The seven female priestesses, clad in deep brown flowing dresses, bedecked with several shells of cowries, dark clay marks on their cheeks and foreheads, did the ritual cooking to feed the people. It was amazing how disciplined these priestesses were and how devoted they were to the god. They didn't speak a word to anyone, as the custom decreed. Not when the priests were watching them like hawks. They were forbidden to speak to anyone, especially not to the men outside the shrine, young or old. Each priestess was supposed to be a gift to the god for seven years at the end of which she was released to her family.

"The god of music wanted London Dry Gin for the libation," the queen mother mocked in a sarcastic tone as she laughed and shook her head. "This was the same drink the Oburonis used as a bait to enslave our ancestors in the past. They managed to get them addicted to this gin and the rest of the plot fell in place."

"Why do you hate this particular god?" the priest asked her again. "Its anger can be deadly to you, to your family and to the entire kingdom."

"Isn't protecting the people the role of the gods?" She blinked repeatedly. "This one failed to do so, therefore, I ask why we continue to waste our sacrifices on it."

"I hate to see what happens to your family at the end of the proverbial seven days," the priest pointed his hand at the queen mother. "My advice to you is to come to grips with your inner conflicts and deal with your personal grief from the past to avoid the wrath of this god."

"Why should I respect a god that committed treason against its own people?" She demanded to know.

"Hmm, who has ever heard of a god committing any kind of treason? Even if it did, are we supposed to disrespect it," the high priest asked her sternly, staring at the woman with an evil eye.

"I blame the Oburonis more than the gods. They knew what they were doing when they brought all those barrels of rum, and let the rum to flow freely. It was to get our ancestors drunk, make war and then became easy targets for the slave traders," she told the high priest.

"You are right that they gave them lots of rum. And when they let down their guards and stepped on the slave boat unsuspectingly, they took off with them in the middle of the night. Before they knew it, they were headed beyond the blue seas to the land of no return," he agreed with her.

"Well, the music also enchanted their spirits, the rum intoxicated their brains and the slave traders outwitted them. And before they knew it, they became sitting crows that waited to be swallowed by Oburoni greed hidden inside the evil arms of history," she said sadly.

"Still, we can't defile the gods, because the consequences are too drastic . . . their wrath and vengeance . . . too deadly. Their anger might follow you and your children to the gates of the world of the ancestors," the high priest told her candidly. "So, it is better to hold your tongue."

"The only way to silence me is to cut off my tongue," the queen mother told the priest arrogantly, defying the priesthood.

"I have heard that the gods sometimes kill their own priests in anger too," the linguist told the priest. "You could be the first one this god reaches out to cut down in cold blood. Don't come crying to me hysterically then."

That hot July afternoon, the high priest poured the holy water on the ground slowly, like water the gods had sanctified to cleanse the shrine and all the participants present, to pacify the silent spirits that were still lingering in the old slave castle. The echoes of the footsteps of the departed ancestors were heard in the courtyard. Their "wailing blues" and screams were heard banging against the endless shoreline. The rainbow priest saw the ghosts roaming around the castle looking for justice, seeking atonement for the pain and suffering that they'd suffered and endured in the past. He quickly went down on his knees and poured libation.

"The spirits reached across the Gulf of Guinea, across the ocean and pointed accusatory fingers at the Europeans and their American counterparts for their role in the slave trade," the linguist said. "The descendants of the Oburonis must make atonement to end the heavy burden of guilt they still bear. They will know no peace and will have no free conscience until they make atonement for the past."

"Though it ended long ago, if anyone thinks that the world has forgotten about the slave trade, then they are living in a fantasy world. The ancestors have not forgotten about the tragedy. In fact, they have decided to avenge the departed victims," Dokuwa said. "That quest has sent some of them on the warpath."

"Until the Oburoni people decide to do the right thing, agree to make atonement," the priest said. "They will hear from the ancestors and face the consequences of the actions of their ancestors."

Zogan asked permission from the elders to do the libation. And when the elders granted the permission, he bared his chest and began to communicate with the ancestors in his silent, sentimental way. He always recalled the ordeal in the land with sorrow and regret.

"What has become more painful is how the descendants of the European and American slave traders have shifted the blame for the slave trade to the African leaders, ignoring the fact that the trade was primarily because of the insatiable appetite they had for our youths—their quest to satisfy their labor needs."

"Well, that does not surprise anyone since they wrote the history books. They wrote them as if our ancestors had invited them over to buy our blood relatives," the priest said with an angry voice. "Our ancestors had never invited them to our shores to buy anybody. They came as human locusts or human pests that simply showed up like ghosts on our doorsteps, unannounced and armed to the teeth looking for slaves for free labor."

"They were greedy and bloodthirsty marauders, people without any kindness or any boundaries to the extent of their brutality. They'd drowned their conscience in barrels of rum and drenched their souls inside kegs of whiskey," the queen mother said.

"You are right. The saddest part was that they gunned down all the chiefs who opposed their evil plots as if they were flies," the war captain lamented.

"The slave traders ruthlessly crushed any opposition to their enterprise of shame. Any wonder then that they'd deleted all the opposition from the chiefs to the slave trade from their records," the chief said.

"Though they think wrongly so, the world has not forgotten about what their ancestors did to this unfortunate continent?" The queen mother cleared her throat repeatedly. "Evil does not easily disappear into thin air regardless of what they think. The memories of their deeds still live on in notoriety to today."

"Well, the ancestors have brought all these embarrassing facts back into the open, parading them before the rest of the world," the king revealed. "Maybe someday, the descendants of the culprits would address this long-overdue transgression in global history, an embarrassment in their heritage."

"The past has turned out to be such a huge humiliation for them. What their ancestors did years ago is just too shameful for their descendants to face today," the queen mother said bluntly. "They are trying to deny that they still carry a heavy burden of guilt in their hearts, but the world knows that they certainly do."

"They tend to develop historical amnesia whenever it comes to the truth about the slave trade and the role their ancestors played," the griot said laughing. "They have tried to twist the history of the slave trade, but the sad truth is that their descendants still have the blood of the millions of Africans on their hands and they would continue do so till the end of time, or till they make atonement and receive a settlement."

Meanwhile, the clouds gathered on the horizon as the priest descended into the world of the gods to convey the collective thoughts of the people to the gods and receive wisdom from them in return. Zogan reported in his baritone voice that "the ancestors want the descendants of those who'd violated Mama Africa and her offspring and did so for such a long time in the past with impunity to return to our shores to make atonement for these transgressions. They must appease the ancestral spirits; otherwise, they would face the consequences—vengeance that would force them to make atonement for the squalid past."

"How do the gods plan to do this?" the linguist asked quickly.

"Well, the ancestors have decided to go on the warpath all over the land, to make the inhabitants feel their presence and listen to their demands."

"How long do they plan to continue to seek this vengeance?" the queen mother mumbled. "Let us say that, like the slave traders did years ago, they intend to bring some anxious moments in their trails till the descendants of the Oburoni traders return to the shores of Africa to make atonement."

"Why have they decided to go on the offensive at this time and not before or later? I mean why now?" the king inquired in a voice filled with suspense and questions.

"Well, the ancestors are very patient. They prefer to act cautiously and with restraint," the priest told him. "They rarely go on the offensive and on the path of vengeance. They do so only after they'd exhausted every possible avenue of peaceful resolution."

"Well, they want the necessary atonement, a ritual that is centuries overdue," the head priest declared. "The sooner their descendants do this the better for everyone involved in this dreadful nightmare."

The king and the elders sat anxiously, wracking their brains, pondering the future and wondering if the atonement could stop the rage of the ancestors. After all, who could forget how they'd killed the young, the helpless and the aged during the slave raids. Who could forget the abductions, the bloody civil wars that they'd incited or masterminded and the prisoners that these wars generated as slave cargoes? And how could they forget the desolation they'd caused in the kingdoms? How they'd gunned down in cold blood all the chiefs that opposed the slave quotas they so constantly demanded.

The priest took a deep breath just before he put the calabash to his mouth and gulped down the palm wine angrily. He became visibly unsteady after gulping down seven calabashes of the foamy dredge. A few of the women giggled when he swayed from side to side, but the comic relief did not drown the tears in their eyes.

The souls of the departed made their presence felt among them and their restlessness and the agony saddened many of the people. They saw the venerable ancestors walking along the beach, restless and angry but refusing to swear or curse the culprits. The spirits saw them and opened their hands and asked for water and drinks of appeasement. So, the people poured the drinks on the ground and placed food by the wayside for them.

"Obviously, this is not the moment for laughter," the queen mother warned the other members of the gathering. Rubbing her eyes, she held her head in her palms for a moment, pondering the anger of the departed ancestors. "Are the gods going to persuade the descendants of those who did this to the continent before they go on their path of vengeance, before the harbingers of destruction reach their destinations of horror?"

"Or maybe, they would make the apotheosis possible."

The high priest pushed away the imported London Dry Gin angrily, indicating his displeasure. "This was what the uninvited Oburoni traders used as baits during the horrible slave trade," the high priest said to the helpers. "The gods don't need any more imported drinks. Instead, give them some local Kantamanto home brew "akpeteshie" hot spirited drink. The gods would drink it immediately."

"We shouldn't give them any more imported drinks," Zogan agreed. He knew that the women were watching to see if he was going to select the imported gin, so he didn't. When he caught a glimpse of the "akpeteshie" home brew, he nodded happily and proceeded to use that.

The linguist shouted loudly, "How long did our ancestors fall for these despicable traps of deception?"

The crowd saw the priest gulped down another round of the palm wine and a large glass of akpeteshie home brew moonshine a third time and giggled. The grimace on his face revealed that the akpeteshie did not go down very easily. He nodded his head again repeatedly as he tried to manage the pain and the pleasure at the same time.

The king and the elders stared at Zogan with some derision. But Zogan, for once, delivered not only a powerful message, but also a surprising warning from the gods.

"The gods have spoken," the war captain declared, and he asked the drummers to play the selected ritual beats for the gathering.

The audience spoke in low tones commenting on how deep into the spirit world Zogan the priest had traveled that day. His red eyes spoke volumes as they bored weakly into the eyes of the audience. The audience sat in silence through the ritual at the shrine, many of them had unpleasant flashbacks from the horrible and painful past.

The queen mother rattled beads suspended around the yellow gourd and she started to sing the blues—the sorrowful dirges of old. No one was in the mood for any more blues. They were tired of recalling these tragic experiences, but since the sun never ceases to rise, they could never forget the ancestors.

Zogan was getting up from the libation mat when, seconds later, the falcon reappeared from behind the blue sky. It circled the shoreline and quickly disappeared behind a patch of dark clouds. Maybe it came from across the ocean or from the sacred shrine of the legendary Chucalissa Shrine, a sacred shrine thousands of miles away.

Zogan's drunken state, the only way he could muster enough courage to confront the dark past, to face the sorrows from the past, to talk about the taboo slave trade that many people dreaded, came only after imbibing several calabashes of palm wine.

Except a few low tones and whispers, everyone was quiet. It was forbidden, indeed a crime punishable with a curse for several generations, to talk during the libation.

He'd done his task very well that day. Zogan congratulated himself. He would continue to speak for the gods and act as the intermediary among the people many years to come, remembering the unborn, the living and the ancestors—if he continued to live a long life.

Throughout the ritual, the voices of the departed could be heard from the dungeons below the Cape Coast Castle. They were wailing, moaning, groaning and crying for freedom.

"Why do you drink so much liquor whenever you invoke these spirits?" the linguist asked Zogan quietly. "Are you trying to drink your life away?"

He paused for a moment, cleared his throat loudly and said, "Not at all. When you are pouring libation in these slave castles, you are invoking the ancestors, calling on several aggrieved souls, the souls of the departed, the souls of the angry victims, the souls of blood relatives, so it is hard to be sober and not get sentimental in the process," he told the linguist.

"Why don't you let the ancestors rest in peace?" the youth asked. "They'd been gone centuries ago."

"When you confront the most difficult and the most shameful part of your history, how could you speak about it or reflect on the horrible tragedy without getting sentimental? How could you deal with the pain and the bitterness the Oburoni locusts had left in the land and in their trails, on our shores, in our kingdoms without invoking the names of the gods or calling on the ancestors to intervene?"

"We understand what you feel," the youth said. "But try to put the past behind you. It might send you into an early grave. You are a valuable asset to this kingdom and we need you around to continue to fill the pot of history for the generations to come."

"Tell me how anyone could delve into the past without the help of the gods?" the priest waved his flywhisk in the air waiting for an answer.

"You are right," the Okyeame said sadly. "You are dealing with the ancestors during the horrible and bitter past, which was the era when bloodshed was all over the land and everyone's soul was on fire." He leaned to say something to the Mankrado, but everyone knew or guessed what he said.

"Well, those were the notorious days, the era of shame and the centuries of dilemmas," Mankrado danced to the war drum beat a little longer than expected. "Those were the days when our ancestors slept with loaded guns next to their beds, with roasted yams and gourds of water in their hunting bags ready to go to war."

"And the men went to bed in their clothes ready to jump out of bed on the spur of the moment to protect their families, shield their villages from the slave raiders and defend their honor," Elder Buamah said. "Men rose to the occasion. And they understood that they better be ready to do battle at a moment's notice or become cowards in the eyes of the women and children."

"What the Oburoni people did to our people, to our land and to our collective future, no one can talk about these without long, deep sighs of agonizing pain. I agree that you can only visit the past with the help of the spirits," the queen mother agreed with him. "But as for you Zogan, this has become an excuse for you to satisfy your drunken cravings for liquor."

"The priest is right, he is absolutely right," the Mankrado, the war chief, said regrettably. His mood was solemn and he had on his war batakari attire, just like his ancestors did centuries earlier. Mankrado's family had provided the war chiefs of the kingdom at the time the Oburonis came and conducted the infamous slave trade and did their havoc in the land. So, to him, the bitterness of the past was a personal family matter as well. The amount of sarcastic comments he had to endure from many people was unnerving.

There were seventeen war captains before him. They were all Mankrados. "You know then why I have such a strong resentment toward the Oburonis. Most of the Mankrados on my father's side had either been killed or taken into slavery during those sad days of horror," he complained.

"Were your ancestors not supposed to drive the Oburoni locusts into the Atlantic Ocean?" Dokuwa asked the war captain trying to annoy him. "Confess to the people and defend your family honor. Just tell us why they failed to drive the Oburoni pests into the Atlantic Ocean."

The mere mention of the death of his ancestors erupted a volcano of anger inside Mankrado. He felt some guilt because his family had actually failed to defeat "the locusts" that came to the land. But he knew the truth, so he decided not to explain anything to anyone. "My family did not send "the human lifters" from across the Atlantic Ocean to come over to defile the land," he told Dokuwa and the rest of the gathering. "When my great grandfather opposed them, they got the rival chief of Zongo to topple and apprehend him. He was exiled and enslaved within weeks."

"Do you want to tell the youth some more about what happened in the past, or do you want the griot to do so?" the priest asked Mankrado.

"Well, all I can say is that my ancestors did their best. There wasn't much my people could do against the Oburoni people with their powerful cannon," Mankrado said. "My great, great grandfather tried to stop them, but three rival chiefs, for bribes of bottles of rum and some of the latest guns from Europe, betrayed him. They let their own people down."

"Split and defeat them was the main strategy the Oburonis used against our ancestors," the queen mother said. "They used their guns to split our groups and then they set one group against the other, tongue against tongue and blood against blood. They shot and killed any chief or king that closed the trade routes or resisted the slave trade in any way."

"I wonder if the slave trade still worries their descendants, torments their conscience or trouble their hearts today," the king wondered.

"Hmm, their ancestors were ruthless and callous at heart anyway," Dokuwa said. "Their children could never forget the stories they have been told about the dark past."

"Who could forget the notorious trader named Don Pedro?" the queen mother said. She sat down and drank a calabash of water. "He was the greediest slave dealer in the land, perhaps the most notorious and cold blooded of all times. I heard that peace was never the same in the land from the moment he stepped on our shores. The youths vanished like flies, and he spilled blood everywhere."

"Well, he raided villages and took more slaves than any Oburoni at the time," Dokuwa complained. "He had the best of time doing this dirty job, he took advantage of the slave women and he drank a lot of rum as well."

"How did he manage to drink three gallons of rum each night?" Dokuwa asked.

"The man had a "heart of stone" and sent more Africans into slavery than any other human being ever did, but the irony was that he was afraid to die. He didn't want to die at the hands of the African chiefs, those that resisted the slave trade," the queen mother revealed. "But what became an obsession for him, though he pretended he had no fear, was his fear of the tiny little mosquitoes. He had a premonition of one day dying from malaria, the pandemic disease that swept most of the Oburoni traders on the Slave Coast, sending many to early graves."

The chiefs and their elders sat about seventeen yards from the black shona stone in front of the shrine and watched the libation ritual from the balcony. They listened to the priest, shook their heads, but they also nodded in agreement once a while—some were still angry over the past. Others decided to put the past behind them, though there was no way they could ever forget what their ancestors had endured in the past.

The king stood up, took seven steps toward the ocean and pointed his golden sword at the blue sky seven times, thrusting it against the blistering tropical sun, toward the dead, toward the living and toward the unborn. He muttered a few words, sat down and held his chin in his palm brooding over the future.

His eyes were fixed on the blue sky as if he was expecting a miracle. Maybe, he was expecting the gods to provide some answers, to convince the Oburonis to make atonement, or to force them to seek reconciliation instead of traveling the road of denial.

Zogan, the priest, told the audience, after he had sobered somewhat, "Our ancestors were at peace with the environment and they were living in reasonable prosperity and comfort for thousands of generations before the European 'Oburonis' arrived with this evil slave trade on their mind. But when they imposed the slave trade on our ancestors, they shattered the peace in the land. The ropes of kinship, which had held the continent together for millions of years, were shattered into several pieces leading to bickering, constant warfare and bloodshed in the land."

"How did this affect the people?" the youth asked.

"Well, instead of unity, there was war. Instead of security, there was fear. And instead of food, there was hunger. Groups went after other groups. The youths could not learn to weave 'kente' cloths, learn to fish, grow yams or make drums because in the chaos, the Oburoni slave traders interrupted everything including even the industries," the linguist said.

"And the young girls could not go to fetch foodstuffs from the farms or get firewood from the forests anymore," the queen mother complained. "They were afraid that the slave traders might abduct them on their way and ship them off as slaves."

"All the peace we'd enjoyed before the Oburoni came, vanished into thin air," the king said. "The traders were like packs of hyenas in the land looking for youths to snatch and use them as black cargoes."

"Even though the descendants of these uninvited visitors deny this reality, our people were living in relative peace before the arrival of the slave traders. Indeed, the slave trade destroyed our crafts, our farms, and decimated the civilization we had," the griot told the youth.

"This misfortune, this horrible Harmattan, which these aliens had forced upon our ancestors, will live on forever in ill repute," the king told the people. "We must make sure that the Oburonis never returned to our land to repeat this evil again."

Queen mother Ayesha leaned toward the king and tried to give him some message, maybe some advice. The other women were glad that she still had a cordial relationship with the king. They weren't very sure if the king would reprimand her after the priest had complained about her criticisms of the god of music. Perhaps the threat of the Oburoni traders outweighed any other issues.

Dokuwa sat on the small "Odum stool" next to the queen mother, then placed her hands in her lap and started watching the priests perform the annual ritual.

"I thought you had disappeared like Kokoroko Mansa did last year," the queen mother asked her. "Who knows what is going on these days?"

"Well, why do you ask that question?" Dokuwa inquired.

"You know how these slave traders came very close to taking everybody from the Slave Coast into slavery," the queen mother said. "But for the wrath of the mosquitoes, these Oburoni predators might have wiped out our ancestors from the face of the earth, and maybe even from the pot of history altogether."

"Aren't you getting too afraid for your own good?" Dokuwa asked.

"Well, the rooster says to be afraid is to live longer, so leave me alone to deal with my fears, real or imagined," the queen mother told her.

Zogan paused to swallow some lumps as he heard the names of the famous kings who were taken to the land of no return in "kunyowu" chains and shackles. "Many were still fighting on their feet when the slave traders took them away," he revealed. Who could forget Nana Adja Mama, who was taken away from the burial grounds of his youngest wife? "Why I couldn't even say farewell to my beloved wife, my soul mate, and the sweetest African honey without being taken into slavery?" Nana Adja Mama fought hard to escape the dragnet but to no avail. He was taken away in chains.

"In retrospect, if the African chiefs could turn back the wheels of time, they probably would fight the Oburoni intruders till the last person dropped dead. Perhaps, they would have found a way to prevent these intruders from ever entering the land and . . . though sad to say . . . nipped the Oburoni plot in the bud.

"I hate to think about the havoc they'd done in the land," the high priest said, inspecting the sacrifices to the gods.

"We could forgive anything, except the way the descendants continue to blame the victims, the chiefs for the slave trade, making our ancestors the culprits in this ugly drama, instead of putting the blame squarely on those who conceived and began the slave trade, where the blame rightly belongs. That is something we would never forgive them," Dokuwa ranted, working herself into a frenzy. She straightened up the adinkra cloth around her waist noisily, enjoying the dozens of eyes that followed her broad and shapely hips. She sat next to the queen mother, wriggled herself in the seat, unconsciously showing her beautiful profile. She proceeded to play with her braided hair, which was neatly wrapped under a gold-plaited headgear. "The gods would not continue to let them get away with this atrocity forever. They would make them account for this horror of horrors one day."

"Who invited them to the continent anyway? Our ancestors never did," the queen mother, who was both a leader and a warrior, asked. "They'd claimed that they had itching feet and that was the reason they stumbled upon the land."

"They suffered from "insatiable greed" than anything else," Mankrado told them, biting into the chewing stick.

"Why did their itching feet become our problem?" Dokuwa asked jokingly. "The itching feet story turned out to be one big lie. They were just covering up their evil plots with this bizarre story."

A mixture of pain and anger went through the queen mother's heart, as she saw images of the ancestors parading around the town square pointing at her, telling her to ask the king to do something about their state of restlessness in the ancestral world. She loosened a small yellow bottle wrapped at the end of her cloth and put a pinch of fine dark brown tobacco on her left thumbnail and sniffed it slowly.

"The ancestors had been very patient. They had made very little attempts of vengeance in the past, but the ancestors would not allow this iniquity to go unanswered forever. They have begun to look for vengeance, to seek retribution. That is because their efforts to reason with the Oburonis had failed. They'd hardened their hearts and the ancestors had become angry over their inflexibility.

Zogan was the twenty-seventh priest from his bloodline to occupy the office of the priest of the Shrine of Music in three hundred years. During his tenure, Zogan had done what the ancestors had expected him to do. He had single-handedly appeased the ancestors, calmed them down when they'd decided to wage a war of vengeance against the descendants of those who had destroyed the continent.

"The time for accountability, the moment of redemption from the old profane histories and the time for making atonement for the horrible past has arrived," Mankrado declared, as he threw his flywhisk on the ground angrily and took a few steps swaying to the rhythmic beats of the legendary "fontomfrom" war drum beat.

"I hate the marks on the walls and looking at the millions who had been lost from our kingdom in this ordeal sickens my soul," he blurted out. And we continue to mourn them with drinks and tears."

"You dance just like your late father did years ago," an old Abrewa lady, told the war captain. She paused and nodded her head admiringly. She was ninety years old, still in good health, had all her teeth present and walked without a cane. She still had a sharp wit.

Mankrado told the old lady, "Well, my father was a good father, but perhaps the ancestors took him away because he did not get the atonement they wanted for them and was not able to appease them."

"Unfortunately, some of the new Oburoni generations do not acknowledge the enormous damage their ancestors did to the African continent. Do they understand that after all these years, they still have the blood of Africans on their hands?" the priest asked.

"Of course, some of them do," Dokuwa said. She hesitated for a few seconds and said, "Others pretend that they know nothing of this ugly history."

"Maybe atonement could end this tragedy once and for all," the queen clasped her hands around the top of her head. "They must show remorse, make atonement and then put down the heavy burden of guilt . . . cleanse their souls . . . erase the profane in their past and get the tranquility they so badly need at home."

Sitting in front of them was Zaidoo, the leader of the "obrafuo" group. These were the descendants of the soldiers that fought the slave traders. His great grandfather confronted the European slave traders in the past, but he did not succeed in his plan to drive them into the Atlantic Ocean.

Zaidoo swung his hatchet in the air and repeated some sacred words as he proceeded to sacrifice the ram to the gods. Zogan stood there and smiled when he smelled the burning flesh of the animal. He glanced at the side dishes the priestesses had prepared at the shrine for the sacrifice and nodded his head showing his pleasure.

"Some day, something would prick the conscience of these Oburonis people and they would agree to make atonement to free their conscience," the high priest said.

Zogan fanned the hearth briskly; he was sweating profusely.

So the priests agree that the mood of the ancestors had changed. It was not the tolerant mood it used to be. They'd recently displayed their displeasure and extreme impatience. They'd raised their voices like the lions roaring in the forests and demanded atonement. They'd looked sternly at every visitor and acted like angry cobras caught between two foes, ready to strike with vengeance.

"But who could stop the gods from doing their divine duties anyway?" Zaidoo asked the leaders. "Which priests dared to stop them from the path of vengeance?"

"The descendants of the slave traders definitely need to give some of the wealth their ancestors had milked out of the land back to the descendants of the victims. We are not asking blood for blood or flesh for flesh, but something substantial to appease the ancestors would be the right thing to do," she told him. "But the time for this has almost run out."

Meanwhile, the breeze from the Atlantic Ocean brought the horrible images back to the onlookers once more. The linguist asked the audience to be silent. And you could hear the gathering heave a deep sigh. "King Gizenga has something to tell you. You must all be quiet so the king can give you his message," the linguist announced with an air of solemn grace.

Meanwhile, the fontomfrom war drum beats filled the courtyard with their sacred calls for unity and valor. There were sentimental dirges to the dead, rituals for the departed and sad sounds from the flutes for the unborn. You could feel the spirits of the lost sons and daughters of the land lingering in the air. You could sense their presence. And you could feel their anger from beyond the grave.

He was the king of the Bakano kingdom, the king of kings. He reminded himself that he was walking in the shoes of his proud ancestors. His grandfather was a stubborn king that gave the Oburonis all they could handle. He recalled how his great grandfather closed the slave trade routes more than a dozen times, and how the governor made him the most wanted king in the land for many years.

He'd been king for ten years, but on that pleasant, cloudless afternoon, he realized the possibility of the descendants of the Oburoni traders returning to the kingdom to talk atonement and to try to rectify the irreverent past.

The king rose and walked up to the podium; the linguist was on his right hand side and the war captain was on the left side. Like a warrior, he lifted his chest like his gallant father did years ago. He started to address the gathering. "Kuse, kuse, kuse, kuse!" King Gizenga repeated. He pointed his royal golden staff at the mighty Atlantic Ocean and sought the undivided attention of the people and the ancestors as well. He straightened the twelve-yard dark adinkra cloth with several symbols that he proudly wore. He gave the golden staff to Botwe, his nephew and the heir apparent, just for a brief moment, to free his hand to place the cloth firmly around his torso.

Botwe adored his uncle the king. He was his role model and his mentor. He had the yearning to become the next monarch, the king of the kingdom.

"These are the descendants of the same people who came to our land years ago to trade in gold, but ended masterminding the evil slave trade," he told the gathering. "So, let us proceed with caution."

"They'd enslaved our people and had destroyed the land," a woman shouted loudly. "Their ancestors brought chaos and misery into the land and death to our people. You must send them back home without asking them anything."

"Their great grandfathers overpowered our ancestors with their cannon and destroyed our towns and villages," the war captain said angrily. "Let them pay for these atrocities."

"The trade in gold became a mere pretext. The traders turned out to be blatant liars. They'd abducted our sons and daughters and forcibly hauled them away in droves like cattle, hauling them across the Atlantic Ocean to the land of no return," the king said. "As if that was not enough for them, they have placed a stigma of inferiority on us and on our children."

"Speak to us, King Batuka. Speak to us from the heart. We are ready to listen." Dokuwa, the female warrior leader, said in a shrill, eerie voice.

"The Oburonis forced the chiefs to sell the cream of their people to them," the king said. "The leaders that had been bold enough to oppose the slave trade, the Oburonis quickly mowed down like weeds."

"Why did the chiefs not fight them to the last person?" Osei asked somewhat childishly.

"The Oburoni would have killed all of them and wiped their villages and towns out completely," the king said. "For centuries, the Oburonis left nothing but bloodshed, desolation and death in their trails," he said. He paused briefly to gather himself.

"Speak your mind, our king," the women shouted. "We would listen; speak to your subjects, our king."

"King Gizenga, they must apologize for what their ancestors did to us in our own land," a woman's voice cut in sharply from the back of the gathering. "We are still suffering from this ordeal today."

"Well, the Oburoni visitors have traces of goodwill, but like their ancestors, they have evil on their minds," the queen mother said. "Beware of what they bring. We have failed to predict what they had in mind once and it is likely we can be wrong again."

"Their ancestors did not know any shame in the past," Dokuwa said sharply, evoking laughter from the people. She adjusted the scarf on her braided hair, knotted it neatly at the back. Her body was full and her wide hips spoke volumes for her beauty. And her war attire, which was secured firmly on her chest, revealed a woman with courage and fortitude. "How do they preach love to the people in one breath and then turn around and enslave them in another?"

"Now, what do they want from us? Do they want to take the rest of us with them to the land of no return?" the queen mother joked. "Tell them we don't have any more youths for them to take away. Tell them they need to start doing their own labor."

"So they have returned looking for more slaves to use as laborers?" Okyeame asked the women calmly. "No, I heard they got machines to do the hard labor for them these days."

"The young people should never forget what the Oburonis did in the land. They must pass this on to the future generations. They must explain to the next generation how the slave traders pushed the backs of our ancestors against the walls, held guns to their heads and asked them to either exchange slaves for guns or face the wrath of their cannons," King Batuka said firmly. "If only our ancestors had access to the same kinds of weapons that these Oburonis had, the history would have been very different."

"Yes. You are absolutely right," Mankrado said quickly.

"Instead, they gave our ancestors the inferior muskets. They gave them guns that exploded upon discharge and sometimes even killed those who fired them."

"What happened when they tried to say no to the Oburoni traders?" Osei, the young school lad asked again politely.

"They threatened to kill every chief or send them and their families into slavery if they did not cooperate," Okyeame said. "They usually set fire to their houses, burned down their palaces, destroyed entire villages and even destroyed whole empires just to flash out the victims."

"Why did they have to face such a dreadful dilemma in their own land?" the queen mother asked.

"Do you know how many victims these aliens forcibly removed from our shores over the years?" Ablakwa asked pointedly.

Dokuwa counted the marks on the walls, but stopped half way. "They were in the millions. The number was so large that the ancestors lost count of it," Dokuwa interjected. "It was a tale of shame on the part of the Oburonis and a tragic drama of betrayal by some of the African leaders."

Chief Saka, the quiet divisional chief said, "The historians, had put the number between forty to fifty million taken out and an equal number dead in the fray, in the gathering process."

"It was such an incredible loss," Amanfule said. "These losses came from the so-called Lower Guinea area: Togo, Benin, Nigeria, Cameroon, Gabon, the Congo and Angola. It also includes the figures from Upper Guinea: Senegal, Gambia, Mali, Guinea, Sierra Leone, Liberia, and the Ivory Coast, and of course, the former Gold Coast, which is now called Ghana."

"Did the Europeans show any guilt over the monumental harm they'd done in the land?" Ablakwa asked. "I mean how did they react to the human toll and all the losses they'd inflicted on the continent?"

"They did not show any guilt, no emotions. None whatsoever," Amanfule said. "A few missionaries felt sorry for the African people, but the slave traders had hearts made of stone. Most of them chose to drown their guilt and shame in barrels of rum and bottles of whisky."

"The European historians reluctantly declared that their ancestors forcibly removed only nine to ten million African slaves, and another ten million died in the process," Chief Saka said. "Their scholars have intentionally minimized the figures to lessen the shame and the guilt they still carry in their hearts."

"Whatever figures you go by, these were really some ruthless, insensitive and bloody traders," Ablakwa said.

"The Oburoni traders on many occasions destroyed whole villages and entire communities without showing any mercy to the victims," Chief Saka pointed out. "They'd ignored all the rules of war as they pushed farther and farther into the interior to round up every youth between the ages of thirteen and thirty-five in their notorious slave dragnets. They killed the "unslavable" infants and aged folks during these raids."

"Their thirst for slaves was so strong that they did not care how much blood they shed to get the "black cargo" to haul away," Mankrado told the audience with candor. "The moon could not stop their love for the blood money, nor could the rain stop them from getting the slaves. The kind of greed they brought is yet to be surpassed in human history."

"How our ancestors even managed to survive the ordeal for nearly four centuries, this systematic and relentless onslaught, baffles everyone," Ablakwa said.

"The blatant denials of some of them when it comes to wrongdoing on the part of their ancestors have added insult to Africa's pain and suffering," Chief Saka said. "They claim what their ancestors did back then was legal and so they do not need to make any atonement."

"But since they have finally returned to our shores, let us see what news they have brought with them," King Batuka, speaking through Chief Saka, the tall, elegant chief, said in a stern voice. "Instead of thunder and lightening striking them down, maybe a huge colorful rainbow with a shining black star in the middle would emerge from behind the dark clouds."

Taking his usual place on the right side of King Gizenga, Chief Saka nodded to the Queen mother and shook hands with the stool father briefly. The mood was grave and anxious. There were no smiles; it was all solemn. He couldn't make the visitors tell the gathering why they'd returned to our shores. They had to wait for the king to complete all the time-consuming protocol before they got the chance to communicate their message.

There sat a delegation of Oburonis from those who had violated the African continent during the slave trade. They sat in the courtyard of the Cape Coast Castle. It was a nice-looking group basking in the sunny weather enjoying the soothing breeze from the Atlantic Ocean. There were lots of suppressed guilt and sadness in the air. You could feel the waves come in at the seashore, and the white sandy beaches quivering quietly.

Why the king decided to let the descendants of those whose ancestors had once raided our shores to return to the African continent was incomprehensible to many. But he did so to let them show their remorse to the whole world—atonement.

This time, there were no hawks circling the coast and no vultures looking for human remains—common occurrences in those dark, horrible and profane days of the slave trade.

Nevertheless, there was tension in the air, on both sides of the fence. The red roses the visitors had brought with them withered quickly and became lifeless or even useless. The king wanted to know if the visitors planned to placate the ancestors and appease the gods, but he made them wait again for another hour.

Meanwhile, the visitors were breathing heavily. Bubba was anxious and restless. Reverend Peterson was reading from his black book. The waiting was killing them. Some feared they could suffer heart attacks; the suspense was unbearable and elevated their blood pressure.

They could not stare down the king and the elders rudely. They knew that the use of the wrong words could trigger the anger of the king, could put an end to whatever agenda they had in mind. It could also bring on the wrath of the king, but most importantly, it could also bring much worse—the wrath of the African gods.

The delegation members looked gloomy in the tropical sunshine. They had to let go of their pride and address the shame they'd inherited. They waited anxiously for the king to agree to listen to them.

"But what can they possibly say that will pacify us? Nothing! No amount of money can replace our losses," the queen mother said.

The king sat with the elders pondering the future, contemplated dealing harshly with the guests, but decided to treat them with dignity and respect so they could work out a solution for a better future.

What he had in mind was food programs that would eradicate hunger in the land, he also dreamed of a continent without the stigma of slavery and a continent on its way to industrialization and with respect all over the world.

And uppermost on his mind, was the idea of calming down the angry gods of the continent and making peace with the descendants of slave the traders.

TWO

REVEREND PETERSON COULD NO LONGER contain the guilt he'd inherited from his past. He'd been born into money, which was wealth that his ancestors had left behind. He had inherited banks, mansions and farmlands from the slavery past. The rumor had it that he had tried to get the leaders to get rid of the ghosts from the past, to end the secret forces that had been haunting him and his neighbors at night for years.

He was the leader of the Goodwill Delegation to the continent, a group that was going to the African continent to atone for the past. They decided to go to the continent because they'd realized that the past had refused to go away. They also believe that the past has something to do with the strings of havocs that had plagued the region. So they had to go to the continent to ask for forgiveness and seek peace.

The venue for the historical mission was the Shrine of Music, the place where many victims were caught off guard, drunk, helpless and spirited away into captivity. The people who came to have fun and honor the god fell victims to human greed of the Oburonis and betrayed by the misfits among their own people. Many people, however, still believe that those who aided the Oburonis were forced to do some of these deeds because of the cannon the intruders brandished in their faces. Time only swept the guilt under the carpet of history only for the burden to resurface in the future, and did so again and again.

Thus, he sat in the front row at the shrine, his hat in his hand, his arms folded after he'd drunk the ritual—"akwaba water." He was glad the king gave them what was like a warm welcome. He glanced at the king seconds at a time, blinking repeatedly, because the missionaries told them that it was an improper decorum or an insult to make steady eye contact with African leaders. So, his eyes rotated from the faces of the leaders to the courtyard of the slave castle, but his heart was secretly pumping with excitement.

They'd obviously waited for this moment, some had yearned for it, but there was still that part of the preacher that somehow dreaded this meeting—this encounter of destinies—a meeting with the chiefs, queens and kings, the leaders of Africa—the chance to finally show remorse and talk about reconciliation.

He was not the only one wondering what was in store for them. The other members were very grateful for the warm gesture from the king and the elders. Though they saw the queen mother kept rolling her eyes at them during the entire time, they under stood why she was doing that. The queen mother had not forgotten the heartbreaks of several mothers over the centuries and the torrential tears they had to use to drown their sorrows.

When Reverend Peterson was a youth of thirteen he and his father were digging at the back of their house when they entered a large pit that had some slender bones. In the past antebellum days the slaves were buried in mass graves with little or no fanfare. This discovery became a burden that followed him like a dark shadow for the rest of his life.

"One day," he promised himself fervently, "as soon as I live and am able, I would personally lead a group to the continent to make atonement for the ugly past. This would be the humane thing to do. I would visit the scene of the crime to ask for atonement. I would ask the chiefs to forgive us our transgressions against the land, and put down the heavy burden of guilt lingering in my heart all these years."

Meanwhile, the mighty Atlantic Ocean was angry that afternoon. The waves were gigantic, almost thirty-feet high and spilling angry foams of surfs. And the breeze was so strong that it kept their clothes flapping erratically. But the weather was the least of their concerns. They were more concerned about what was going on inside the minds of the king, the queen and the elders.

He was glad that the delegation was finally in the lions' den. He respected the king and the elders and he understood their concerns. All he knew was that the members of the delegation carried the hopes of millions of people who wanted some kinds of closure to the slavery in their past. These were people of conscience, responsible and religious people who wanted the opportunity to put down the heavy burden of guilt they'd carried in their hearts across several generations.

As Reverend Peterson sat on the elegant mahogany chair in the front row at the entrance of the shrine with his fingers crossed, he leaned toward Brandon and whispered something into his ear. He told him he was relying on him to make sure that the mission did not fail. The delegation members were relying on the goodwill of the African leaders.

"I wish we could get the forgiveness we need from the chiefs as quickly as possible," Reverend Peterson told Brandon frankly as he wriggled in his chair uneasily for the twentieth time. As the members of the delegation waited anxiously, you could hear the pounding of their troubled hearts and the occasional loud exhales of pent-up tension.

"Well for nearly four centuries of slave trading and another three and half centuries before atonement and closure, a few hours of waiting should not be that bad, not for the role their ancestors played in this horrible crime," Brandon told the preacher bluntly. "The suspense, the few more hours of waiting, is killing everyone."

"I guess you are absolutely right, though sitting here and not knowing if the elders would reject our proposals is really rough on us," he made his way to the balcony to exhale and to put the pressure aside for a moment.

The king intended for the visitors to appease the ancestors, make atonement for the past and leave here with final peace in their bags. But was he right when he wanted them to concretize their remorse with a reasonable atonement to demonstrate that they were truly sorry?

Whatever they thought, the king deliberately kept them waiting to prolong the suspense, maybe this was his way of getting his personal vengeance. Or maybe, he wanted the ancestors to deal with them directly before he got to them.

Meanwhile, the fragrance of Egyptian musk mixed with myrrh and basil leaves was in the air, and the white suds on top of the palm wine were foaming aggressively, leaving an air of a major milestone in the making.

Reverend Peterson had been on missionary assignments to Africa on three separate occasions. On all these occasions, he loved the reception he'd got and was impressed with the hospitality and how receptive the hosts were to his coming to seek closure to the horrible past.

At the shrine, the reverend saw the Africans pouring libation and preparing sacrifices for the gods. He saw the blood-soaked parts of lambs on the hearth, the priests on their knees pouring homebrew whiskey on the ground to the gods. Bubba was so disappointed and felt very uneasy about it. But why he was so much against the rituals, he did not understand.

These were the very practices they'd preached against in his church.

The delegation quickly realized that the king was a shrewd leader, someone who was very much in control of his kingdom. Though the tragedy happened long ago, the hurt was still very visible, it was too deep for anyone to conceal completely.

"We can forgive you for what your ancestors did. We can even strike a new relationship with you and your people," the priest told Bubba privately. "But we can never forget the "black eye" your ancestors had given us in our own continent."

"That is exactly why we are here today." Bubba told the elders earnestly. "We are here to say that we are sorry, show our remorse and make atonement for this ugly past."

"Well, we can help you put down the heavy burden of guilt in your hearts, but we can only do so if you make some sort of atonement." Zogan the priest repeated. "It has taken you too long to do this ritual."

Those who got angry over the visit of the Oburoni delegation knew that was not the wisest thing to do. "For crimes committed centuries before everyone present here was even born, why should people still get so angry?" the king threw his hands in the air. "It wasn't the modern generation that did it, but it was their ancestors that conducted the slave trade in our land centuries ago."

"Quiet. The king is still on the floor," the linguist told the gathering, ending the sporadic mumbling.

"Maybe the visitors would remember what our ancestors suffered during those dark and ugly days of the slave trade," he said. He wished everyone in the kingdom would agree with him. "We are hoping that the Oburonis would give back to the new generation a fraction of what their ancestors had taken out of Africa centuries ago."

The griot sat in the middle of the gathering on a small wooden stool brooding over the future. There were several youths next to him. They gathered to hear him tell them about the past. He strained his neck to look at the marks on the wall. He reluctantly showed them the marks of shame, symbols representing the number of people who had been taken away as slaves from the Bakano kingdom. He also showed them the few jawbones of the enemy traders on the palace walls. These were the few bittersweet victories our ancestors had over these slave traders.

"Though the past has defeated the present, these gallant heroes would always be in our hearts," the king extended both arms toward the blue sky reaching out to the ancestors. "We would never forget them."

"You are right, your majesty as the griot broke into a sad song. Kondo, the song said, went to the Oburoni people's land, but he did not return. And since he did not return; the elders agreed that we must declare him a soldier missing in action. And we need to sing a dirge for him."

"So, many of our people disappeared one by one, they left in the night, but in groups of hundreds. It was an era of evil, an era of tragedies and an era of shame for both the descendants of the traders and for their victims.

The children continued to sit by the fireside, at the feet of the griot, to learn more about the history. The smoke from the fire kept the mosquitoes away long enough so the youth could soak in the history from the best in the land, from the mouth of the griot, from the highest authority on African traditions in the kingdom.

Since there were next to no written records in the land and no one could write down the dates and the major events, the griot was the expert on the history, the sole authority on what went on in the land. His knowledge came from the thousands of songs, proverbs and adages which had been compiled and committed to memory and passed down over the years to several generations.

"How long did the looting and the exodus of the victims last?" Osei, the youth leader asked, breaking the silence

"For nearly four centuries, these Oburonis raided the land and took advantage of our youths, and bullied our ancestors," the griot sang in a sonorous alto. His sad and trembling voice brought tears to the eyes of some of the youths.

At that point, some of the women wanted to ask the Oburoni delegation that was seated in the front row at the shrine to explain why their ancestors did what they did to the African people. They wanted to know how their ancestors treated their fellow human beings like lower animals.

"I don't believe that you have the courage to come back here to our shores. Is it the guilt from all the horrors from the past that is still weighing heavily on your conscience? Or you have just returned to the scene of the crimes of your ancestors just to view the legacies of the past?" the queen mother waved them off angrily. "Your faces show that the guilt from the past is killing you."

"Really?" Bubba laughed quietly, squirming and dying to respond to that.

"The ancestors should seize the chance to retaliate, deal some deadly blows in retaliation," Dokuwa said. "We should seize and subject them to the same fate that our ancestors suffered."

"Let them speak, let us hear the "amanie" that they have brought," the queen mother finally said. "They are anxious to deliver their message, but the king has kept them waiting. He is not in a hurry to hear them."

"But we need to get on with the ritual, we have to hear them. Either you send them back to where they came from or you deal with whatever mission they have brought," Chief Saka insisted.

"The European slave trade was mainly along the West African Coast, and the Arab slave trade was along the East African Coast. Whatever differences in routes existed, both of these slave trading activities decimated the African people and shattered their security and confidence. They'd destroyed the land and supplanted the culture that our ancestors prided themselves on," the griot told the youths.

It was from these slave castles on the coasts of the Atlantic Ocean that the Europeans ran the slave trade. It was from behind these impenetrable structures, which you might mistake today for luxury palaces, majestic and impressive-looking edifices. And yet these were once the abodes of horror and the fountains of human depravity," the griot said.

"How much money did their ancestors make out of Africa's miseries?" Osei asked pointedly. "I imagine quite hefty sums of blood money."

"Well, they have our ancestor's blood on their hands even today," the griot mused.

"Why did their God allow them to live off the slave trade for so long and at the expense of the African people?" the youth wrote down some of these facts.

"They got a lot of loot from the slave trade. In fact, their ancestors claimed that it was perhaps the most lucrative trade they had ever indulged in," the griot continued. "But all the profit they made came at the expense of the misery of the African slaves."

The linguist remarked, "Their conscience has secretly tormented them all these years. Maybe that is why they have returned."

"Don Pedro for instance was a heavy drinker before he came to the continent, but the shame and the guilt turned him into a bee, into such a heavy drinker. He tried to drown his guilty conscience in barrels of rum and gallons of whiskey just to stay sane," the queen mother said.

"It was the guns that the Europeans brought to our shores that fueled the slave trade. The Oburonis wanted only slaves in exchange for these guns, so our leaders had to comply with their demands or face some drastic consequences. If our ancestors wanted these guns to protect their families, villages, towns, and even to defend their kingdoms, they had to accept the quotas that the slave traders demanded," the griot said.

"At the peak of the slave trade, the Oburoni traders refused to accept even gold in exchange for their guns. They wanted nothing but slaves in exchange for these guns," Mankrado revealed. "Of course, they did not care what these guns did to the African people. In fact, it was a great pleasure to them anytime the guns generated lots of prisoners of war, which meant thousands of slaves for them."

"How did they get neighbors fighting against neighbors?" Teacher Johnson asked. "The Oburonis were behind many of these inter-group wars. They were the people that fanned the flames of old quarrels in the land and incited endless inter-group wars."

"Well, these traders proceeded to arm the different factions and sent groups fighting against groups. The horrific and bloody civil wars that ensued among the Yoruba people lasted for decades. The wars between the Asantes and the Fantes led to the capture of several prisoners of war on both sides, victims the leaders exchanged for more guns to defend themselves and protect their kingdoms. And so the wars between the Ewes and the Akwamus also produced a lot of slaves during the slave trade."

"What did the Oburoni traders do to the chiefs that defied their orders?" Osei asked, and started to write down the answers in his black notebook. After that, he underlined the words bloodshed and profit several times.

"The Europeans traders quickly deposed them, got rid of them and replaced them with subordinate chiefs who were more willing to accept weapons, trinkets and barrels of rum as bribes. The traders preferred stooges, people who were willing to do whatever they wanted," the griot said.

The youth had heard about his great grandfather's tragedy—after seven days of hot pursuit in the forests—just as he returned to his palace, tired and exhausted, he was seized and sent into captivity. His family continues to pour libation in memory of his great grandfather every year, and they have done so for centuries.

"They were not stooges, they were traitors," the youth remarked.

"In an atmosphere of the survival of the strongest, which the Oburonis created in the land, several African chiefs and elders fell for the tempting bait of weapons, trinkets or rum, which the Europeans dangled in front of them like baits," Mankrado said. "The chiefs, out of fear, sometimes cooperated till they got tired and then the relationship with the Europeans ended in a stalemate. Then the Oburoni people proceeded to court the next nearest chiefs, and then armed them heavily to attack those defiant leaders."

"There had been some defections from the ranks of the chiefs, but it was rare because those who turned against their own kings became outcasts in the land," the griot said. "It was also a crime to shed the blood of anyone or to sell members of your own group to the Oburoni slave traders, unless the victim committed a capital offense, treason or slept with the chief's wife."

"These were the demons, which destroyed the solidarity of the people, and played into the hands of the European and American Oburoni slave traders," the griot pointed out.

"Maybe the Oburoni delegation is here to atone for all these profanities in our history, these past deeds that are still disturbing to many of us even centuries after all these deeds," the queen mother wiped her eyes and waited for her turn to speak.

"It is about time these Oburonis address the past, make the necessary atonement, so we can heal," Chief Saka said, looking piercingly into the faces of the delegation.

"Why are they so concerned about the past now?" the queen mother asked. "Maybe the guilt and the embarrassment have finally overwhelmed them. Or maybe the wrath of Mother Nature has begun to put some fear in them."

"Definitely the wrath of Mother Nature is nothing to joke with," the griot rattled some seven shells on the ground. "I wouldn't be surprised if the angry outbursts of Mother Nature have become a serious problem that'd set their conscience on fire, forcing them to come down to Africa to make the atonement that the African ancestors had requested years ago."

"Have they finally run out of excuses?" Zogan the priest asked laughing.

"If the initiative for the trade came from us, as they claimed, then why did their ancestor-traders need all those impregnable slave castles—to avoid the anger of the Africans? Why did they erect the thickest of walls to hide themselves? Why did they need those heavy cannons?" the king asked briefly.

"They couldn't come up with any more excuses. They also used to argue that all these happened before they were born, so why should they be held responsible for these past crimes?" Mankrado remarked. "They usually do not mention the fact that they'd benefited from the proceeds and from the fruits of the slave trade."

"This time there will be no attempts to blame the past on the victims, or on the descendants of the victims, on the African chiefs or on the few misfits who had collaborated with the slave traders," Chief Saka said. "But were they not the so-called religious people with the deep faith? So, I ask why they were so eager to buy their fellow human beings."

"No number of bales of King Cotton could cushion their guilty hearts and no amount of sugar could hide their bitter taste of shame. Why have the descendants of those whose ancestors masterminded the slave trade, those who had executed this diabolical plot against the continent of Africa, not been forthcoming with sincere remorse for the tragedy? This has puzzled many African people, especially the way the Europeans have not tried to concretize their empty words of apologies with some sorts of solid atonement," Mankrado remarked, cleaning his rings.

"What Africans and the Africans in the Diaspora have received as reward have been empty, self-serving words that are equal to dodging responsibility for the slave trade," the king remarked.

"You know it is not easy to accept guilt," the queen mother said. "One of the most difficult things to do in life is to admit that you are wrong and then show the guilt openly. Obviously, the bigger the crime, the harder it is to admit the guilt. But they have at least started to admit wrongdoing on the part of their ancestors."

"Those, whose ancestors came from Europe, from Portugal, Spain, and Holland, England and from the American Northeast, those who masterminded the slave trade, must bear the lion's share of the blame for it. They must make atonement and seek reconciliation," the king was angry.

"Why are they not trying to put the continent back where it once stood before their ancestors descended on our shores like hyenas looking for the next youth to enslave?" the queen mother asked. "What a shameful way to make a livelihood—out of African misery—and did so for many centuries?"

"It is our hope that the descendants of the Europeans and their cousins from the Americas, the North East slave traders and the plantation owners of the former Old South, must confront the past and take responsibility for the mistakes their ancestors made." The griot repeated.

"They'd stigmatized the African people and tainted our history forever," the king declared. "Who would deny that the slave trade has destroyed global respect for the continent of Africa or had placed a badge of shame on the continent and on the faces of the perennial progeny of Mama Africa forever?"

"The slave trade is the main reason that Africans are seen as an inferior race around the world today," the griot shrugged his shoulders. "Is this fair to a people that once worked like beasts of burden to help the white Oburoni people to get to where they are today?"

To add insult to the monumental tragedy, many have denied that they have benefited from the fruits of the slave trade, in spite of all the profits their ancestors had made from the slave trade enterprise, from plantation slavery and from the amount of wealth which they had passed down to their children," the queen mother said.

The king continued to ignore the members of the delegation. "Do they know that they have to make atonement?" the king asked. He whispered to the linguist to ask the members of the delegation to state their business. He sat on his golden stool, straightened himself. He was looking stern and regal in his demeanor. From his persona and the aura of dignity around him, who could deny that he represented the best in African royalty?

The king couldn't ignore the past—nor sweep it under the carpet of history. His goal was to help the visitors to confront the profane past and make atonement. And with the atonement, they could help them to lay down their heavy burden of guilt.

Seated on his golden stool, the king asked the members of the delegation to state their business and some of the women tried to walk away, too angry to hear what the Oburoni delegation had to say.

THREE

T HE HARMATTAN SEASON HAD ALWAYS been a difficult time for the African people. And the queen mother was no exception. The weather was dry, though it was cool in the mornings. The afternoons were hotter than the clay ovens and it made people thirsty. It also brought on cracked lips and wrinkled hands, just a few of the problems that the Harmattan always brought in its trail.

Dressed ostentatiously in her Kente cloth, Dokuwa tied a brown, elegant headgear on her head. She always looked pretty and seductive. She loved to wear her gold jewelry, especially her gold necklaces and large bracelets, which she showed off on special occasions. No matter how loud the elders complained about her vanity, she refused to change her ways to please them.

She hated the Harmattan weather because it made her whole body stiff and left her body aching all over. And she suffered from fatigue because the Harmattan made her easily tired. And to her, the Oburonis were like another brand of the hated Harmattan in the land. They had also drained the sap out of everyone's body. And all the inhabitants could do was to stay out of sight moaning and groaning like a childless mother.

"I hate the dry Harmattan winds that came from beyond the Atlantic Ocean. I hate the waves rocking the Oguaa beach and banging against the pristine shoreline in anger," the queen mother complained bitterly. "It feels like the ancestors are taking their anger on us, instead of penalizing the culprits who had defiled the land."

"The weather didn't make a difference in the trade, nor did it slow down the activities of the slave traders," Dokuwa said. "The castle is still buzzing with activity, the dungeons are still jam packed to capacity and the sailors are still waiting on good tides to haul away their "black cargo" to the land of no return."

The weather, however, did not always cooperate with the slave traders. The angry waves, sometimes thirty feet high, delayed the trip to the New World for weeks and even months.

The king also hated the harshness of the weather, but most importantly, he detested its insatiable greed. He hated the voracious appetite and how it sucked the moisture out of everyone and drained the water out of everything around. He liked how it was cool in the mornings, but watched the damp air dissipate into thin air by mid morning, then it was followed by the blistering heat that overpowered everybody and left many panting for breath and craving water. The least of the discomfort were the many fallen yellow leaves under the trees.

In spite of the bitter weather, the Asafo soldiers did not give up on stopping the slave boats from departing from the African shore. They fought hard, using the strategies their fathers taught them and with the few weapons they'd got from exchanging slaves.

Whether the ancestors participated in the trade voluntarily, or did what they did in the interest of self-preservation, the king knew the ancestors have always been restless and are still ashamed of what happened in the land.

He knew vengeance belongs to the ancestors.

In fact, the cold Harmattan nights required blankets and piles of clothes to stay warm. It also brought cracked lips and holes in heels for several people. The women knew this did not help those of them who were looking for spouses among the eligible bachelors. Many single women tried to defy the Harmattan to find their dream husbands.

The queen mother cared less; she felt these unions simply made it possible for the women to get more children who later became victims to the Oburoni slave dragnets.

The king remembered how long time ago his great grandfather was meeting with the elders, one of his royal duties, when he got word that a mysterious group named "the Oburoni ghost people" had come ashore riding on the cold breeze from the Atlantic Ocean. He quickly sent the Asafo soldiers to stop them. But how could the soldiers stop the gun totting Oburoni intruders, a different brand of the Harmattan from the boisterous Atlantic Ocean, from coming ashore?

"They disobeyed the king when he told them that he didn't want them in his land," the queen mother said. "They disregarded his wishes and forced their way inside the land anyway."

"Whether it was the lure of gold that brought them or the critical need for labor that propelled them to the pristine shores of our aged continent, no one definitely knows," the linguist said.

"I think the king was right when he said they had a plot and that it wasn't their itching feet that brought them," Dokuwa shrugged her shoulders, her braided hair was getting a lot of attention from many men.

As Zogan the priest maintained, "It was either the twisted fate of this continent that brought them to our shores, or the divine ordination of the gods, the pantheon of deities in the land."

"We know that it wasn't the rivers or the streams or the wisps of the deep blue sky above or even the impressive vegetation or the breathtaking scenery," the high priest denied. "It also wasn't the many venerable mahogany and ebony trees on top of the endless range of mountains, some of which reached breathtakingly into the heavens as they towered over the dense forests that brought the Oburoni strangers to the continent."

Why did these different-looking people force their way inside the continent when the inhabitants did not want them in their fold? What actually brought them remains a mystery to today?

"Perhaps the main reason, as many scholars have pointed out, was the greed they had in their hearts, though they tried to pretend that they came simply because they had itching feet, or wanted to help our ancestors to help themselves," the king told the gathering. "The main reason, as far as I know, it was mainly because of raw human greed."

"Don't forget that it was the Oburonis' critical need for cheap labor—African human resources—beasts of burden—heavy muscles to save their immense dreams of economic paradise in the New World," the griot said. "These forces propelled them past the geographical cysts our ancestors had erected around the continent, which had held them away for ages."

"Well, though they denied it, King Mansa Musa's tantalizing display of gold also lured them like bees to the African beehive. Mansa Musa, the flamboyant king blessed with lots of gold, dazzled the Europeans with his gold collection during his pilgrimage to Mecca," the griot told the gathering. "He had gold in quantity no one ever did then or to today."

"He was one proud and wealthy ancestor," Chief Saka remarked flatteringly. "Nobody ever repeated that kind of wealth anywhere."

"He displayed so much gold. He definitely dazzled the audience with more gold than any human being had ever displayed at any time according to the eye witness accounts," the griot continued as he chewed some kola nuts and swallowed the caffeine. "He was overgenerous and gave so much gold away on the journey to Mecca that the price of gold plummeted in Egypt for ten years. One can safely say, though the Oburonis would disagree with this sharply, that he was the richest person that'd ever lived."

"It was either the tales about Mansa Musa's gold or the obsession to find another route to Asian spices that drove the Portuguese adventurers, the Spanish, the Dutch, the British and the other Europeans on to land their caravel vessels on the African shore," the linguist pointed out. "But the saddest part was that they had forced their way in and were sitting on our doorsteps ransacking the land for booty, gold and slaves."

"Which was worse, the rapacious Oburoni locusts or the blistering seasonal Harmattan winds?" the queen mother joked. "Everything was dry, arid, and uncomfortable in the land. The gushing winds were bitterly cold in the morning, blisteringly hot in the day time, and painfully cold at night. But we still could endure the bitterness of the weather, but the Oburoni intrusion, was forever like the death grip of a lion on the neck of a helpless antelope."

In fact, doing battle with the Harmattan winds and the insatiable greed of the Oburoni slave traders at the same time was like fighting a bunch of wild, greedy and ravaging locusts and packs of voracious hyenas at the same time.

"Who in his right mind would invite the old man Harmattan to his home, bringing the dry and bitter weather—the harshness and the severity—so much havoc in its trails?" the queen mother asked. "Who wants the dry skins, the cracked lips and the thirsty tongues anyway?"

"But I think the agony, the despair and the bloodshed from the Oburonis were far worse than the Harmattan," Dokuwa remarked.

The leaves on the trees turn brown during the Harmattan season, falling nearby, underneath the trees, not too far from the roots. The brushes and the leaves quickly dry up and lay ready for sparks of fire. In fact, the least spark of fire usually ends up in acres of land burning down sending the 'grass cutters,' the squirrels, the cobras, the lions and even the almighty pythons out of their underground abodes for dear lives and looking for hiding places.

If they had to choose between the two evils, the people would prefer the Harmattan any day to the Oburoni influx.

"Usually many people pray to the gods that should they survive the two curses, the harshness of the year's Harmattan and the plague the Oburoni locusts had brought to the land, they would do something special to honor the ancestors," Zogan said as he continued to purify the land with the sacred water from the Ayensu River.

"The past was very unpleasant," the queen mother said.

"They promise to appease the ancestors—pour libation should they survive the scorching rays of the blistering sun. And they promised to sacrifice roosters, rams or even calves should they live through the Oburoni ordeal."

"The effects of the Harmattan on the women are used like yardsticks for the youth to choose their spouses. The season is regarded as the best time for a man or woman to select a mate," the linguist joked, though it has a lot of truth in his case. "The Harmattan always separated the truly beautiful women, and handsome men, for that matter, from the artificially decorated ones. Though everyone feels the effects of the harsh weather and the intrusion it causes on their personal lives, they go through the Harmattan without the usual cracked feet and the nasty, ugly chapped lips. The men watched out for those women who still meticulously kept themselves from the debilitating effects of the harsh weather. They got marriage proposals to begin new lives.

"They hold their own gracefully and do so with admiration," the queen mother said.

"The Oburoni locusts proved to be far more deadly to the land and to the people than the Harmattan," the linguist declared regrettably. "And while the weather did some havoc, the Oburonis were much more aggressive, much more brutal. They stayed in the land for centuries, massacred the people and crushed their souls. And even long after they'd departed, the impact of their activities have lingered on in the land," the griot concluded. "In fact, these intruders conducted the slave trade for over three and a half centuries. Believe me; they were much more voracious and much more destructive than the old man Harmattan."

Meanwhile, the priest in the white flowing 'agbada', who had been lost in thought for minutes, finally woke up, rose to his feet from his lazy chair. He took his small bell, rang it seven times and woke up the ancestors to hear once more about what the slave traders had done to the villages, the kingdoms and the civilization in the land, gut-wrenching stories in the pot of history.

Who can explain how such an evil twist of fate plagued the African people in their own land. The kings and the elders didn't want to wait to see how long the exodus and the looting would last. They didn't want to lay any more wreaths and shed any more tears. They were tired of the onslaught. It was simply a losing cause. The invaders had more powerful guns than they did—superiority of technology—weakness against brute force—fueled by greed? They wanted them to depart the land in the night just as they arrived at night.

The rhythmic drums echoed the voices of the fallen heroes. They announced the untold havoc done to the continent. Though the slave trade had ended centuries ago, the people still remember hearing echoes of desperation from the underground dungeons, from the forests and from the grasslands. They still hear their endless gurgling sounds of death, their hysterical screams of pleas against the howling Harmattan winds, from the greedy, bottomless ocean and from across the mighty desert.

Also they hear the booming sounds the European cannons that reverberated against the white sandy, pristine shores and echoed into the endless rows of grasslands, across the thickest parts of the virgin forests, next to the notorious "coconut grove."

They still see the youths still fleeing from their abductors. How it was never a choice between running for dear life and staying behind. Their anguished faces made the decision a forgone conclusion. For when death and slavery stared them in the eyes, they had only one choice. The youths simply split in small groups and went in different directions to evade capture, hiding in the nearby bushes and panting for breath like the leopards.

The Oburonis used their guns as the weapons of coercion to force our African ancestors to play the role they really didn't want to play in the slave trade—collaboration.

The Oburoni demanded quotas from the chiefs to fill their slave boats. If the chiefs came short of these slave quotas, they drew the anger of the Oburoni traders who became displeased and retaliated, drenching the land with rivers of blood.

It was the cannons the Europeans wielded on our shores, not the lure of the arsenal of luxury goods that the aliens brought to exchange for prisoners of war, which fueled the slave trade. The African leaders had to choose from broadcloth, trinkets, brass pots, chamber pots and guns and ammunition in exchange for their "priceless youths" or face the Oburoni cannons.

The monuments these Europeans left behind are constant reminders of what the traders had inflicted on Africa and how they'd changed the lives of our ancestors forever. But the most horrible wound of all was the manner in which these aliens eclipsed an African civilization that was at its apogee at the time they showed their ghost faces.

Obviously, though the Harmattan weather was bad and uncomfortable in the land, it was nothing compared to the chaos the Oburonis brought on their heels, or what their American counterparts introduced into the land from the Atlantic Ocean and from the American Northeast.

The havoc they'd left behind in their trails had been horrible, but the unkindest had been the sunken spirits and the psychological scars they'd left behind. In fact, they had stamped an eternal badge of inferiority on the forehead of every African, regardless of whether they lived on the continent or lived in the Diaspora.

This stigma of inferiority has become the indelible force of degradation that has prevented the continent from making the necessary transition it needs to take its place proudly in global politics once again, as it did in the medieval period and in recent years in the modern global economy.

Africans and the people of African descent in the Diaspora have still been trying to overcome racial barriers. They are trying to cut down forests of discrimination and climb psychological mountains of hate, and conquer the many obstacles in their efforts to survive and achieve.

How can Africans forget the tragedy? Even the new generation knows about what the Europeans did to our ancestors. They know about the abductions, the killings, and the confrontations, the dethronements of leaders and the intense pain and suffering. These are events no one could ever easily forget. These are tragedies written in heavy casualties, in bloody raids, in inter-group wars and in unparalleled misery.

The lives of the inhabitants had been spent dealing with abductions, bloody slave raids and the ensuing chaos, the destructive forces that'd engulfed a once relatively peaceful and prosperous continent. They've buried their dead, mourned the departed and tried to rinse off the blood and cope with the pain, but they have still not been able to put the past completely behind them.

If there was an award for resilience in history, for enduring bitter hardships against incredible odds, Africa definitely deserves that award. Her courage, endurance, resilience and survival in the face of incredible odds went beyond the experiences of other continents. Many people still wonder today how a continent could endure so much, but continue to stand on its feet today.

The ancestors refused to give up. They did not want to let go of the past, or preside over Africa's disappearance from history. They did not want to give up on the future.

Some of the Europeans like to say that the continent has recovered from the cataclysmic damage that their ancestors had done to the land. They do delude themselves that the population has recovered from the temporary itch they'd inflicted. But the empires they'd destroyed have never made the dramatic comebacks they'd described, and the people are still struggling to emerge from the ashes of the slave trade. They are still battling mountains of racism and jungles of inferiority complex.

"How could human beings from halfway across the world inflict so much pain and suffering on their fellow human beings?" the priest lamented. "Why could Mother Nature allow such a horrible tragedy to befall her offspring in her old, beloved continent?"

In spite of the false claim by the Oburonis that they'd brought light to a dark continent, faith to the heathen and civilization to the backward, the Oburonis have rather done more to extinguish whatever light the Africans already had in the land before their arrival.

If they think that the continent has recovered from the chaos of the slave trade, then they better think again. The people are still dealing with the post-traumatic effects of the slave trade to today. The stigma of inferiority from the shameful slave trade is still plastered on the faces of every African that lives on the continent or inhabits the Diaspora.

As the years rolled by, however, the African people have struggled to overcome the disruption in agriculture and the stagnation in industries—interruptions that'd lasted over several long centuries.

The psychological insecurities from the past have continued to follow Africans everywhere. Is the slave trade not the root cause of Africa's inability to make great strides in the modern economic world?

The griot wondered out loudly, "Would the African continent have continued to be the shining example of civilizations in the world, what it once was, if the Oburoni traders had not descended on it like foraging hyenas and destroyed almost everything we had?"

"Though we may never know, maybe the continent would have exceeded all expectations and continued its leadership among global civilizations," the linguist answered.

The Europeans and their American counterparts control the bulk of the fiscal resources in the world today, the very people who ironically climbed to their pinnacle of prosperity with the help of African blood and sweat, must take steps to rectify the lingering post-traumatic plight of the African people. They must also offer some help to those Africans who live in the Diaspora. Though the tragedy happened centuries ago, they must not assume that the victims have recovered from the slave trade or from the effects of plantation slavery. The trauma has been very deep and so prolonged that time has not rectified the identity crises and stopped the degradation of the victims.

With the voices of the ancestors ringing in their ears, speaking loudly through Mother Nature, the chiefs firmly believed that the descendants of the slave traders would return to their doorsteps one day and bring bouquets of red roses to show remorse and rectify the plight of the victims of their ancestors' crimes.

They must do something about the pain and suffering from the slave trade past. They must bring drinks, rams or cattle to appease the ancestors and calm down the angry spirits. Then, after appeasing the gods, they must proceed to make concrete material atonement to help the African people and those who live in the Diaspora to resolve the lingering trauma.

How long must Africa continue to wait for this atonement? The truth is that the ancestors cannot wait forever. They are tired of all the carefully crafted words of apology, sugar-coated excuses, words that have no essence of culpability and are devoid of accountability and liability.

Though many Europeans and Americans have admitted wrongdoing on the part of their ancestors, they are yet to come forward with any concrete atonement package for the pain and suffering of our ancestors. What they've offered so far have been hollow pronouncements, devoid of any sincere remorse. It looks as if they have not realized the enormity of what the continent had suffered from the iconoclastic slave trade, the labor that saved their grand economic dreams of paradise.

Where are the offers of atonement for the victims or the necessary terms of appeasement of the ancestors? The continent continues to suffer in silence and the African leaders are struggling to break into the modern global economic system just as the Asian countries have done in recent years, but with next to no success.

Maybe the Europeans and Americans must reciprocate the help from Africa—put Africa back on its feet.

"This atonement is long overdue," the African chief mentioned.

"They certainly had their tongues in their cheek, whenever they offered their sugar-coated words of apology for the slave trade," the linguist pointed out. "They'd never showed much sincerity in their remorse. They just spoke those words of apology because they know very well that the world was watching them. That the world knows about the horrible atrocities their ancestors committed against Africa and against the people of African descent in the Diaspora would be an understatement."

"They just made the apologies when they did because of the tremendous burden of guilt they'd inherited from their ancestors and still carry with them today," the queen mother said. "But deep down them, it appears many of them have no remorse for the profane past."

"Well, if the media hasn't exposed the horrors of the slave trade and plantation slavery in the libraries and on the Internet, the descendants of the Europeans and the American traders might have continued to bury their heads in the sand even today. Apology would still be the last thing on their minds," the king said. "It leaves you wondering whether these empty words were simply meant to help the new generation to lay down its heavy burden of guilt and end the shame they'd inherited from their ancestors."

In fact, the Africans have realized that these empty apologies were just other instances of the West throwing dust into their eyes. What is the benefit of the empty words for the African people, the victims of this brutal trade?

Why an ancient continent has been overwhelmed and traumatized—the continent that once occupied the forefront of human progress, which had once enjoyed an enviable place in global civilization—baffles many historians.

Europeans, in trying to get Africa to fulfill their labor needs, sacrificed Africa's future on the altar of European and American orgy of greed.

What a noble gesture, the Africans believe, as they continue to nurse the hope that there would be terms of atonement sooner or later to appease the ancestors and to rectify the profane slave trade past. Instead of continued denial of wrongdoing, they would accept blame on behalf of their ancestors. Instead of the continued heavy burden of guilt on their conscience, they would put down this heavy burden. Instead of passing this profane past to their children, they would give them a future free from this heavy burden of guilt—a future with a clean conscience.

FOUR

THOUSANDS OF MILES ALONG THE African shoreline, the voices of the slaves reverberated against the coconut groves. The encounters with the slave traders were filled with horror and tons of guilt. There were many lingering questions about the sordid past, over the old nightmare. Not many people were anxious to find out what had happened during the European encounter with our ancestors, but Modibo and his friend Kamkam decided to do exactly that. The two were history students at the University of Cape Coast searching and researching the slave trade nightmare. They were curious about living in a city that the Royal African Company of England made the headquarters of the British slave trade to Africa.

The Cape Coast Castle was a majestic and elegant architectural masterpiece standing against the blue sky on the African shoreline, but sad to say, it was also the vortex of evil—the hub of the British slave trade to the continent.

What the two researchers found were not only amazing but also attention-grabbing. The Cape Coast Castle, the majestic Tudor-like aristocratic mansion was the residence of several European missionaries, administrators, governors and slave traders. It was also the house of torture, a building of shady commercial deals and definitely a palace of sorrow.

It is no coincidence that the European version of the accounts of the slave trade is filled with self-exculpatory statements. The European historians had spent most of their research time trying very hard to make a scapegoat of the victims trying to put the blame on the shoulders of the African victims.

The more these scholars, Modibo and Kamkam, learned from the African griot, the more curious and excited they became. In their quest, they'd found out the role our ancestors played in the notorious slave trade. They knew what roles the Europeans played, but they also found out how they used chicanery to get whatever they wanted from the chiefs. They knew that the slave traders completely overwhelmed the African people with their firepower—their cannons.

The military might that they'd used in the encounter had not been highlighted in the history of the infamous trade. They European scholars always find themselves looking for African scapegoats for what their ancestors did.

When King Djata no longer wanted to exchange slaves for guns, the Oburoni governor gave him seven days to change his mind. When he refused to cooperate, the Oburoni governor removed and sent him and his family into slavery. He took this stand because though he needed the guns, he knew that this was an immoral practice for a king, an act of betrayal for someone who was charged with the responsibility of protecting and safeguarding his people.

When the governor heard about his defiance, he threatened to remove him from power. So, he stopped cooperating with the governor completely and he even became belligerent toward all Oburonis that ventured into his kingdom. The truth was that deep down him, he was opposed to the slave trade. And he finally stood up and forbade the Oburoni slave traders from marching their slave caravans through his kingdom.

After King Djata made himself clear, the governor who reigned from the Cape Coast Castle like a medieval tyrant, decided to teach the king a lesson. He, therefore, sent a massive force after the king. But when the king was nowhere to be found, the force took Quao, the next big fish, the heir apparent to the Bakano throne. They took him by force into custody. The king heard about the tragedy and resented the fact that such a fate had befallen his protégé, Quao, his heir apparent.

When Modibo got the opportunity to find out what became the fate of a member of his clan, the heir to the Djata royal family, who ended up in the land of no return, he jumped at the opportunity to find out what really had happened to the royal prince.

The story of this man, Quao Ohene Djata, was intriguing. He was the heir apparent to the Bakano golden stool, when the governor's palace garrison from the Cape Coast Castle abducted him when he was on his way home from a funeral. He was taken as a slave and locked up in the dungeon beneath the Cape Coast Castle for weeks. The Bakano kingdom heard about it and rose up, marched to the castle to free him. They charged at the castle, the impregnable stronghold, firing volleys from the impotent guns that the Europeans had supplied to them.

The Oburoni slave traders in the castle responded with the utmost display of deadly force. They fired their cannons with utmost brutality against the inhabitants mowing down hundreds of the attackers in cold blood in the blistering African heat. The cannons took down hundreds of soldiers splattering blood everywhere, on the greens and along the beach. The rest of the forces retreated into the nearby forest, into the savanna and inside the "coconut grove" bidding for time.

As for Quao, the unfortunate victim, seven weeks after the bloody encounter, the slave traders hauled him in the middle of the night through the door of no return. They placed him on the boat at night, though he was kicking and screaming to get his freedom back. He did not get on the boat without a last minute effort to free himself. He attempted to jump into the ocean and drown himself, but the slave traders had extra guards present to prevent him from doing so.

Though that was his last day on African soil, his people did not give up on him. They actively continued to ask the governor to return him to the kingdom and when that failed, they conducted a series of guerrilla attacks on several Oburoni traders, disrupting all slave caravans that traversed the Bakano kingdom.

In retaliation, the people of the kingdom virtually attacked any Oburoni they laid their eyes on, whether he was an innocent missionary, a government official or a slave trader. The rules of law no longer applied. It was retribution in everyway possible.

It turned out that Quao Ohene ended up on a tobacco farm in North Carolina, where he organized several protests against the plantation slave owners. He hated losing his freedom, but even much more, he hated not being able to succeed his uncle, King Djata Gizenga, as the next king of the Bakano Kingdom.

It was extremely hard for Quao to adjust to slave life because of his royal ancestry. Never before had he been so degraded and humiliated in his life and so he didn't want his slave master to get any labor out of him.

But the ordeal got tougher and tougher for him. He'd run away thrice from his master. And thrice he eluded the patrol that had chased him with dogs. He'd escaped and hid in the marshes for six months at a time, eating rodents and sometimes even feeding on snakes. He came to town at night to steal supplies from the plantation owners, but he had to stay clear of the dogs. He had some friends among the field hands who helped him to survive in the marshland and he managed to evade capture for more than six years.

Though he never gave up, this ordeal fatigued his body. But he did not give up the struggle. The years in the marshes wore him down. The thought of being enslaved alone tormented his soul for years. He struggled to stay out of sight during the day. But his mental health was failing. His physical strength was still there, but the idea of being captured at any moment, lynched and possibly even killed gnawed at his soul. He also thought about the patrol shooting him in cold blood in the marshes. But his determination to go back to his kingdom alive, to return to his homeland, to inherit the Bakano throne one day and to claim his birthright in Africa kept him alive.

Though he never gave up, he stopped fighting extremely hard to evade his captors because he did not see a way out of the quagmire. He did not see an end to his captivity. How long could someone live in the marshes evading the patrol?

One day, however, a falcon appeared to him mysteriously in a nearby oak tree; it came from nowhere. It landed on the oak tree in the marshes not very far from his master's plantation. It was as if he were day dreaming. The bird was there fluffing its colorful plumes and was saying something to him.

In the dream, he was swimming against the tide with all his strength and he was headed toward a sinking boat as he searched frantically for a lifeline, an escape route. But it seemed he could not find one. "Your struggles would soon be over," the falcon whispered in his ears. However, he simply brushed the message aside as a joke or a bad dream.

At thirty-seven, he knew that he was at the crossroads of his life. He thought that his quest to return to the motherland might never become a reality, but he knew that no Oburoni was ever going to get any labor out of him. He wondered what the slave driver wanted in the marshes in the broad daylight. "Master Reynolds wants you back on the plantations," Jason told him.

He came out from his makeshift bunker, put down his clubs, hurried toward the field hands. The meeting was mutually friendly, a great reunion, but Quao still had some suspicions. The ordeal was over, and the master he had hated all these years decided to forgive him and give him a second chance?

"He wants me back for what?" he asked the field hands quickly.

"Master Reynolds has a change of heart. He wants to give you a full pardon, set you free without any whipping and lynching," Jason told Quao. He still had some fire left in his belly and thought about continuing the resistance, but he decided to seize the opportunity to leave with the other slaves in the full glare of daylight.

He didn't know whether he should be happy, angry or sad. He didn't know if the message was true or if it was simply another trick to entrap and execute him. He was a sworn enemy of the slave holders and he never wanted any favors from them.

But at that point, it was wise to leave the marshes behind. He joined the rest of the field hands. He ate some home cooked meals for the first time in years and slept in a slave cabin for a change, though he hated the scent in his old, moldy slave cabin.

However, hours after he arrived, his master called him into the "big house" to his living room and told him about the arrangement between the governor in the Gold Coast, now Ghana, his home country and the king of his kingdom. It was to swap him for some British slave traders who had been seized by his people. Quao stood there, looking around surprised. Here was his master with the greatest news for him, the news he thought he would never hear, but there he was debating whether to shout like someone possessed with the spirit of Dente, cry tears of joy, or continue down his path of resistance.

He was leaving the land of no return. He was returning home to the Bakano kingdom. He was happy inside, but he refused to show much emotion in the presence of his master, because he'd nursed so much hatred for this man over the years.

If the prize for his persistence and dogged determination was worth the same as gold, his twisted fate was about to take an unexpected turn for the better. It was giving him back the dream which had never deserted his soul. It gave him a return trip to Africa, the chance to go back to his Bakano kingdom and live like royalty once more, in essence, to be all that he could be.

However, by the time he left his master's living room, he had seen some transformation in himself. For one thing, he had been scrubbed clean; they got the mud off his feet and he had his hair trimmed and the maggots off his shoes. He had lost his front teeth so that prevented him from smiling very much, not that he had much to smile about anyway or had anything to celebrate, especially not after what he had been through in the marshes.

But the images of snakes charging at him in the marshes and dogs chasing and sending him deeper into the more treacherous parts of the marshes were over. Though he knew that they were over, these images continued to haunt him in his sleep and in his dreams. He realized the time he had spent in the marshes were the toughest challenges any living being could ever face.

Life was no longer a guarantee. But he never gave up on being the prince that he once had been. His thoughts about what his royal and aged uncle was doing back home in the Bakano kingdom kept him sane. He was optimistic about the future.

He was very much worried in the marshes because he knew what the patrols were capable of doing to him. He had no doubt how ruthless they could be, if they ever caught him. The more he thought about his physical condition, the more he cherished his temporary freedom. In his mind, it was better to be a free slave in the malodorous marshes, and swamps than to live in the shackled confines of a moldy slave cabin working daily from sunup to sundown.

If the master slave-relationship was supposed to be based on some sort of mutual cooperation, there was no love lust between him and Master Reynolds. He had caused all sorts of problems for him. He had incited seven rebellions against his master.

He had destroyed his crops and he had deliberately set fire to the cotton fields. He wanted one more chance to get even with his master, perhaps his last act of defiance as a slave before his supposed journey back to freedom. He wanted the opportunity to burn down the Reynolda mansion, the master's big house. But Jason, his closet confidant and the head field hand, made sure that he did nothing of the sort, because the patrol could slaughter all of the slaves on the plantation for such a bold act of defiance.

"Your freedom has come, take it, and hold on to it dearly," Jason told him as he helped him remove his field hand clothes and replaced them with house Negro clothes. "No one ever gets to go home from here. Look at you. Aren't you the luckiest slave that has ever lived?"

"Well, I'd never given up on my dreams," he told him. "And that made all the difference."

But the one thought that dominated his mind, the source of sunshine to his soul, the key to his continued survival was the desire to return home one day and rejoin his people. Still, he did not believe what Master Reynolds had told him. It was not enough to convince him that it was real and not just a figment in his vivid imagination. It was like living in a dreamland.

He hated the land of no return. He knew that some of the slaves only tolerated the Carolinas. Others identified with the fortunes of their masters in Tennessee and in Mississippi, but to him, there was nothing lovable about these plantations and nothing likable about the slave owners—not as long as he was a slave in the land of no return.

He knew that his fate had been sealed; he had to work till he died on the plantation as a slave. But his pride as a prince from Africa never died within him. His hopes had never failed and his soul had never wavered.

Why did the master send for him? He wondered why? Why did the other field hands help to wash him clean? Maybe the running, the sickness, the barking of the hunting dogs and the starvation in the marshes were about to come to an end. Maybe his master had a change of heart. But most importantly, maybe his luck had changed for the better.

Master Reynolds could not look him in the eye when he entered the room. He turned his back to him and gazed at the cotton fields through the window the whole time they encountered each other. When he spoke to him for the first time in seven years, he did not look at him or tell him that he was sorry for what had happened. He noted that they both were still angry and filled with vengeance in their hearts.

"Why did the man refuse to look at me?" he pondered. "Maybe he had started to feel some guilt, after all the suffering he had put me through. Maybe all the efforts he had made to bring me in dead or alive had started to torment his soul. Though he was a brutal slave owner, maybe deep down inside his heart, he had some softness; he was still a human being."

"The governor in your country need you back home in exchange for twelve of my people, white traders. I see where you got your stubbornness from, your folks had kidnapped them from a village on the African Coast," he rattled a bunch of keys in his palm, his back still facing him and his eyes glued to the window, perhaps he was surveying the meadows, the cotton fields. "It is not a matter of whether you are going back home or not, but it is how soon we could find you a passage on a ship leaving from the northeast bound for Africa headed back to your home country." Master Reynolds told him.

"Yes sir, master," he finally said to him. That was the first time he had spoken to him in seven years.

After all he had been through over these few years; he thought the news would be exhilarating or mind-blowing. Unfortunately, however, he had no immediate feelings of joy and no spontaneous outbursts of jubilation. His heart had become immune to any sort of good feelings or any joyful news. Obviously, nothing excited him anymore.

Would he have had the opportunity to go back home, if his folks had not abducted the twelve Oburoni slave traders forcing the governor to request his release from his master in exchange for these hostages?

Which of his memories were worth salvaging and which ones were so bitter that he wanted to leave them behind forever? He knew that he had to get rid of his experiences quickly because they had been extremely negative.

When he got to the slave boat to the notorious "Liberty Express," he took one long look in the direction of the Reynolda mansion and watched the tobacco plantation from the distance and he instinctively let out a deep sigh of freedom. "You will pay for all these brutality several generations to come," he told his master and the other slave masters angrily. "If you think you will continue to get away with these forever, you must rethink the future."

He was going back home. He was expected to be in a happy mood, but he was more shocked than happy. The truth was that he had one in a million chance of ever returning home from the land of no return. He was returning to his motherland a free man.

It was something he never expected. He was going to be the very first to ever return to the Bakano Kingdom, to the bosom of Mama Africa, from the land of no return. "I hope I am not dreaming. I wonder if the return journey home is actually a reality and not a fantasy or a wild, vivid dream."

He was leaving the world of slavery behind. He was going back to the other world of freedom. He was going back to dignity, to the other side of humanity and to the other side of the Atlantic Ocean. "I will know kindness and love again in my life. How will I fit back into this old world of dignity and privilege, a world that I have left for years?" he asked himself. He sat down calmly, pondering over these questions.

The head slave offered him a handshake and a warm embrace. "Your freedom has been handed back to you, now make the best of it!" he told Quao.

What does a man do when his or her cherished dream comes rushing back—his soul yearning to become the next king in the Bakano kingdom—a legendary king. This dream was about to become a reality, in spite of all the incredible obstacles he had to overcome in the Diaspora. He would be king in two years.

FIVE

H E HAD AN EXCITING AND eventful life. He'd been intoxicated with the Blues. In his dreams, he was feeding on barbecue ribs and beer to wash it down. How could he not do so when he lived in Memphis, a city known for its music and its extraordinary world-class culinary arts? How could he not have the time of his life when he could go to Beale Street and dance to Rock and Roll or listen to the Blues? Whether it was the cuisine, the music or the warmth of the people, he thoroughly enjoyed the Bluff City, the music, the food and the warmth of the people.

It was the fun, the beer on Beale Street or the seductive, exquisite looking women that enthralled him.

"Life seems to be going great," Brandon remarked, "In fact, it is going quite smoothly. It couldn't be any better with all the good food, pulsating music and good-looking women that were present out there in full force."

Behind this façade, however, there was somewhat a different reality. In the streets, in the schools, in the churches and at the board of education and even in city hall, there were rumblings of the aged profane past coexisting side by side with the roars of modernity and the dawn of new technology.

"Many businesses have moved outside the city, relocating outside city limits. They were moving from the inner city farther east to the suburbs to the affluent neighborhoods. We know the laws of supply and demand dictate business behavior, but why some of these businesses have moved into the neighboring states puzzles many of us," Trent remarked, bluntly.

"Did the trend begin because the city elected its first African-American mayor in its history?" Brandon asked. "Or like many major cities, was it a quest to move away from crime in an inner city? Or did the European-Americans or the bulk of the business owners feel threatened by the new political realities in the city? Did they develop a sense of insecurity because of the change in the power dynamics?"

"If race is the reason they are moving, they are not saying it openly," Steve pointed out. "Those who have moved say quickly, rightly or wrongly, that they've moved away because they wanted to escape the high incidence of crime in the inner city."

Why are the public schools in these suburbs getting heavily overcrowded with migrants from metropolitan Memphis schools? Why have some of these schools actually doubled their enrollment, sometimes at the expense of the exodus of the migrants from Memphis?

"Well, they could run away from the racial problems, they could put a distance between them and the problems in the city, but they are simply postponing the inevitable," Trent flipped through the newspaper. "Are they not missing the golden opportunity to confront and deal with the profane past, with problems that hold back the city?"

"The city would overtake them once more, when it wins the annexation fight in court," Brandon concluded. "They could run, but they could not hide from the dragnet of the city."

Memphians have tried to take down the old curtains of racial barriers that have been so closely woven into the cultural fabric and the ethos of this historic city, but the progress has been a slow and painful one, though the process still actively continues today.

It seems Memphians live in a city of contradictions, a city in which you hear great soul-searching songs of integration, great recipes of collaboration, but you still hear racial slurs in the streets. You even hear pejorative racial terms, though this has become less frequent with the passage of time. You hear allusions to the past muffled in their tracks and even sometimes you hear them in deliberations at the various levels of government.

Though many people deny the truth or run away from it, there is guilt lingering in the hearts of the descendants of those whose ancestors used to own Africans as slaves. But because this is so embarrassing for them today, some simply try to shift the guilt to the victims. You see a visible conflict in their conscience.

"How do we solve the problem of racism on both sides of the divide in this city?" Bubba asked Trent, after a meeting in the famous hotel downtown.

"Well, the good news is that things are improving in Memphis, when it comes to race matters," he said. "But there has been a lot of movement of citizens to the suburbs and out of state. But the paradox is that the cultural fabric of the city has remained stronger than ever before."

How can you live in America, in such a beautiful city, in a land known for its freedom but continue to experience racial conflict? It seems like a dream from which people will wake up one day and be told that what they see before them, what they experience on regular basis, shaped heavily by the burden of the profane past, is not real and that the modern racial problem is just a façade, a fiction—just a chimera in their imagination.

To say this is by no means to yield to existentialist despair.

The optimists still see signs of hope and progress on the horizon. They see visible signs of progress among the new generation. They see hope on the horizon when one sees small boys and girls of all races playing basketball, football, or baseball together in harmony in the streets, in the parks, on school playgrounds or competing together on school teams dying for victory. One sees sunshine in the sky when these young people depend on one another regardless of race, color or national origin to win or lose championship contests. Though the color of their skin is different, they realize that their destinies are tied together. They are lumped into one big mass of humanity, a rainbow of a melting pot which many of their ancestors thought could never happen.

When one sees these youths sitting side by side in classrooms, in the cafeteria, oblivious of race or when one sees them working on projects together day in and day out, becoming oblivious of their skin color, then one begins to breathe sighs of relief. Then one sees some hope for a country that champions and cherishes freedom, but has been plagued with a baggage from a complicated past of slavery and racial inequality.

Those who are looking for racial harmony have operated behind the scenes, in the spirit of collaboration, in the hope of a better future . . . for a Greater Memphis . . . for more triumphs in music . . . for more successes in sporting activities . . . for more businesses in the city . . . for low-level crime, for a safer city, for a city where the children are getting the best education the city could afford, regardless of skin color.

The truth is that several people in the city are afraid to face the stark realities. Some of them are saying things that do not come from their hearts and are doing things that are sometimes far from the true dictates of their hearts. Publicly, they put on a façade of racial collaboration, but privately they still harbor the irreverent past in their hearts. They harbor thoughts on both sides of the divide that they dare not reveal publicly.

While some on both sides of the divide reveal what they truly feel in their hearts, and verbalize these thoughts with conviction, others choose to be much more reticent and diplomatic.

From both sides of the racial divide, Brandon and Bubba, have tried to find a true solution for this inexplicable schism in the social fabric of the city. They seem to be making some progress. There are few signs in the city that say so. But they also realize from the hectic fights from all sides over city and county school merger issues, and from city and county government consolidation rancor that the collision of the past and the present was far from over.

These are the realities that each person who lives in Memphis and in several cities across America must deal with each day. People confront these unwritten social realities judiciously, but many others have simply ignored them. They secretly hope that these muted and muffled tensions in the city would not explode into uncontrollable racial inferno, which will engulf their city, burn down their property and endanger their families.

There are people who simply do not care about the racial divide and operate their daily lives as if this problem does not exist. They believe ignoring it is an excellent way of dealing with it. But the sooner they wake up and acknowledge the existence of these problems, the better for everyone, because these problems will certainly rear their ugly heads again and again.

The fact that the city had two separate school systems, two separate governments and several separate neighborhoods means that the city must acknowledge and address the dichotomy, the racial divide. It must attend to the dualism in many things in this beautiful, musical, historic city.

The inhabitants of the city are constantly reminded of the death of the legendary African-American civil rights activist in this city, how he sacrificed his life not only to bring this city together, but also to beat the warning drums for the country, to make this country a better place for all.

Six

"I T IS TIME FOR YOU to confront the past. You must return to the scene of the crime," the voice told him repeatedly. "You must return to the African shores, to the continent that had been put through this trauma and make atonement."

He heard the charge repeatedly, but since he did not believe in superstitions, he refused to believe that the call was genuine, that it was reality.

Still, Bubba groped for the patience and courage to deal with the tangibles and intangibles in his life and the plethora of problems in his world. He lived in a city in which the concrete issues and the glut of imponderables that the irreverent past has imposed on him, on his folks and on the society in general continue to haunt many people.

Then one summer he had dreams that he was at a barbecue feast and the propane grill caught fire, exploded and burned uncontrollably for a good thirty minutes. The guests took off running for dear life, the children were screaming, but he stood firm to put out the fire with the keg of black cherry punch. He knew that was the final sign for him to cross the Rubicon, to do something about the problem before the city explodes into another conflagration.

He'd brooded over the problem long enough. He'd been faced with the dilemma of denying the past, or confronting it and seeking a permanent resolution or even walking away from it like a coward. The guilt from the past, his father's stern warnings before he passed on and the thought of change were too painful dilemmas for him to confront, so he could only hold his head down, heave a quick sigh and inhale the burning propane.

For one thing, he was a rebel at heart—strong, bold, and proactive or dedicated to the ideals of his heritage. His neck was huge like an oak tree, or rather like that of a superstar in one of the favorite pastimes. His mouth was thin, but slightly protruding under his sharp blue eyes that looked like those of a hawk looking for birds of prey.

He was partially bald and sweated profusely in the heat of the summer, but he even sweated when the weather was cool. He usually wore overalls with red suspenders, and cowboy boots, typical fashions in the region. He idiosyncratically used his two thumbs to raise the two red suspenders over his huge chest and tapped his shoes on the ground to emphasize his points anytime he spoke.

In his heart of hearts, however, though several of his friends couldn't say the same thing, his mind was not locked into the racist past, nor was he someone who has personally discriminated against African-Americans, he never did that knowingly, not overtly. Since his great grand father once owned several slaves in the state, he decided to do something about the burden of guilt that he'd inherited from his heritage. He wanted to mash some of the chunks, which were still sitting at the bottom of the pot of history.

Sometimes he debated whether there was the need to do something about the profane past of slavery because it definitely troubled him. He knew he had to quit pretending that time would eventually drag the burden of guilt into historical oblivion. But he knew time has not eased the pain, he hears the sad blues echo the past at every turn. The fields continue to scream with sad, screeching voices from the past.

How many dreams about the ghosts of slaves from the past did he have for the past five years—uncountable? How many skeletons did he come across digging behind his barn? How many voices did he hear screaming in his great grandfather's mansions in the middle of the night?

He was very much into the church. That had intensified his guilt and tormented his soul. He would get his friends to do something about that part of their heritage. He was losing sleep over it, and he agonized over leaving the same baggage of slavery, which had been bequeathed to him, to his children and grandchildren. He could lead a crusade to end the guilt over his ancestors earning their livelihood from the miseries of their African slaves.

The race issue was a priority for him. This was a matter he knew he needed to find some sort of resolution. He knew they had to come to terms with the past. If it takes leading the fight for apology, remorse and atonement, he knew he must do exactly that, to ease his conscience.

Fortunately for him, several of the old guard from the turn of the century had passed on, so the climate became slightly better to do something about a past that used to be "a taboo" to meddle with. He still cherished his ancestors, but he felt the time has come for his generation to set its own generational agenda.

When he began to get his congregation to tackle the burden from the past, he was seen by many as meddling in things he should have left alone. He was confronted with his toughest challenge that involved race and racial integration in the schools. He had to debate whether he wanted to continue to separate the races or to bring them together with a common destiny.

He was sure that integrating the school systems would benefit everyone better, but sometimes the reality was like a double edged sword cutting into his heart.

"More taxes for the suburban cities, so I can send my children to those areas where my cousins live, or send them to the parochial church school and pay the astronomically high fees so that my children can experience life with mainly their own kind, or should I rather send them to the city schools for free in order for them to experience the realities of modern multi-racial America?" Bubba asked his wife, Louise, who looked as confused and as worried about the future like her husband?

Louise had never worked a regular job a day in her life, but supplemented the family income with "old money" from the slavery past she'd inherited from her great grandfather. But that pot of black gold money had almost dried up and the family was staggering under mountains of private school fee debt anyway, so the two were seriously considering all their options.

But time was not on their side. School was about to reopen and the children had to know something soon. Bubba felt that he had to make a decision about where to send the children and that decision had to be made pretty soon.

A round-faced principal in an expensive suit sat at a huge mahogany desk and smiled dryly at them. "Mr. and Mrs. Bubba Reynolds, I presume?" he asked. Mr. Clark, the principal asked, sounding rude and indifferent. No matter how well he tried to camouflage his feelings, it was obvious he did not think much of Bubba and Louise. Maybe they did not come from a privileged background like he did, with lots of money like he did. Maybe they did not attend the best schools in the South, Wake Forest, Duke or Vanderbilt, Tulane or others.

For the first time, Bubba knew that maybe class was more important than race. The snobbish attitude of the principal nauseated him and helped him make up his mind and very fast too. "Yes, I am Bubba and this is my wife Louise," Bubba replied, looking at him dead in the eye and not flinching. He had already sensed the principal's condescending attitude and noted even his secret resentment toward him and his family.

"Well, we have tried to work with you and your wife in the past, but your children cannot enroll in this institution this fall if you do not clear the balance of fees you owe the institution," Mr. Clark told them bluntly.

"What options do we have, Mr. Clark?" Bubba folded his arms over his chest, breathing heavily,

"As much as I would like to help you, I am very sorry to say that you have run out of options. Believe me, what I am telling you is not personal; it is simply school policy."

"Well, what a pity. We will go and try to borrow some more money from the bank and see what we can do before school starts on Monday," he told the principal. "But our chances look very slim at this point."

"I know. Well, good luck to you and your children," Mr. Clark told them as they headed out the door. He had a feeling that was the last he'd seen of them. "The semester opens in a few days, so you need to pay off the balance as soon as possible."

"Thanks, maybe we cannot continue to pay all this money," Louise told Bubba curtly. "This principal has promised to give the children not only the best education possible but also some sort of partial scholarship. He'd promised to keep them safe and well-educated, but the only thing we have noticed from all of his promises is that we are drowning in a pool of debt."

"I made a promise to my children I cannot break," Bubba said, sounding angry and resolute. "But maybe this is one promise I have to renege on, unless there is a sudden miracle. It is becoming ridiculous the way the bills from the school keep on mounting and mounting."

"And . . ." Louise said, watching Bubba with a dry smile. "What do we do next?"

"The promise we've made to the children to uphold the dreams of our great grandparents from the past, the dream of keeping our children in parochial schools separate from the mainstream for the reasons I told you before, we cannot continue to keep," Bubba told Louise and dropped his head as if a ton of brick had fallen on him.

This was perhaps one of the turning points in Bubba's life.

"I am glad you have finally seen the light," Louise smiled. "I was wondering how long it would take before you came to your senses and to that realization."

"Well, as Mr. Clark was talking . . . do you think he will give them any sort of partial scholarships next year to ease the pain?" Bubba asked Louise.

"Hell, no," she answered quickly. "He thinks we are dummies anyway. And how can he give scholarships to the children of dummies?"

"He broke his word to us, to this family, and he did so twice already," Bubba said. "It is like he is just taking us for a ride, playing with our emotions and our children's future."

"Well, all we have to do is to forget about this money and send our children to the public schools where most of our neighbors send theirs anyway and get to brag in our face about basketball state championships, and great soul musical concerts," Louis told Bubba.

"That is okay," Bubba told Louis. "I know several doctors in Memphis that went to the public schools. Dr. Itzkovitz, our family doctor, went to Central. Dr. Bencerdes, the dentist went to White Station. They went through the public school system right here."

Days after they'd left the principal's office; Bubba became a very relieved person. He no longer has to sit before Mr. Clark's Sanhedrin again. But most importantly, he was no longer worried about the high fees and the pressure of losing face with his neighbors. He was no longer guilty of shielding his children from the naked multi-racial reality of modern American society, a nation that is increasingly becoming pluralistic, though it still has all sorts of chunks in the melting pot. He was no longer afraid of his children going to Goodview High. And he was also not afraid of his children playing on the same teams as the descendants of people his ancestors once owned as slaves. He just wanted them in school, good schools getting good education and playing on winning teams. "The textbooks are the same and the teachers basically went to the same local colleges and universities anyway," he rationalized. "So, what is the big fuss?"

He couldn't have said the same thing a decade before, nor was he willing to travel the same road of integration that he'd decided to cruise on that day. "It was not cool to do that in my family then and it was frowned upon to the point they could disown me. But that was yesterday," Bubba told himself.

"It would be a new experience, but as the other parents have done, we can also adjust to the change," Louise took a big gulp of her iced tea, "Who knows, we might even come to like it better."

"But how do I react if Rickie, my teenage son, falls in love with the big derriere girl from across the racial divide?" Bubba looked worried as he stared at Louise. "What do we do? Just say love is love, no matter . . ."

"Why are you worried about these unnecessary things? Are you the one falling in love with her derriere?" she joked, but pointedly.

"Hell, no, I can't even handle you," he said and shook his head.

"We would cross that bridge when we get to it," she told her husband. "Just let that one rest till . . ."

"Well, maybe the future would take care of itself," he told Louise resignedly, though secretly the possible interracial paradigms confronting him were still secretly gnawing at his soul. "I have got to bite the bullet somehow, once and for all. But it is not easy to shed my old spots."

As they drove home, they looked up into the blue, sunny sky and saw the colors of a rainbow in the sky. They were surprised to see the many colors and the deep black star in the middle. But he was still worried about his children's social life in the public schools. He was still battling his guilty conscience and he was still fighting his past.

When you live in a city that has a racial divide, it creates separate lives for different segments of people. Many people's attitude to education has been based on the fusion of all the students into a single unit. The city must boast of a school system in which any student can attend any school and get the best education possible.

On the contrary, the reality is that African-American students and poor whites fill the inner city schools while the affluent white students dominate the county schools, most of the time with better facilities. When would change come to such a beautiful city and to many other cities around the country? All they have to do is to use the resources to enforce the standards everywhere for all the children.

For the young adults, there is hope because most of them have grown up in an atmosphere of integration. The ghosts of the past do not preoccupy the minds of most of these youngsters in their day-to-day activities. Many African-Americans, Hispanics or Asians effortlessly sit side-by-side Caucasians in the cafeteria, in the libraries, on the fields and in the parks. They even do interracial dating, though many of them, taking cues from their parents, do so cautiously.

Also, during competitive basketball, baseball or football games—in those situations, no one is thinking along racial lines at that time—the determination to emerge winners becomes paramount in everyone's mind. It doesn't matter if you were white or black, yellow or brown, Asian or Hispanic, the team depends heavily on everyone to cruise to victory or snatch a win out of the jaws of defeat the hard way. Whether it takes a Hispanic, a Jew, a Caucasian or an African-American to score that buzzer beater, the team needs someone to score the point. In the end only one phrase really mattered to all of them—"We won. We are the champions."

For several adults, however, it is still a struggle of uneasy coexistence, of trying to dream of a one big, harmonious racially, inclusive city held together by barbecue parties, rich musical heritages of rock and row and blues, annual festivals and team sports, while at the same time trying to let go of the baggage inherited from the decadent pasts.

Bubba continued to ponder the fate of his region from his swivel rocker. He has always defended his ancestors for standing up like men and women to defend their way of life when the sacred moment of honor and duty required the sacrifice of them. He had a great affinity for Southern cuisine. He loved fried chicken, barbecue ribs, turkey and dressing, fried okra and gumbo. But above all, he loved the warmth of his people. He cherished his voluptuous women and his religious fervor, but the signs of the time meant they'd to drastically change their thinking with regard to certain things.

Healthy lifestyle and racial toleration are in vogue.

Some whites have the feeling that their ancestors had been wrong in owning African slaves and in treating them harshly. And some still ask whether that was the moral thing for their ancestors to do even back then? Whatever they think, Bubba knew that they still carry a burden of guilt in their hearts from the profane past of slavery.

But others maintain that not all their forebears had slaves, and those who did had no alternatives back then, and that slavery was the only way of life many of them knew. They couldn't just stand aside and let go of their heritage without fighting for it, They couldn't forfeit their property that had once been tied up in mainly African slaves and they couldn't just walk away from the Northern intrusions and offensives like cowards.

It was good old Southern noblesse oblige.

They had to stand up and be counted as people of honor, as true Southerners, and as people who had kept the faith and the dream alive. They had to uphold the historic solidarity ideology that had prevailed in the Old South, adhere to what the good old Professor James R. Chancey describes as the "Proto-Dorian" ideal.

Has time dissolved the past, and swallowed its racist institutions?

On the other hand, how do African-Americans forget stories of distant uncles being lynched in the past? These are tales, long ago forgotten by some, but are still as fresh in the minds of many as if they'd happened only yesterday. They couldn't very well put the past behind them. They couldn't pretend that opportunities are equal, when their names, their skin color, in some cases, are constant reminders of the scars from the unequal slavery past.

If they move to the suburbs, live next door to the whites there, will they be accused of betraying their own or lowering property values for others? And will they be viewed as unwanted residents in these areas, subjected to constant harassment, or welcomed with open arms, and be at peace with their neighbors? Would the true melting pot sit on their porches?

As the days come and go, the years rolled by reluctantly dragging the profane past screaming along like a carriage behind a reluctant horse and the seasons continue to change, giving way to years, decades, centuries, Mother Nature struggles to deal with the past in the present, to get some justice for the aggrieved.

Obviously, this is a struggle to embrace progress and modern technology while the chariots of fire from a turbulent racial past continue to pull the city sometimes in the opposite direction. It is also a battle between old father time and the new forces of mother progress.

It is gratifying that the millions of Africans who were taken out of Africa to the Diaspora have been enjoying free productive citizen status for centuries, they could vote and even get elected to high offices, but the irony is that they continue to encounter mountains of discrimination, as the country continues to deal with both the guilt and the anger from the slavery past.

In fact, the forces of reconciliation have tried to heal the old wounds that slavery had left on the descendants of the victims. They have tried to create a better future for everyone, starting with apology and some remorse, though doing so have not been easy.

The nation has tried to say that it is sorry for the past of slavery, for the horrendous atrocities committed against the African people on their own continent, and for the tremendous brutality the former slaves had endured across plantations and fields in the former Old South in the New World, even up North in Ohio, New York, New Jersey, across the Caribbean, and spanning the Americas to Brazil.

Still, these efforts to rectify the past have been sweet empty words without any sincere remorse or any concretized acts of atonement. The time for sweet honey coated apologies is definitely over. It is time for atonement and the final reconciliation.

Would Africans on the continent and African-Americans in the Diaspora be expecting programs for the enormous liability America owes to Africa and to the people of African descent who live in the Diaspora? What of the Europeans, those who started the slave trade, what do they owe? What should the Portuguese, the Danes, the Dutch and the British do?

What would stop the African victims from thinking that every Caucasian person they see walking around owes their ancestors and them something because of the profane past of slavery even though their ancestors had nothing to do with the slavery legacy?

Each city, town or community has struggled with the past differently. Some cities have been managing the dialogue between the races very well. Others have let it get out of hand and exploded into open confrontation, and even at times some have ended in uncontrolled calamitous conflagration, through issues such as annexation, the merger of both inner city, and county governments and attempts at the consolidation of educational opportunities for students of all the races. But the most incendiary issues have been centered on racial profiling.

Bubba smiled. He'd taken the right step. He'd crossed the Hernando-Desoto Bridge. That was the moral thing to do, he conceded to his wife. He knew that if he wanted to let go the guilt from the past, he must travel the right road—atonement—no matter how symbolic or substantial.

SEVEN

T HE AFRICANS PREFER NOT TO talk about the European slave trade to Africa, a tragedy which officially ended more than two hundred years ago. They had been dealing with the aftermath of this catastrophe forever, it seemed, by trying to suppress or ignore it or, if they decided to do so, by pouring libation to the ancestors and to the gods.

The descendants of the Africans who forcibly, or voluntarily, participated in the slave trade still feel the shame and the pain from the past. That is why many Africans do not want to talk about the slave trade, because it was not only immoral, but also an embarrassment for them. In spite of the fact that their ancestors more forcibly than voluntarily participated in the slave trade, they still bear some responsibility for the slave trade. Their ancestors had the most difficult dilemma. It was if they participated in it they were immoral, and if they didn't, they ended up as slaves themselves. It was a no win situation for them.

King Gizenga, and the inhabitants of Oguaa, around the Cape Coast Castle areas, has been the shining example of the several initiatives in play to remember the departed victims, honor the ancestors and to help the returnees, the descendants of the victims who live in the Diaspora to make an active connection with the continent if they so desire, to reactivate their identity and to find their roots.

Of course, the Panfest Historical Theater Project, the brainchild of the likes of Mrs. Efua Sutherland, has become a cultural paradigm that creates a hub for Africans born in the Diaspora and on the continent to break bread and dialogue over the slave trade past and plantation slavery, to seek common grounds and plan collectively for the future.

Ayekoo to such progressive Pan-Africanists, to the governments that are fostering this solidarities, all those chiefs and kings reconnecting severed historical links and reuniting DNA to DNA.

King Gizenga led a group that wanted to find closure for a bloody, bitter and brutal past. He decided to break his long code of silence and address the bitter past openly in the presence of the ancestors and before the descendants of the victims who had returned to our shores from the Diaspora. But he must ask for the atonement that the gods have asked from the culprits.

During Panfest Festivals many of the offspring of the victims have returned from countries such as Trinidad, Jamaica, the Virgin Island, Brazil, Montserrat, Cuba, Haiti, Canada, London, Lisbon, Madrid and the United States to attend the soul to soul festival in remembrance of the victims. The idea is the reuniting of the victims from all over the Diaspora with the continent to create a positive approach in forging ahead in a global environment.

Jim Jacobs, for instance, came down to the festival that hot summer from Kingston, Jamaica because he found his roots in the former Gold Coast, renamed Ghana. It was because the new tool of DNA has positively linked him to the Ga group in the Accra area in Ghana. He didn't want to leave the connection just on the romantic level; but he wanted an effective connection with his Ga roots. He wanted to break bread with his newly discovered cousins, uncles, grandfathers and grandmothers since the DNA evidence positively linked him to the royal family in the Teshie-Nungua area in the capital city in Accra.

He was ecstatic that he'd found his long-lost relatives. And he'd found his roots. The Hesse Odamten family welcomed him with open arms. It was his ardent desire to become part of them and so the members went to great lengths to extend warm hands of hospitality to him. The African family tried to foster this newly resurrected kinship bond with the returnee Jim Jacobs, the outspoken Jamaican born with his idiosyncratic dreadlocks.

There he stood in the middle of the compound; his clothes, hair style and songs routed through Jamaica, but his spirit and soul were deeply rooted in the continent, in Teshie-Nungua. He was the soul brother from Jamaica, who spoke Jamaican dialect with the African past yearning for his African identity.

King Gizenga knew that his forebears had played a role in the slave trade, whether it was forcibly or voluntarily, they did. This has continued to plague his conscience. He did not want the returnees to continue thinking that the African chiefs had invited the Oburonis and sold their own to the Oburoni slave traders, and did so gleefully. He knew that his ancestors, his predecessors, many of them Gizengas were guilty to some extent of collaborating with the Oburonis to enslave his own people, but it was in response to pressure and coercion. But as the king, he was tired of carrying this burden of guilt in his heart. The idea out there that his ancestors betrayed their own people as leaders when they needed them most troubled his soul exceedingly.

He knew that his ancestors were reacting to the insatiable demands on the part of the Europeans for slaves. They were trying to survive an impending holocaust, which the Europeans had created and master minded on the African shores using their guns and cannons as dragnets.

The king looked troubled and unsettled. "What my ancestors did was in the past, but if an apology could alleviate the pain in any way, we can do that. As a matter of fact we have rendered several apologies to our blood kinsfolk in the Diaspora and did so on numerous occasions and in many places already."

Since he felt that his ancestors did the wrong thing in the past, he led his sub chiefs to apologize to the descendants of the victims and to those who live in the Diaspora. They had to address the turmoil raging inside their conscience over the dark past. They had to come to terms with it.

King Gizenga, decided to render a fresh apology on behalf of the ancestors at the Cape Coast Castle once again and make atonement for the role their ancestors played forcibly or voluntarily. "We are sorry for whatever roles our ancestors played in the past to part our bloodlines," the king said. "These drinks and sacrifices we have for the gods."

"It is the proper thing to do. These sacrifices to the gods, the traditional African ritual of remorse, would lead to atonement and reconciliation," Zogan, the priest said.

A delegation of chiefs decided to do the same on the road on behalf of the African continent. They headed overseas to pay their homage and render their heartfelt apologies to those Africans who live in the Diaspora. The chiefs chose Washington D. C., New York, Atlanta, Memphis and several other cities in the United States for these symbolic rituals of remorse, atonement and reconciliation. "In fact, this is like apologizing to ourselves because these folks belong to the same bloodline as we do. They are our descendants, our own relatives," Togbe Gbedro Zendo X said in his quiet demeanor. "Well, we need to make the atonement since the gods are asking the descendants of the Oburonis to do the same at a much more dramatic level, that is if they want to live in peace," Zogan told the paramount chief.

In fact, many, if not most, Africans experience flashes of anger and pain whenever they think about the European slave trade to the continent. Though the tragedy happened centuries ago, the thought of the tragic event still stirs anger, pain and even remorse in their hearts. Africans still feel a sense of humiliation, a sense of degradation whenever they remember this tragedy. They resent the idea that this tragedy took place on their shores and that their ancestors couldn't stop the carnage. They are surprised that the gods didn't use the blistering heat or the bitter Harmattan winds to kill these intruders. They wondered why they allowed them to do what they did in the land.

The slave trade was nothing that pleased the African leaders, because it was a dark horrible institution that the Oburonis brought to our shores and literally imposed on the chiefs. Africans refer to the slave trade as "death is better than". In fact, many of the chiefs had been coerced by circumstances to participate in the slave trade and they did so largely because of the instinct of self-preservation.

"It was either the chiefs and kings found the slave quotas for the Oburoni traders or became slaves themselves, when these greedy Oburonis came for their "African cargo," King Gizenga explained.

This destroyed the continent, a land which was in the forefront of human progress and civilization at the time these Oburoni traders arrived. But they ended up destroying the agriculture, empires, industries, but the most damaging impact had been the permanent stigma of inferiority complex that they'd pinned on every African on the continent and around the globe.

While Africa was heavily destroyed and had lost its valuable human resources, its gold had been looted and its sense of confidence had been shattered, the descendants of the slave traders still enjoy the proceeds from what the blood and sweat of the slaves had succeeded in creating for the Europeans and their American counterparts. The Africans see how their ancestors helped these Oburoni to reach their dreams of economic prosperity and material comfort in the New World and in Europe. The question is do these countries know that they'd attained such high levels of material prosperity today with the African help? Do they realize that they'd climbed on the shoulders of the African slaves to get to this material opulence?

If the Oburoni people were responsible for the exodus of our kinsfolk to the Diaspora, why do the African leaders have to cross the Atlantic Ocean to the New World to render several apologies to the victims and make the ritual atonement for this tragedy? Why should the victims apologize for the crime and not the vice versa?

Indeed, the continent had waited many years, after the slave trade ended, for the Europeans to return to the continent to show remorse, render apology and make atonement. We feel America and Europe would some day have a change of heart to address the past and, most importantly, make atonement for the past to calm down the ancestors and appease the angry ancestors of the continent.

Do they know that before their ancestors came, Africa had not been in such dire circumstances? Agriculture was thriving in several places in the so-called West African Slave Coast. There were so many thriving empires on the so-called Slave Coast, democracy in the kings' courts, abundance of food and security. However, almost all these ended with the advent of the Oburoni European slave traders. It was as if, since their advent to the continent, the Oburoni traders had put a curse on the continent and have destroyed this once very proud continent in many ways.

In a sense, they are largely responsible for making the continent the laughing stock of the world today. The face of Africa today is painted in famine, civil strife, economic stagnation, rampart disease, some of which can be attributed to the lingering effects of the slave trade and to the degradation they'd inflicted on the African people during the slave trade.

Did the descendants of the Oburoni slave traders know what their ancestors did to the continent? Can Africa ever be able to rise out of the ashes of the slave trade and plantation slavery and thrive once again or become collectively-actualized?

What of the inferiority complex the slave trade and slavery had imposed on the African people? Can they overcome them without the help of those who had caused them?

Knowing which family brutalized their ancestors, the fear of who has whose DNA, or the fear of knowing that the Oburoni people snatched, bought or hauled their ancestors out of the continent, has become very troubling to several people. These links are no longer fabrications or exercises in speculation. Several have been authenticated with faces, blood content, of vital and irrefutable DNA evidence.

On the contrary, though they will not admit it openly, many of the descendants of the slave traders are still better off materially today because of the help they'd received from the African slaves and the benefits from the fruits of the slave trade to Africa and the wealth from American plantation slavery in the New World.

It was an enterprise of shame—money for African blood and flesh.

With the huge profits they'd made on each leg of the trade, by their scholars' admission, the slave trade had been described as the most lucrative commercial enterprise that they'd ever undertaken.

"Hadn't they realized that the trade in human flesh and blood was an immoral and shameful enterprise that degraded Africans?" the king asked the griot. "My feeling is that they knew that it was wrong, but the huge profits they made from the trade forced them to disregard all these rules of ethics and their own religious precepts. The huge profits from the blood money forced them to close the door to morality."

"Well, it is surprising why the so-called leaders of global civilization did not know that it was wrong to forcibly haul millions of people, about forty million in all and another forty million dead in the chaos, out of a continent to a land of no return to labor and to do their dirty chores for them for free?" the griot looked at the several marks on the wall in the king's palace and shrugged his shoulders. "These are just some of the burdens these "shameless locusts" had imposed on the continent."

"Their argument that it was legal then to trade in slaves and that it was sanctioned by their faith to trade in slaves is a lame excuse for a civilized group of people," the king said. "Which global organization or body must determine culpability? Or are the descendants of the slave traders too sacrosanct to be held accountable when it comes to global justice?"

"Well, maybe the world court does not have jurisdiction over the case because of some limitations and circumstances," the griot remarked. "But they have got to look into this critical matter if they are truly independent . . . and ready to show Africans that their interests would be equitably represented at the global court."

"It is just not right for the African leaders to continue to ponder why the gods allowed this horrible twist of fate to overtake the African continent. People all over the world are asking these same questions as to why the gods did not stop the invaders, the slave traders in their tracks?" the king asked one hundredth time.

"When you ask the chiefs, you saw the guilt, remorse, anger, and even the silent shame on their faces, anytime they tried to explain what really happened in the profane past. When you asked them about what drove their ancestors to do what they did, they usually choked on their words, too bitter and too overwhelmed to explain the past," the griot said.

"Maybe they had to do what they did just to live to see another day in their own land," King Gizenga lamented. "Our fathers had very little freedom in deciding what they did or did not do when it came to the slave trade."

"With cannons looking them in their faces, they better complied or died," the queen mother said.

"Our ancestors had been wrong, and we have no problem in saying that we are sorry for what they did. We are asking for forgiveness on their behalf," Zogan said, when he poured the libation. "But we know that if the Oburonis did not use their cannons to intimidate them, or their guns to kill them, our ancestors would more than likely not have collaborated with them."

Shallow and muffled voices of apology have been heard from some of the Oburoni people too. Even some governments have offered some perfunctory apologies. But several of them are still too proud to admit their guilt openly. They have continued to deny any wrongdoing on the part of their ancestors. "So, they continue to carry the burden of guilt with them and prefer to pass it on to the next generations."

"They sold their own people, the European scholars love to say," the griot said. "This is nothing but a strategy the Europeans have used repeatedly to shift the blame to the African victims. And to Africans, this is like adding insult to the crime or adding pepper to the wound."

The griots, the African storytellers, however, have vehemently disagreed with those who want to sanitize the history and twist the facts to exonerate the European and their American ancestors from accountability for the slave trade. "We still remember how the slave traders came to the continent uninvited, used brutal force, muskets and canons against our ancestors. We tell the young about what these Oburoni traders did to our ancestors and how they used a lot of brutality against our people, especially against the youth, in rounding up and hauling away the sons and daughters of Mama Africa," he said.

"Why are the descendants of those who introduced the trans-Atlantic slave trade into Africa still denying that it was their forebears that introduced the hauling of Africans out of the continent across the Atlantic Ocean to the New World?" Danquah, the head griot asked calmly. "Why have they refused to accept responsibility for the truth?"

"If they own up to this crime," queen mother Nana Binto said, "then we can talk about how to forgive them and help rid them of the guilt, rid them of responsibility from the destruction their ancestors did to the continent. They must realize that while they got the help from Africa to build the foundations for their economies, the Africans have been dealing with the lingering effects of the help in calamities for centuries."

"Why have they refused to make atonement for the pain and suffering that their ancestors had caused the African people?" Dokuwa asked looking unhappy and distressed.

"What atonement would be appropriate in case we agree to do something about it?" Bubba, the owner of two antebellum mansions in Mississippi, asked pointedly. "Remember the present generation did not catch any slaves. It was just something that we had inherited. Those who actually caught, bought owned and brutalized the slaves had died and exited the scene centuries ago."

"We are not talking about any outrageous atonement," Danquah told him, sharply. "For one thing, you could never repay all the liability you owe the African continent. You cannot even put a price tag on the lives of the forty to fifty million victims, let alone pay for the pain and suffering. The victims would, however, be willing to accept a fraction of the huge profit that the European countries that participated in the slave trade are willing to part with."

"Maybe we might even write a rain check for what we owe?" Bubba joked. "Or maybe we can even put in place some programs for the descendants of the victims to soften the hurt from this terrible global horror."

"Well, we have to work something out," Danquah said. "We need to come up with the terms of atonement, a package, which would not bankrupt the coffers of any government."

"Which countries are expected to make the atonement?" Bubba asked.

"The initiative must begin with Portugal, the first country that started the slave trade on the African continent in the first place," Danquah said. "Then the other European countries must make their atonement for the slave trade. That is the only way the anger from the past would end in peace."

"The actual victims who suffered directly during the slave trade have long been gone, and we have no idea who actually deserves to get the atonement today, that is, even if we want to give something for the horrors of the past," Bubba said. "Try to take comfort in the fact that we want to make the atonement, but we just don't know how or whom the beneficiaries must be."

"Give it to the women; they can manage it better than the men," Louise said jokingly. "The men would squander it on liquor and on women."

"Louise, get serious. It must belong to everybody, men, women and the children," Bubba reminded her,

"Just joking, just joking," Louise said quickly, her hands up in the air.

"Give it to the African people collectively, sir. Give the atonement to the African countries, particularly to those that reside along the former African Slave Coast. Give it to those whose descendants had suffered the worse twist of fate in the world, the worst brutality the human race has ever witnessed. Those who have long been forgotten in the shuffles of history and had been left to deal with centuries of posttraumatic stress from the slave trade," Danquah told Bubba.

"What is the atonement specifically for?" Bubba asked impatiently. "Is it for the millions of victims, for the pain and suffering or for the destruction in the land?"

"Only heaven knows what our ancestors had gone through during the slave trade. We are talking about the brutality which the Oburoni traders, your ancestors brought to the continent," Danquah reminded him. "What of the four centuries of free labor your ancestors had enjoyed out of the slaves, what kind of amends do you plan to make for it?"

"Don't even discuss that," Bubba said sharply. "We can never repay the African people for the centuries of free labor they had given our ancestors."

"Perhaps atonement can help you escape the wrath of the angry gods of the continent," Danquah said.

"Why do you think that this is the right solution?" Bubba asked.

"Maybe that is what is on the minds of the Africans who live in the Diaspora and on the minds of the leaders on the continent," Danquah said, looking worried. "You can never repay all that you owe the African people from the past. Those who know about the past are not thinking about any country paying Africa all that they owe from the past. Any reasonable atonement would not be refused."

"It does not matter if you did the slave trade and plantation slavery. The reality is that you've inherited the fruits of the slave trade and you have benefited from plantation slavery, the griot said. "The Africans are still struggling today, some still live in abject poverty partly because of the mismanagement and corruption of their leaders, but most importantly, because of the lingering effects of the catastrophic slave trade that your ancestors and the Arab slave traders conducted on the continent centuries ago, we need some form of accountability."

"You mean business, don't you?" Bubba asked, folding his sleeves hurriedly.

"Well, Africans could take their case to the world court and officially demand that something be done about this crime against humanity," Danquah said. "Maybe this would be too embarrassing for the countries involved, for those whose guilty conscience from the past only sleeps comfortably under the carpet of history when it comes to the European slave trade to Africa and plantation slavery all over the New World."

They said goodbye; Bubba took his Bible and went to an evening worship. "Here comes the falcon; it has arrived on a mission. It is circling the shrine, swooping down the edge of the legendary Mississippi River. It has stirred the river, suddenly bringing the past alive again. The urgency to resolve the burden from the past has never been greater before," Trent told his friends.

"Someone better revisit the injustice your ancestors did to Africa and make atonement for it to avoid the wrath of the ancestors," Danquah said angrily.

EIGHT

B UBBA KNEW THAT HE HAD to do something when he couldn't sleep in peace at night in his own mansion. He knew that he still carried a heavy burden of guilt from the past on his conscience. He was pondering how to put a past that continued to rear its ugly head every night to rest once and for all, even though this tragedy ended centuries ago.

A battalion of ghosts, appeared every night in the forms of African youths with shackles on their feet, iron collars around their necks and identification brands on their foreheads, stormed the mansion with impunity. How could he have a sound sleep when he suffered from anxiety from these ghosts from the profane past haunting him in his dreams and threatening to wreck havoc on him?

In his barn, he saw an African slave, who had lost both of his toes, brandishing a sword in front of him in anger, and he stared and pointed his finger at him angrily. When he was digging in the fields behind the barn, he saw skeletons of dead field hands hurriedly buried in shallow graves. The blood from these African slaves had been dripping from his hands, especially the death of the runaway pregnant slave women who had been suspended from the post and whipped mercilessly till they died. He knew that his past had some brutality, exploitation and hypocrisy buried in the bottom of the Mississippi River.

He had tried to confront the past that year, remorseful and pertinent. But every time he tried to come clean, to pour out his guilt into the open, he saw his great grandfather asking him to leave the past alone. He was, however, still fighting these realities. Bulldozers had destroyed many of the former plantations, leveling the burial grounds of many of the slaves and Native-Americans. But what had transpired in these lands could no longer be swept under the rugs of history.

He tried to organize a group to revisit the past, but he received a stern warning in the mail to leave the past alone. It was, however, becoming increasingly obvious that he could no longer continue to deny the part of his heritage that committed these atrocities and fight against the need to do something about the past. He knew that the earlier he and his people lay down this heavy burden of guilt the better for the children and the next generation.

All over the country, his region had this dark cloud looming around the land. It continued to give a negative global image to his region. In spite of the fact that there were many good people with warm hearts in his region, the dark clouds from the past continued to distort the true character of his people.

Though the idea was in conflict with his regional pride, his mind was inundated with endless thoughts about how to rectify the profane past—support for the cause of reconciliation, since not many of his cronies were anxious to rectify the past and make atonement.

He was determined to do whatever was necessary. But several of his friends and cronies continued to deny the past, and wanted him to do the same, but he felt the special calling to start a movement to end the guilt and to make amends for the tragedy. He knew that it would take a lot of controversy to make any atonement.

If he was still debating what to do, his brush with death cleared all those doubts and started him down the road of reconciliation. In fact, he had his death bed conversion when he was involved in a headlong collision, pinned under a wrecked car, and fortunately for him, an African-American mechanic saved his life by pulling him from under the burning vehicle a few minutes before the vehicle exploded into an inferno.

It reminded him of another descendant of African slaves who had saved several Europeans who had been thrown overboard. This man single-handedly pulled several of these victims to safety when their steamboat overturned in the middle of the treacherous currents of the Mississippi River. Bubba's encounter, however, was much more personal and very much an eye-opener for him.

Definitely, this timely rescue from the grip of death, from being burned to death, forced Bubba to develop a much more tolerant attitude toward African-Americans. After that incident, he was no longer afraid to speak his mind on race issues, no matter how hurtful his views were to the people who refused to see anything wrong with the past.

Maybe it was real. Maybe it was an illusion. But Bubba's conversion also coincided with his neighbor, an old man named Curtis, going into his barn in the night looking for a quiet rendezvous from his troubles. His world was collapsing around him. His health was failing and his wife had level four cancers. Though he least expected to see anything in his backyard, he came face to face with a ghost from the past standing in the middle of his backyard. The apparition stood still; it was unresponsive, but his demeanor was that of someone that was filled with a lot of anger. He also looked like someone who had vengeance on his mind. It was the ghost of an African slave who had brutal lacerations on his back, perhaps from the proverbial thirty-nine lashes. His flesh was badly torn from his back, and it was hanging like a piece of red meat from the butcher shop. Blood was still oozing steadily from the wound.

Curtis remembered the role his ancestors played in the ugly drama of plantation slavery. He remembered from the pictures on the wall how many slaves his great grandfather owned in the 1850's. He tried to forget the look on the face of the ghost and the horrible shape, the state of pain it was in. But the more he tried to block it out of his mind, the more it stood there terribly angry, looking at him, though it said nothing to him. How could he live in peace, or how could he have a free conscience, when he still carries a heavy burden of guilt from the past? How could he ignore what the silence of this solitary ghost told him without opening its mouth and uttering a single word?

Bubba knew that the river was brownish and it was filled with the mud from the past, so were the treacherous currents that rumbled in anger under the legendary bridge. Bubba heard the bluffs of the mighty Mississippi River howling, beckoning to him to do something about the past. He heard some of the victims of his ancestors still screaming for mercy, and all these mysterious noises stirred some guilt inside him.

The agitation over the past coincided with the old human skeletons that he'd found in the old cotton field earlier that summer when he was digging a hole, obviously the remains of the victims of his ancestors' slavery past, a heritage of brutality and a life of oppression. These were things in his past that he did not ask for, but he'd inherited them by virtue of being born in the region. He, however, refused to continue defending the ugly past and its institutions. He personally felt that atonement was long overdue and time has begun to run out.

He must accept his heritage and maybe personally make some sort of atonement and live in peace thereafter, ending his family guilt. But how could he convince his folks, the die-hard conservatives in the region to also take this monumental step, a move in the right direction?

"We can't continue holding on to this sagging load from our history forever. Honestly speaking, I am tired of defending all the evil things in our past," Curtis declared sadly. "I didn't ask to be born in this part of the country, but though I am not ashamed of being born here, I am not going to continue to condone the evils in our heritage, nor am I going to let my region off the hook either."

"I strongly feel that it is time to get the past behind us. At some point, we definitely have to lay down this heavy burden of guilt in our heritage, and we must do so once and for all," Chris Boyd, the carpenter from Alabama said.

He could hear voices from the marshland, the voices of runaway slaves in hiding foraging. He could also hear the barking of the dogs and the galloping of the horses and the curses from the patrol that were in hot pursuit.

To Bubba, the voices from the past, the spirits of the ancestors were chilling and eerie. They remained restless, dissatisfied and distressed. They were demanding penitence. They wanted redemption, expiation and atonement.

"Why are you so worried about the past?" Bubba asked Curtis. "I don't understand why you keep raking the old stuff from the old bygone days."

"Every time you go into the barn and you constantly see the ghost of the young black man, who had been badly beaten, bleeding profusely but saying nothing to you, would it induce fear or guilt in you?" Curtis asked Bubba and Chris. "What do you think that does to me every time not only as a human being, but also as a man of faith?"

"Well, though this is really sad, it does not totally surprise me," Chris said. "I told you to leave our bloody past and all that guilt alone. Forget about what our ancestors did in the privacy of their land."

"You see my conscience keeps telling me to do something about this past," Bubba said. "Maybe, this would help the victims to make strides toward equality and economic progress in this great land of ours that we call the land of opportunity."

"Whatever we have to do so I no longer have to see this solitary ghost in my barn staring at me silently and penetratingly like an African cobra snake, let's do it," Curtis said, almost choking with anger, guilt, worry and anxiety.

"Indeed, this is the beginning of a new century, so this is the right time to move toward redemption and racial reconciliation."

Indeed, this is "the season of atonement."

"This is not fair to us. Why do we have to pay for crimes our ancestors committed centuries before we were even born?" Jim, the young leader of the group, remarked. Looking at his grandfather's picture on the wall, he wished he could have escaped the wrath of the victims like his great grandfather, but since that was impossible, he simply gnashed his teeth and swallowed his agonizing thoughts. "We have inherited this baggage from our forebears, a heritage we'd been born into and a past that, fortunately or unfortunately, whether we liked it or not, has been passed down to us."

"I know we didn't ask for it," Curtis told him.

"So tell me, Mr. Knowledge Head," the young barber said. "I know you were born into it, but haven't you benefited from the fruits of slavery from your heritage? Aren't you proud of your great grandfather's

old money, and the name he'd made for himself and for the family with
the proceeds from his great grandfather's plantation?"

"Yes I don't have a choice in my relatives. He was my grandfather, my
flesh and blood," he blurted out quickly. "I am proud of him regardless
what he did or how he lived."

"But how about how he and the others exploited my ancestors,
using them as slaves, milking them for centuries of hard labor and
abusing them on the plantations and fields?" the young barber asked.

"How can we atone for something that happened centuries and
countless decades ago, centuries before we were even born?" he asked.

"If you have benefited from the fruits of the old, tragic past, how
could you continue to harbor the ghosts of the past in your heart and
not let go of them?" Trent, the young activist asked the old man.

"If apologizing for the past means turning your back to all the evil
things your ancestors did, rejecting what they'd cherished most and
put their lives on the line for, why would you hesitate to let go of this
horrible burden of guilt that'd tormented your soul for so long?" Steve
asked.

"Well, no matter how brutal the past, it is not easy turning your
back on your heritage, no matter how wrong our ancestors were," Jim
admitted. He was suffering from a serious conflict in his conscience. He
had several friends who were very critical of his region in more ways
than he knew.

"Very easy, Jim," the barber who was also an activist said, tapping
his feet to the legendary blues music of Memphis and nodding his head
to the beat. "I think you should apologize, show remorse, and move
into a more glorious future."

"You feel we must make atonement for something that happened
years before we were born?" Jim asked him, gritting his teeth in
suppressed anger. "You've got to be joking, right? Why should we do a
thing like that?"

"After all, DNA and Internet technology have brought the old
realities back into the open for the wide world to see. They are
revealing the ugly details of the slavery past which involved several
families. And if you truly cared about the future of our children and
their grandchildren, why should you pass this heavy burden of guilt

on to them without resolving it once and for all, so they could go on to enjoy a better future?" the barber asked him bluntly.

"You don't understand how hard it is . . . how much agony this means to us," he said. Jim slumped in his chair with a sunken heart, pounding the arm of his chair with his right hand in frustration. "You are asking us to make atonement for the ancient deeds of our ancestors—well—regardless of how long ago? And you think the atonement would help the victims heal faster and better and—you suggest we should even ask for forgiveness—make atonement on African shores."

"Well, why not?" the barber asked. "That would be a great idea and indeed a noble thing to do. Think it over, Jim."

Early that Thursday morning, a week after the Protestant Fundamentalist Convention voted on the Resolution for Atonement, Bubba and a dozen other church members, conscience on fire, roses in hand, goodwill on their minds, boarded an airplane at the Memphis International Airport and headed to the heart of Africa on a special mission—to settle the past, a vivid, philanthropic dream. Chris thought the plane would fall from the sky, ending the mission to Africa. The civil war dead and heroes from their resting places would strike down the members of delegation.

Bubba's upbringing in the church and the lessons he'd learned from his father, who had been the deacon of his church and his three month stay in a seminary, had all reshaped him as a moderate on racial issues. But the turning point was his close encounter with death from being rescued by an African-American from under a burning car.

For that reason, he individualized the burden of guilt from the past and made a lot of effort—for his folks to put down the heavy burden that they still bore in their hearts—culminating in a dramatic rendezvous with the chiefs and kings on the former African Slave Coast.

The Fundamentalist Church had decided to send the delegation to Africa to convey their heartfelt apologies to the African people, to present the leaders with the terms of atonement for the tragic past of the slave trade and for plantation slavery. The terms the delegation carried were sealed, but these were the terms of atonement that the congregations had collectively decided.

Making atonement for the past has become a raging issue and a soul-searching challenge. And especially for the descendants of the former slave owners this was an issue waiting for resolution. If the goal was to atone for the profane past, placate the African continent and pacify the people of African descent in the Diaspora, then why were the descendants of those who did this still hesitating to do what needed to be done?

Many of the descendants of the slave owners have experienced a change of heart. Many have decided to open a door to a new chapter in race relations in a manner the world had never known before. Though the decision didn't please some of the members, the leaders decided to do the right thing and go forward with the mission anyway.

So the date for the departure couldn't come fast enough for some of the delegates, but for a few of the members, the date of departure was a day they dreaded. Why rake a past that had been hidden and treated like a taboo subject all these years?

Several families and hundreds of church members were at the Memphis International Airport to see the delegates off and to wish them luck. The pastor tried to play down the mission because he did not want the excessive publicity to overshadow the true humanitarian goals of the trip. He had to remind everybody involved that this was not a publicity-seeking mission, but rather a genuine mission of reconciliation. Though there had been a few discussions in the past between the African chiefs and the European-American missionaries, there had never been a mission of reconciliation like this before.

It was not surprising to see Bubba's excitement, and the anxiety he had as well. He still firmly believed in his heritage, but he also knew that it was time for his folks to make peace with the past. He knew it was time for them to put down the heavy burden from the profane past.

There was a farewell party the Saturday before—a sendoff party for the members of the delegation. It was where Bubba ate barbecue ribs, drank some beer with several congregation members and well-wishers. From the balcony of the church, he could see a new moon on the horizon. Bubba was very excited and had a sentimental discussion with Reverend Peterson, the leader of the delegation. The three-time

missionary to Africa told Bubba that their great grandparents would
have been very proud of their decision to rectify the past. Though this
did not put Bubba completely at ease, it reassured him that they were
traveling on the right road.

On the day of departure, obviously, the immediate family members
of the delegation were at the airport, though many were very uneasy
about the trip to the heart of Africa. The well-wishers filled the check
out counter area to capacity.

As Louise looked at some of the faces at the airport intensely, she
let out long, deep sighs. She was worried about Bubba's safety. She
had a deep love for her husband, a strong affinity for him; a bond she
knew would keep them married forever, though Bubba sometimes had
doubts about where the relationship was heading.

There was Rosemarie, the old syrupy lady who shed tears silently,
because her great grandfather, who was deeply involved in plantation
slavery, had left her so much wealth that it had caused her a lot of guilt.
She loved to give lavish parties in her home, barbecue feasts in her
backyard and pool parties in the summer. Though it had been difficult
to admit it, she had always felt guilty because she was so fabulously
rich. And she knew that most of the wealth came from the "old money"
that came from the cotton boom in those days of plantation slavery.
She was part of a family from the slavocracy that'd made tons of money
from the cotton boom in the Old South—thriving at the expense of the
African slaves.

So she was extremely excited about the proposition and felt some
relief when the mission finally became a reality and got off the ground.
She figured out that the mission would make it easier for her to enjoy
her wealth. She would not have to look back on the dark pages from
the past. It would also have absolved her from whatever wrongdoing
her ancestors might have been guilty of. She'd put the biggest offerings
in the collection plate in church, the biggest donation for the mission,
because she wanted to sponsor the mission in order to empower the
members of the region to rectify the past.

Bubba seemed both excited and anxious to make history. Before the
trip, he had toured several mansions in the rural district to chat with
the owners, to tell them about the mission to Africa and what it might

mean to them. He even told Chris that the journey would end the visit of "Joe the Ghost" to his barn every night.

Chris seemed strangely unmoved by the mission though it could end the apparition in his barn—he was quite nervous about the consequences of the mission for him; it might bring on some more havoc.

"Good thing we have finally decided to confront the past," Bubba told Chris.

"After all these years, isn't it amazing?" Chris smiled broadly, heaving a sigh of relief.

"Can you imagine the sort of reception the African people would give the members of the delegation when they arrived to reopen the old bitter wounds of the slave trade and American plantation slavery?" the lady shrugged herself.

"How in the world would we know that?" Louise laughed and pulled her eyebrows.

"I have prayed a lot over this mission, ever since the news broke out," Ms. Violet said. She was the wife of the Global Ministry director, another powerful voice behind the movement for reconciliation. "All we can do is to put this mission in the hands of a higher power."

"I hope the mission would mean the end of the guilt inside our hearts," Bubba said.

Bubba ignored his fears and anxieties or maybe he pretended to do so. Though it was hard to hold down his zeal, he carefully went through the departure protocols at the Memphis International Airport, checking out every detail of the process on a piece of paper.

"When you meet the chiefs do not let your guilt disarm you. Do not start shaking in your boots. You already know who is your armor and shield," Reverend Botch, the global evangelist, told the members of the delegation. "Remember you are representing our ancestors, those who fought and died for our heritage. They are resting their hope on you, and you must bring them nothing but honor in the end. Therefore, be as strong as steel when you enter the lions' den to work with the African chiefs."

"I can see the anger of the chiefs already. I can feel the indignation of the inhabitants, but the scariest of all, I can sense the rage of the

African ancestors toward the delegation," the deacon said. "They have been waiting for a very long time for this day of reckoning."

"All they want is some final closure to centuries of bizarre nightmares and degradation," Reverend Peterson remarked.

The pastor of the church was the central force behind this unique mission. He had thoughts to do something about the profane past since his childhood years. His initial idea was dismissed as sublime stupidity. But the combined congregations finally came to a positive resolution. The delegation carried the terms of atonement from his church group and from hundreds of other congregation members, but it also carried the remorse, the hope and red roses from many of the members to the people of Africa.

"The ritual might end the dark past of our heritage that'd been tainted with slavery," the reverend said. "We are setting free the children of the region and liberating generations yet to be born by this very mission."

"Why are we addressing the past at this point in time?" the deacon asked. This was the question on his mind as he prayed over the mission.

"Well, it is very important that we make the atonement now before some lunatic somewhere decides to . . . the world on fire," the reverend told the deacon and groups of well-wishers, tense and breathing heavily as he sighed deeply.

"Well, that will be such a shame, and a very sad day for the world."

"But if you think we are nervous now, wait till more facts emerge from the archives to the Internet revealing more about the slavery past," he told them. "These are very embarrassing revelations."

"It is surprising that the Africans had not considered any legal avenues to settle the pain and sufferings of their ancestors in the past and all the aftereffects the new generation still experiences," the reverend remarked.

"Well, I guess we are doing the right thing then and at the right time," he admitted. "I suggest we speed up the process and get it done as fast as possible."

Other missionary groups were scattered all over the airport in large numbers ready to send off the members of the delegation to Africa with a bag of atonement, bouquets of flowers, letters of remorse, anything they thought could alleviate their personal or collective guilt. They brought any symbolic objects that they thought could free them from the past with them. Some wanted personal letters tossed into the ocean. Others wanted beads thrown into the forests, and Bibles placed under stones on the grasslands.

On the other hand, it was the twilight over the Old South as many ultra conservatives also made their presence at the airport known in the glaring morning sunlight. As the rising sun simmered through the glasses, they tried frantically to block the delegates from boarding the plane. They thought the mission was a dishonor not only to them, but also to their ancestors. Regardless of what the logic was, they felt that it was not going to bring any closure to the sordid past of slavery. At best, they thought it would simply stir a mixture of anger and anxiety in many people.

On the contrary, however, many of the congregation members in the audience felt it was a new day and that things would change. Many wished they could personally make the journey to Africa to experience the actual moment of the apology, to show their remorse and to make their own atonement. They wanted to witness the moment when the delegation reveals the terms of atonement to the African leaders at the Panfest Festival in Cape Coast, Ghana. They wanted to see the look on the faces of the inhabitants, the expressions of joy and closure.

"Everything would be all right," Bubba said, holding Louise against his heavy shoulders, fighting back tons of suppressed emotions that rose and fell inside his soul. He remembered the last service the congregation had, an emotional revival, which happened two days before the journey. The descendants of the former plantation owners, those who wanted the delegation to convey to the African people how sorry they were, stood by nervously whispering their thoughts and saying their last minute prayers.

"Are you sure, they won't retaliate against y'all down there?" Louis asked Bubba. "Aren't some of the chiefs still very angry over what our ancestors did and are seeking atonement?"

"But they didn't sound as if they want to retaliate," Bubba cut in sharply.

"Do you know that for sure?" Louise looked at him and at the powerful rising sun.

"Well, the advanced squad of missionaries returned just last week and said the African leaders do respect our decision to return to their shores to apologize and make atonement. They said that they want closure to this historical calamity," Bubba told her.

"That sounds like great news," she said.

Louise was extraordinarily sweet to Bubba for a change, as she wiped the gentle tears that rolled down her cheeks. She let Bubba's hands go for a while and rubbed her eyes for a few seconds, making sure that what she was experiencing was reality and not a figment in her vivid imagination, or that she was not daydreaming. "Knowing you, don't go there and be secretly mocking the proceedings, laughing at the chiefs."

"I am a changed man, Louise." He remarked pointedly. "You know better than that. Why would I do that?"

"Just make sure that you take a good care of yourself, till you return safely back to Memphis—see you in one month. I tell you again, please give the African people their respect and our heartfelt apologies," she told him.

"By all means, we would do so. Just pray for us, you hear?"

"And please don't look at another woman while you are over there representing the church," Louise told him. "I'm just joking with you."

"Louise, quit mocking me. You know me better than that by now," Bubba told her.

"Well, when you see all those pretty women with their broad hips, vibrating behinds and great lips down there, who knows whether the devil will get into your head to please your flesh?" she said teasingly.

"You know how devoted I am to you," he confessed, with a twinkle in his eye. "I told you there would never be another you."

"Then, please don't follow each of the women with your eyes as you usually do in the mall," she laughed as she moved next to the reverend.

"Well, you know I am a deacon in the church, so give the man of faith a break, give me the benefit of doubt," he said to her.

"Being a deacon doesn't mean too much of anything these days and you know it," she said.

All the procedures were observed. And the members of the delegation saw many eyes staring at them with gratitude as the announcer's voice blurted out: "Flight 777! I repeat Flight 777 boarding begins in fifteen minutes at Gate 234." The intercom sounded loud and clear signaling the beginning of a new era in race relations.

Bubba knew the moment of truth had finally arrived. He was about to confront a past, which had plagued him, tormented his conscience and troubled his soul. "Here we go Louise. We are going to be gone for a while, for a couple of weeks, so say your good bye now, Louise," he sniffed noisily. "And give me the biggest kiss you have."

"Come on, this is a temporary goodbye—it is not like you are going through "a door of no return," she joked.

"Watch out now, that is nothing to joke with," he warned her. "How badly are you going to miss me? Are you sure you won't lose your mind over missing me?"

"Bubba, don't push your luck now," she told him fondly. "It is only a few weeks, so I can put up with that."

"Oh well. This was a good try anyway," he said.

Bubba kissed Louise passionately but quickly on the lips, broke free from her raspy arms and took his tote bag and dragged his suitcase filled with the hopes and dreams of many, the blazing morning sunrise, passport, shot records and his great black book in hand and headed proudly toward the boarding gate. The last hug and kiss from Louise were firm, tight and memorable.

"I have been through several emotions—love, greed, gluttony and even hate—but guilt is the most difficult passion to get rid of. But we have begun the process of putting this guilt from the past behind us once and for all," Bubba told the reverend. The last thing he heard was Louise's last shout of "I love you Bubba, and you be safe now. Give them whatever they want."

Bubba then disappeared, olive branch in hand, atonement in his pocket, setting out on a journey he felt strongly would bring about the much needed relief. Bubba was somewhat uneasy inside because he was trying to shed his past, change the cloaks he was born with—his heritage.

"It is such a strange twist for Bubba and his former secret society members—the diehard folks who once said they would die before they let go of their heritage—go to the African continent to make the past right," Louis told the church secretary as they both walked in the parking lot to their cars, brooding, in a very pensive mood.

"I still don't believe this is happening. Either I am dreaming or hallucinating," the church secretary said. She heaved a deep sigh, shook her head and sat on the hood of her car watching the plane from the parking lot still trying to make sense out of the events that morning.

Louise and Elaine, the church secretary, watched the gigantic plane the Boeing 747 disappeared into the blistering early morning sunrise. And with the huge plane also went her husband for twenty seven years, and the apologies, the dreams and the hopes of her people. They kept their eyes on the plane from the ground till it disappeared into sunny clouds.

The members of the delegation threw their lot into the sunny, silvery clouds above, carrying the hopes and dreams of the future generations in their hands. "Would they bring back with them a future free from the guilt and shame from the profane past of slavery?" the secretary asked Louise quietly. "Would the mission succeed?"

"Wouldn't that be great, if we can finally put this heavy burden of guilt behind us once and for all?" Louise asked Elaine.

As for Bubba, he sat in his window seat in the plane, watching the clouds raced by like the years, the decades and the centuries. He looked into the faces of the other members of the delegation and noticed the same guilt in their hearts. He knew that he was not alone in the guilt.

Then the plane gained altitude, steadied itself. Hours later, they would be in the heart of Africa the place they would execute their mission the next few weeks.

NINE

THE DELEGATION ARRIVED TO THE blistering muggy, hot December weather with the guilt inherited from the past and they nursed a faint hope of success for their mission. Many of them were filled with optimism. The warm weather felt great on their bodies. Though they did not say it loudly, it was such a great relief to them from the winter cold they'd left behind in Memphis hours earlier. But then they'd to deal with the blazing African sun and the ancestors for the next two to three weeks.

Keeping a positive outlook was the best way to go, they agreed. It was not unexpected that Bubba, Reverend Peterson, and the other members of the delegation would be apprehensive about what they would find on the continent or how the chiefs and their elders would receive them.

In fact, they didn't know what to expect when they arrived at the Kotoka International Airport that warm December evening.

They were pleasantly surprised. As people who had heard so many negatives about the African continent, what they encountered was a surprise to them. It wasn't because they were afraid of the people or hated the land or the environment; it was just because of their past and what they'd been told about the continent. Many of them admitted that they loved to travel to exotic places, to meet new people and to experience different cultures. However, with the barrage of misinformation they'd received from the media over the years, the idea of making a trip to the heart of Africa was seriously troubling to some of them.

They'd resolved to go on the mission to the continent to rectify the past, to make atonement for the irreverent past and to go before the African kings and chiefs to make peace over the past. The feeling inside them was like how an arid desert would yearn for torrential rains.

Nevertheless, the idea of going to a continent on which their ancestors had once enslaved and brutalized the inhabitants raised some red flags for some of them. Most of them had lived in America and Europe all their lives, and had never stepped out of their countries. Some of them had witnessed racial issues flaring up sometimes in cities and even in the countryside. Can you imagine what was going through their minds as to what to expect on the former African Slave Coast, the country that has now been renamed Ghana? How many of them had flashbacks about the nightmare their ancestors had caused the African people on their continent during the slave trade?

Contrary to their expectations, they arrived to a warm 'akwaba' reception at the airport. Except Reverend Peterson, a regular missionary to the continent, it was the first time for all the members of the delegation on African soil. Many, if not all of them, were surprised by what the airport looked like. It was not a jungle; it was just like any small airport anywhere. After the constant barrage of negative images from the media, and the brainwashing they'd received from American and European media about Africa being no more than a jungle filled with exotic animals: lions, leopards, cobras and naked and starving people, what they saw was a great surprise to them.

The few who were there to welcome them were warm and courteous to them. They opened their arms to them and made them feel welcome to the country. "They are so friendly," Bubba told Reverend Peterson. "I never expected them to be so nice to us."

"I told you they are some of the friendliest people on the planet," Reverend Peterson wiped the sweat from his brow.

The ride in the Mercedes Setra van to Las Palms Hotel, the modern five star hotel on the breezy Labadi Beach, with coconut trees surrounding it, located on Teshie-Nungua Road, a suburb of Accra, the capital city of Ghana, was as pleasant and delightful as it was educational.

But how many of them felt some pity for the cruel hand their ancestors had dealt to the African people on their own continent as they rode silently away from the airport?

Meanwhile, the gentle breeze from the Atlantic Ocean soothed their souls and calmed down their nerves as they made their way toward the exquisite-looking beach front hotel. The friendly but curious looks from the indigenes along the route calmed down whatever fears they had. The warmth of the people and the glow of the African setting sun, the rows of coconut trees along the road and the breezy air were so enthralling that they thought that they were on a warm tropical paradise and not in the heart of Africa.

But they were in Ghana-Africa, the mother of all the continents.

Next day, the ride from Accra, along the asphalt highway along the Atlantic Coast, was equally mind-elevating and tremendously instructive. The beauty of the undulating grassland, the intermittent hills and valleys along the two hundred mile journey to Cape Coast in the Central Region, was refreshing. The group members rode in silence and spent the time pondering the number of slaves that'd been captured and marched along the same route, or had died on these hallowed grounds. Maybe the number was in the millions, they reflected.

"Be very careful with the mosquitoes. Don't let them bite you," Reverend Peterson warned the members, but he was very serious. Some of them were already slapping off the mosquitoes. "They cause malaria; a horrible disease which left untreated can become fatal in a matter of days."

"What do you mean fatal?" Bubba asked. "We had all the shots the doctor prescribed and we had taken the anti-malarial tablets as well, so what do you mean by fatalities?"

"Well, you think that you are safe. But the truth is we have very little or no immunity against the malaria parasites, so they could infect and overpower our bodies easily," he told the members of the delegation as he tried to instill some fear in them.

"That was in the past. This rarely happens these days, so don't get too worried about catching the disease."

"This mission is tormenting my conscience already. When you added the malaria scare to it, you have increased my worries," Bubba told the reverend. "I thought malaria is the last thing on this beach that anyone wants to catch."

At high noon that Saturday, the griot led the members of the delegation in front of the Cape Coast Castle as they watched the gigantic waves of the Atlantic Ocean crashed angrily against the pristine shoreline. You could hear the booming voice of the dead repeated themselves in these gigantic waves as they smashed against the rocks time after time and again and again.

The members of the delegation came to seek reconciliation. They needed redemption and peace. And they hoped that they would not encounter any problem in getting what they wanted.

Fortunately for them, the chiefs were in a pleasant mood and the town was bustling with all sorts of mirth. Maybe time had healed some of the past wounds. They thought.

The European and American visitors were curious about the monuments their ancestors had left behind on the shores, especially the majestic slave castles and the cannons at the gates. But since the African people hated the memories these artifacts stirred in them, the members of the delegation were careful not to offend their sensibilities by saying any negative things about it. They tried to show a lot of empathy and sympathy for the victims of the past. They'd noticed that with the passage of time, the rocks on which the castle stood had become moldy and the powerful waves of the Atlantic Ocean had gradually chipped bits and pieces away, dumping them into the wide open mouth of the insatiable Atlantic Ocean.

The members of the delegation were not tourists, so they couldn't go to swim at the beach, but they managed to eat the delicious-smelling "zuya khebab" culinary delight under the thatch roofed shades. Many of the visitors carried the idiosyncratic bag packs, wore the tennis shoes and donned the blue jeans. They were on a special mission. They had to return another day to the shores of Africa to take advantage of the pristine beaches, the unpolluted gentle and natural breezes.

This was an urgent mission. Reverend Peterson glanced at the brushes. "Well, I see the notorious coconut grove in the distance, the resting place of many slave traders, the notorious place that people dread to talk about," he told Bubba. "The irony is that the slave traders who refused to drink the African concocted "anti-malaria mixture" died from the disease, and the servants hurriedly buried them in this coconut grove."

"The servants laid them to rest in shallow graves in this coconut grove without any fanfare?" Bubba asked naively. "Dark pebbles, clustered mahogany woods and brown coconut husks led to the unmarked grove-cemetery."

Whatever they felt about those Europeans who were buried in the "coconut grove" they said very little about it, as they stood in the heart of Africa, facing the Atlantic Ocean as they reflected on the gravity and the sheer scope of the slave trade. The rusty cannons, legacies of the horrors of the past, shocked them. Their sight made them realized the enormity of the crimes of their ancestors.

Some of them felt that those buried inside the shallow graves would probably have been proud of the atonement they came down to make, but a few thought that they would rather turn in their graves.

Even the lighthouse on top of the adjacent hill, which was directly overlooking the Cape Coast Castle where the sentries used to spot the incoming pirates, or reported hordes of invading African soldiers to the castle, caused some of them to break down in tears.

They had conflict in their conscience.

Some of them headed to the old Portuguese chapel. This was where the Europeans baptized every slave that they shipped from the Cape Coast Castle. Bubba would make his way reluctantly to the notorious dungeons and the legendary governor's mansion, but they were very much saddened was very much troubled that afternoon.

Bubba saw the birds circling the shoreline, flying in all directions. It was hard for them to listen to the moaning of the slaves that had been brutalized and victimized in those filthy dungeons. He knew that the tourists that described the scenes to them had not exaggerated the suffering inside the structures, because he realized that they did not even paint half of the horrors that went on inside the dungeons.

The festive voices of the slave traders drinking rum and partying in the courtyard were silent. Nobody heard their drunken curses and intoxicated exuberance. All they heard were the gut-wrenching miseries of the victims from the dungeons below.

In the silence, the delegation members heard the Atlantic Ocean roaring angrily and reaching out to them. It was calling on those who inherited the fruits of slavery to atone for the deeds of their ancestors, to account for what happened on the hallowed grounds centuries ago. You could tell that their hearts were weighed down heavily with the burden of guilt from the profane past. You could tell that they were ill at ease and their guilty consciences were bothering them and their souls were on fire.

"You must, of course, accept wrongdoing before we can even consider any terms of atonement," the African griot told Bubba and the other members of the delegation in front of the thousands who had trickled in to the Panfest, the African reunion of victims and tourists in Cape Coast, Ghana.

"Well, over the years, we have built several hospitals and schools along the former Slave Coast for the African people, It means that we have already done a lot for the people," Bubba told the griot. "We have done enough in the past to open a dialogue between the tragic past and the present. I hope that some of the aid we have given you could be a starting point."

"Your ancestors had destroyed our continent. They'd put a knife on our cultural ethos and shattered it into fragments. They'd made us to become people in perpetual conflict."

"Though we have tried to survive as a people, we are still reeling from the effects of the nearly four hundred years of trauma."

"Too little too late or perhaps too insufficient," Mankrado told them. "You need to do something that will bring true healing to the continent. Stop reminding us about the small things that you have done for us in the past."

"Something like what?" Reverend Peterson asked, quickly.

"To make up for the destruction, we want you to put the continent back on the road of progress," Mankrado told them. "You must put us back where our ancestors used to be before the Portuguese arrived to overwhelm the continent with their cannons, inflicting the horrible 'mfecane' on us."

"You are blaming us for too many things?" Reverend Peterson asked.

"Well, we were once a very proud people and we might have continued on the road of progress, if they did not derail our dreams," Mankrado said. "They did not only decimate a continent that was relatively happy before your ancestors brought an insane orgy of slave trading, they also spread death and destruction in the land, sealing the fate of this unfortunate continent forever."

He counted several cowry shells on a table as he sat down to drink some palm wine.

"We are willing to face the past, but we cannot go back to recreate everything and correct all the injustices that our ancestors had done." Reverend Peterson revealed.

"As Africans, we are tired of being the laughing stock of the world, the direct result of the slave trade. You need to do something to help the African people cope with the stigma of slavery which your ancestors had imposed on us. The most important is that you must help Africans to join the modern economic system much more effectively. You must ensure that we are accorded the same level of respectability that other rising countries from Asia do enjoy," the king told them.

The griot, Mankrado, King Batuka and the elders went to the Uhuru Palace in Bakano to look at the records of the slave trade, which the griot have kept over the years. These were invoices, receipts and inventories that spanned over forty-seven generations, starting from the innocence of the pre-Oburoni era to the centuries of tumultuous scrambles for loot, for African cargo, and the ensuing bloodbath.

When the griot and the scholars calculated the number of youths that had left the continent from the door of no return at the Cape Coast Castle alone, it was approximately fifteen million—a fraction of the forty to fifty million slaves in all that had been forced out of the continent to the New World.

"How worse could it get when missionaries ended church services by marching the African converts into the dungeons below the slave castles and shipping them out. The African people still wonder today why the Oburoni missionaries tricked their converts and marched them into slavery after church worship," Mankrado remarked angrily.

"Why? Why did they have to stoop so low by using their religion to enslave us?

"We are not here to defend the past, we are here to make atonement," Bubba told Mankrado. "We can't tell you why our ancestors did all these things, but definitely it was because of the money."

"They took advantage of our ancestors. They took advantage of our continent. Maybe they did so because, at the time, they thought these deeds would never come to light," the queen mother said. Her angry face was spewing steams of anger in the blistering Harmattan heat as she fought the mist from the Atlantic Ocean. "But the world knows these secrets now. They know about what your ancestors did during the slave trade and the burden of guilt you have inherited from them. Therefore, you definitely need to make this atonement."

"You have much more guilt compared to us. We have admitted that whatever mistakes our ancestors made or the things they'd been forced to do were wrong and immoral. We have apologized and atoned for these several times already," the king told them.

"We understand all that," Bubba told the elders. "What do you want us to do about this?"

"We would make it possible for you to put down the heavy burden of guilt that you and the descendants of the slave traders still carry," the king told them. "But you must be sincere and accept responsibility for the past."

"Your majesty, we used to be in denial, but lately we have had a change of heart," Bubba told the king. "At this point, most of us want to do the right thing. We want to put a distance between the shame in our past and move into a much more peaceful future, one without any burdens of guilt."

"The gods had let your people to get away with this for so long. But the past has started to rear its ugly head in many ways, and trust me, it is not going to get any easier for you and your offspring, unless you sue for peace," he told him. "Unless you make the atonement, you would suffer from these dark clouds of history."

"We have brought you red roses and sincere apologies from home," he told the king and the elders. "Maybe they don't mean much, but this is a sign that we have decided to address the past."

He was not telling the king and the elders anything that they hadn't heard before. He wasn't confessing to them any guilt they didn't experience themselves. He was simply excited over the chance to bare his guilt to free his conscience.

"Your people cannot keep postponing the atonement," the king said. "The more you deny the guilt, the longer you prolong the agony and the stronger the wrath of the African ancestors."

"But we'd succeeded materially throughout our history. We have been blessed with material prosperity at a level other countries only dream about in their history," Bubba said.

"You could run away from your past and from the things you had inherited from your ancestors. You could try to deny that these events do not concern you, simply because they happened way before you were born, but you could never run from the wheels of justice—escape the wrath of the angry gods, from justice for the victims," the griot told Bubba.

"Are you saying that the gods are angry with us and will punish us because of the slave trade?" Bubba asked pointedly. He was still on his feet, suddenly animated. "Aren't the gods supposed to aspire to higher ideals than vengeance and taking their wrath on people?"

"Listen to who is talking about morality of gods," the king remarked sarcastically. "Listen to your words and set them against the deeds of your ancestors in the past. Why did your ancestors march their new coverts from worship services into the slave dungeons? Why did they haul our youths out of the continent as if they were cattle? And why did they tell our ancestors to gather treasure up in heaven while they looted our gold and abducted our children to sell for the blood money?"

"We have a change of heart. That is why we have come back here. We know we cannot correct the past, but we can make atonement for it," Bubba told the king, restating the mission of the delegation.

"Unless you make this atonement, you would continue to face the wrath of the ancestors. They would demand accountability from you," the griot told Bubba. "They would destroy your peace in many ways."

"What will the gods do?" Bubba asked. "Our mission is to make the past right."

"The gods would need libation and sacrifices to extend forgiveness to you and your people," the griot told Bubba. "That is the only way to end the wrath of Mother Nature and curb its voracious appetite."

The members of the delegation stood on the African shore facing the vast Atlantic Ocean during that hot afternoon. They spotted the falcon flying toward the old abandoned British slave boat. It was headed for the infamous "coconut grove" the place of poetic justice for the greed and callous Oburoni slave traders that died from malaria. This spot became a symbol of the struggle between good and evil, and greed and need. The grove epitomized the pinnacle of vengeance for the brutality in those days of horror.

Then the slave traders sometimes ironically became victims themselves—the quick death they suffered at the hands of the tiny mosquitoes. Though the impotent guns of the Asafo soldiers couldn't eliminate them, the mosquitoes ended their dreams and aspirations quickly—cemetery in the "coconut grove"—poetic justice.

"The Oburoni traders that our Asafo soldiers could not defeat, the mosquitoes were able to infect with malaria, sending them to early graves," the queen mother said. "They died quickly like flies."

Then the delegation watched the falcon flew over the Atlantic Ocean and headed toward the other side. The priest revealed that it was headed toward the Chucalissa Shrine in South Memphis in the New World. It flapped its wings loudly and then it quickly disappeared beyond the blue ocean, outside their view.

The messenger didn't want the falcon to rest on his shoulders with its sharp claws, but he wanted to find out how much it knew about the mission. If the falcon was in close touch with the spirit of the ancestors, then it knew about the unresolved burden in the history. It knew that blaming the victim for the profane tragic past no longer made any sense to the victims. It also knew what it would take to get the descendants of those responsible for these tragic deeds to lay down their heavy burden of guilt.

Maybe the time has finally arrived for both the victors and the victims to confront the profane past with empathy, sympathy and understanding. Maybe the moment of truth and the time for reconciliation has finally arrived.

Is this the moment everyone has been waiting for? Are the Americans and the Europeans ready to express their remorse and make atonement for the past of slave trade and plantation slavery?

On the other hand, are the people of Africa also ready to reciprocate the goodwill, ready to forgive the Oburoni people for the past tragedy if they agree to make atonement?

"How do you address the paradox of slavery in the land of the free? What do you do to turn a legacy of brutality and exploitation into a spirit of reconciliation and progress?" Trent asked probingly.

"Is it possible that the anger of the African gods could remain active forever?" the head shaman of the Chucalisa Shrine asked. "How could you ignore the anger of Mother Nature when you see its force in progress? How could you prevent her from visiting her wrath on the future generations?"

"High, Reverend Peterson," Bubba said, waving gently to the pastor. "It looks as if we have got ourselves into more trouble than we have anticipated. Don't you think so?"

"Well yes, you are right, Bubba. But don't jump to any conclusions as yet, because this thing can turn around quickly," the Reverend told Bubba. "I detect some softness in the elders and a willingness on their part to put this difficult past behind us."

"No number of church worship, no amount of offerings could heal the raw painful regrets that several generations before us have felt and still carry in their hearts today," Bubba told the preacher.

"But how have we addressed it?" he pressed Bubba for an answer.

"We know the sort of past that was passed down to us. They are recorded in books, symbolized by old slave cabins, posted in antebellum plantation homes and preserved in rusty slave shackles. They are also recorded in leg irons and chains of torture, remnants of which are scattered all across the consecrated region even today."

"That is why we are trying very hard to do something about this," Reverend Peterson told him, earnestly. Their hearts could no longer contain the guilt. Time and events have changed, creating different paradigms of existence from what their ancestors had experienced in the immediate past.

"Reverend, how do we make a clean break with the past?" Bubba asked, while he was reading his favorite pages from his sacred book. The guilt still lingered in his heart, though he wanted to get rid of it very badly.

Meanwhile, the legendary Mississippi River, affectionately known to many in the region as the Old Man River, has continued to roll downstream with fury, struggling desperately not to expose the old buried secrets of the region. Maybe, the time has come to stop denying the past and allow the old man river to wash away the burden of guilt they've inherited and end the feelings that'd plagued them all these years.

How can the world forget what the European slave traders from Portugal, Spain, Holland, Denmark, and Britain and the American slave traders from the Northeast, from Rhode Island, New York, Connecticut, and Massachusetts, did to Africa during the slave trade? The descendants of the plantation slave owners in the Old South must also confront what their ancestors did to their slaves. While they could never pay for the forcible exodus of the more than forty million Africans who ended as slaves on the cotton plantations, tobacco farms, rice fields, gold mines and on sugar cane fields in the New World and worked as field hands, they could make at least a reasonable atonement for the profane past.

Maybe the ancestors have been watching them like hawks.

The slave trade made the Africans the most widely dispersed people on the planet. They are found everywhere, from Brazil, the Caribbean, the United States, England, Holland, Canada, and in many other countries outside the continent of Africa.

Many of these countries are great today mainly because of the help Africa had given them in the past. They'd built the foundations of their economies on the sweat and blood of the African slaves.

Today, they are admiringly democratic and law-abiding, but are their hands still not dripping with the blood of millions of African victims that'd perished in the forests, on the grasslands, on the mountains, in the valleys, on the high seas, and during the notorious slave raids. But many also died in the privacy of the plantations in the Old South, and in the gold mines and sugar cane fields in the Caribbean and Brazil.

The role my African ancestors played or were forced to play is still unpleasant for me to talk about today. But the only consolation is that if the European had not supplied the guns to our African ancestors and had not overpowered them technologically with guns and cannons, the history would have been different today.

The most logical course of action for the descendants of those who did this is to rectify the past, is to make atonement.

Maybe the time for the final reconciliation has finally arrived.

The profane past must not continue to haunt you anymore. We must not allow the negative forces of the ancestors to continue to seek vengeance for the past.

The only path left for you is to show the rest of the world that you have a change of heart. Let the world see that you are remorseful for all the free labor and for the brutalities the African people had suffered during the slave trade. That you regret all the horrors your ancestors did to Africa in the past and are ready to say to the rest of the world that you are truly sorry and that you are willing to make atonement and seek reconciliation.

Sitting on one of the green benches at Tom Lee Park on the banks of the Mississippi River, Bubba heard the voice of the African poet reading one of his masterpieces to the children:

> It was sunrise, and the griot was talking about the past.
> The dark past lit with all the modern bright lights.
> The ugly truth had emerged in the broad daylight.
> This is the truth that can no longer be suppressed,
> Because the ancestors are angry and on the move,
> You must face the profane in our pasts.
> You must admit guilt and make atonement
> The world is obviously at a crossroad.
> At an epochal juncture in history;
> You need to end the guilt from the past,
> And lay down the heavy burden of guilt.
> What you have carried for so long

You must seek the road of reconciliation,
Still the African lioness sits and waits;
Her loud voice roars over the mountains,
Echoed loudly across the luscious grasslands,
She prowls across the virgin forests;
And waits patiently for the atonement,
But how long must she wait?
Before she makes her move?
To unleash the wrath of the gods
The time for atonement has come.
The gate of history is wide open.
You should say on behalf of your forebears
That you have a change of heart
That your remorse is sincere,
You would heal the wounds of Africa.
And lay down the heavy burden of guilt,
That you still carry from the past,
Then purge your guilty conscience,
And end the shame and suffering.
Speak to the African ancestors
Put forth the package of atonement
Bow your head in shame no more.
Do something about the past,
To receive forgiveness
And reconciliation!

"On the other hand, the African descendants of the victims must be able to forgive the past," Chukwuyo, one of the old African-Americans who live in Memphis admitted, seated at a sports bar and barber shop combined. "A lot of progress has been made since I was ten years old. It is about time we must also put the ugly past and the sufferings of our ancestors behind us.

"Are you telling me that all the white folks have to do is to say that they are truly sorry for what their ancestors did?" Kevin, the young barber, asked with a skeptical look on his face. "For all the horrible things they did to us, are you saying a simple remorse will get them off the hook?"

"Son, listen. The slave trade ended long ago and plantation slavery ended in a bloody civil war in which hundreds of thousands of these very white folks died in a horrible bloodbath, so the masters have also suffered tremendously . . ." Chukwuyo said as Kevin cut in sharply. "We have to swallow the bitterness from the past and extend forgiveness to them at some point."

"What about the departed ancestors, the victims whose lives were lost in the forests, in the Middle Passage across the Atlantic Ocean and on the plantations, or even at the hands of lynch mobs up North, were they in vain?" Kevin asked angrily.

There was a long pause. The old man was fidgety and meditative. He raised his head and stared at the young man intensely. The silent voices murmured from the past and he pondered whether he could forgive those as well. This youth, the old man thought, was a youth with the right sense of history, but he lacked the maturity to deal with the horrors from the past.

"Son, you have no idea how much brutality went on in this land in the past," he said with teary eyes. "When our people have been so violated, so badly abused and so miserably degraded, we can never completely recover from the agony. We just got to put the hurt and the misery behind us and continue to live in the present."

"Is the atonement for the pain and suffering still in the works?" Kevin asked, drawing his attention to the controversial issue of sending a delegation to Africa to atone for the slave trade. "Or is it still the same old pretend it had never happened strategy inherited from the past?"

"Well, I know we need something concrete to help us start the healing process, but that belongs to the ancestors to decide. We can never recover even a fraction of what they owe us or let alone expect them to pay the debt they owe our ancestors for the free labor," he told Kevin.

"In this country, all I know is that everyone pays if they have inflicted pain and suffering on anyone, if they are liable," Kevin asked. "Why should the descendants of these folks go free or walk away from their liability?"

"If we can't solve it, let the gods handle it on our behalf," he told Kevin again. "We might be going about it the wrong way, if we take matters into our hands."

"But why can't we get some atonement for the pain and suffering from this ugly and horrible past they'd inflicted on our ancestors or had forced on our people?" Kevin, the young barber worried. "You need to tell me because I've been trying very hard to put the past behind me. All I want to get is good education, a decent job and the ability to take care of my family, but I have not had much success in doing any of these."

"What do you mean by not much success?" Chukwuyo asked, pointedly. "Didn't you finish high school with a diploma? Didn't you get into the Community College, the highly rated local community college in the city?"

"Yes, I did. But I kept dropping out . . . the courses are tough, quality professors, but the past still catches up with me every time I hear the professors talking in class about how my folks have suffered so badly in history, especially during the slavery past," he told him.

"That is why we need a resolution for the past to deal with the undeserved stigma they'd placed on every African in the world," Chukwuyo said.

"We need the forty acres and a mule that they'd promised our ancestors years ago, plus some interest too," Kevin joked. "No, just a couple of billions to set up businesses and perhaps scholarships to correct the idea that slaves could not own property and that they were not supposed to read and write in the past. That is truly a great idea."

"That is a great idea, but we need reconciliation as well," Chukwuyo, the old man said in a shaken voice, "I know the heavy burden that they still carry is because of their failure to make atonement and ask for reconciliation—the keys they need to free themselves."

"You can sense the tension and the guilt in the elevators, in the stores and in the work places," Kevin said. "I wonder if it is simply an ordinary fear, or if it has something to do with the guilt from the past?"

"Well, it is because some folks still carry the guilt to their homes, to the work place, to government jobs at all levels and it is true some even carry these feelings to the churches and into the legislatures."

"Well, you are right. But we need some form of dramatic apotheosis for the past. The burden of guilt is so huge and so ingrained in everyone that we need some "reasonable economic package" no matter how "reasonable" to shake the continent back to economic, political, and cultural reality," Pete, the other customer, told the old man resolutely. You could hear the bitterness still lingering in the man's voice after all these years.

The seventy-year-old man got out of the chair and the twelve-year-old boy who has been waiting for his turn for a radical fade haircut sat down. The old man paid for the haircut with fifteen single dollar bills, shook hands firmly and sat back down to socialize in the shop a little longer. "What good would any money do to the dead ancestors?" he asked himself.

"What kind of haircut do you want, son?" the barber asked the thirteen-year-old-youth in a firm but friendly voice.

"A fade, sir!" he said quickly, he'd already decided on what he wanted. He knew where he was going and what sort of cut should define him.

"Are you sure your mother will not put you out of the house with that kind of "bad, radical haircut?" Kevin asked him firmly, but he later on broke into a hilarious laughter with the others.

"I want something that can knock the young girls out and make many of my friends jealous when I make it back to school after the two week suspension, come this Monday morning," the young boy told him.

"Son, I got you," he told the young boy reassuringly.

"Well, apology is the right thing for them to do. That's really not asking too much of them, is it?" Christopher, the old man, asked the barber, still gulping down some of the rum he'd mixed inside a coke can to calm down his nerves. "I still love to get the rum down. That was part of the bait that broke the will of our ancestors, got them in trouble in Africa long ago, if you still remember your history."

"I don't need to apologize to Ms. Churches, the Caucasian teacher," the young boy said. "I didn't do anything wrong. She just hates me and constantly picks on me because she does not like me, maybe because of you know what I am talking about . . ."

"Son, we are not talking about you apologizing to anybody or for anything. Are you guilty of something at school?" Kevin asked him quickly.

"It is my fault! My fault!" he said loudly as if the barber and the rest of them had ear problems. "I am sorry, I thought you were talking to me," he said.

"Well, stop blaming our ancestors. They did what they did because the slave traders held their guns to their heads. They either sold their own or got taken as slaves or died for not producing the slave quotas. If that is not what we call self-preservation, then tell me what is. It is as ridiculous as being arrested and handcuffed in your own residence for burglarizing your own property, while you struggle and looked on helplessly screaming obscenities," Kevin said mockingly. "The ancestors do teach lessons the hard way to those who blame them arrogantly and foolishly by hiding in their towers, torturing the facts and drawing some uninformed conclusions from the records and from six week visits to the slave castles on the African continent. The gods definitely reveal themselves to them, sometimes dramatically."

"I need some beer after all that tough talk," the old man said.

"For all the havoc their ancestors had wrecked on the African continent, which included the raids, the burning down of villages, the abductions and the mowing down of African chiefs who protested the onslaught, why do they still blame our ancestors for the slave trade?" Kevin asked. "Why did the slave traders hide behind those impregnable strongholds if our ancestors sold the people to them voluntarily without any coercion?"

"Well, that is because they prefer to shift the guilt to the African people, the victims of this wicked trade," the old man said unhappily.

"That is simply as ridiculous as it can get. The Africans still can't get their acts together today because of this prolonged psychological trauma your ancestors had created in their past," the barber said angrily.

"They go on six weeks of research on the continent, then they think they know all there is to know about the slave trade," the barber remarked. "These empty barrels are the most dangerous minds when it comes to the racial discourse."

"The ancestors would teach them the historical reality as opposed to the created fiction or sanitized half truths they keep on espousing and teaching," he pointed out.

"Well, all I know is if you mess with the ancestors, they will mess with you as well," the barber joked. "And they will sometimes embarrass you publicly or in your own home too."

"You are absolutely right," he agreed.

"If the descendants of the slave owners face the truth, it would set them free and bring some sort of healing to the victims as well," Pete, the young barber, said as he swept and clustered the cut hair and dirt from the floor into two small separate piles. He collected both into one huge pile and threw the pile into the dumpster.

"Well, once the terms of atonement sound reasonable, we have to forgive them," he told the barber. "We have to finally help them to lay down their heavy burden of guilt, because that is the only way forward for everybody involved."

"Just thinking about how the forgiveness can set them free sends angry chills down my spine. At the same time it also makes my heart leap with joy if this could really happen, because the world would become a better place for everyone to live in," the barber said.

"It will not end racism overnight, but it will make it easier for all the parties involved to bury the past and move into the future trusting one another a whole lot better," he told the barber.

"Meanwhile the guilt in their hearts is destroying them like the ravaging power of a terminal cancer, the old man said.

"It is in the hands of the ancestors now," he told him.

The old man then left for his old decrepit house next to the projects, half a mile from the barbershop. He wanted to get to the mailman before the hoodlums got their hands on his social security check. "These young boys live in homes without adequate direction and if this is what the future looks like, I wonder where we are heading," he mumbled to himself as he walked faster, leaning on his walker and headed toward his residence.

"This burden will live on in notoriety if the guilty refuse to swallow their pride, show remorse and seek reconciliation. There is no reason why they must continue to lower their heads in shame forever whenever they hear about what their ancestors did in the past in Africa, or did on the plantations in the New World," the barber said. "All they need is to apologize for it and make atonement."

"Atonement will end the guilt. If they found it compelling enough to make the atonement, it would halt the wrath of the ancestors as well," the silent voices said, breaking their silence.

TEN

BUBBA HAD BEEN WRONG ABOUT the African chiefs. They also felt some guilt from the past. And he was right that they had to make atonement, though the victims in the bizarre enterprise of shame were their ancestors. He wasn't the one to insist that the Africans ought to do something about their guilt, if they had any.

He knew that his people had more to feel guilty about. He'd realized that the old ugly mansions across the South, the old money and even legendary ancestors were some of the most enduring legacies from the slavery past. The old court houses and country clubs had been places where the slave trade took place.

What was his responsibility in this ugly drama? All the old plantation homes with barns and boundary posts separating one cotton farm from the other belonged to his great grandfather.

He hadn't minced words in saying that his great grandfather was one of the most successful cotton planters in the Old South. He was quick to admit that he was one of the richest cotton farmers in the state of Mississippi. But he was quick to point out that his great grandfather treated his African slaves humanely, though they could not walk away from the field. He still earned the reputation as a "hard-handed" cotton planter that worked his slaves very hard.

He wondered why the past has refused to die and the brutalities from the past are still driving some issues today. Bubba complained. "People still act as if the slave trade and slavery ended only yesterday. It is causing a lot of tension among people, though all this history happened way before we were even born."

"The victims want to put the past behind them as much as possible, but the experience was so brutal that the effects still linger on even to today," Verna told him after the meeting.

Verna, the church secretary had shuffled through her old books from her great grandmother the day before. She untied the red ribbon around the eighty-year-old box, which still held some revered documents in one piece, to find out the old secrets that had been hidden from the family in those aged documents all these decades.

"Did you find out any new secrets?" Bubba inquired.

"Oh yes. The ancestors passed down all they knew to us. They wanted us to know about the many tragedies and the few triumphs in our past. They wanted us to never forget what they had suffered in our history and remember how the past was extremely brutal," she told Bubba, who happened to be one of the deacons in the local church.

"The past had been ugly, but it is over. Our ancestors did the best they could for their slaves. They took care of their food, shelter and clothing. And you would agree with me that it took a lot to do these things for them," Bubba admitted. "I am not trying to apologize for slavery on behalf of my ancestors, far from that, but they tried to do their best."

"Well, I just feel that, instead of letting the next generations to still face the future with the same old baggage from the past hounding them, it is better to move forward redeemed, united and not as different races or different folks," Verna declared. "So if it is atonement that the Africans need, we must find a way to make that happen."

"We are working on it. But how do we deal with such a past that many people look at differently and they have a right to do so. But we are working on a proactive plan to settle the issue once and for all."

Verna who was also an African-American schoolteacher asked the European-American lady in Mississippi what she felt about the past and how it has impacted her life. "Do you feel you have any responsibility for the slavery in your past?"

"Well, I regret the past. I have a lot of regret in my heart for it. But I have African-American relatives. I have lost relatives many decades ago, because they left Tennessee to live up North to pursue their dreams," the lady told him.

"So was it the lack of opportunity in the South which sent several of them up North to sow their wild oaks?" the teacher asked her, pointedly.

"Yes, that too was one of the reasons. But the racial barriers in the South played a big part too," she confessed. "In fact, it had a lot to do with their leaving the South for what they thought was a milder racial climate."

"What is the relationship between you and these African-American relatives today?" she asked her calmly.

"My mother's grandmother had slaves. I know their names and I have seen their faces. I have heard their stories, but they are my family. Their descendants still live in Shelby County, Tennessee, today," she told him.

"Did your ancestors own many slaves?" she asked. It seemed strange that she let her anger aside and the tone of her questions was being very polite.

"No, my grandfather had only five slaves. He had a family that he would never have divided. They became one family: the Kellys. White people were hired and they did some of the dangerous work too. In my grandfather's house, a white woman did the housework. My African-American "great-great aunt" Polly simply looked after the children, including my grandfather who had a love affair with a black woman, also a Kelly," the teacher said apologetically, trying to compensate for the past.

"How do you feel about being related to the descendants of former African slaves?" she asked the lady calmly.

"I feel no regrets about that. Long ago when I was about twenty-one; I met a young black woman in Winston-Salem, North Carolina when my band was playing in a nightclub over there. We were dressed in the same kind of clothes—flannel shirts and jeans. We very much looked alike. We started talking and I realized that her great grandfather was my grandfather. She was a Bailey from Shelby County, Tennessee. She's my cousin. We are of the same blood and of the same family. Her face resemblances mine and the rest of the white side of my family, though she is African-American, we had several things in common."

"Have you tried to reconnect with anyone from the African side of your family?" she asked her, probingly, "that is if you are of the same blood and you love them so very dearly?"

"Well, I respect and treasure the African side of my family. My mother knew and loved them too. Of course, I know about the horrible past, so I hate the idea of slavery. But I still honor and love my African relatives. As far as it goes, they are my blood. They are part of my life. They guide and protect me. I never knew Polly or Ted Bailey, they died long before I was born, but I still cherish their memory because they are part of my bloodline. We are part of the same family tree."

"Are you ready to apologize to their descendants personally for the slavery past?" she asked her again.

"I hate the fact that my ancestors conducted the slave trade in Africa and I regret how the white side of my family from Tennessee forced them to work on our farms and to do household chores," she said.

"Why are you so sorry about what they went through?" she asked.

"Well, as I look at the African side of my family, I know that they have my DNA and I feel nothing but sorrow in my heart that their ancestors had to endure so much brutality during slavery. Personally, I will apologize to them and tell them how sorry I am that this had happened to their ancestors in the past."

She refused to condemn the past, though she knew that it was tainted. But she sometimes felt very uncomfortable about this heritage. She was torn between respect for the sacrifice her ancestors made for her heritage and the shame and embarrassment the slave trade and plantation slavery had brought to the region.

"Maybe, the rest of the world, especially the victims of your ancestor's crimes would be ready to forgive the dark, horrible past of slavery. It would definitely relieve you of some of the pain and shame. Maybe it would free you from the heavy burden of guilt, which you and your descendants have carried in your heart all these years."

"Though we still hold our ancestors dear to our hearts, we can't wait to lay down this heavy burden of guilt," she confessed to him. "We are ready to move into the future without the burden."

"What are you doing personally to put down the heavy burden of guilt," she asked her.

"The slavery lingers on in our history and it will never go away and be forgotten. But we have tried to do something about this tragic part of our past and for that matter, about the American past," she replied. "I extend a lot of love to my blood relatives on the African side of my family. And I feel sincere remorse. And I offer my sincere apologies to them. Maybe that's all I can do for now."

"You know what your ancestors, especially what the Europeans did to the Africans on their own continent was more than horrible?" she straightened up the strings on her purse.

"What do you mean? Are you talking about how they bought the slaves or how they shipped or hauled them away?" she asked politely.

"How they invaded their land, raided their villages, abducted some of them and forced the chiefs to exchange their own people for guns and it was wrong how they hauled them out of the continent in droves like beasts of burden to work as slaves for free for centuries," She wanted to know how much she knew about the genesis of the burden that she'd inherited.

"I agree that the past was shameful, indeed, it has been very embarrassing to several of us. How the traders abducted or bought the slaves and kept them in captivity in the dungeons and loaded them on the jam-packed slave boats, was absolutely horrible. Anything to make the past better for all the victims will be the right thing to do. What else can make things better, I don't really know," she said candidly.

"Well you must listen to the Africans and do whatever they are asking for," she told her, bluntly. "I think they want some form of compensation, amends for the past, nowhere near what your ancestors owe them."

"Well, this is not a past we are very much proud of anyway, but we cannot turn our backs on our heritage completely either," she sighed deeply. She was battling the guilt inside her and trying to conceal the remorse in her heart at the same time.

"The world knows that the Portuguese conceived the idea, masterminded and started the slave trade against the African people. Though we cannot say that this was a sinister plot of genocide, which they'd conceived to destroy the continent, the truth is that it'd brought enormous suffering to the continent and to the African people," she told her. "Because of new technology, the world knows about the hidden horrors in your past, which you have sanitized and hidden from the rest of the world."

"Well, as I said earlier, we can't go back to correct the past, but we are willing to work for harmony in the future as much as possible," she said.

"It is amazing today how the truth about the past is all over the Internet and in the libraries for the world to see. The activities of the Portuguese, the Danes, the French, the Spanish and the roles the Dutch and the British played, especially how they came to monopolize the lion's share of the slave trade, reaping tremendous amount of wealth out of the misery of the victims, have all been placed on the web for the wide world to see," she told her.

"Well, my ancestors were Irish and some of them were sharecroppers in the South," she explained, defending what role her ancestors played directly. "So just like the African slaves, they were field hands and suffered in the fields as well."

"Since your ancestors, regardless of their origin, still carry some collective burden of guilt from the past, are you willing to make the atonement in order to get final reconciliation? Don't you need to make peace with the world, beginning with Africa?" the teacher asked her.

"Well, I don't know exactly what they want, but we can try," she told her.

"Well, they are ready, but you know you have to reach out to them?" the teacher asked her, determined to find out her position on the question of atonement.

"I don't suppose we can ever pay back the heavy debt that we owe the African people. Those who'd been forced out of their continent to work for us for free for centuries," she told the teacher passionately. "We cannot change the past, but we can try to make amends for it.

That is if they would permit us to do this according to terms that are reasonable."

"You are right that you can never pay back all the money that you owe the continent, but you can show your remorse. You can atone for it. This would lead you down the path of forgiveness and reconciliation," She told her.

"If the atonement is reasonable and meaningful, and not short-sighted, we can make it," she said, though uneasily. "I hope it won't come to where we have to kneel down before some African gods and beg for forgiveness, or where we have to sit and watch them slaughter some cows, sheep or roosters, with blood all over, in the name of apotheosis—to cleanse our hands."

"Well, they want atonement, some form of restitution. It does not have to be a huge sum that will bankrupt any country involved. The truth is that you can never repay the monetary debt, which you actually owe the African people," she told her again, getting a little emotional. "We are talking about nearly four hundred years of free labor, of brutality, of lashes, of slave raids and of pain and suffering."

"You know those who had started the slave trade and those who began all these evil things are dead and gone," she said defensively again. "We, the modern generation, have not enslaved anybody. But, on the other hand, we are just trying to stop this heavy burden of guilt in the past from plaguing our children and their children."

"We know that your generation did not commit many of these atrocities against Africa. We know the generation of traders who went to the African continent to get the slaves, and those who tortured and murdered the slaves on the plantations are dead and gone, but the fact remains that you have benefited from the fruits of the European slave trade to Africa and from plantation slavery in America. This makes you somehow liable for the profane past," she told her bluntly, reminding her of what benefits they'd received from the slave trade.

"Yes, as I told you earlier we certainly feel some guilt in our hearts. The whole thing is a silent shame," she sighed. "We the present generation did not directly do these things, but we are willing to make amends, if that would help bring some sort of final reconciliation."

"You are a descendant of those who have benefited directly or indirectly from the slave trade and plantation slavery," she reminded her quickly.

"Well, you are right. For a long time, we have denied these things, and erroneously blamed the African chiefs. We have been hiding our heads in the sand, but we are now ready to face the truth, to atone for it, to get a brighter and better future for everyone."

"The whole world is expecting you to do something about what your ancestors did to the African continent. They know that your ancestors had arrested the continent's development and had put a perpetual stigma of inferiority on the African people," she told her.

"You are not serious, are you?" she asked her, feeling surprised." "What do you want from us? We can't go back into the past and correct everything, rectify every wrong, stop every brutality and take back every crack of the whip."

"Yes, I know that. But you must show genuine remorse, offer a sincere apology and not recite empty words that have no sincerity. Africa has no more use for perfunctory words. The people of Africa and those who live in the Diaspora are like stones in rivers, they have seen it all, and dealt with the currents every day. So they have no room for legal niceties and florid jargons with twisted logic. They need some atonement for the past. The world is waiting for a more remorseful apology from you, preferably a small ritual somewhere on the so-called African Slave Coast, and that is what the African chiefs and elders have been waiting for."

"Is that all you want?"

"No. That is not all we want."

"What is next then?

"We want to see some concretized deeds from your people."

"How do we do all the things you are asking for?" she asked with mixed feelings.

"Well, the truth is painful. For one thing, you can no longer blame the African chiefs, many of whom your ancestors had forced with their cannons to cooperate and get them the slaves, or if they failed to do so, they were mowed down like grasses," she told her.

"They played a role in several of the transactions too, I remind you," she said forcefully.

"But you must admit that your ancestors introduced the trans-Atlantic slave trade to our shores, and you, the Dutch and your British ancestors were responsible for the lion's share of the slave trade."

"Well, teacher . . . it is not that simple . . ." she remarked. "The slavery past was long ago, and it is much more complicated than we are both willing to admit."

"Well, the truth will continue to hang around your neck like a dark cloud. You can no longer suppress, twist or even erase these crimes from history because the anger of the departed spirits is everywhere, proclaiming the truth to everyone."

"What do you mean by hanging around our neck?" she asked her quickly.

"I don't mean that they are going to drag you to the wheels of justice anywhere to answer for these crimes against humanity," the teacher told her. "It would probably never come to that, but regardless of all the pontificating, it is Africa's prerogative to let the world court hear the case."

"You mean some people are even thinking about settling this at the global court?" she asked exasperated, and in total disbelief. "Oh, my goodness! I don't believe they are going all out to rectify the past?"

"If the African ancestors, the deities that have been on the path of vengeance, have decided to take matters into their own hands, the more forward-looking leaders will have to comply with their wishes," she told her.

"But what of the role your ancestors played in helping the Europeans in the slave trade?" she asked.

"Did the African chiefs ever invite your ancestors over to the continent?" the teacher asked her. "Your folks forced their way into the land and claimed that they only stumbled upon the continent. But do you not know what they really wanted or what was on their minds when they arrived?"

"Gold and maybe, slaves," she told her.

"Wrong. They needed labor for their plantations," she told her.

"Slaves," she said. "You are right," she told the teacher.

"Well, you sounded like an honest and humane person and you claim that you love the African side of your family, but what I see in you is someone who is still battling a lot of guilt, fighting several secret forces deeply buried inside your heart," she told her.

"It is not inside my heart, I think it is deeper than that. It is inside my soul and certainly inside my psyche as well," she told the middle-aged teacher quite frankly. "Why we couldn't easily let go of anything that hurts our soul so badly, something which gnaws so greedily at our essence, and tears apart the cultural fabric of the nation, I still cannot understand."

"I guess the final answer lies with us and the spirit of the ancestors. That is whether you believe it or not, your fate is in the hands of the angry ancestors of Africa."

When and where does the peacemaker come in? Whether now or later the one designated to make peace would come to the scene.

Brandon Beringer, the chosen one, rode on the gentle breezes of the Mississippi River, danced on its gentle bluffs and gathered his courage to reach the shrine to direct the mission of reconciliation. His role is to bring about a more harmonious future in the land for everyone.

The gods reaffirmed Brandon as the chosen leader for this unique mission. He must preside over the atonement. The ancestors had selected him—among several talented individuals—to lead this unique mission, to direct the quest for redemption.

Brandon went to the Shrine of Chucalisa to eat some of the barbecue lunch. He ate two slabs of ribs, some coleslaw and potato salad. And he drank two glasses of black cherry punch to wash it down. It did not take him long to realize why Memphis has the title the barbecue capital of the world.

"Mine, mine, mine, this is the best barbecue in the whole wide world. And if this is not the best place for barbecue in this country, then think again, I declare," he told himself, but Trent and Steve, his two closest friends, heard him and started to laugh at him.

"You're just crazy about them ribs," Trent joked. "The barbecue has got hold of your brain and has driven you crazy, so you are always singing its praises."

The three friends dashed to T. O. Fuller Park and played some basketball. During the game, according to an eye witness, the giant falcon swooped down, circled around Brandon's head as if it wanted to lift him up into the sky. It landed on his shoulder and spoke some spiritual words to him, but did so quietly. Brandon was embarrassed before his friends, but he heard the words of the falcon, nodded, but appeared to take exception to the message the falcon gave him.

When Brandon returned from the Shrine of Chucalisa to his residence, the sky was filled with dark rain clouds, large patches that were racing angrily toward the almighty Mississippi River. He turned off the television, because the flashes of lightening continued to interrupt the reception.

Surprisingly, his friend who was fast asleep on the couch in the living room did not wake up. Brandon tried to wake her up, but the beer hangover from the previous night prevented her. She simply opened her eyes briefly and continued to sleep. She felt so relaxed and so protected in his presence that she did not even care to wake up in spite of all the lightening and torrential rain. She depended on him totally to protect her from the demons that plagued her. Maybe she was taking a break from the things that'd made her depressed and anxious.

Brandon was worried about his mother's safety. So, he got on the phone to check on her. But he had to get off because there was too much lightening or electricity in the air. He didn't want to get electrocuted or get shocked and burned without fulfilling the mission.

Meanwhile, on the other side of the city, it seemed the sky opened its gates when the rain started to come down in torrents. The streets became suddenly filled with flash flood. The cars were traveling slowly, wading through the muddy flood with their blinkers on. The rain god took over the evening, and ended the festivities on Beale Street, sending the thrill-seekers home.

"No one is trying to go anywhere in this rough weather," Louise told her daughter. The weather was horrible and the dark clouds of retribution hid inside the heavy rains. Meanwhile, the booming sounds of thunder reverberated against the river banks, shaking the Desoto-Hernando Bridge repeatedly, echoing the demands of the ancestors for atonement.

And for the thousands who made the trip to Memphis for the Blues Festival that weekend, those who could see or hear and smell the fun, the rain was such a heartbreaker, a complete hindrance. It was standing in their way. The music was good, the food smelled delicious, and the entertainment in the air was pulsating. But from the heavy legs of the rain, they knew that Mother Nature was not going to give them the opportunity to party that night. The gods of hedonism must wait till Mother Nature was willing to give them permission.

Maybe Mother Nature would be fair to them. She might take Friday night from them, but she might allow them to have the time of their lives on Saturday and Sunday, the main reasons they made the pilgrimage to the historic city in the first place.

The Blues Festival on Beale Street attracted fans primarily from the Mid-South, but some visitors also came to the festival from as far away as California, New York, Michigan and Hawaii. Some came from overseas seeking the thrill of their lives. The overseas visitors came mainly for the barbecue and the music. They came mostly from Europe, from London, Amsterdam, Paris and Frankfurt, and some came from Asia.

There were thirteen couples from Tokyo, Japan, but their obsession was more with Graceland and the legendary King of Rock and Roll rather than the blues festival on Beale Street. These tourists, Europeans as well as folks across the United States came to enjoy the festival, but most importantly, they came on the annual spiritual pilgrimage to honor the King of Rock and Roll and to tour the Graceland Mansion. The amazing thing was that some of these tourists were not born at the time Elvis Pressley was performing his musical magic, but they were in love with his music. The Visitors Bureau expects between one to two million visitors annually. Some have done these tours five years in a row. They have returned to the city for the good times, and the chance to honor the king of rock and roll seven years in a row.

If you want to see the joy and satisfaction on their faces then go to Elvis Presley Boulevard and watch these tourists climb the stairs into the historic Lisa Marie airplane. They enter this plane as if they are going to heaven. They depart energized, sanctified and even touched. You could tell that the tourists become very satisfied for being that close to the departed hero, the legendary Elvis Presley. Some of them snapped endless rows of pictures of the Graceland Mansion and anything that reminded them of the king.

Most of the outside visitors did not care much about the history of the region. The visitors from Beijing, Singapore and Seoul come looking for sight seeing, some culinary delights, the blues and rock and roll music. These tourists do not care about any racial issues. Even if these issues existed, they do not notice them and no one throws any of these issues in their faces. These tourists have always been embraced by all segments of the Memphis community.

You could see them armed with their cameras, dancing shoes and tote bags, but the main thing on their mind—the opportunity for fun and a taste of the best barbecue in the world. The city of Memphis has been the barbecue capital of the world for many years. Though New Orleans and St. Louis have disputed this claim, Memphis has always managed to put its best foot forward and has held its own very well when it comes to barbecue.

When these visitors are back in their home countries, the people of Memphis imagine that their visit to the city would be memorialized in postcards, pictures, videotapes, tee shirts and other memorabilia. Several could see themselves returning to visit Memphis, to Graceland and to the legendary Beale Street, doing the pilgrimage for many years to come.

The visitors say that there is something special in the air in Memphis. Maybe it is the food or the music or just the soul of the city, which makes this place a very friendly, lovely and gentle city for many visitors. "It is the water," someone said jokingly. "Perhaps, it is the mud from Mud Island or the bluffs of the Mississippi River."

"Maybe it is the small shrine called Chucalissa, or the tiny peninsula sitting in the middle of the legendary Mississippi River overlooking downtown Memphis," Trent said sarcastically. "Maybe the soul of the city is Mud Island."

The tourists usually walk the historic Beale Street with pride, inching their way on the red cobblestones from one end to the other, covering the three hundred yard walk. You could see them moving their bodies to the rhythm of the blues or to the pulsating beat of ravishing rock and roll. They often stopped in front of some of the legendary night clubs to dance away the evening or to buy beer.

There must be about one hundred bands playing on Beale Street on these special Saturday nights, and they go all out to entertain the tourists. Beale Street is bustling with music, beer and barbecue. It certainly comes to life with an assortment of animated music from some of the legendary musicians in the clubs that line up both sides of the red cobblestone street. The sight seers, some with beer cans in hand, walk arm in arm with their partners.

Most of the tourists stay in groups, understandably uncomfortable in some of the small dives, but most of them love to mingle on Beale Street freely. The crowd on Beale Street that night was made up of Hispanics, European-Americans and African-Americans, Asians and tourists from several countries. But the bulk came from the neighborhood. There was a large throng from rural Mississippi and Arkansas. They came from Senatobia, Greenwood, Little Rock, Sikeston, New Albany, Marion, Olive Branch and Byhalia. They descended like hungry wolves ready to devour life, eat, dance and party. They were ready to push the gusto back into their lives.

With the blues, rock and roll and even gospel music vibrating all around, the crowd had to choose the brand of music, the food or the artifacts they wanted. Historic artifacts representing the heritage of the city were in great demand. You could see the joy in the faces of the people buying beer, tee shirts, barbecue sandwiches and some of these artifacts.

The city has deservingly claimed many titles including the birth place of Rock and Roll, the home of the Blues, and the barbecue capital of the world. The city has lived up to these reputations, but not without the envy of the neighboring rival cities. There have been claims by neighboring cities that their cities had better barbecue, more vibrant rock and roll music and a richer cadre of blues music than Memphis.

That Friday evening, the tourists and the visitors from mainly rural Mississippi threaded their way on the cobblestones of Beale Street and gravitated to other parts of downtown to avoid the rain. The thousands of people who arrived from far and near were looking for nothing but plain old fun, They did not pay to walk the historic Beale Street, but most of them were expected to get hotel rooms in the downtown area, buy beer, go into the clubs or eat in the restaurants. In return, they expected the organizers to provide smooth and flawless music, the food must be tastier than anything they'd ever had and the atmosphere must be more compelling and vivacious.

Outdoors, the tourists used their umbrellas to keep on moving, but they had to flee to take cover from the rain. "The rain must give way. I know the rain would stop so the party can go on," the visitor from Byhalia, Mississippi said.

When the stormy weather finally abated, the bands on Beale Street woke up from their slumber like sleeping lions and roared loudly at the top of their voices. You could hear the pulsating drums, the loud trumpets and the saxophones from the various clubs filled the air. You could see the dancers go crazy with joy, showing their newest moves as they gulped down beer like drunken bees.

The sponsors were happy for the tourists who spent all that money to come to the festival. Those from rural Mississippi, most of them were regulars anyway and those from other states usually have their money's worth whenever they came. And they needed all the safety and security the city could provide them to have the time of their lives.

Alonzo, the chair of the Organizing Committee, scheduled the Blues Competition Saturday morning and the Barbecuefest as the last event for the evening. Many visitors had brought their rain gear with them, but they were still very much disappointed because of the strong winds and the pile of mud in Tom Lee's Park.

Whenever the weather became a major disruption in the festivities for the weekend, the organizer, Alonzo, must move some of the events to the nearby secure locations, but the atmosphere in these places were not the same as that of Beale Street, where the sonorous blues were pulsating against the red cobblestones on the legendary home of the best barbecue in the world.

"For three years in a row, the festival had been drenched in the tears of Mother Nature and in the floodgates of the angry ancestors," Pete told Alonzo. "How do you manage to pick the wrong date for the festival each year, and did so three years in a row?"

"We cannot complain about Mother Nature. We are at the mercy of the weather. Mother Nature could make or break the festival anytime. It could make the festival enjoyable for everyone or waste the money and time of everyone. And that includes African-Americans, Hispanics and European Americans, and it does so without any distinction. For she treats all races, men and women, both the rich and the poor alike," he told Pete, though he couldn't deny the connection between the timing of the festival and the torrential rains.

The weather was calmer on the West Memphis side of the Mississippi River, but rougher on the Memphis side. Crossing in between the two places were the gigantic legs of an onrushing tornado, which was headed directly toward the eastern part of the city. It was rushing at the soul of Memphis, trying to dash the hopes and expectations of the musical fans.

"The weather looks very scary," Bubba told his wife Louise.

"I don't know if this is the deadly tornado that the meteorologists have predicted a week ago. If it is going to be anything like the one that had ripped through the downtown area a few years ago, then we have a very big problem on our hands," Louise complained to her husband, Bubba. Louise who had been so upbeat about the Festival on Beale Street earlier that morning that she skipped several other functions, had to run for dear life from the inclement weather.

"It is very dark everywhere. The storm on the horizon terrifies me," Bubba told her and started running toward his barn. "Look at the funnel clouds crossing the Mississippi River, which are headed toward Memphis. I am afraid this tornado is going to destroy the city."

"What do we do to be safe?" Louise asked trying not to appear distraught or over worried. She continued to pack some of her essentials before the storm arrived. "How best do we survive this?"

"Mother Nature is tying to have her way with us once again," Bubba mumbled to Louise. "That is the way it had been during the last three festivals. Maybe, I hope there is no curse on this city. I don't know what we can do to change the torrential rains and the mud on the ground, let alone the onrushing tornado."

"That's the second time this year that we needed shelter from the wrath of Mother Nature," she told him.

"Well, running to the shelter has become such a ritual that maybe we ought to just pack our belongings, move into one of these shelters and stay there for the rest of our lives," Bubba said jokingly.

"This is not the time to be joking. We need to leave right away and head for the shelter. The funnel clouds are headed directly our way," Louise told Bubba, anxious and panic-stricken. "Let's get going, honey. The monster tornado is almost in our backyard. It looks like it is a huge one, maybe a killer tornado."

"If it touches down in our house, I don't want us to lose all our valuable family papers, the lifelines of this family," Bubba said.

For Bubba, this was about the antiquated antebellum house he'd inherited from his grandfather. The twenty room antebellum home was built in the 1840's. It had twelve bedrooms, six bathrooms, seven halls, a large ballroom, four large porches and seven fireplaces.

"Who wants that stupid, ugly haunted mansion anyway? Have you lost your mind? This is an old slave mansion that is filled with ghosts. Who wants to live in an old mansion haunted by the ghosts of African slaves anyway?"

"Don't talk about my family property, you hear me," he told her angrily. "I can forgive you everything, but talking about my great grandfather's mansion that means the world to me, shows that you have crossed the fine line."

"Whatever," she told him sharply. "I just don't enjoy sleeping in haunted mansions, it does not matter how huge they are."

Though they were arguing over his alleged affair as the tornado made it to the top of their house, Louise held on to Bubba's midsection in the basement with all her strength, as if he was an unshakable pillar of strength for her.

Seconds later, the tornado actually tore the roof off the old antebellum mansion shaking it off its foundations. The twirling winds tried to suck them both out of the basement. It was like a powerful vacuum sucking everything in its trail, but Bubba held on to the iron bar in the middle of the basement, while Louise held on to his torso as tenaciously as she could, her eyes were closed and her teeth clenched.

Louise smiled broadly after she released her hold on Bubba, unable to look him in the face. She was amused that she was still holding on to Bubba for dear life, in spite of her demands for divorce from him a few hours earlier.

"Easy, easy, easy, let go of me, let go of my stomach. The tornado has passed, you must let go and move on as you said," Bubba laughed, still reeling over the accusation. "One day, you will realize that my love for you is completely genuine."

The inhabitants of the historic city of Memphis, those that have inherited "old money from the past" as well as the inhabitants of Whitehaven and North Memphis scrambled for survival in their homes. So were the neighboring small cities such as Marion, Forest City, Jonesboro, Arkansas, Grenada and Byhalia, Olive Branch and Holly Springs, Mississippi. The inhabitants have all taken shelter waiting for the monster tornado to make its way through the area. Many thought about how to protect their houses from the fury of Mother Nature. They have always been resilient and this latest disaster was not any different.

Bubba didn't run away like many others. He didn't succumb to panic, not even when the tornado was almost in his backyard. Instead, he snatched his great grand father's photo from the wall. It was the one in which his old man was standing tall and towering over his "precious" African slaves. But unfortunately for him, the strong tornado winds ripped the picture from his hand, destroying one of the last vestiges of the past that his ancestors had bled and died for.

Basil, Bubba's neighbor, hurried his four children into the basement shelter. His barns and porch were all gone. He was no longer expressing regrets over the five thousand dollar investment he had made five years before to build a shelter. "Y'all get down to the basement before the tornado tosses you little rascals away like dolls," he shouted.

"Dad, we hear you, but are you sure we will all be safe in that small, iron coffin you built down there?" Jerome asked his father jokingly. "I hate to die inside the tin box you call a shelter. This is worse than a slave cabin."

"Well, the basement is the safest portion of the building, so rush down here or risk being lifted up and tossed about like a piece of doll," he told them earnestly.

"I don't want to die either. How much time do we have before it hits the house?" his youngest son was panting for breath,

"The longer you stand there asking your silly questions the better your chances of getting killed or getting blown away," Basil told his sons.

"Why do these tornadoes love to destroy our side of town each time they come through anyway?" Jerome asked his father. "Why are we always the target for these tornadoes? Are you sure that they are not killer bees in disguise?"

"Killer tornadoes and destructive hurricanes have been rampant in the West Tennessee area for years, and this has been going on in this part of the state since time immemorial. So are earthquake tremors and the floods from the angry soul of the Mississippi River," Basil explained to Jerome. "But this is not the time to ask these questions."

These tornadoes and hurricanes have constantly interrupted the rhythm of life along the Mississippi River banks and on the quiet vast grasslands in the Delta. The rumor has it that these hurricanes have always followed the route that the slave traders used centuries ago. The hurricanes normally start from the former so-called African Slave Coast, usually from the West African Coast, from the legendary Gulf of Guinea. And then they head to the New World to America, to Brazil, to the Caribbean, to Cuba, to Jamaica or to Louisiana, Florida, Alabama, Tennessee or Mississippi.

They spread havoc and terror mixed with other messages from Mother Nature across the land.

"Maybe the spirits of the dead from those dark days of slavery have risen to seek vengeance," Bubba told Basil, who had moved to Memphis from rural Mississippi. He was the descendant of a rich plantation owner in the state of Mississippi.

"What was slavery doing in the land of the free anyway? In terms of material success, this country has been blessed. It has become the land of great prosperity," Basil told his sons. "We still have the monkey of plantation slavery on our backs though, something we are unable to shake off no matter how hard we try."

"Well, without the slaves, the experiment in economic prosperity would not have been possible," Lou reminded his father promptly.

"Dad, why do you talk about the slave trade and slavery so often and with such fear as if these were events that'd happened only yesterday?" Lance asked his father bluntly. "Is your conscience bothering you? Do you still carry some of the guilt from the past in your heart of hearts? Or have you been keeping some family secrets from us?"

"Well, this is our heritage, regardless of how wrong people think our ancestors were," he told his son. "This is the only heritage that we have inherited, so we cannot turn our backs on it."

"The Civil War was fought one hundred and fifty years ago, dad. And our great grandfathers shed a lot of blood in that war for whatever crimes they'd committed against the African slaves. They'd died trying to pass this heritage on to us," Lance told his father. "We're supposed to have been absolved from the guilt by now, judging from the volume of blood they shed defending our heritage, and standing up to the North by defending their way of life, a life uniquely based on plantation slavery."

"Well, son, as much as I hate to admit it, the bloodbath during the Civil War did nothing to wash away the heavy burden of guilt, which we have inherited from our forbears and still carry in our hearts even to today," he confessed to his sons. "It is sad that our ancestors still lost our way of life, after all that dying and bloodshed. Indeed, this is a very painful truth for everyone."

"You sound as if you have realized that our ancestors were wrong in enslaving Africans," he told the father. "Do you think enslaving the African people was a terrible blunder?"

"Maybe at that time in the past it wasn't so bad to own slaves, but today it definitely is the wrong thing to do," Lou, the other son, blurted out quickly.

"Our ancestors made a terrible mistake by going to Africa to haul the African slaves out of the continent by the boatloads, getting them out tightly packed like cattle, and then putting them to work on their plantations for free," Basil said, as he finally admitted that his ancestors did something wrong.

"But Dad, that was then and this is now. No one is even dreaming of making a living anymore from king cotton or owning anyone from Africa as a slave to do any work," Lou reminded his father. "The past is over. This is the present, with its new realities of factories, machines, tractors and harvesters."

"The American dream of prosperity came partly from African slaves who worked for free under pitiful and desperate conditions. Do you know how many slaves perished on the high seas and how many others died on the sugarcane farms or in the cotton groves in the Old South, unsung and unappreciated?" Lance asked his father, with sadness in his voice.

"I have no idea," he told the son. "Tell me what you know."

"Our ancestors were wrong when it came to slavery. Though the South has survived, maybe it was a blessing in disguise that it did not prevail in its plantation slavery lifestyle."

"Do you think the past has anything to do with the disasters?" Lou asked his father. He was still skeptical about what was going on.

"The tornado which is halfway across the Mississippi River, which is rushing toward our home, is probably a message from Mother Nature, from the profane past," his father said to him. He suspected there could be accountability for the past, but refused to consider the disasters as part of it?

"If it is true, then this is really bad," Lou told his father. "We need to do whatever it takes to stop these disasters."

"These are natural disasters that'd begun years ago, before many of the people who live in the land today were even born. Do you think the ancestors swore an oath of vengeance against the region?" he joked. "Maybe, they'd declared to go on a rampage and commit these deadly acts of vengeance if they were not appeased."

"You mean the land would no longer know peace, if there was no atonement?" Lou asked and he was also confused by all that was going on.

"These are empty threats. Are we modern people, or do we believe in superstitions, believe in some mysterious world of ancestors? Tell me how can the spirits of the venerable dead hold the people of today a hostage to a dead past?" Basil asked his sons. "I can't believe the nonsense coming from you."

"Why wouldn't you believe it?" Lou asked him, quickly. "Then what is causing these disasters with such spontaneity?"

"What of the deep Protestant evangelical heritage with which most of the people have grown up? I mean both the victims and victors who live in the region, don't you believe that they'd washed their guilt and purged their souls already?"

"What about what our ancestors did to the Native-Americans' land?" he asked him.

"I told you never to criticize the South," Basil cut in sharply, staring at his son sternly as if to suffocate and squeeze the sap of life out of him. "Don't you ever point accusatory fingers at your heritage?"

"I am just telling you the truth, what you already know. I don't care how badly it hurts, but it is time to make atonement for the past," he said to him boldly.

"Why should we be desecrating the memory of our forebears by making atonement? Our ancestors fought and died gallantly for the region, for our heritage and for their birthright," he warned Lou, shaking his head and waving his finger at his own son.

"We've got to atone for the past; otherwise, we would continue to battle the wrath of Mother Nature," Lou told his father, very bluntly. "The tornadoes in the region do not seem to know any end."

"These victims have been dead centuries ago, son," he told him. "So what has that got to do with these disasters?"

"But the ghosts that still roam this mansion in the middle of the night scare me," he told him.

"Are you pretending that you've never heard the slaves pleading for their lives in the middle of the night in this mansion?" he inquired.

"I have never heard or seen any ghosts from the past in this mansion," he told his son. "What you see is not real. It is all in your imagination, my son. You are probably seeing things, or maybe you are even insane."

"One night, I heard voices in my room and saw ghostlike figures crawling around," he told his father. "It was very scary and unnerving for me."

"Maybe you were having a bad dream or that was just the ancestors' way of telling you to stay out of their business," Basil told his son jokingly, though he was very serious.

"Do you really believe that?" he asked his father.

"You better leave the past alone, otherwise the ancestors would strike you down," he replied. "Or maybe they may even kill you on the spot."

"I have done nothing against them. I am just not proud of what they did to their African slaves in the past. That is all."

"Don't point fingers at the ancestors in their graves. You are acting as if they should undo the history," he told his son plainly. "We can not remake the past that ended centuries ago. We can only move forward and watch our steps in the future."

He held on to the iron rail because his life depended on it. Basil closed the shelter, placed the hatch into the lock and slumped into the old worn out couch like an African mummy that was laying restless in the desert next to his children. He'd bought the shelter five years ago. It was compact, maybe no more than twenty by fifteen feet. But they needed this iron shelter for survival against this raging tornado.

"I can feel the tornado directly on top of the shelter," Lou told the rest of the family.

The monster tornado swept violently through the house, probing for any villains. It tried desperately to suck Basil and his sons out of the shelter and toss them into the gusty, angry winds, but they miraculously survived it all. Lou had secured the latch to the iron shelter just before the powerful wind gust. Was it destiny or fate?

The next day wasn't a pretty sight—it was such a bloody scene in this beautiful city. But the good news was that most of the city had escaped the wrath of Mother Nature once more. The irony was that during such disasters, Mother Nature did not distinguish between African-Americans, Native-Americans, Hispanic-Americans or the people of European descent on its path of vengeance.

The mystery was you could hear the voices of the victims of the past screaming, moaning and whispering during the violent encounter with the tornado. In the deadly columns of the tornado that had destroyed many things around, you could feel their presence. You could see their arms of vengeance reaching high into the dark sky, tearing down buildings, destroying telephone poles and cutting up utility wires.

The spirits were out in the city with their hands out looking for appeasement, asking for atonement and seeking reconciliation.

Still, after all these years, they still hadn't found a credible resting place to lay down their angry souls.

After the dark menacing clouds on the horizon and the gusty and twirling tornado winds from the bluffs of the mighty Mississippi River had died down, you begin to cherish more the gentle sounds of the musical blues or rock and roll in Memphis.

"Maybe the slaves sang the blues in the past on the plantations, but wait and see what song the angry ancestors of the land will sing today on their behalf," the shaman of the Chucalisa Shrine said.

Uncle Stanley died a violent death, but he did so outside the confines of his wheelchair. He had always wanted to be free. He wanted to be free from his wheel chair and then also from the past. The tornado killed him, but before he died, he told himself that he should have worked harder to make atonement.

Most of the city ended up in several shelters. They were seated in the basements as if these structures were impregnable fortresses. It was as if they thought that the force of the tornado could never penetrate the walls of these basements to hurt anyone.

The old cotton farmer at the barbershop, who had had his fair share of tragedies, was the last one to arrive at the shelter. He had lost his two sons and six grandsons in a deadly house fire the year before. He had witnessed his family's old plantation mansion that had been built in the1850's gone up in smoke. He wondered whether that was the end of his family's dreams or whether that was the last he had seen of his most cherished possession.

"How long are we going to be held hostage to the past?" Basil asked. Then his mind wondered back and forth thinking about the destruction.

"You have a heavy burden of guilt. The past has refused to go away. The whole world is watching to see what you and your folks would do about the past—the slave trade—plantation slavery—the antebellum mansions," the African-American lady told the man that was agonizing over his heritage.

"Well, those of us alive today didn't do anything wrong and you know it," he told the lady, angrily. "I was born only yesterday; I'd never owned a slave, and I had never treated any African slave badly in my life."

"You are right, but you are a product of the past," she said.

He stood there like a deer caught in the headlights of a car, his jaws dropped and he could not utter a word. His heart started beating very fast. His guilty conscience was troubling him and he wondered what could save or set him free?

"Oh no!" he gasped as he reached into his pocket for his keys. "Don't ask me to reveal the secret, because I'd taken an oath never to reveal it to any one," he pleaded with the old lady. "I swore on my grandfather's grave never to reveal the dirty, little secret."

"Oh, well, why was an oath necessary if you were doing the right thing?" she asked him sharply.

"Yes, I swore never to reveal some top secrets," he told her, feeling uneasy.

"I am all ears," she told him, as she strained her ears to listen to the confessions of a guilty person.

"Why can't we let the past be the past and move into the future?" he asked her sharply. "Who cares about the past anyway? I thought whatever happened in the past is over and done with."

Though people thought the past is wrapped up under the carpets of history, it is very much alive and active today."

"Um, listen to me, it is just a matter of time before the past catches up with everybody," Pete told the old man pointedly as he walked past the dozens of antebellum homes making his way to the haunted Montross House, and headed to the post office to mail the letter to the governor. "Why these young folks continue to act the same way as their great grandparents "the old timers" did during the horrible days of slavery beats my imagination."

"Who knows why? They are probably trying to deal with the realities of the past in their own unique and painful ways," the old man said. "Personally, I can understand they don't want to let go of their heritage, but they cannot stop the wheels of progress either. They have a difficult dilemma because they want to enter and live in the twenty-first century, but one way or the other; they still want to hold on to their heritage.

"The old strategy of hiding the facts of history, behind a jumble of misinformation and then adding more insult to the gruesome injuries the African people had already suffered from slavery, by blaming the tragedy on their chiefs, no longer works. You could no longer victimize the African people in the media through negative pictures of diseased and famished African people as if those realities made their ancestors ideal for slavery," Pete told the man.

"Well, our people have mellowed, though when it comes to race matters, the new generation has refused to denounce their ancestors. "Please give us some credit," the man pleaded. "We have met you half way. You have noticed that things have steadily improved over the years, in the course of time."

"Today, the truth is that both races and groups have to face the ugly past and turn it into a usable present. We must make these ugly profane events fit into twenty-first century realities. We are one people on earth and obviously we have one destiny—the progress of humanity.

"Well, we know our ancestors were not right in what they did during the slave trade, but we just don't want to let go of the only heritage they had left for us," he stared at the long rows of antebellum mansions in his small rural Mississippi town. "Our grandfathers were people who led simple lives. They were our heroes. They lived, loved, played, fussed and did things their way. But they were not like our great grandfathers in the 1800's, because they didn't own slaves."

The old courthouse still stands today with the red and black rebel flag still flapping noisily as it has done for countless years. The old grandfather clock on top of its summit has survived many years and had seen bad and good weather. The base of the flagpole has turned into a resilient anchor for a decayed past, but the rusty cake of cemented deceit and oppression has continued to haunt many segments of this small city.

The mere glance at a Southern Belle in the past, fueled by years of inferiority complex, sent many African slaves and free ones to their doom, to the lynching posts. These victims screamed their innocence at the top of their voices, but they died in the woods anyway, stifled and silenced forever.

The sort of injustice they had received in the court houses, in the nearby woods, on the adjacent cotton fields and in the privacy of the plantations would never be completely known.

"Even though some knew that slavery was bad, most of my ancestors fought and died for it during the American Civil War. They did not run away, but died on their feet fighting like valiant warriors," he told him hesitantly.

"Those were some bloody days," Pete remarked.

He rubbed his eyes and acted as if the silent voices from the past had overwhelmed him. "In those days, my ancestors counted their property in the number of slaves they owned. And the possession of many slaves meant status, power, prestige and wealth."

"I knew your ancestors were fighting for a cause, though it was a losing cause. At least, they stood for something they believed in," Pete told him.

"I am surprised you agreed with me on that point," he confessed.

"Well, I can definitely say that cowards, they were not. They stood up to the challenge like valiant warriors, fought and died gallantly with honor. They stood, fought and died on their feet. Though the lifestyle they fought and died for, the old ways that meant so much to many of them, could not be saved, they lived and died for what they thought was the cornerstone of their way of life."

Crowded panoramas of flowers, magnolias, azaleas, lilies, red and white roses mark where they have rested their hopes and aspirations for centuries. Sentimental tombstones and rows of graveyards still line up nearby battlefields, which contain the souls of those who loved the Old South and its plantation lifestyle, its fundamentalism, its noblesse oblige, its Cavalier ideals and its special codes of honor.

"Well, thanks, I know they died fighting for our heritage, though they knew all along, maybe even from the very start of the conflagration that it was a losing cause," he agreed. "But they dared not believe that they were supporting a losing institution."

"Did you say you were going fishing this afternoon?" Pete asked the old man.

"I sure did, and you must wish me luck to catch some good looking catfish and buffalos," he told Pete.

"Well, let us go fishing another day. Bye for now, my friend."

ELEVEN

H IS FACE LIT UP. HIS heart quickened and his spirit was jubilant. Though Brandon was not a conceited individual, he felt like the most important person on the planet after he'd finished reading the interesting prediction on the ancient papyrus tablet. He felt that he was someone special; though he dared not disclose everything he read to his friends till the right moment came.

The text deepened his belief in the ancestors. For once, he understood much more what the ancestors went through and what they felt. He just wanted to represent their wishes much more forcefully, to give them what they wanted—atonement.

The dreams he'd had over a year ago made more sense to him now than ever before. He knew it was not a useless journey into nihilism, because he was going to work for a very important cause.

He could choose the past and the old ways of doing things, just like his father or forebears before him did. He could also continue to live in the profane, oppressive past of inequality and subjugation without desecrating the memory of his ancestors. But he knew that he could not go back in time to become a field hand or a house Negro, not even if he wanted to.

He'd been positioned to make some dramatic changes. He'd been given the rare chance to make reconciliation in the land of dreams—help those still carrying heavy burdens in their hearts to purge their guilty conscience, but only if they agreed to make atonement for the profane past.

"The time has come to make a decision," he told himself. He was at a crossroad. It was as if he was standing on the banks of the mighty river, and faced the most difficult decision in his life. He could have stood there staring at the swift currents of the river for endless hours, unable to take a deep plunge into the rough, rushing currents down below him. Or he could dive into the muddy river, swim against the currents and try to reach the secrets at the bottom. But he could also take an easy way out by simply reneging on his dreams, turning his back on the writings on the tablet.

These were all rough and painful roads to travel.

Facing the famous bridge, he stood chest deep in the muddy river as he battled the treacherous currents of the mighty Mississippi River. So, why did he struggle so frantically to stay afloat? The river had swift currents that pulled him under, but then he reemerged on the other side of the Hernando-Desoto Bridge. He didn't know where it came from, but an extraordinary force from a protective hand, pulled him from the bottom of the river to the surface. He was glad that the swift, treacherous currents and the ugly secrets underneath did not overpower him, leaving him lifeless in the mud at the bottom of the legendary river, never to be seen or heard from again.

The initiation ritual was getting closer and closer. The sacred mission that was supposed to lead to atonement and final resolution was around the corner. He had to make his final decision to lead the movement or went underground and lived the rest of his life like a coward.

There was only one option that was open to him as a member of the Chucalisa clan.

Law school and a career as an attorney in the public defender's office or a career with the FBI or the CIA sounded attractive, but they had to wait. His roommate did him a favor, when he screwed up the opportunity for him, though not intentionally.

He probably got his priorities mixed, but as an inner voice revealed to him later on, the ancestors never meant for those options to become his realities. They knew that it was better for him to rather listen to the falcon and serve his people and his ancestors dutifully. He must become an instrument of the ancestors, someone who represents their desires and verbalizes their wishes.

How did the falcon know about his whereabouts? How did it know that he was trapped under the treacherous currents of the muddy river under the bridge, was at the verge of drowning and came to his rescue? Did it hear his scream for help or did the gods send it there to come to his rescue?

Whatever it was, this bird pulled him from under the treacherous currents to the surface of the muddy river. And then it comforted him. It kept him alive for a purpose—perhaps to lead the sacred mission to the promise land of reconciliation.

When the sharp claws of the falcon pulled him by the shoulders from below the muddy river, he was happy and grateful. He tried not to bring up any of the dirty secrets buried in the bosom of the old man river. So, though he drank some of the muddy water involuntarily, it was better than drowning.

Brandon, the muscular-looking leader, decided to step forward to the political scene. He was the leader of the Youth Reform Movement that sought to end the bad blood between the races. He wanted to bring peace, the one thing that had eluded his region for so many centuries. He would silence the ghosts, if he knew how to do so. He would also cleanse the land from its tainted past and rescue it from the wrath of Mother Nature, if the forces would let him.

His meting with the leaders of the Heritage Preservation Group had left more questions than answers in everyone's mind. He wanted to discuss the multiracial platform he had carefully crafted and his goals to help all sides involved in the complicated, protracted racial discourse to come to a final resolution.

He puts flyers in many public places, goes on speaking tours to spread the word and he tries to conduct interviews in the media promoting racial reconciliation. However, the more he pushes forward, the more the movement gets rejected. But he is determined to bring about change.

His confidence amazes his friends. Trent and Steve, his two closest friends, support him unconditionally. He is dynamic, charismatic, and has a strong sense of humor. He is able to plant hope in the hopeless, vision in his visionless friends and supporters whenever he speaks to them. He is good at convincing his supporters that the time has come for everyone in the discourse to make a rendezvous with the past, to come to terms with the conflicts and rectify things. But to succeed, he must bring the conservatives in the fray on board, in spite of their stiff opposition to his plan.

"It is the beginning of a new era. We must not make the same mistakes our ancestors made in the past. Every group must walk on a much more inclusive road. And if that means a progressive multi-racial path, a colorful rainbow in the blue sky, so must it be," Brandon told the small group. They shook their heads and ignored him angrily. Some dismissed him as a rabble raiser or someone who would soon fade away into historical obscurity, if they just continued to ignore him.

"Why are you putting the blame on us?" an old lady asked Brandon angrily, "Why don't you blame the other side of the divide as well?"

"I am a product of two worlds: Native-American and Africans who were brought to America in slave boats—I can't run away from any of these two heritages. I must confront and deal with both worlds like a warrior."

Both heritages are equally important to him.

He discovered that though America was not the only country that possessed and used slaves in the history of the world, the harshness of the slavery and the sheer level of brutality involved in keeping the institution under control surpassed those of any other region in the world. Though the Greeks, the Romans, the Egyptians, the Ottoman Turks and the Persians had all used slaves, their institutions pale in comparison to what the African slaves suffered in the New World.

"I think our ancestors made a serious mistake when they did the slave trade," the old man flipped the pages of the newspaper repeatedly as he read about the plantation documents in the archives over again.

"When did you come to that conclusion?" Brandon inquired.

"I realized that a few years back, but maybe their conscience went to sleep and did so for a very long time."

"Don't forget, it was their intention to continue to use the free African labor forever. And you cannot tell me that they did not know that what they were doing to the African slaves was wrong, immoral or unacceptable even within their own faith," Brandon remarked.

"They knew they were wrong, but they just pretended not to know that it was wrong because they made so much money from the institution," the old man confessed.

"Let me reserve my comments on that issue," Brandon told the man.

The historians and the novelists have revealed to the public and to the global community the nature of the slavery that their ancestors had practiced.

People probably don't even know this. Africans got next to nothing for the slave trade and for their pain and suffering. And yet the continent paid a heavy price for the tragedy. This unhappy continent toiled in vain to help the European planters in the New World reach their dreams of prosperity, self-sufficiency, utopian dreams of democracy, religious freedom and exalted expectations of material prosperity.

But the African chiefs were cheated, bullied into cooperation and exploited brutally because they got virtually nothing out of the slave trade.

"It was that anger that set the restless souls and spirits of those that perished at the bottom of the Atlantic Ocean centuries ago to foment disaster everywhere," Trent suggested.

"Did the departed African slaves get behind the deadly winds from across the Atlantic Ocean to the western hemisphere demanding appeasement and reconciliation?" the novelist asked in his writing at the risk of his life.

"But these powerful forces are certainly on a deadly rampage across the land. Only atonement for the past, the legend has said, can stop the gods on the path of disaster."

"He is just the messenger doing his job; there is no need to crucify the prophet. He was simply delivering the message from the angry gods to the people," Brandon watched the events to unfold, concerned.

"Who accounts for the souls of the millions of African slaves that were lost in the bloody raids, in the tropical rain forests and at the bottom of the ocean during the notorious Middle Passage?" Trent asked passionately.

"Though the story of this great land has been written in slavery, in forced labor, in bloodshed and in guilt, it has also been written in progress, freedom, religiosity and tremendous economic prosperity," Brandon pointed out.

"But how long do we continue to hide the heavy burden of guilt from the past under a façade of freedom, prosperity and innocence," the curious youth asked his father, feeling a pang of guilt in his heart at the Cotton Exchange in downtown Memphis.

He looked ashamed and alienated when he raised his head to view the legacies of Jim Crow laws in the land. "Why do we have four old restrooms side by side in the far corner?" he asked.

"Because there was the one for white men only, another for colored men, and then one for white women and lastly one for colored women, all of these were standing side by side. These were the shameful legacies that old Jim Crow had left behind," the youth leader mumbled.

"You must stop talking about the past," his father told him quickly.

"Well, I noticed these separate bathrooms for the first time when I was only ten. However, after forty seven years, it seems nobody pays any attention to them any longer. Society has made some progress in race issues, though we are yet to atone for the past and get it completely behind us."

"Time has started to heal some of the wounds from the past, but unfortunately these legacies still exists all over the region and are scattered across the country. They are like funnel clouds of tornadoes ready to cut miles of paths of disaster across the region." Reverend Peterson said. He was a deeply religious individual who genuinely wanted to steer his region past the heavy burden of guilt into a new era.

"The time for atonement is at hand," Brandon whispered.

"You are right. And we cannot afford to let this opportunity slip by," he told Brandon. "This is the right time to get it done."

"It has been tradition not to question the ancestors and what they did in the past," Edward Reynolds said. He was the leading cotton farmer whose ancestors owned the most antebellum mansions in Forsythe County, including the Graylin Mansion.

"But how long shall we carry this burden, this baggage in our heritage? How do we explain to our children what our ancestors did to their slaves in the past?" Bubba asked Christopher, the old man, after a brief pause. "I know some of us don't want to hear the truth, but our ancestors were wrong, so we must rectify the past."

"What happened during the time of slavery was in the past," Christopher told Bubba. "Why are you worried about something that happened centuries before you and I were even born?"

"How in the world can we continue to serve our faith meaningfully, when these ugly deeds in our past continue to stare us squarely in the face? Do we purge our souls or do we confront the past headlong and deal with it in a much more realistic way?" Bubba asked, after a brief moment of soul-searching.

"Even if we want to, what is the right atonement for such a tragedy anyway?" Christopher asked. "I mean what would be a fair atonement for the past?"

"How do I know?" Bubba asked. "But, I guess it must be quite substantial?"

"You need to ignore the history and act as if you know nothing about these events. Bubba, we now live in the present, you hear me?" Christopher Reynolds asked, breathing heavily as he spat the gooey tobacco from his mouth on the ground everywhere.

"Hi, Kevin, please get me some lemonade to quench my thirst," Bubba asked him politely.

"Yes sir. Whatever you want me to do, sir," Kevin said respectfully as he moved to the kitchen with the speed of lightening to bring him a glass of iced tea seasoned with lemons. "You need more than lemonade and iced tea to quench your thirst and ease the guilt burning inside your soul, sir."

"You mean we don't have to continue to carry this heavy burden of guilt in our hearts forever?" Bubba asked in an irksome tone.

"Don't you think that we have got to do something to contain the dark clouds of guilt that have tainted this deep blue sky? How do we stop the powerful wind gushes from the Atlantic Ocean from destroying everything in their path when they come ashore? How do we appease the ancestors?"

"These are subjects you'd better leave alone. Trying to fight each disaster is like trying to prevent a nightmare and trying to predict what Mother Nature would do," his father told him firmly, playing with his suspenders on his overalls. He looked like a man whose conscience had been soaked in a river of guilt. "You should never undermine or belittle your heritage. Your ancestors fought and died for it. The damned Yankees denied you your past way of life, but they could never deny you your heritage. This is all you have left from the past."

"But is there anything we can do about the profane in our past to make things better for the next generation?" he asked his father pointedly. "These dark pictures I see with my own eyes are troubling to my soul."

"We cannot correct what our ancestors did to their slaves centuries ago. Son, since it is impossible to do anything about the past, I suggest you leave it alone before someone hurts you," the old man mumbled after pausing for a few moments as he chewed his tobacco angrily. "These are taboo subjects. You can gnash your teeth, bite your tongue or chew your nails, but you can never openly discuss such natters."

"But what do we do with the millions of descendants of the victims who continue looking for justice?" a nearby youth asked. He had been listening avidly to the discussion. His great grandfather once owned about a thousand slaves on his plantation. They lived and worked on his Reynolda Plantation. "Don't you think that we owe it to their descendants to say to them that we are sorry for what'd happened to their ancestors?"

"Certainly, Mr. Reynolds, we must do our moral duty," Klein said to him calmly. "Maybe we can no longer be silent. Maybe, we need some kind of social programs to correct some of the wrongs of the past."

"Is it possible that the spirits of the dead can torment us?" the seventy-year old cotton farmer asked the youths after a short pause. "Some of us are anxious to do something about the past. Maybe, we ought to satisfy Mother Earth and these angry gods to stop them from their path of violence."

"We don't need the devastation and despair, which they have left in their trails," Klein said sadly. "We ought to make the . . . atonement and restitution . . . end this guilty bandwagon."

"How can we fight against the wrath of Mother Nature? As humans, we are no match for her power," Christopher Reynolds said grimly. "There would be thousands on our doorsteps, if we admit wrongdoing, or apologize to anyone for what our ancestors did to their African ancestors or try to make atonement."

"But, honestly speaking," Klein told the old man, after a brief pause, "don't you think that we need to swallow our pride, put our fears and guilt aside and do the right thing, do what the African ancestors have demanded?"

"Listen very well, son, the demands for atonement from the descendants of the victims would overwhelm us, if we try to do something about it. Some might even try to pay us back in our own coins, or try to do to us some of the very same things that our ancestors did to their ancestors."

"That's not true," Klein said quickly. "Many are ready to forgive us, though they might never forget the wounds. Don't you think that they definitely need this atonement to start the process of healing?"

"As far as I am concerned, we will need to put the lid back on this ugly past," the old man said with some trepidation. "Every generation must follow this rule. That is the only way out of this difficult dilemma. We must put the lid back on the past."

"The dead would raise their voices loudly and fill the land with their angry voices echoing voices from the dark," the old cotton farmer said. "The past has refused to die a natural death. We must accept and not ignore it, or we have to face the consequences."

"We need to ease the tensions from the past, so we can free the next generation from this heavy burden," Bubba told Klein, though he still refused to denounce his heritage.

"With all the information out there, hiding the past looks difficult in the future. The descendants of the victims might start thinking about accountability for the past," a deacon of the church finally said, unable to continue to swallow his thoughts.

A flock of falcons circled the trees and quickly flew away confusedly, fading into the thickest parts of the nearby woods making strange, swooshing sounds. Their sharp red eyes had words of vengeance.

"Bubba, do you think we have the courage to unveil this new proposition before the entire congregation tonight?" Louise asked her husband.

"Well, I am not sure. It would be like swimming upstream against the swift currents of the mighty Mississippi River without life jackets." Bubba joked, with a cynical smile.

"You would run into a firestorm of protests if you introduce the proposition at the meeting," Klein cautioned Bubba.

"Well, but I don't see why they should get angry," Bubba said hesitantly. "We have almost run out of time at this point in time."

"Why the past continues whirling through time and space without fading into the usual historical darkness, no one really understands," Trent remarked. "The ancestors had not been able to cross over to the land of the ancestors to eternal rest, so that has been a mystery to many people."

Meanwhile, Trent and Steve felt a column of wind stirring from the Gulf of Guinea in Africa, twirling across the Atlantic Ocean headed toward the Caribbean region. The misty tumultuous waves were like monsters with several blackheads of terror riding on top of the waves with frightening fury. The desperate cry of the people who had been caught in the wrath of the rough waves of Mother Nature filled the islands for days.

"Where is the armor against these disasters? No one has any means of stopping them. The more we try to do so, the more we realize that there is no power strong enough to stop them. Maybe we must do what the ancestors have asked for," Brandon remarked.

"Who knows? Maybe it would continue forever," Trent said.

It wasn't the best of weather that morning. There were gushing columns of wind that spewed across the heartland, letting loose columns of pent-up anger from many people. Some people closed their eyes as they saw the dark clouds of nature approaching their mansions and businesses. What it took years to build, the tornado took only seconds to destroy. Some of the old homes were flying into the air like bales of cotton reduced to piles of flying debris.

"I hate it when Mother Nature destroys the legacies of the past, because these are pieces of living history reserved for the next generation," Steve said with his tongue in his cheek.

"If you think these are the kinds of history worth preserving for the future generation, then think again," Trent told him firmly. "Why preserve a tainted past? Remnants of old mansions and decrepit-looking barns in old abandoned cotton farms are not worth preserving."

"Why are you so critical of everything?" Steve asked him, grinning.

"It is because these symbols of a past are filled with hatred and oppression," he commented. "They are not the best representation of the land of the free and the brave."

"Well, they might represent a past that not everyone is proud of, but they are still part of our national history, part of who we are as a people," Brandon said. "I do believe strongly that we must leave these legacies intact for posterity to render their own judgment about the past."

The shrine of Chucalissa was rumored to hold the key to end these mysterious forces. In great weather, we admire the gods. But in bad weather, unfortunately, not even the priests could stop these forces from haunting the land and tearing through the prairies or from leveling acres of houses in the heartland.

Many power lines were down, homes wrecked, businesses demolished, and lives were lost in the gut-wrenching disaster. The air was filled with the noise of chain saws, the screams from victims and the agony of the bereaved. But the survivors have banded together, whether they knew the victims or not to offer some help to them.

The Reynolda mansion had been rehabilitated and repainted. It became one of the best surviving architectural legacies of the region. It was a majestic-looking structure, a masterpiece designed with ancient Tudor aristocratic motif and it stood proudly against the deep blue sky. It was a nostalgic symbol of a decayed past, but in spite of its majesty and glory, it was the vortex of the forces from the past. Though it was very lovely, people hated what it stood for.

A mile from the mansion was the large cotton field, surrounded by old oak and sweet gum trees. These were old cotton fields that seemed to have seen better days. The Reynolds had made tons of money in the past from the cotton boom in the region; they got it from the cotton their African slaves grew on these fields. But with the money came a lot of guilt from the past too, from the free labor they'd used on the plantation and did so for centuries.

Christopher Reynolds, the old cotton farmer, who was dying to tell the young boy all about the past, finally broke his silence. He had seen enough to want to vent his innermost feelings. He had to travel a full circle into the past to gather his thoughts. He sat down with the boy under the oak tree smoking his pipe and rubbing his red eyes, sighed repeatedly. He was about to vent out the guilt in his heart.

"As the legend has it, the past was difficult. We have lost everything, but the chosen one from the Old Mound of the shrine of Chucalisa has risen to appease the aggrieved souls and bring this elusive peace and harmony into the land," he told Klein, the young man. "He will shake the land and sway the tall, aged oak trees. He will not fail to bring in his quest, though he would have to face the storms to bring about the peace we need in the land."

"Our great grandfathers thought they got the key, but it did not work they way they wanted it. The past has become bittersweet. It'd exploded into a nightmare, into bloodshed, into huge losses and into embarrassment too," he told Klein.

"Maybe we need to burry the hatchet, and deal with the problems better, to bring harmony into the land," Klein told the old man. He was obsessed with doing the right thing. "Whatever it takes to reach final reconciliation, let us do it."

He was worried about the disasters and the agony. "I am tired of carrying this heavy burden of guilt around my neck like a shackle, this heavy baggage from the past. I am almost eighty years old and I don't have a lot of time left, but who wants to die unredeemed?" the old man asked.

"That sounds like the right thing to do."

"You know something else?"

"What?"

"Well, I want to say to the victims how sorry I am for what my ancestors did in the past. I want to ask for forgiveness and make my personal atonement," the old man told Klein.

"Well, there will definitely be peace and reconciliation some day," Klein said confidently. "But when that would come about depends on what every one does. But I would love to see this reconciliation before our time is up here on earth, before we depart this life."

"I wonder when is that going to happen." Klein said inquisitively, looking at the old man as if he knew that he was a deeply troubled man with contradictions in his conscience. With his lung cancer, he had very little time left to resolve the serious conflicts still lingering within him.

"I know some people are still in denial, but I hope this reconciliation happens before I . . . the end of a journey," he told Klein.

Another tornado started to twirl in the sky, sending Memphians and the inhabitants who live in the smaller cities around the area to take cover in their basements and in their makeshift shelters. The wind tore down buildings, leveled trees, and downed power lines. And like a burglar, it exited as quickly as it came in.

The damages were many and widespread—antebellum mansions were ripped off their foundations and carried several yards away from their foundations. Dozens of barns were destroyed.

The irony was that the one-hundred-year-old courthouse was the first structure ripped off its foundation. With it came down the old aged grandfather clock, which had sat on its summit for more than a century. The flagpole fell on the asphalt with the old red and black flag still attached to it, intact, as many people on both sides of the divide exhaled sighs of relief.

"Help! Help! Somebody, help me!" the old lady cried out from underneath a pile of debris, but her voice was so faint that it took rescuers another fifteen minutes to get to her. The damage had been done.

"This is not fair," Bubba said repeatedly. "The inheritance left from the past from my great grandfather the tornado has torn down, and blown away." Bubba's two mansions were all he had left from what he'd inherited from his ancestors. Would he rehabilitate the mansions in memory of the hectic struggles his forebears made during those horse drawn carriage days, during those days when cotton was king, which climaxed in the bloody conflagration during the Civil War? Or would he simply demolish the remnants because of what they have come to represent today?"

He'd realized the past had conflicting messages. So maybe he was even secretly glad that the tornado destroyed the mansions and reduced them into piles of debris. He wasn't the type of person that easily believed in divine retribution, but he was very grateful that the disaster had spared his life during the violent encounter with Mother Nature.

"Maybe, the dark forces from who knows where got the best of us, perhaps it was poetic justice from the past," Bubba told his pastor. He had escaped death by hiding inside the basement once more, but he was used to Louise screaming on top of her voice for dear life anyway. The winds of the tornado, however, lifted the mansion off its foundations into the air like a bird, slamming it on the ground fifty yards away.

At one time, the winds were spinning furiously like the cotton gins from the past, reaching high into the sky, and spewing nothing but bales of cotton, the silvery profane debris in several directions and into the neighborhoods.

"Another round of disaster has come to pass," Klein told Bubba. "We need to do something to lessen these devastations in the land. If we cannot prevent them—maybe we must press for some sort of resolution, or sue for peace."

"What can anybody do about the situation? These are natural disasters," Bubba said angrily, as he collected some vital papers from the pile of debris in front of his lawn. The houses on the hill were torn down so badly, he hardly recognized them. The wrath of Mother Nature has slammed itself once more into the area reducing it to debris from a discarded past.

"As I told you, the past has nothing to do with these tornadoes or hurricanes. I simply want to continue to believe that these are just natural disasters with no connection to the past," the cotton farmer insisted. He was still playing a tune on the fife that he'd inherited from his great grandfather. He wasn't going to die from these violent storms he hoped. So why worry about them?

"Listen to the agony of the victims . . ." Klein told him. "How long can we let this continue? How long shall we hold back and watch the region suffer these devastations? What else do we need to convince us that these are more than likely from the past?"

There was the blues singer, and he was also guitar player, who was singing and playing sad tunes the entire evening. He was obviously drinking the rum and smoking his brown, home-rolled and stinking cigars again. "Maybe the atonement is long overdue. Maybe the time for change has come. Don't run from it. Don't ignore it. We need to just step to the table and face up to it."

"Indeed, the ancestors, though angry, determined and resilient, prefer an amicable resolution to their grievances—atonement," Trent told the old man.

The time for redemption has come.

The next day, the rain fell on what was left of the iron roofing of the mall. It was loud and persistent, drenching the piles of debris below. It destroyed many store shelves, iron chests and left over merchandise. The broken shelves were scattered across the street and ended up in the parking lot as unwanted debris. It showed how the finest of material things could easily be reduced to piles of debris in a matter of seconds.

Since the wind actually blasted the roof off several houses, including the neighborhood schools, it sent the children hiding beneath their beds. Lightening struck a tree in the yard and set it ablaze. It was as if someone had deliberately tried to burn down the neighborhood in one thick, smoldering conflagration.

In the evening, the young boys and girls went to bed early so that they could get up and go to the other school across from theirs, the rival school they've been taught only to "hate" and compete against as rivals. This reality of attending this rival school made the disaster much more bitter and distasteful for these youths.

Beneath all these storms, were souls that secretly beamed with optimism for a better future, for an era filled with racial harmony and the modern progress of material comfort?

Brandon stood there, with his impressive frame, knowing very well that he was the chosen one for the times. He stood near the disaster zone, pondering what to do next as the trees continued to rustle and the foliage moved erratically in the enchanted woods. He felt an incredible urge to do something to rectify the past and to end or lessen the number of disasters.

He stood at the edge of the forest, in the sacred shrine wondering what the final resolution of the mission was going to be. He wondered how much cooperation he was going to get from all the parties with stakes in this critical matter.

There was a brief moment of solitude as Brandon studied the script on the ancient tablet once more. He gathered his thoughts together pondering what exactly his role as the chosen one was going to be. It struck him; the thought of being the instrument of harmony and the mediator, the reformer that would challenge every one, all the parties.

The priest told him that he had to sacrifice his own future for the cause. He could no longer live in obscurity and anonymity. This mission required tremendous sacrifice on his part, so he could no longer hide behind his fears. He had to confront the future headlong like a warrior. He needed to be on the offensive.

He was prepared to give everything he had. He was prepared to sacrifice everything or to even lay down his life, should the ancestors even ask that of him. However, his greatest concern was that his life would never return to what he had once enjoyed. But as much as he regretted the loss of his simple unassuming life, which would be gone forever, he accepted the privilege to lead.

Suddenly, just as he was beginning to have doubts as to whether the others would agree with him, the falcon reappeared from above the trees once more. Maybe it returned from the ancestors. Its amber eyes glowed against the green leaves and its colorful plumes radiated a mixture of wrath and hope, but the olive branch in its beak delighted all who saw this bird of destiny.

Still, his heart was filled with hope. He would help the continent rise from the ashes of the past. As he took inventory of the last months, he felt a yearning to know more about how he could chisel a more equitable future for everyone. He didn't have to look inside a crystal ball to see what was in store for him and for his followers, it was written in stones on the ancient Egyptian tablet, retrieved from the heart of the continent of the Pharaohs—Africa.

He was held spellbound by the political landscape—he must show the way. He must lead the people into renewed prosperity, industrial resurgence and shape the conflicting forces of the new dawn. He must save his city, and for that matter, help his people bounce with gusto.

He was at the crossroads of his life, as he waited patiently for the charge from the falcon for the all-important mission. He heard the screeching voice of the falcon and saw the copy of the old Egyptian tablet it carried in its beak. He closed his eyes to receive the charge, which was written on the seven ancient papyrus rolls, on the revered tablets.

Then something touched him, sending tons of inspiration into his heart, as he stood at the edge of the woods, tablet in hand, ready for the mission of destiny.

TWELVE

B RANDON WAS CONVINCED THAT THE only route for peace and serenity in the land was to help all the parties in the fray to let go of their anger and guilt. He was the type that was heavily involved in the shrine activities, but he convinced the priests that an elaborate apotheosis by all the people involved was the key to racial harmony in the land.

This was revealed to Brandon in the mysterious charge written on the ancient Egyptian papyrus tablet.

He stood at the foot of the Great Smokey Mountains looking at the breaking of the sun in the morning as it headed toward the Mississippi Valley, traveling with superfluous alacrity toward the Delta. This was in the land of blue and green grasses, where cotton once used to be the almighty years ago. They hated for him to arrive. They hated his point of view, though they needed some fresh voices in the political tug of war.

He realized that this was the dawn of a new era, though the pessimists might try to ignore this fact or might even try to derail his wagon of hope. The ancestors would usher in a new era filled with possibilities for all the people and from all walks of life.

He carefully folded the papyrus rolls one by one, putting them in his coat pocket, next to his heart. He smiled broadly, flashing one of his infectious smiles of optimism. He gave one of those soft and amiable looks which set many hearts ablaze as he invoked trust and confidence in several hearts.

The falcon was on hand to neutralize the forces that disagreed with the mission of reconciliation. It told him to be wary of those who wanted to continue down the path of denial, down the path of chaos and down the steps of regress. The falcon circled around his head; it did this whenever it saw or sensed danger. It did not allow the plots against him to materialize. It did not allow the critics to silence him or suppress his ideas.

His critics might mock his vision and they might even mock his style, but the one thing they could never mock was his strong-minded determination, his resolve. They have called him several names, but the one thing they could never call him was a coward, a cynic or a pessimist.

"Can the falcon throw me a lifeline if I needed one? It sounds ironical that I should depend on this bird for survival, but I think what I need most, apart from the vigilance of an eagle, is constant guidance." Brandon joked briefly around his friends. "Though you might lose your life bringing this about such a great and unprecedented deed for all the people, don't you think it is worth risking your life to save all the generations to come?"

"Absolutely, you are right," he smiled.

The time for the mission was, however, left open-ended. The falcon did not want to impose any time constraints on him. Brandon left that to the priests to decide. There were several priests working with him. One was Choctaw, another was Chickasaw and the third was a Ga priest from Ghana, from the former Gold Coast. There were others from Whydah, Calabar, Abeokuta, Dakar, Banjul, Anecho, Notsie, the places of origin of several people who live in the African Diaspora.

"Stop hesitating, Brandon," Trent told him. Trent had been Brandon's friend since grade school. He knew that it would take a unique individual like Brandon to go on the mission. He started to tease him again about the falcon, though he knew that without the falcon, the chances for the success of the mission were very slim.

"I thought you had changed your mind," Brandon exclaimed.

"Where is your spiritual anchor?" Steven asked teasingly. "I mean the falcon, your mysterious friend."

"Oh, the falcon, the bird of knowledge and hope, is on the way," Brandon teased Trent back. "I have been ready for the mission months ago."

"How do you know the falcon is on the way?" Trent asked again, teasingly. "You look weird talking to this bird the way you do all the time. Some people even think that you have lost your mind."

"Why don't they keep out of my business?" Brandon shot back briskly, smiling. "I am going to be on my own for a while. But do you realize what a great disadvantage that would be for everyone who is interested in the cause."

"It is a sacrilege not to appreciate the power of the creator," the priest told him curtly. "In the end, this good mother earth that we all live on, the gods will rise up and see everyone through—the intended destinations. Though they would not tell you their plans beforehand, they will be solidly behind you."

Brandon and the priest could hear the falcon in the woods in the Shelby Oaks Forest. It was still communicating with the ancestors. It perched on an old oak tree on the other side of the bluffs of the legendary Mississippi River, where the tall sweet gum trees and the newly cultivated bamboo grove met. It was facing the windward side of the shrine, overlooking the mighty Mississippi River.

The python of the shrine merged from the basement. It crawled lazily around the hearth next to the sanctuary. Maybe it was looking for prey or maybe it was just simply fulfilling its priestly obligations. It coiled around the legs of a seven-year-old boy who started screaming at the top of his voice looking for help. It was sacrilege to kill or harm this python. The shaman heard his screams and untangled the snake from the leg of the boy. He was excited to be free from the serpent. It was a messenger from the ancestors and only priests knew whatever message the python brought that day.

Brandon recited a short passage in his head. Then with the speed of lightening, the falcon emerged again from behind the tall sweet gum trees to deliver the charge to Brandon, the descendant of a long line of shamans who was ready to take center stage. He has always wondered whether he had been chosen for the task because of his family name or because of the writing on the sacred Egyptian papyrus tablet.

The falcon had changed his mind. It had altered his thinking. He was anxious to go on the mission. The fear in him had quickly disappeared. He'd been transformed into a powerful crusader ready for action, ready to bring about peace among groups, arbitrate quarrels among enemies everywhere.

He walked to the hearth in the sanctuary thoughtfully. He was in his purple robe, a small hatchet in hand and a prayer on his tongue. He wanted to make sure that the mission would be successful and would not end in a wild dream of nihilism.

Brandon remained motionless, figuring out what exactly the mission required of him. He knew that he could not move till the bird had finished its sacred task of consecrating his body.

But if accepting the mission kept him excited and charged up with enthusiasm, he didn't show it openly. At such a relatively young age, he knew that becoming the torchbearer for his folks, both past and present, was such a heavy responsibility. And in a lot of ways, he was committing himself to a very dangerous mission.

"The people are solidly behind this mission of reconciliation," he said. "A brand new dawn has arrived in this land. And all the parties involved must take advantage of this groundswell of goodwill."

"For me, accepting the challenge is like stepping into a deep hole filled with challenges, which I cannot get out of," he confessed candidly. "I cannot abandon the boat or allow myself to be kicked off course. I have to see this mission to a logical end."

"Why are you so obsessed with this mission?" Trent, his friend since grade school, asked him. "You think your little friend will make a way for you at all times."

"I feel the same way about it too, but the other folks continue to cling so hard to their old ways. They continue to cherish a decayed past to the point that it is upsetting to me and derailing the better future agenda. They prefer to carry the heavy burden of guilt, which they'd inherited from their ancestors, for the rest of their lives," he told Trent.

"You are absolutely right," Trent, his friend and confidant for almost all his life, told him shaking his head. One could see that his eyes were filled with more questions than answers. "Some people never want any kind of change; they don't want to even consider anything that is different. They are so set in their ways that they prefer to live and die with the past intact and strapped to their hearts."

"We must confront the past at some point in time for the sake of our children and for better mutual coexistence," Brandon told Trent. "It makes no sense to keep running away from the past instead of confronting and addressing these shameful legacies in our histories."

"Do you agree that this is the time to confront the controversial issue of atonement?" Trent asked pointedly as he looked at Brandon, whose eyes were searching endlessly for answers,

"Well, how in the world do you expect me . . ." he said before Trent interrupted.

"You are the hope for the future," he said. "You have to make reconciliation a reality. You must save this land for the future generation."

He sat with his hand on the enchanted black stone in the sanctuary of the Chucalissa shrine. He knew that there was no turning back, because he'd given his word and he'd received his charge. This was a pact that the falcon had delivered. Then he made his way into the abandoned mound and knelt down to receive the last critical words of advice from the higher powers.

"Why postpone what would happen anyway?" Brandon asked his buddy. "I might as well bite the bullet."

"It is time to step up to the task like a brave son of the cause, a messenger of the ancestors and bring about the final reconciliation. Everyone is depending on you for a better future," Trent told him bluntly.

"You are right. It is time to begin the mission," he said calmly, though he dreaded what he had to go through to bring it about. But he was ready for the sacrifices, the challenges and certainly the opportunity to serve the land.

The ancient Chucalissa legend had predicted the ushering in of a new era of peace and progress for cities, for states, and for the entire country. "If I am the agent of reconciliation, which this land has been waiting for, then let us mend fences and build bridges," he mused.

"You are that messenger of hope and the leader who will preside over the final reconciliation. You certainly are that special someone, my friend," Trent told Brandon. "You are the legend. I am just surprised that the one the people have heard so much about turns out to be my buddy."

He closed his eyes briefly and heaved a deep sigh and said, "Stop saying all these nice things about me. Say no more. Believe me, if I can roll back the profane part in our past, I certainly will. The truth is that, though I seem skeptical at times, my heart has never wavered. It has always been filled with optimism for a better future for everyone."

"Do you still have doubts about why the gods have selected you as their messenger?" Trent asked his friend once again. "You are such an ideal candidate for this pioneering mission. It couldn't happen to a better person, because of your abilities, character and general frame of mind."

"Why do you repeat what others have been saying behind my back in my face? But will all the parties understand the signs of the times and work with the same ideals?" Brandon asked

Brandon placed the red goblet of whisky on the steps of the shrine and stepped back as he pleaded for peace. "No need to see a people brutalized in these modern times. How I wish I could speak to those who burned crosses in the front yard of the family house of a young couple in the small rural Mississippi town. In such a country town, with a façade of peace and quiet, a place so serene and so rural that it has one traffic light, why should there be racial and ethnic conflict flaring up among people of different races in such a very quiet and rural environment?"

"There you go. You do realize the depth of the problem. We have minds to change. In the end, there would be deeper racial understanding on all sides when your crusade takes hold of their hearts, minds and souls," Trent smiled proudly as he raised a symbolic olive branch high above his head.

As soon as he raised the olive branch toward the blue sky, the fear in him disappeared. His heart was filled with hope and optimism for the future. He felt completely at peace within himself, if only for a short while.

Some more tornadoes had ripped through the land destroying everything in their paths. They'd destroyed the trees, grasses, insects, animals and several houses. Several antebellum mansions had been targeted, battered and then finally shattered into a million pieces of debris.

He saw the ominous clouds darkened and the deadly wind lashed out with a level of ferocity unknown in the land. It was as if the gods were trying to destroy everything along the path of the wind primarily to get people's attention.

Looking into the sky, Trent saw a bright yellow rainbow, the unexpected symbol of peace. It appeared on the horizon out of the dark clouds, maybe it was signaling the new dawn of peace and reconciliation. The rainbow emerged just before the wind gushes reached their maximum speed, twirling with anger and leaving a trail of devastation behind all over the land.

"This is a special epoch and a unique era. All those who would live through it would never forget what they'd seen, they would have had a rendezvous with history," Brandon commented. "I mean the fear and the destruction in the land would have subsided, but how could anyone forget the wrath of Mother Nature, and its efforts to cast a spell on the people?"

"In this great land of Native-Americans, Europeans, Africans, Asians, Hispanics, homosexuals, lesbians, White supremacists, African-American race-mongers, feminists and single-parents, where many ancestries and orientations have been meshed together in one gigantic melting pot, why has the land continued to experience so many disasters?" Trent asked bluntly.

"I am not so sure about what you mean, but these myriad of heritages aside, we need an arena that allows peace and mutual coexistence for all," Brandon said with conviction.

"That includes freedom from the wrath of the elements too," Trent nodded. But he knew that freedom was impossible, freedom from the elements, but also from the spells from the shrines . . . following the dictates of the ancestors, it was obvious.

The Native-Americans in Buxton called these tragic events "the raw force of Chucalissa" and "the power of the angry ancestors of old seeking vengeance." The head shaman vividly recalled the "Trail of Tears," how the group lost its land, the march through hostile territory, the death of many innocent children and women, and the gut-wrenching scenes of people dying from starvation, snake bites and chicken pox—why did the powers in the land displace them and sent them into an arid wilderness, away from the burial grounds of their ancestors and away from their gods? They shed tears along the route and cursed their enemies. But they refused to resign to fate.

On the other hand, the people of African descent have labeled these mysterious forces "the centuries of the Plight of the Mandinkas." They say openly that the battalions of demons and spirits in the land seeking vengeance and retribution for the profane past have broken loose and have left trails of blood, miles of desolation and plenty of agony in their trails.

"But just as they came in the night, these ancestral spirits must depart the same way, at night," Brandon said as he stood at the entrance of the shrine and spoke to the priests. The priestesses were burning the choicest part of the beef on the altar; they were burning out of control. The priests had to slow down the fire, if they wanted to appease the ancestors.

His mother, who had raised him with such an honor, was not surprised he was the chosen one who could bring peace and reconciliation to the land. The mother was Zakiya, and she knew that her son was special for two reasons. He was the descendant of the great Chief Batahalia, the most powerful high priest of the Chucalissa Shrine and he had the same authentic birthmark on his forehead as the legend had predicted.

The mother, Zakiya knew that since his childhood, her son was always yearning for something greater than himself. She knew that her son possessed extra occult powers that gave him an advantage over his friends and colleagues. But where these unique powers would take him, and to what tasks, she did not know.

"He is the chosen crusader; he must guide the mission. The land will know no peace, unless he tells the people how to attain the peace," the head priest announced to the small gathering of onlookers who made it to the shrine mainly to eat some of the barbecue ribs and drink some of the black cherry punch. His mother looked on and you could see the pride and satisfaction in her heart, though you could also feel her fears.

You could see a mixture of suspense and grief in Brandon's eyes. As much as he inhaled rapidly because he dreaded the task, he somehow came to cherish the opportunity to help those who still carried such a heavy burden of guilt from the past in their hearts. He wanted to help them end the torment they'd felt all these years.

He was the final peace broker.

"The falcon will spell out your role. It will reveal the time to you and who will fight alongside you. But you cannot be afraid when the falcon gives you the signal to act. You must, thereafter, act quickly, fearlessly and wisely," the priest told Brandon, who closed his eyes during the entire conversation because he was overwhelmed by emotions.

"Do you realize how much responsibility you are putting on me?" Brandon asked respectfully. "Do you also know how these folks are so set in their ways and determined never to make any atonement?"

Even the ancestors were worried about his safety. They trembled and shrieked that he might not survive the next series of ordeals. The falcon cried in horror, but all it could do was to spread its protective wings around him.

Amazingly, while many did not make it through the hurricane alive, somehow, Brandon survived to fight for his cause another day.

This disaster will go down in history as one of the most horrible tragedies the land has ever seen. What brought on Hurricane Katrina into the land like a wayward, misguided missile to torment the people? It arrived in broad daylight. It was on a tragic mission in the legendary and beautiful city of New Orleans. Maybe, this disaster had picked the wrong city, flooded the city that least deserved its wrath. Why did it put one of the most beautiful cities under siege, bringing this legendary tourist haven to its knees?

They wondered if they would survive it, live through it or succumb to it. The hurricane, which started from deep inside the Atlantic Ocean and worked itself up to category five hurricane shortly before it touched down on the shore, was as outrageous as it was destructive. It sent everybody running helter-skelter for dear life, young and old, rich and poor, and African, Hispanic, Asian or European, or black, yellow, brown or white. It pounded and flooded many houses in the city until these dwellings looked as if they were inside the floodgates of hell,

It was painful to stand on the bridge to witness this once beautiful and legendary city disappear, flooded and inundated with billions of gallons of sea water, nearly obliterating one of America's finest treasures. As if that was not enough, it was nauseating to see such a beautiful city become a hub for looters, hooligans and thieves.

From the safety of his nest, Brandon saw how the flood had buried the roofs of some buildings. He saw many victims stranded in the attics of buildings screaming for another chance at life. He saw people waving flags from roof tops asking for help. How could he help? What could he do to ease the agony of the victims?

The falcon had put a spell on him to stay in his nest for his own safety. Though he tried very hard to extend a helping hand, he was not able to do so. The falcon wanted it that way. He had to wait for his turn, for the opportune moment to start his crusade.

Many innocent victims were trapped on rooftops. There was an endless cycle of looting, rape, sniper gunshots and other crimes too horrible to describe.

This hurricane would go down in history as the disaster that had put a chokehold on the most powerful nation on earth and nearly won the battle. It had placed its sinister grip over the main superpower in the world and did so for weeks, if not for months. The event challenged the entire emergency disaster apparatus of America and then it became obvious that its response came somewhat short.

Meanwhile, the price at the gas pumps escalated all across the nation. Food became scarcer and drinking water became a luxury in New Orleans, not to mention how it affected prices of products in other parts of the country. Those were some rough and miserable days in New Orleans and all across the nation.

But while our sympathies are with the victims who got caught in the wrath, the world watched in absolute horror and bewilderment as this hurricane taught America, the greatest country on earth, a lesson in disaster control.

When the hurricane struck, it brought ashore wind gusts of over one hundred and fifty-five miles per hour. The ferocity of the winds created such a powerful surge that it destroyed the levees, sending massive volumes of water into the city of New Orleans, unfortunately a city that was below sea level.

Was it a mere meteorological event or some sort of retribution from the ancestors, as some critics have suggested?

This legendary city, one of the most ideal places on earth for holidays in this beautiful land was under water. It was under siege from Mother Nature. There were tense and anxious moments for the victims and concern for them from the entire country. There were no Mardi gras dances then, no pulsating drums of mirth and bizarre costumes contests, but rather desperation in the eyes of several unfortunate victims. How could such a legendary city be subjected to such monumental despair?

The aftermath of chaos, the lootings, shootings, rapes and orders "to shoot and kill," did not make things any easier for the rescue workers. Some even became targets of the very people they were trying to rescue. Many of the victims were acting out their bitterness and desperation. They were taking their hunger and anger out on the very forces that were trying to help and protect them.

Nevertheless, the city refused to lose its soul. It was very resilient. It clung to its faith and vowed not to be written out of history. It refused to give up, or let alone, perish. It was determined to survive to celebrate another Mardi Gras. It was resolved to continue the tradition of pomp and pageantry. It would once again reclaim itself. It would dry its soul from the flood waters and continue to be a fun place, an entertainment treasure not only for this great nation, but for internationals as well.

While the number of people who actually perished or the exact amount of damage the hurricane had done might never be known, this mind-boggling catastrophic destruction will never be forgotten in the annals of American history. The images of desperation and the suffering and the resilience of the people would never be forgotten.

Hurricane Katrina was just one classic demonstration of the fury of Mother Nature. Whether we are talking about the tornadoes touching down in Oklahoma or earthquakes destroying parts of California or floodwaters inundating the towns along the banks of the Great Mississippi River, or fires engulfing the heartland, there is always the question why Mother Nature can easily destroy everything within a matter of seconds that humans have taken years to construct. And it does this despite all the modern technologies and monitoring devices in place today—the wrath of Mother Nature cannot be easily contained. And if they needed redemption from these disasters, they would have to demand it, work toward it and then achieve it

One day, early in the morning, another tornado ripped through America's heartland, uprooted houses from their foundations, destroyed businesses, tore down utility poles, ripped off signs from buildings and lifted automobiles into the air as if they were toys. The force picked up some children, catapulted them into the air and slammed them on the ground like dolls. No one had any idea how many houses had been flattened or how many people had perished in this tragic event.

The weather forecasters, who have been wrong on many occasions, had been right that time. They had predicted the disaster, but they had no idea about the extent of the damage on the way.

The old farmer watched the tornado tore through his house, lifted the roof into the air like a kite, reducing it to a pile of debris as it came back down. He was lucky to be alive. Bruised and shaken, he was thankful that he only suffered minor cuts on his face and arms.

He realized the misfortune of his neighbors. The tornado lifted them through the roof, tossing them into the dark sky just as it did the refrigerator, the freezer and the stove. The next morning, they found the mangled bodies of four of his neighbors in the middle of the street on the asphalt with blood still oozing from their muddled bodies. The sad part was that the oldest couple had been talking with their children on the phone seconds before the tornado lifted them to their doom.

During the ordeal, his heart started palpitating like an axle, and his nose started bleeding hike a fountain as he caught a flying pot. Bubba Mansford remembered it all. How could he forget how he was tossed around inside his trailer park like a football? How the tornado lifted and landed him on the ground one hundred yards away from its foundations. He could remember the ordeal clearly, moment by moment. But what hit his wife and made her paralyzed in one leg, he could only guess. He thought it was a cooking pot or a piece of debris from the kitchen sink.

People could not forget the dark clouds that reached into the heavens, lashed at the land with its deadly columns of twirling winds that reached high into the heavens as they twirled around like black thunder, destroying everything in their path. The pain that left him angry forever while his heart searches for forgiveness still remains today.

In the adversity, the small community became intoxicated with joy when it found an innocent child, who had lost both parents and was presumed lost, but was suddenly discovered hours after the tornado had subsided. She'd been tossed away, but was sitting comfortably under a couch, though dehydrated, among a pile of debris. This infant landed safely yards from the home, alone, but still alive and relatively in good health. What protected this little infant from harm during the tornado has been a major mystery in this small town. Maybe, the mother shielded the child or maybe the ancestral spirits protected this infant, but her survival was a small victory over Mother Nature in this small, bucolic and peaceful city.

The majority believe that this was simply another natural disaster, the result of the recent massive changes in the weather. Those who think it was the work of the angry ancestors were entitled to their opinions as well, since this is America, the land of the free where people are allowed to think what they liked.

But there has been something sinister about these disasters and the manner in which they have been destructive and have done so very frequently lately—they have become much more mysterious and fearful. How do you comfort the victims, especially the senior citizens who were living on fixed incomes but had suddenly lost everything at the hands of Mother Nature?

"Oh my God! Oh my God!" Gabriel, the seventy-five-year-old retired cotton farmer crawled out of the debris, freed his arm that'd been trapped under a canister and screamed repeatedly. He remembered standing face to face with the eye of the tornado, the objects flying around him, and thought the ordeal lasted forever, but the violent winds lasted only about fifteen seconds, but no more than a minute. He remembered the power went out quickly, as a matter of fact it did within seconds, but it'd left decades of hard work and a lifetime of properties in ruins.

Gabriel remembered the excruciating pain from the canister crushing his arm, the electric cooker that was filled with scalding chicken breasts, hitting him in the chest, leaving its burn marks. He collected the remnants of his possessions that morning, which were few and miserable-looking. The wind had scattered away his vital possessions. Only a few old pictures, two raggedy pillows and an old heater were left for him to take away to his new makeshift tent.

In the end, he was very disappointed over his loss, but he was thankful that he was still alive. He knew that he had to live like a nomad for some time, but there was nothing compared to escaping with your life. He regretted that Mother Nature did not give him adequate warning before it tore through the land, destroying what he had acquired over the years. He was, however, glad that he'd escaped with his life and he did not end up as one of the casualties in the disaster.

On many occasions, it began with a light rain and then strong wind gusts followed which then escalated into tropical storms, which demolished road signs, smashed down traffic lights and tore up roofing sheets from houses, driving fear and terror into the hearts of the inhabitants. These wind gusts sometimes became full-scale powerful hurricanes that traveled with superfluous alacrity and left miles of destruction behind.

When a single hurricane makes landfall three times in twenty-four hours, blasting everything in its path with one hundred and sixty-five mile an hour wind, and when cars are completely submerged in flash floods in the streets, when mosquito-borne diseases began to plague the people, do you then begin to believe that probably something other than climate change has something to do with these cycles of catastrophes?

Maybe this is simply superstition.

When the dispossessed take inventory of their lives and then muster the courage to visit the devastation that was left of their homes and find that thieves had already looted the remnants of their hard earned wealth, the few items that survived the storm, brings nothing but pity for these unfortunate victims? Should nature put a curse on the criminals that did the looting?

How do we expect the bereaved to bury their loved ones and come back to normal life as if nothing catastrophic had happened? How should society best help them to cope with their losses?

The manner in which the people have risen heroically to the occasion, battling the hurricane, rescuing the victims and started to rebuild the devastated areas has been amazing. But it would take more than weeks, months and even years to recover from such mammoth catastrophes.

Those who had risked their lives to save those of others receive praises and awards. The leaders extend their powerful shoulders for the victims to lean on for comfort. Though a panacea, these leaders raise the spirits of the discouraged and try to get them out of the doldrums of despair. They ease their worries, and assure them that they feel their pain.

These leaders give the victims promises of hope, saying to them that though things look bleak and hopeless today, there will be a better tomorrow. They promise that the city, the state or even the nation will help them to rise from the ashes of devastation, from the throes of violence and hope for a better tomorrow.

Nevertheless, in some cases, after the initial shock wears off, what you see are people who had become just the victims of yesterday's disaster, just the statistics of the last earth quake. They are desperate for help, but could not find it. They are the victims of the last disaster in the endless cycle of disasters, the desperate and the homeless of the last tornado, or the unlucky casualties of the latest drought or flood waters.

THIRTEEN

B UBBA SAW THE WIND GUSTS ripped through his barn and it was just like a twirling cyclone racing through it. And he was shocked how it destroyed everything in its dark path including houses, shacks, leftover antique slave cabins, livestock and pets. As the wind reached the plains, the hills, and the valleys, it left pools of crimson red blood across the land. It was unusual for him as a man of faith to think it was something else other than geography or natural forces behind these disasters.

Then, it was even more incredible for him to admit for the first time that perhaps maybe the past had something to do with the catastrophes in the land, that it was the work of evil forces.

He started to believe the superstitious and the fear-mongers.

As the survivors worked their chain saws with alacrity, and the bereaved got ready to bury their dead, he began to become more convinced that maybe some other forces had something to do with the disasters, to think more along the lines of the superstitious people.

The chain saws were punctuated by loud noises from fallen trees, stumps hitting the ground as the rescue workers tried to make the roads passable once again. Some of the trees had brought down power lines and were still hanging from people's houses. You could see the streetlights on the ground. Some were sagging, dangling aimlessly in the air. And some of the lights were still on, but were pointing the way toward no particular direction.

In the midst of his problems, Bubba received a call from his daughter Helena in California that she was reading a book when a 3.5 earthquake hit the city shaking her violently on her bed and scaring the life out of her. She told him that she got outside as fast as she could and took cover in the nearby park just in case the big one was to hit the city.

Bubba was overwhelmed by all the disasters. He had never had a conversation with a shaman before, but this was a rare moment for him to talk to someone of a different mind-set, of a Native-American heritage to get another point of view. He wanted to see how much the past still holds the present a hostage. How much bitterness was still out there in people's hearts?

"Hi Shaman Batahalia, what do you know about these disasters?" he came out and asked him directly.

"What you have seen is the wrath of Mother Nature. You have seen what it has done to the land. We have to end the anger of the spirits and the vengeance of the ancestors," the shaman pointed toward the sky.

"Well, I have seen all that. But are these not natural disasters," he asked the Shaman.

"Well, these are not just natural disasters. They are evil omens coming to the land from several sources. But the ancestors have something to do with it," he told Bubba, feeling uneasy. "It didn't have to be this way, but what a pity it has come to this," the shaman said.

Bubba sat down quietly and watched the Shaman discuss the disaster at length and listened without saying a word.

When Brandon, the chosen one, came to the scene, he bowed to both of them gently, greeting them politely.

"I hope you have brought peace in your bag?" the Shaman joked.

"Yes, I think I have. We have to make peace with these conflicting forces. I think that would be a noble thing to do." Brandon said earnestly, slumping into the chair in frustration.

At the meeting, he watched the expression on the faces of the group of housewives trying to rebuild, his own face became sad and his muscles twitched nervously as he thought about the complexity of the solution ahead.

After a short pause, he gathered his thoughts together and made this statement: "Though this is still such a sensitive issue, we are amazed by how far Mother Nature is willing to go to make her point."

"Making peace would end these disasters," Brandon said. "By the way, who knows what other ways to bring an end to these disasters?

"Not really!" the Shaman said.

Brandon hesitated. He was trying not to reveal what the falcon had told him. He reached into his handbag and pulled out a slab of the papyrus tablet and read it intensely, nodding his head repeatedly in the process.

Meanwhile, the head priest emerged from the shrine, with some barbecue he had made from the lambs they'd sacrificed to the gods earlier on. Ayesha was delighted to eat some of the leftovers. Trent wanted some of the barbecue ribs but hated he had to wait in line for his turn. As for Steve, he wanted some whisky with the barbecue but he had to settle for some black cherry fruit punch.

Brandon didn't want any part of the meat. Instead, he wanted the priest to put the meat in the sanctuary to calm down the anger of Mother Nature and to stop disasters, whether we are talking about tornadoes, earthquakes, hurricanes, droughts or floods.

"Well, the descendants must come to the Shrine of Chucalissa to ask for forgiveness," the priest declared, after he'd washed his face with the holy water and invoked the spirit of the ancestors.

"We need to redeem the land. That is if we want to live in peace and harmony with Mother Nature," Trent told the priests.

"Who knows when this peace will come to pass?" Brandon asked, hesitating to look into the crystal ball and unwilling to delve into the occult world. "No one, but the ancestors have the answers to these questions," the shaman declared.

"We cannot turn our backs on the past and expect to live in harmony," the priest cautioned as he made a list of animals for possible sacrifice to the gods. "The gods are definitely angry and we need to appease them if we want to live in peace."

"I can tell that they are hungry for some fresh sacrifices," the priestess told the Shaman teasingly. She had a lot of apprehension in her voice. She then took the mixture of eucalyptus, myrrh and basil leaves and sprayed the room with a generous amount of the mixture as she lit the incense. "The ancestors are angry and atonement can calm things down."

"Well, you are trying to judge my ancestors by today's values instead of the values they'd lived by centuries ago," she replied. "Maybe, what they thought was moral back then is not moral today. So, you must not judge them too harshly."

There was a minute of an uneasy silence as he inhaled repeatedly.

"We know how horrible the past was. Back in Africa, from behind the slave castle walls, many European gun dealers exchanged millions of guns with their stooges and a few African renegades for prisoners of war, with those who agreed and collaborated with them on the Slave Coast to acquire and ship out millions of African slaves," he said painfully.

But the griot has told them what some people did not want to hear. That the slave dealers removed some chiefs from power or enslaved and even killed others, because they did not provide them with the right quota of slaves.

"Why do you trust the griot's version of the story?" Lady Eleanor asked the Shaman.

"Naturally, I trust the story, because we know that there was critical shortage of labor in the New World, and the European planters had an acute need for labor on their plantations," Brandon said. "In fact, the need was—don't deny this historical reality—such a make or break situation for the Europeans in the quest for "economic paradise, religious freedom and dreams of material wealth in the New World."

"Well, Brandon," Lady Eleanor said angrily, "How much of the slave trade was your ancestor's inability to fight off the Europeans and how much was because of the old prophecy that Africans would be the hewers of wood and drawers of water for the European people?"

"Is that what you think was the motive force behind the movement of people—the exodus—of the people?" Brandon asked. "Are you putting the blame on some ancient prophecy written somewhere in the books?"

"Do you know about this prophecy?" she asked.

"This is not a true prophecy," Brandon said angrily. "I wish you wouldn't hide behind any wild predictions to justify the carnage your ancestors had committed against my people."

Lady Eleanor retreated to the back of the room with a dozen of her church members to ponder the solution Brandon had suggested to them. His letters to the Ladies of Progress Club, though completely ignored and never acknowledged, was very persuasive. The most recent letter that he sent to Lady Eleanor, the leader of the group, was much explicit about atonement.

There was a fifteen-minute interval. Everyone outside the room could hear the animated discussions from the ladies deliberating in the executive room, though they had no idea what in the world they were so excited about.

After an hour of deliberations, Lady Eleanor and her compatriots emerged quietly and took their seats. Brandon hoped they could be on the frontline in his mission of reconciliation. He looked into their faces and saw signs of hope.

"Can you tell us once more what exactly you mean when you speak of atonement?" Lady Eleanor asked Brandon pointedly. She was tense and appeared to be in a pensive mood. "Just give us a rough idea; we are not looking for specifics."

"Be as precise as possible," Jolene Bridges said, as she wrote down the minutes of the meeting in shorthand and did so as meticulously as possible.

"First there is a need for a sincere apology for the past, and we are talking about a heartfelt expression of remorse and not just a mere perfunctory statement of apology. Then you must make atonement, a reasonable gesture to concretize the remorse," Brandon spelled it out without any hesitation. "This is not to bankrupt any coffers in any way."

"Whom do we apologize to?" Jamie Bridges asked quickly, still writing down every word on the yellow pad as if her future and the destiny of the next generation depended on it. Her background as the granddaughter of Colonel Bridges, a major leader in the Confederate military during the Civil War made her particularly interested in the atonement issue, though she tried very hard to appear as disinterested a recorder as possible.

"For the forty million slaves your ancestors forcibly removed out of the African continent without any compensation for the free labor they got out of them for nearly four centuries, you need atonement," Trent explained with details. "They left an equal number dead from slave raids, inter-group wars, which they actively encouraged. They even fanned the flames of inter-group wars, and they sometimes even initiated some of these wars and waited on the sidelines for the booty—slaves and more slaves, but rarely some gold.

"What else?" Lady Eleanor asked.

"Then you need to apologize to those who live in the Diaspora who had experienced plantation slavery with all the brutalities, oppression and exploitation that their ancestors suffered," Trent continued.

"Did we promise to give to each liberated slave "forty acres and a mule?" she asked anxiously. "Didn't we deliver on that promise long ago?"

"No. These were major violation of human rights and the victims need an apology and some sort of concretized atonement at some point."

"In many cases, the European Christian missionaries were simply trying to convert the heathen Africans into souls for Christ," Jamie Bridges said, reading a quote from an old antebellum plantation record. "The book was solidly behind my ancestors as the basis for what they were doing in the past."

"Well, that was simply the cloak your ancestors had used to camouflage their real intentions when they entered the so-called African Slave Coast." Trent told the group. "The real motive was economics. They particularly needed labor on tobacco, cotton fields and sugarcane plantations. They had to satisfy their sweet tooth for sugar."

"Stop the lies. Our ancestors did not go to Africa purposely to catch slaves. They did not do anything against the African people," she told Trent, brushing her blonde hair back repeatedly as she made some notes on her pad. "I know that all they wanted was labor on the plantations and the chance to civilize these heathens."

"Well, they removed these Africans as slaves from their homes and brought them across the Atlantic Ocean half way across the world against their will to work for your ancestors for free," Brandon declared. "The hauling of these slaves for many centuries was contrary to the natural laws of human nature, especially when they did so for centuries and got away without any compensation."

The ladies shook their heads in disgust. They did not like what they were hearing. They sighed heavily and sounded as if they were about to explode over what they'd just heard. Like people who wanted to hide their guilt under the carpet of history forever, they were uncomfortable with the references Trent made to the deeds of their ancestors.

So they excused themselves once again to reconsider what they'd heard from the team. As for Brandon, he stood his grounds and refused to support their romantic views about the past. He was quite emphatic. He wanted them to acknowledge some wrongdoing for slavery, he told them. He must live up to the dictates of the mission as contained in the ancient hieroglyphic texts given to him.

The mission, the charge he'd received, had some strict guidelines. There was no room for backing down in the face of opposition from the descendants of those who needed to sue for peace and seek reconciliation.

The secretary led the way and brought them back to face the team, the seven-person crew, the bandwagon of reconciliation.

"Our great grandparents did some terrible things to their slaves, but while we cannot change the past we can try to make up for it one way or the other," Lady Eleanor stated, after they emerged from the round of discussion. She straightened up her beautiful blonde hair once more, and did so repeatedly. "The past was really horrible, though we know this. You still can, however, understand how hard it is for us to turn our backs on our heritage as well."

"We can't continue to suppress or ignore the past," Brandon told them. "All you have to do is to atone for it and then you can continue to look on the rest of your heritage with pride, without the heavy burden of guilt you have carried for centuries."

"The irony is that our ancestors thought that the time for accountability for this would never arrive," Lady Eleanor said. She sat on the chair to try to stop herself from hyperventilating angrily in front of the other members of the committee. "The reality of the past is a bitter pill for us to swallow, but we think, though reluctantly, that maybe after a sincere apology and atonement, which are all probably long overdue anyway, we would put the past behind us and calm down the elements in our world."

"Well, maybe we need to let go of this heavy burden of guilt anyway," Jolene said, still reluctant to turn her back on her ancestors. "But this heritage is all we have, so we can't denounce it completely either."

"A lot of blood was shed in this land," the preacher said. "Some of the bloodshed was in self-defense. But violence against anybody, against even slaves, was not the right thing back then and it is not right even now. For that reason, we will agree to make a reasonable atonement."

"The country has moved past this "ugly past" and has experienced a lot of economic progress, but how can people still be stuck in the past looking for answers to the problems of today by raking the old dirt?" the old tobacco farmer asked angrily.

"How can you even contemplate blaming all these disasters on the past of this country? Does it make any sense? Maybe to you, but maybe not to most of us," the preacher said. "It is just a natural progression of the weather changes in the land."

"What is the atonement for anyway?" another youth asked.

"You mean you don't know?" Trent asked. "Just as we take life for granted, it is the same way that we take the past for granted. Let us remember that a country cannot shed its past. It must live and deal with it and make the best of it. The past might have been tainted and cloudy, but we can use atonement to transform it into a usable past."

"How do we do that?" the farmer asked, skeptically, looking at Trent and the rest of the team with curiosity, thinking what if they were right. "I know what you feel about the past and I know what we could do, but I am hesitant because I am not so sure atonement is the solution."

"Atonement would lift the dark clouds of suspicion, hatred and vindictiveness from both sides of the divide," Trent said. "It would set your people free from the ancient burdens of guilt that they'd inherited and still carry to today, and it will give voice to the oppressed and the voiceless and free several generations from the blame game. And all the accusatory finger-pointing from this side of and across the Atlantic Ocean would cease."

"Are you sure?" the preacher asked. "It sounds too generous to be true."

"Until the atonement, the angry voices of the ancestors will rage on and the restless spirits will continue to roam the land freely, creating havoc and devastation," Trent said, partly cooperating and partly shocking the group.

"We can't promise to support everything you want, but if it will free our children and their children from this heavy burden of guilt, then you have our support," Bubba, who'd been listening carefully, broke his silence and said frankly.

Brandon wanted to jump up and celebrate the breakthrough, but he had to restrain his enthusiasm. "Your support has given the movement the boost we need to continue moving forward. Thanks a lot for the kind gesture on your part."

Brandon was a tall man with powerful muscles. He spoke softly, but when he spoke, he did so with authority in his voice. He harbored deep convictions about the past. His rough life growing up in South Memphis prepared him for the task ahead.

Was he a radical transformer and a peace maker? Or would they listen to his suggestions, which could help them let go of the guilt and put down the heavy burden they'd inherited from the profane past?

"You mean that they don't have a change of heart?" he asked her quietly.

"They appear rattled, but deep down, many of them are still unredeemed from the values and convictions their ancestors had in the past," she said. "They don't give a damn about what happened in the past."

"That is the problem right there. If I can figure out how to make them understand the past, make them obedient to the cause, to support the effort, the mission would definitely succeed," Brandon declared.

Jolene, Brandon's significant other, rubbed his back as he wrote another round of petitions to some key groups soliciting their support and cooperation. "There has been some softening up among your critics, and I don't know if that is a good sign or not," Jolene said. "But your hard work is beginning to yield some positive results."

"That is a lot of progress for groups that didn't even want to listen to me a few months ago," he told her.

Brandon returned home and pondered the future. We have made some progress, but the atonement will be the true test of this progress.

FOURTEEN

I T WAS SUNRISE ON THE banks of the almighty Mississippi River. The barges were busy traveling down stream or inching their way against the currents going up North. The birds were singing with joy in the old oak trees in the woods on the banks.

Meanwhile, the initiation ceremony must not be delayed. It must be done to give Brandon the extra power he needed to succeed during the mission. The source of his power must come from Mother Nature and the priests conferred these powers on him.

Trent stood next to Brandon, his friend forever, waiting for the command, making the two warriors anxious and determined to succeed where the critics said months ago that it was impossible for them to make any inroads, let alone make any progress.

Brandon sat at the Shrine of Chucalissa, on top of the abandoned mound complex and waited anxiously for the beginning of the ritual. He was debating whether he should continue the crusade for atonement and reconciliation or stop it and fade beyond the dark clouds of historical oblivion.

He went into the nearby woods to ask the advice of the ancestors and to communicate with the spirit of his great grandfather, the greatest priest of the shrine.

He was on his way to the shrine when the falcon reappeared. Though he didn't want the falcon to repeat the gory details of the past to him, he listened vaguely to what it had to say. But it reminded him of the horrors and the brutalities his ancestors suffered over the years.

Brandon had done some work of reconciliation earlier on as a community organizer.

"Definitely, you must do so, though success was a long short at best," Trent told the priest vaguely. "Perhaps he could use the unique powers you have conferred on him to bring this about . . . even then how to reach the ultimate goal of reconciliation was another problem."

"It would require Brandon knocking on a lot of doors to make this dream of . . . you know you won't be celebrating complete success any time soon," the priest told Trent and Brandon frankly.

Well, Brandon had always been a diehard activist and was always on the frontline of the struggle. "He is trying to put a shameful past behind him, but this is not an easy thing to do."

"The more things change, the more they stay the same," the priest told Trent, repeating an old saying firmly. "Brandon knew that fifty years ago, he could not attend the same school with students of European descent in many places, but he has that choice today."

"You are right. The truth is bitter, though it is very simple," Trent said. "Then he should thank his gods that he didn't live during the yesterday years."

"But he can do something about this. The Chucalissa shrine can give him the inspiration he needs to change things," the priest assured Trent as the two of them watched the orderlies prepare the sacrifice for the ancestors.

"He is doing the right thing by staying in touch with the falcon, his guardian angel," Trent remarked quietly. "At first, I thought it was ridiculous and silly, but now I have changed my mind."

"Well, he would need the help of the falcon to complete the near impossible task, which he'd set his eyes on," the priest confessed frankly. He had lots of optimism in his voice but he had some questions about the mission.

Brandon came back with a smile on his face. "Everything would be all right," the falcon assured him. "Just make sure you complete all the sacrifices that are needed."

The mention of the name of his ancestor brought flashes of painful memories to him and sent eerie shivers down his spine. He sat on the stool thinking about the ritual and the fortification. He thought about the sacrifices and the spells the ancestors had ready for him.

He had known for quite some time that the gods were trying to work something out, but he did not know that he would be directly in the frontline in the movement of reconciliation.

"Was it fate, destiny or simply an accident of history that placed him in that role, directing the movement toward reform, peace, and the final reconciliation?" Trent asked himself.

Brandon left it to the aged priest who nearly starved to death, after a ninety day fasting, to appease the gods. "You must guide the movement every step of the way: otherwise, it will not succeed," the aged priest told Brandon, his stern eyes radiating an austere demeanor.

Brandon's life would never be the same again. From the moment the Chucalisa priesthood decided that he was the chosen one for the special assignment, he became a celebrity in many circles. He wore the red robe to the inner shrine and ate some of the sacrificial lamb. He was to work toward getting all the parties in the horrible racial discourse to end their anger, and to lay down the guilt in their hearts.

"I never thought that the gods would target me for such special duties," he reflected as he drank another cup of coffee. "I know that my great grandfather was a legend in the Chucalisa priesthood, but I am still not happy about being the one chosen to guide this movement."

"You are a unique individual with extraordinary talents and qualities. This coming from your friend, you better believe that it is genuine and true," Trent told Brandon truthfully. "But I think all these have gone to your big head and got you intoxicated with the idea of changing too much too fast."

"You are just jealous of me," he told Trent.

"I don't envy you: I only admire your courage and your resolve," he told him. "But you have to work with people who feel you are still just a step above a slave, people who share little or no sense of equality in their bones and people who have refused to open their narrow minds to the enlightened wheels of progress."

"Well, I tell them not to hate the messenger," he retorted quickly, laughing. "These are very difficult times and we have complex problems to deal with. Some of these problems are self-inflicted, but it has a lot to do with global forces churning everywhere."

Brandon sat on a stool and closed his eyes behind the blindfolds as he drank the bitter juice of wisdom. He saw a streak of shiny lights above the trees. He knew that he was not daydreaming, and he was also not hallucinating. However, he was pleading fervently for a better future for everyone. Minutes after he started dreaming, he landed on the shores of Africa, pondering the predicament and the plight of his ancestors.

He saw himself roaming the insides of several slave castles. He leaped into the slave castle on Goree Islands in Senegal. He then went to the city of Whydah in Benin. He landed in Port Harcourt, Abeokuta, Lokoja and Ibadan, places in Nigeria. He ended in the slave dungeon in Cape Coast Castle and then Elmina Castle in Edena, both located in modern Ghana. He resented the shackles he had on his feet.

He was sweating profusely inside the dark dungeon. He had no fresh air and there was virtually next to no sunlight inside the eerie labyrinth of concrete tunnels. He could smell the putrid air, a mixture of sweat, excrement and fermented urine. He could hear the sighs and groans of the slaves. He could see the marks on the stone walls. He could feel the intensity of the struggle between good and evil. All he could do was to curse the hands of evil, the forces that destroyed his people.

"Who thrust the leadership upon you?" his aunt asked him.

"Well, this leadership is a curse, son, it can cost you your life" his mother told him, sighing deeply and showing him a picture of his uncle who was brutally lynched some fifty years ago somewhere in rural Mississippi. His mother Edna was at the shrine and was telling him that she wanted him alive and not dead, so she challenged him to abandon the mission and return home. His mother's eyes were tired and red, obviously the look of someone who was extremely perturbed by her son's mission. In her mind, the task resembled her own brother's crusade against bigotry thirty years before Brandon was even born.

"Your uncle tried a crusade to bring the races closer together, but he ended up dead," Sandy, Brandon's aunt, said. She was sitting across from his mother. "I don't care one-way or the other whether you continued the mission. There is not much you can do about the racial divide. It will be nice if you would just go about your business and ignore the racial conflicts, because you would be putting your life on the line."

"Son, stop meddling in white folk's business," the mother yelled at him, sharply. "These folks don't play. They will hurt you, just the way they did your uncle years ago."

"They are beginning to listen to me," he told his mother and aunt politely and calmly. "They are beginning to acknowledge some wrongdoing over the past."

"You don't know what they will do to you, do you?" the aunt asked him firmly, patting him on the shoulders softly. "I wish you had seen your uncle Molevi when he was going through with his mission."

"What happened?" Brandon asked quickly, hoping for the worst story from her auntie's mouth.

"Well, they put a label on him, and the next thing you know, they lynched and killed him," she told him. "He was hanging by the neck from the old oak tree, which is still sitting in the square today. They wrote the "N" word on a string around his neck."

"They are waiting to do the same to you," his mother repeated.

Though he did not want to end up dead like his uncle, how could he forget the words of his great grandfather who had been the high priest at the Chucalisa shrine for more than three decades, the one who asked him to work toward atonement and reconciliation? His grandfather had a round face, a powerful jaw, and a deep baritone voice that frightened everybody whenever he spoke. And then everyone feared him because of his special occult powers.

Brandon was pushing for atonement, but he had to earn the trust of the people, he had to prepare them to accept the idea, and convince them to agree that atonement would make the future brighter.

When the city became flooded, Brandon guided the group that worked tirelessly to fill the sand bags to save many homes on the banks of the Mississippi River. The crew spent hours at the flood zone in

North Memphis. His powerful muscles easily carried three sandbags at a time, while others struggled to carry even one. Maybe he used some of his supernatural powers to carry these sandbags; people had the thought, but did not say it loudly. They simply swallowed these thoughts.

How many young people would battle the flood of the century and would continue fighting very hard for two solid weeks to save others? When the owners of the houses became tired and needed some help, Brandon asked the Youth Corps to step in and help with the rescue effort. He knew that without the sandbags, the flood would have destroyed several more homes, rendering hundreds of people homeless in the city. The floods might even have reached downtown and destroy some of the vital businesses, the critical lifelines of this historic city.

Again, like many of the unexplainable disasters that had plagued the land, this particular flood, which became "the flood of the century", was perhaps the ancestors' way of bringing up the past.

"But some of us believe that this is simply another natural disaster," the old cotton farmer said. "I know others think that someone is punishing us for something that our forebears did in the past."

The superstitious actually said that the flood was the ancestors crying over the past, so they decided to flood the land with their tears. Others simply said that the city was due for one of those historic floods anyway.

Was it just too much rain up North that caused the flood downstream in Memphis? Or was it the profane past that collided with modern forces? The irony was that many actually believed that the flood was punishment from the angry ancestors?

In spite of their efforts, the flood still invaded and destroyed several homes anyway. It caused millions of dollars worth of damage to homes, businesses and to the city. Brandon saw the chance to help the homeless victims, so he and his friends got busy helping all races of people in the city and he cared for all those who were in need.

He didn't want people to drown in the raging flood. He didn't want people to defy the orders to evacuate, though several people did so anyway. Unfortunately, a few still perished in the swift currents of the rising floodwater.

Brandon and Trent were resilient. And Memphians were resilient as well. They'd worked for seven weeks combating the rising tide. Brandon and his team were so dedicated to the task that they were the last to leave the flood zone, though others abandoned the task after seven days. The climax was when they rescued a desperate family with seven kids that had very little food left for them.

"It's so nice to know that people still care," the old tobacco farmer said to them. "We will never forget the way the three of you risked your lives, cruising down the rough Mississippi River for weeks saving victims who were trapped in their houses."

"Well, we are happy we could be of service to people. We just want to make a difference." Brandon forced Trent to land the boat on the banks of the Mississippi River next to the bridge. He wanted to go to the nearby motel for a good night's sleep, after a good meal in one of the diners on Beale Street.

"Trent, Steve and Brandon, the three of you were like angels sent from above to help the poor and desperate in the hour of need," the preacher told them. Reverend Peterson embraced them warmly and nodded several times in approval. He appreciated and admired the yeoman's work they did. "Your parents ought to be very proud of you two young men for all you have done for the people of this city. Who would not appreciate your help to Africans, Hispanics, Asians and Caucasians?"

Naturally, the people took notice of their dedication and steadfastness during the disaster and appreciated their efforts. Their actions were very different from the other youths who just stood by and watched the disaster unfolded and didn't care less about it.

When Brandon returned to North Memphis again to ask the people for an audience, even the ultra conservatives, the diehard cotton farmers who'd vehemently opposed his message earlier on, before the epoch-making flood, who even plotted at one time to get rid of him, gave him the cooperation he needed for the mission. He had many ears willing to listen to his message of hope, his mission of atonement and his program of reconciliation.

Each year, the rains came and drenched the land for weeks and did so till the river rose and sent the floods downstream to inundate the land. Many were tired of the cycles of rain and flood, the breaching of the levees, which left acres of cotton fields submerged under the water, and rendering hundreds of people homeless.

The people remembered the intervention of the Army Corps of Engineers and the efforts they made to contain the flood. Nevertheless, it was a race against time; it was man against Mother Nature; and the spirits of vengeance against a city with a unique destiny.

But this happened in Memphis, Tennessee, the sister city of the legendary city across the Atlantic Ocean—Memphis, Egypt. This is a city that has ties with the Old Mother of rivers, the legendary Nile River. Whether the statue of Ramsses the Great, standing tall and majestically overlooking the river, could save the city from more flooding or whether the gods of the Chucalissa Shrine could protect the people, that was left to the invisible powers to decide.

Unfortunately, however, they couldn't save everybody. A few inquisitive, adventurous youths who tried to swim in the river against the strong raging currents, ended up at the bottom of the river just like the profane secrets from the past. Some were never seen or heard from again.

The prediction that someone would rise from the wet banks of the river and from the Shrine of Chucalisa to attend to the needs of the people and to stop the disasters in their tracks suddenly proved to be right.

"The chosen one would rise from the ashes of the past, from the Shrine of Chucalisa and redeem the land," the clairvoyant told the people seven years before the beginning of Brandon's mission of reconciliation.

"If you have any doubts about whether you are special, the sacred tablet with your name on it should erase any doubts still lingering in your mind. You have been marked at birth, for some reason to achieve greatness," the mother told him. "You don't know how much you look like a throwback of your grandfather."

Of course, there were rumors in the city that he used his occult connection to bring the old folks, who would rather die than listen to him, to have a change of heart, to listen to him. But whatever suspicions they had about him, he erased with his charisma, respect for others, amiable demeanor and service to the people.

However, Brandon was oddly concerned about the dark clouds of racism and the strong undercurrents of hostility. He didn't like the idea that his friends were teasing him about his interest in the falcon—the force behind his occult powers. But he noticed that they were only teasing him when he was not using the bird to rescue them from their problems.

"You must decide not to back out of the mission. Just get ready to continue it for peace and for equity in the land," the falcon whispered once again into Brandon's ears. His eyes widened when he heard the message repeated. Brandon saw the bird at least thrice a week. It descended from the trees in the morning and landed at the shrine. It came down gently and sometimes rested on his shoulders, an embarrassment to him among his friends.

He never tried to reward the bird whenever it appeared. Why do you refuse to help some one who'd helped you so immensely? But he was under strict orders from the high priest never to feed the falcon. The ancestors strictly forbade anyone from doing so. So when James Murray Potter tried to feed the bird, Brandon was so furious he nearly pounced on him.

"Why do you want to destroy my lifeline, the falcon? Why didn't you ask me if you could feed the falcon?" Brandon asked James, as he tried to explain the situation. He cleared his throat several times, as if he wanted to start the sacred chant, but he restrained himself at the last minute.

"I m sorry, it was not my intention to harm your friend," James told Brandon looking very concerned. "Please don't turn him against me; I have enough trouble in my world already!"

"If you make the gods angry, you will never live to attend your parties, drink your booze and go hunting again so leave my friend alone. Otherwise, it will leave you sitting on the floor, dead, leaning against the edge of the bed. There would be nothing the paramedics could do to revive you. You will never live to see daylight again. That is a promise."

"You are carrying this thing too far," James told him frankly.

"Do you know how much the falcon means to me?" he asked James.

"But you can't turn your back on an old friend, Brandon, not because of a bird," remarked James, apologizing fervently. "I am sorry. I did not do it intentionally. I just wanted to start my own connections with the falcon."

"No more silly pranks from now onwards," Brandon told James laughing. "You have my forgiveness."

"Don't get sidetracked. You are the torchbearer; that is a mission from which you can't get distracted. Not because of these petty squabbles," the voice of the falcon said mysteriously and flapped its wings loudly. Even though Brandon could not see his friend, he could never mistake its scratchy, whisky voice. He could not mistake its bright, guiding spirit.

"Why don't you let someone else guide the mission, since it is so dangerous?" Brandon asked the falcon quietly. "I have a life to lead, friends to hang with and a lovely lady to love. I mean someone who loves me dearly. Is it hard for you to understand that?"

"You are dreaming," the falcon said, as it flapped its wings erratically again. "You are going to provoke the gods to become angry with you and your people. If you fail to accept this mission, there would never be a chosen one for another one hundred years to bring about peace."

"What do you mean there would never be another one?" he asked seriously.

"You are a rare star who showed up on the horizon. You are not even supposed to lead your folks, let alone lead an entire movement for reconciliation. You remain the greatest puzzle in modern history," the falcon told him frankly. "You are a rare genius, a rare gem in the annals of history—maybe a phenomenon that would be remembered for a long, long time."

So, he accepted the challenge to continue the task to rescue the people without any more reservations. "Since you said the task would free the land, I will do whatever you want me to do to appease the ancestors, and to bring about this reconciliation."

"No matter what happens, you must never forget the fact that you are the chosen one," the falcon told Brandon quietly. Then it flew away with joy, saying loudly: "You remain the one and only leader of the cause—the one chosen to see the mission through—the final peacemaker."

"There would be a breakthrough soon, so we can get things to where they ought to be," he told his mother.

She was convinced that her son was destined for great things in life. He was born under a lucky star and his abilities are also superior. Anyone who questions his authenticity would fail; because in the end, he would not only triumph but also prevail over his critics and detractors.

"Son, can you share with me what the falcon usually tells you, whenever it comes to you?" the mother asked him, mumbling to herself. "Whatever it is, it surely sounds powerful and convincing to me, though it looks odd and crazy to other people."

"Well, nothing much, mother. Nothing very important for me to tell you, mother," Brandon told his mother slightly irritated, though he was smiling through it all, flashing the same pleasant knock them dead smile he'd always had when he spoke to people.

"I just want to know what this strange bird has been telling my son," she joked. "Is that asking too much of you?"

"This does not concern you, mother . . . just the same old you are special story . . . someone trying to recruit you for something, the sort of things you are really not interested in, but a mission you cannot turn down either," Brandon assured her.

"Son, can I tell you something?" she asked him tenderly, her hands on his shoulder.

"Why not, mother? For once, are you sure it is not one of I am not feeling good about the future stories," he asked her mother hugging her warmly.

"I know you would one day go places, with or without your parents in the picture," she told him.

She nodded her head repeatedly, though seriously speaking; however, she wished the falcon would step back and leave her son alone to enjoy his youth, to live his precious life. If guiding the movement was too dangerous a task for anyone, why then did the falcon choose her son for the dangerous mission? She wondered.

Then there was the mysterious old man who visited Brandon. This was the man who also tried to keep company with him on a few occasions. There was the rumor flying around that the man made a sacred pact with Brandon to do something special for his family in particular and for everybody in general. The man brought him some special gifts, some came from the ancestors, but it seemed Brandon did not intend to use them. Maybe he was interested in them, but his attitude was very much indifferent to the gifts.

While he was avidly interested in the Chucalissa Shrine, but had turned down the gifts was puzzling. So, many people said that the mysterious falcon and the visit of this strange old man, a man from the underworld of mysticism, were the spirits behind his mission.

It seemed, however, that it went deeper than that. Brandon was always very much concerned about racial issues in the city, but he had always swallowed his thoughts and kept whatever was worrying him under tight control. He did not want to get the authorities angry and hot on his trail for inciting racial dissension and riots among the youth.

Brandon, a robust, handsome youth, was filled with the sap of life and wanted time to enjoy his privacy and to enjoy his life while he was still in good health. He very much did not want the political divides to hinder his life or make him miserable.

"Do you agree to lead the people on the path of atonement and reconciliation?" The falcon asked him the tenth time.

"Yes, but I am not going to risk my life unless I have some assurance that I would be safe. So, only time will tell when I'll be ready for the kind of sacrifice the mission requires of me."

At any rate, though reluctantly, Brandon followed the instructions of the chief priest and lifted the small sword in his hand. He pointed it toward the blue sky, and thrust it with his muscular right hand up above his head. He lifted it toward the blazing morning sun and smiled. At that time the sun exploded and the silence gave way to a spontaneous explosion of sun blast.

The priest lifted the special Chucalisa Star of Leadership from the table, the legendary symbol from the ancestors and the Star of the Volta and pinned these medallions on Brandon's chest, one after the other.

"Though you still harbor some fear, this is the final sign from the ancestors," he told him firmly as he pinned the last one on his chest. "From now onwards, you have the backing of the gods and the ancestors to go on the mission."

"What do I do now?" he inquired politely.

"It means there is no turning back because there is no human being that can turn you around," he assured him. "You are the torchbearer for many, indeed, for the cause. You have been assigned the task of fulfilling the Chucalissa mission—atonement."

"What does that mean in plain language?"

"It simply means that you will become the final peace broker."

The strong wind gush symbolized the beginning of his new life, his new state of mind. For a man who was fed up with the racial tension, who wanted to change things, to organize the voiceless or to give the people a better future filled with peace and safety, he got the chance to get a step closer to his dreams.

The future of the people, and indeed the collective destiny of several groups were closely tied to him. The change was that he was no longer very much afraid of the dangers, not too much.

Immediately following the ceremony at the shrine that afternoon, there was the threat of another menacing tornado twirling around the city sending everything flying in the air, leaving houses in shambles. This terrorized the people, dampened their spirits.

No one ever believed that anyone could ever take on such an onerous and dangerous mission, or even gather enough courage to suggest the ritual of atonement to the parties involved. But he did so for reasons only known to him and his team.

Those who spoke about his mission spoke in low tones. Those who criticized him did so behind his back. This was because they did not want to cross swords with someone who was heavily into the occult, or speak evil of the torchbearer of such an important mission.

"He is nothing but a foolish dreamer," the old cotton farmer said to the young boys. "If he thinks he can convince us to make atonement for the past, then he is not being honest with himself. He would be in for a rude shock."

"Well, I like what he says about goodwill towards everybody across the globe and those of us with burdens from the past should lay down these heavy burdens of guilt," Bubba told the old farmer.

Reverend Peterson said, "We need to do that for sure."

"But at what cost?" Louise asked Bubba and Reverend Peterson.

Brandon Beringer was the name his parents gave him. They were the descendants of Native-American and African ancestries. But he would become known in the land as "Brandon, the Trail Blazer," or as some called him, "Brandon, the Peacemaker." Though his closest friends nicknamed him the prophet, he did not believe that he was a prophet. He categorically rejected that name or any reference to any prophecy.

He was tall, about six two or more and he was a physically powerful presence. He was very agile and walked with much confidence. When he walked, he pounced on the ground as if he could crush the earth. He was always deep in thought and had an aura of dignity around him. Some of his supporters say that he was a throwback of the legendary Ramsses the Great of Egypt, Chaka the Zulu of South Africa or the Great Osagyefo, Kwame Nkrumah, the Nzima legend of Ghana, maybe the qualities of all these individuals meshed in one person. He was the best of many worlds, the accomplished leader of the youth and the torch bearer for many.

Looking into his dark ebony eyes and sizing up his dark lips, one does not have to wonder why he puts fear in so many people, evoking respect from many men and women. He was someone on a mission to change his world. He definitely intended to make things better. He wanted to create a better and a more livable world for everyone, white, yellow, brown and black—a rainbow world.

He carried himself proudly. His demeanor was always serious, yet he looked friendly whenever he approached anyone. His heart did not always tell what he was feeling inside. But he was a very nice and likeable person. He could easily win the celebrity of the year award anywhere. And that is if his critics, those who had vowed to derail his dreams, could allow that to happen.

"Pick up the mantle, you have been charged with the mission," the falcon returned.

"It is too late to go back on my word now, I know," he pointed to the falcon. "What chances of success do I have?"

He stood at the edge of the green wooded area, felt the heavy star around his neck and had no choice but to look ahead with hope and optimism.

"Son, that is not in your hands; you had no voice in that," whispered the falcon as it stretched its powerful wings over him protectively. "That was a decision made by the ancestors, years before you were even born. So, just get out there and they would fight your battles for you."

"How can I convince those who continue to cling to their heritage?" Brandon asked the falcon calmly as he tried to reason with the messenger.

"They can cling to the profane past, but the reality is that they are doing this against a backdrop of angry souls roaming the land seeking vengeance," whispered the falcon. "These gods are definitely out of patience. They can no longer wait, not anymore. They are out there, roaming and seeking vengeance."

"Would they agree to abandon the path of hatred and lay down the heavy burden of guilt that still lingers deep inside their hearts?"

"When you take up the mantle, you would receive some more guidance and support from the ancestors and from the gods. They will guide you carefully to overcome these problems," the falcon assured him.

"You ought to understand the power of the ancestors by now and we have already briefed you on that," the old man said, looking at him intensely as he added, "Stop doubting the ancestors and leave their plans the way they are."

"Do you know this task is a difficult burden for anyone to carry?" he argued.

"Your burden is light compared to those who still continue to carry around their necks the burden of guilt from the past," the old man explained to him, candidly. "They have a harder choice to make. They have to choose between their heritage and their future."

As he left the shrine, the falcon returned to perch on his shoulder and to give him some more assurance. "Of course, don't waver, because the ancestors and the gods are all behind you," the falcon whispered to him again.

Byhalia Buffalo, also known as Bright Blue Skye, one of his ancestors, who had worked in the movement his entire life, appeared to him in a vision from the blue sky and rode on the wings of the falcon to lend him his support.

"Son, I confer upon you "the Sacred Order of Byhalia" the ultimate power of the gods," Byhalia Buffalo told him that hot afternoon, shaking his right hand firmly. He rubbed his left hand gently on his forehead. "Only you can set the angry spirits of the ancestors free, spirits that are still roaming the land in pain. You must relieve them of their pain and help them make the transition to the world of the ancestors. Anyone who poses any danger to you and anyone who tries to destroy this mission or the messenger, the ancestors would readily confront. These are your marching orders, my son, and word up."

"If you would stick to your word to protect me," Brandon told Byhalia Buffalo, breathing heavily. He knew that he could not turn down or walk away from the task. "Consider me the man for this historic mission, I will be the instrument of peace and prosperity, and I will not let you down."

"This is truly an historic moment," the old man said gleefully. "I never thought I would see the day that these two medals, coveted prizes that I seriously craved, but could not receive, conspicuously displayed on my grandson's chest as the chosen one. We are very proud of you."

"Thank you for your confidence in me," he declared.

"I presented you with the mantle of a torchbearer to signify that you are the chosen one. Shall we say that the moment for the final peace and reconciliation in the land has eventually arrived?"

"Yes," a strange voice said quietly. "The time has come. The moment of truth has come. This ritual can no longer be delayed."

"Well, the leaders of the land might have done their best in fighting for peace in the land. How can we forget the likes of Crazy Horse, Sitting Bull, King Gizenga, Queen Nzinga, King Uganda, Nat Turner, Kwame Nkrumah, Osei Tutu 1, Chaka the Zulu, Sojourner Truth, Booker T. Washington, W. E. B. DuBois, Malcolm X and Martin Luther King? These were the fearless fighters, who broke down some of the barriers."

"I stand on all their shoulders to become the ultimate leveler, the true peacemaker, though the road ahead still worries me," Brandon told Trent.

"You better stop complaining and start connecting with the parties involved," Trent said. "Time is running out. The gods and the ancestors want action and no more worries and complaints from you. They are solidly behind you to succeed."

"Is that all the sympathy I get from you?" he asked quietly.

"You heard me the first time; you are absolutely right," the head priest said once again. "The past has defeated the past."

The priest squeezed a small note into his hand and winked at him. "You are the descendant of the great King of Chucalisa, a throwback of your grandfather the Fearless Beringer, and you would live up to that name," he read it to himself, and he watched his eyes beamed with pride. "There is a lot resting on your shoulders, on your decisions and on what you decide to do."

The mission was obvious. The priests sacrificed several animals on the hearth to the gods that afternoon to solidify the mission. The shaman cleansed the shrine for the next big event, the Soul Festival of Legends. He burned a mixture of Egyptian musk incense, frankincense and eucalyptus to placate the gods. The smell was strong, but pleasing and stimulating to the ancestors and to the gods.

The lightening flashes blinded the children temporarily and the thunder that came seconds later nearly broke their eardrums. The breaths of the angry souls reached up into the heavens once more as columns of tornadoes, twirling violently in the dark ominous sky flattened everything in their path. Maybe the ancestors from the past have started to look for redemption.

"The conservative head priests may not be in favor of your choice as the chosen Chickazana, perhaps they wanted one of their own to play this sacred role," a mysterious but firm voice said, a revelation that did not startle him, because he'd already heard this in South Memphis.

He saw his dead grandfather in his vision. He was wearing silvery attire and was walking toward him. He started to scream to get his attention and to tell him that he had been searching very much for him, just to have a word with him, but he got angry with himself when he realized that it was just a dream and not reality.

"You have to take up the mission. Remember that many souls and spirits are counting on you for their freedom," the spirit mumbled in a low voice. "Listen, son, there is no turning back now. You need to start running, holding the torch high."

Trent walked toward Brandon and greeted him in his usual unique way, a hectic handshake and a snap of the fingers. "When is the dance of the week being held? Are you going to go or not?"

"I don't know yet, buddy," Brandon said, reading the seven large crystal balls in the backroom of the shrine and trying to decipher the meaning of the oracle. "These crystal balls say little or next to nothing to us about the blight in the land, if that ever exists at all."

"Maybe it is just your superstitious imagination that is goading you on to such bizarre conclusions," Steven said, teasing Brandon for being so immersed in the occult.

"The consensus is for you to move forward. It will take someone like you from your unique origins, ability and preparation to do this right," Trent said. "Maybe the time has come for a national soul cleansing, prayer, libation and meditation to bring about the reconciliation we need."

"You mean a complete apotheosis?" Brandon asked.

"Something of that nature, to that extent," Steven said.

"If you think that we need to get a broad-based support for this cause, it means we must work harder or maybe even work around the clock," Trent said, secretly laughing at his friend's point of view. "The program might be too drastic for some people at this point in history."

He went to bed that night, inspired by the powerful voices he had heard, words which reverberated throughout his intriguing world. Inside his soul, he was positive that the gods would finally do something about the past and keep it from destroying the present.

"We can not go back to correct the evils of the past, but we can make people accept responsibility for their ancestors' actions or their own actions and lay down the heavy burden of guilt they carried. He also was positive that the modern generation of the victims would be willing to forgive those who have carried this burden of guilt for so long and across several generations," Brandon said, inspired by the revelations.

Seven eagles and seven doves, each one with colorful plumes that had been freshly fluffed, flew past their heads with each one stopping briefly to circle around Brandon's head quietly and landing on top of his head for a second or two. They came to pay their homage; they came to bless his mission. Then they took off as quickly as they came. There was a piercing ray of light directed at his head. The source of that ray of light, which was pointed directly at his head, has remained a mystery till this very day. Nevertheless, it gave him the final powers he needed for the task ahead.

"How do we end this vicious cycle?" a cotton farmer asked him, sounding irritated by Brandon's hard criticism of his heritage. He was also offended by his quest for atonement for what he described as "raking a dead past."

"You need to make atonement for the past," he told the farmer. "Just think about it as the act that would allow you to lay down the heavy burden from the past."

"Why are you so sure that this could do it?" he asked Brandon.

"We need to cleanse the land and the nation, rituals that must follow later."

"We can apologize, but I don't see us making too many amends for the past," the farmer pressed on stubbornly. "We don't want to disown our ancestors, because some of them died just so they could pass this heritage on to us."

"That is exactly the key to the reconciliation," he told him. His eyes opened widely. He smiled broadly, his hands clasping each other very firmly. "It is your turn to consecrate this heritage and make it worthy, and a timeless gift for generations to come."

"Well, we need to calm down the Atlantic Ocean, silence the angry spirits and appease the gods," Trent suggested.

"Maybe we need a National Day of Apotheosis, a day for coming to terms with the past and of making peace, a day of reconciliation," Steve suggested.

"The need for atonement and final reconciliation had never been greater,"

FIFTEEN

B RANDON KNEW THE ONE HUNDRED and fifty year anniversary of the American Civil War was months away and decided to speed up the process of reconciliation. He noticed the anger and guilt that still lingered in people's hearts on both sides. He wanted allies in several camps to champion the movement of reconciliation; to help people on all sides of the divide to get along.

In a nation reeling with guilt from the past, he was tired of people still trying to sweep the past under the carpet of history, ignoring the hurt, running away from the shame and hiding the shame of the past from the world.

"You can't teach me about leadership because I was out there organizing, and I don't need for you to question my bravery, I'd seen a race riot on the streets before," he told his friend. He was once caught in the middle of a racial confrontation which took place when the police shot an innocent boy who was armed with nothing but what turned out to be a toy gun. There was violence, there was looting, there were several warning shots and there were several arrests. The incident changed his life forever. From that day forward, his perspective changed completely—he wanted a meaningful resolution of the racial stalemate.

He knew it would take a sincere apology, with some form of reasonable atonement, according to the shrine leaders. He would have quoted some figures, what he thought should be done, but he knew that would be counter-productive. He wanted the movement to continue gradually, with the states apologizing for the profane past, one after the other.

"It is encouraging to hear that several states especially the states of North Carolina, Virginia, Arkansas and New Jersey have apologized for slavery already," the young historian said at the festival in Memphis. "Virginia and the Carolinas were among the states that used to rely very heavily on slave labor either to grow cotton or tobacco. Though they are indeed conservative states, they have become progressive and forward-looking in their thinking, more in line with twenty-first century realities."

"If these apologies are sincere, with genuine remorse, there is no reason to deny them forgiveness. We must give them the opportunity, help them to lay down the heavy burden of guilt from the past," he repeated emphatically.

"We need to put the past to rest," the old man declared. The aged man was swinging in a hammock tied between two old oak trees. He had on his old blue jean overalls with red suspenders, which were so bright no one could miss his presence. He had silver hair loaded with wisdom, layers of wrinkles adorning his once handsome looking face. His nose was aquiline and his lips very thin. The blue in his eyes was extra pronounced and contrasted sharply with his extraordinary gray hair. It took a man of courage to put the past behind him and a look of optimism about the future, a hopeful sign for everybody.

His goal was to bring change when it came to his children and grandchildren, to make a better world for them. His son-in-law Bubba was busy getting folks to join the bandwagon of reconciliation, though the old farmer was still trying to screen his grandchildren from the modern forces of integration.

"Bubba is such a fine young man, and he would make sure this thing got some leg, so we can rest in peace," he said.

"Well, he still has to get past the folks who feel that they owe no apologies to anyone, especially no apologies to the descendants of the old slavery past," his lady friend told Ayana, the sharp-looking beauty queen from rural Mississippi.

"The modern generation thinks that it is not guilty of anything," remarked Martel, the young African-American activist.

"And they have a case, because they did not enslave anybody, so is it really their responsibility to do anything about the sufferings of the victims of the past? The heritage of slavery has simply been passed down to them by virtue of birth in the region," Edna, the middle-aged lady from Castalia Heights explained.

"What of the fruits of slavery?" Martel asked. "They are still in denial saying that their ancestors did nothing wrong, in spite of the free labor they got, and the cruel and unusual brutality against the African slaves."

"Well, to most of our folks, the slaves served, died and exited the scene, and the modern generation seems to be moving on well with their lives," Bubba said. "But the problem is that the past has refused to disappear and has refused to be swallowed into the abyss of time."

"And I bet you some African-Americans are doing extremely well in the system in the United States. Some of them are even doing better than some poor whites. So why can't we put the past behind us, once and for all and move on?" Louise remarked. "We need to leave it alone."

"You are absolutely right, honey," Bubba replied, as he chewed some Carolina tobacco, spitting the gooey, yellowish mess everywhere, looking conflicted—guilty and angry at the same time.

"Why is making restitution for the past such a bad idea?" Trent asked Bubba pointedly. "The movement to appease the souls of the African slaves, those whose spirits had been restless from the time they'd been taken from Africa, overworked, brutalized and killed continues. Mother Nature has joined the movement looking for ways to appease the ancestors."

"Well, we need to get the atonement movement on a faster pace," Steve told the groups at the meeting at Audubon Park. "We cannot continue to sweep everything that happened in the past under the rug of history, especially not in this modern age of technology."

"We know, but why not give us some time?" Bubba asked, sharply.

"It is because modern technology has all the information posted publicly out there, on the Internet," Steve told him. "Even there are details about toes chopped off, castrations, whippings till the flesh came off, and several brutalities, which have all been posted for the world to read."

"That is not pretty, is it?" Bubba asked Steve quickly.

"These are the actual facts, are they not?" Trent pointed out. "These are the "raw facts" that they have put out there."

Bubba sighed deeply. "We better get a group out to apologize and make the atonement before it is too late."

"Well, in 1998, the Southern Baptists apologized for slavery at the Southern Baptist Convention, and it was such a noble deed on their part," Brandon said. "Weren't they impressive?"

"It was absolutely incredible!" Steve replied. "They'd made a three sixty degree turn in their beliefs."

"And several states have followed their example. Though a few states might take a few more years, or even decades to come to such a change of heart to render apology for the past, many states have willingly done so," Trent told Bubba. "Obviously, some states might never apologize for slavery, but this is a free country founded on such strong convictions, whether they are right or wrong convictions."

"We don't need a presidential apology to pacify the people?" Bubba asked. "That will probably never happen."

"Well, through the instrumentality of Steve Cohen, the white Congressman from Memphis, Tennessee, the United States Congress passed an apology resolution. Later on, the United States Senate also passed its version of apology resolution," Brandon pointed out. "These were unthinkable landmarks of progress a few decades ago."

"The apology from the Southern Baptists is very significant, because who can forget how this particular protestant group provided the biblical justification for the slave trade and for slavery in general especially during those difficult antebellum days of racial oppression," Trent pointed out firmly. "In the antebellum days, some of the churches went out of their way to provide the grease for the wheels that drove the slave trade caravans and the horse drawn carriages that moved plantation slavery."

"You are right, but what a shame though? Bubba asked. "Aren't they ashamed today that their churches assured the planters that they were doing nothing the Bible did not endorse?"

"But is it not amazing how this conservative and deeply religious group, in a true Christian spirit, experienced a change of heart and decided to render an apology for its slavery past, an institution that they'd helped to defend fanatically in the past. They were the strongest defenders of the institutions of the Old South," Trent said.

"In the apology, they have openly admitted that slavery was not the right thing for Christians to do, and that they were sorry for all the hurt that they'd caused the African people and the people of African descent who live in the Diaspora," Brandon revealed.

"Nature loves happy endings," Steve noted and smiled. "How did the victims receive the apology?"

"I don't care how angry Africans and African-Americans are, or how high their demand for atonement is, this is an apology they must accept," Brandon decided, and sighed. "Since the move by the church was such a gigantic shift from their position in the past, the victims must give these Baptists the forgiveness they so very much deserve and need."

"Believe me; you don't know how much courage it took for the group to do what they did," Bubba confessed and nodded proudly, repeatedly.

"What of the pain and suffering they'd inflicted over the years?" Trent wondered. "What do they intend to do about it?"

"Well, the apology was such a gigantic step for the church. But I can see that you want something else from the people," Bubba observed sharply, still trying to resolve the conflicting passions within his own soul.

"You are absolutely right," Brandon said.

"Well, the fact that the people of African descent still struggle with racism and discrimination in America today is a major reason for the reconciliation movement to move at a faster pace," Trent said.

"Though slavery ended in America years ago, the scars the slave trade and plantation slavery inflicted on African-Americans have not disappeared," Steve revealed. "Indeed, some of these wounds are still as fresh and as severe in their effects today as if they'd been inflicted just a few years ago."

"You are not telling me anything that I don't already know," Bubba interjected calmly. Obviously, his conflicted conscience was tormenting him. "I know about the past, because I am a product of the South."

"Bubba, you don't have to testify here," Louise told Bubba, looking embarrassed. "You can keep all your great grandfather's dirty little secrets to yourself."

"Louise, watch out! It is easy for you to say," Bubba shrugged off her bluff.

"Still, the obvious disparity in the distribution of the wealth in the land, in spite of the several years of hard work by the African people, indicates that the playing fields are still not even," Steve quoted some figures.

"Many are doing very well though," Bubba argued.

"Well, in fact, African-Americans do not receive their fair share of what they ought to get and neither do Hispanics or Asians. It is obvious that when it comes to jobs, schools and accommodation, the past is still echoed in many decisions," Steve pointed out.

"We all know that Africans provided the much-needed labor to industrialize this country," Trent argued. "Why not follow all these apologies with some sort of atonement, some sort of reward, and no matter how symbolic?"

"But what of the idea that the slaves were brought to a better civilization here in America, right?" Bubba asked with some hesitation. "Or that doesn't count?"

"That was the old argument or strategy the slave holders used. They tried to paint the Africans as dumb, foolish and degraded and needed to come here as slaves for American civilization. Fortunately, however, that idea has collapsed completely as thousands of people of African descent had personally toured Africa and have discovered the truth about the state of the continent.," Steve told Bubba and the rest of the audience.

"You mean some African-Americans have returned to Africa to live over there?" Louise asked. "I did not know that. Who sent them there?"

"They went on their own to "the dreamland" and to "the tropical paradise" they have so badly craved, in spite of the challenges they are likely to face over there. They know that the continent can provide a tropical non-winter lifestyle for them and some of them are taking advantage of the gold, copper, diamond, coffee, cocoa and even the oil boom on the continent," Trent told Louise and Bubba. "Africa has so many natural resources, plus they have so many seasons to grow food."

"Good for those who went back to their ancestral land? I didn't know that some went back home," Louise added, surprised.

"With all the gold, the diamonds, the bauxite, the tin, the manganese, the copper, the coffee, the cocoa, the oil, and all the other natural resources that Africa has, can we safely say that Africa is the most endowed continent on the planet when it comes to natural resources?" Steve asked the crowd.

"The dreadful things African-Americans have discovered in their past history, especially the manner in which the European-Americans treated their ancestors all came to light with the accretion of knowledge, on the Internet," Steve said. "These truths traveled from the archives to the Internet."

"Are these the reasons the descendants of the victims of slavery have intensified their demands for atonement?" Bubba asked bluntly. "Do they know that America can never repay the liability it owes to the people of Africa and to the people of African descent who live here in the African Diaspora?"

"Yes, they do know that. But all they want is some atonement from the descendants of the former slave masters," Trent told them. "In fact, they want some reasonable atonement for the past. They want some reward money or programs."

"We don't have that kind of reward money," Bubba brushed it aside.

"Well, as outrageous as it sounds, some people even want some sort of arrangements or programs to make up for some of the slavery past. They know you can never pay whatever you owe," Trent explained.

"Well, it is going to open a Pandora box, you know?" Bubba asked Trent.

"I don't see why this has to be a problem, when other victims in American history, the Japanese, Native-Americans and others, have received apologies and compensations for their various past sufferings or grievances," he told Bubba. "Admitting guilt is the hardest thing for the collective ethos of a nation to do. But those Native-Americans, whose lands had been taken away from them and who were nearly obliterated from history through genocidal policies in the past, have received an apology and some form of atonement."

"Well, we stole their land, right?" Bubba argued.

"Then the case of the Japanese Americans, those Americans whose rights had been abrogated or violated when they were huddled into internment camps during World War II, had been told that the nation was sorry," he explained to Bubba. "They'd received some form of compensation."

"Then, the victims of the Tuskegee syphilis experiment, whose health and human rights were violated, had been given an official apology and some form of acknowledgement," Steve also pointed out.

"For African-Americans, because the crimes during slavery were million times bigger than all the crimes in American history combined, the nation has hesitated to offer any sort of atonement for the past. But to apologize for slavery is an acceptance of guilt for a past crime," Trent pointed out. "And in America when you admit wrongdoing or guilt, you must make some form of restitution."

"Hmm, there is a genuine fear here," Brandon revealed sighing.

What is the fear here?" Trent asked.

"It does not only bring the brutalities of the past into the open, the fear is how America can make atonement for such a horrible past? What kind of restitution would the victims expect from America the wealthy superpower?" Brandon asked. "Another fear is that the slave trade and plantation slavery crime are so enormous that any kind of restitution would be too much for the nation. How do you pay for the labor rendered by more than forty million people who had worked for free for more than three hundred years or more?"

"Impossible!" Trent said, laughing and shaking his head from side to side. "And they have to add the interest too?"

"This could be worked out in a country that is famous in its history for its numerous great compromises. Maybe some forms of programs for Africans on the continent and for African-Americans in the Diaspora would be acceptable," Steve said.

"Some people feel that the wounds of the African-Americans are so deep that no amount of atonement could appease the descendants, but that does not mean it is impossible to ever appease them. Others feel that the nation does not have enough resources at this material moment to atone for this burden in its history," Brandon said.

"Well, we admit the slavery past was horrible, but it was so long ago," Bubba argued.

"But we can help you make atonement. You can never know unless we try to design the terms of atonement. We can design terms that would not bankrupt the countries involved, especially these terms would be such that they would not derail the economy of the United States of America."

"Though we are busy pointing fingers at the people from the Old South, the role of the traders from the American Northeast, those who journeyed to Africa to round up and trade the slaves, must not go without accountability. The slave traders of Rhode Island, New York and New Hampshire must step up to the global arena and make voluntary atonement for what their ancestors did to Africa," Trent said, openly.

"We must condemn the slave dealers and the slaveholders in no uncertain terms," Brandon said. "But should the world hold their descendants still accountable for what their ancestors did to the African continent and to the African people centuries ago, causing millions of victims to be dispersed all across the globe? Only time would tell."

"Though Europeans are quick to deny this, they have derailed an African continent, a continent that was once ahead of many others when it came to civilization," Steve repeated. "The slave trade brought the continent to its knees. Since then, it had been struggling without much success to rediscover its past glories."

"But the slave trade ended centuries ago, so why are you blaming the Europeans?" Bubba shook his head.

"Well, that is because after the prolonged assault on its human resources ended, the long-term psychological trauma inflicted on the inhabitants of this once very proud continent continues even to today," Trent explained.

"The time has come for the descendants of the victims to receive the same kind of treatment as other victims in history: atonement. If it is money or some sort of programs, it must not destroy the national economy of any nation involved, whether European countries or Americans," Trent emphasized. "But we definitely need something that would calm down the ancestors."

"In fact, the wheels of time are not on the side of the skeptics of the atonement movement," Steve said. "The new technology of DNA, the most modern technological tool of identification our age has invented, has resurrected, and with great intensity, the discussions about the slave trade and plantation slavery."

"Well, it has brought these subjects into sharper focus and stricter examination. The new technology has made it possible for historians to trace the ancestral links of African-Americans directly to African groups on the continent, and then specifically and directly to groups on the former so-called African Slave Coast, especially to the five major hubs of the European slave trade to Africa: Senegambia, Ghana, Benin, Congo and the Nigerian Delta," Trent declared.

"How many of these descendants of the former slaves would trace their ancestry to Cape Coast in Ghana, the headquarters of the British slave trade to Africa, we will never know," Trent commented, emphatically. "But the invoices found in the Cape Coast Castle, which were written in blood and sweats, housed in boxes of miseries, do identify several British nobilities and merchants that have heavily invested in the slave trade."

"The ability to link the slaves directly to their African kindred has new implications that must speed up the movement for atonement. It means ancestral ties that had been hitherto completely obliterated in the shuffles of history, can now be traced to specific African bloodlines and to even specific families. It accentuates the fact that the genetic bonds of African-Americans to the continent of Africa are no longer fictional. They are more real than ever before. And it is not only shocking to the senses, but also proper for some form of atonement to be paid for what had happened in the past to prevent a strong backlash from a dead past," Brandon remarked.

"The subject of slavery that used to be shrouded in myths and blamed on the African victims, is no longer an abstract subject that can be ignored," Steve pointed out. "The crime has become very clear and the perpetrators of these grisly deeds in the past, the Europeans and American slave traders and slave holders, must become involved in these conversations of atonement."

"The DNA evidence has reaffirmed the guilt of Europeans in continental Europe and the role of American slave traders from the Northeast." Brandon said. "How the Portuguese, the Dutch, the Spanish, the Danes, the French, the Belgians and the British, and many other Europeans actually brutalized Africans on their own continent and did so for centuries must be reopened and addressed by the perpetrators, instead, do we need an international organization to pursue Africa's claims?"

"The Portuguese, who were the people who first started the brutal slave trade and the other Europeans who joined in the orgy to forcibly remove the Africans from their homelands, and then shipped them in droves to the New World, must own up to the role their ancestors played and rectify the past," Trent said angrily. "They must make atonement for their ancestor's enterprises of shame, or face the wrath of the angry gods of Africa."

"The Africans, who had been victimized in the Americas, particularly in the Old South and in the privacy of Southern plantations, must receive some form of atonement as well," Trent said. "Indeed, the gesture would lead to a lot of healing on the part of the victims both in the Diaspora and on the African continent."

"Maybe, it is a good thing for Africa that the DNA technology has reopened the shameful and painful wounds of the past. Though slavery had ended several centuries ago, the continent is still suffering from the lingering effects of the brutal past. Atonement can concretize the authenticity of the apology with programs or money to set up businesses for the descendants of the victims," Steve said.

"The victims of slavery are not backing down. The tide is accelerating toward some kind of restitution. The horrors of the slavery past have come to light and many more revelations will come to light sooner or later. Families who directly brutalized Africans can be unearthed from the DNA machines in the laboratories," Trent noted.

"What would be the reaction of the descendants of the victims if they found out the names of specific families that'd brutalized their ancestors?" Steve asked.

"That is why these nations must address the atonement issue and put the issue finally to rest," Steve said,

"One more reason, atonement is needed is the after effects of slavery have continued directly or indirectly in the job place, in the schools, in the courts of justice and in the streets of America, in London, Paris, Madrid, Copenhagen, Amsterdam, Birmingham Alabama or London, England, Oxford, Mississippi or in Memphis, Tennessee," Trent pointed out.

"The issue of apology must be handled very carefully, because it is not an accusatory process to humiliate the Old South region, or Northeastern American slave trading families, or an effort to castigate the European slave trading nations such as Portugal, England, Spain, Holland, Denmark and Belgium.

"It is mesmerizing how the British government had once lived off the misery of Africans and did so for centuries during the slave trade era," Trent emphasized. "Who can forget how the English economy, its shipping, banking and gun manufacturing sectors, were heavily predicated on the African slave trade, driven by African blood and rose and fell on the forcible exodus of African slaves?"

"How do you know all this information?" Trent asked.

"The parliamentary debates indicate the hectic role the British lobbyists played to make sure that the British parliamentarians did not abolish the trade, thereby disrupting the English dependence on the European slave trade to Africa," Brandon said. "The economies of the shipbuilding hubs in Liverpool, the gun production in Birmingham and even the banking commercial entrepreneurs in London were solidly dependent on the European slave trade to Africa. How can the British continue to live with themselves knowing that, for centuries, they lived off the melancholy of Africans with some of their own lobbying their parliamentarians to continue the slave trade indefinitely to avoid the economic collapse of cities such as Birmingham, Bristol, Manchester and even London, technically the spine of British economy for several centuries?"

"And where is the justice for Africa today?" Trent blurted out. The end of the slave trade and the cataclysmic Civil War in America had led to the evolution of the application of machinery for tasks in the industrial era. However, the damage to Africa had been done and the denial of the past has only added some insult to the injury

"If it is not a movement to humiliate the descendants of the slave traders from Europe, it is also not aimed at penalizing the descendants of the slavocracy of the Old South, the people who used African slaves to support their lives of leisure," Steve said. "It is a movement to get some fairness and seek reconciliation between the descendants of the former slave holders and the descendants of their victims."

Then the other side of the issue, which many people do not seem to be discussing or fail to bring into sharper focus, is the insensitivity of the descendants of the people of Europe, the main architects of the crime, the master-minds, the executors and certainly the primary movers and shakers of the slave trade. How much of the guilt should modern Europeans share for the role their ancestors played in starting the slave trade?

Of course, it is clear now that the slave trade did not come about as a result of any African need or needs at the time. It was primarily the European craving for free African labor. The fact that the Native Americans tried heroically but came short of providing the labor, and the fact that the indentured servants could not provide all the labor they needed forced the Europeans to go to the so-called African Slave Coast looking for the slave labor from African shores.

Should the Portuguese and the other Europeans be asked to atone for the slave trade? To make amends for conceiving the idea, starting the slave trade, gathering the slaves, filling the boats and hauling them out of Africa to the New World? Why should the Portuguese, the Spanish, the Danes, the French and most particularly the Dutch and the British, those that seized the lion's share of the trade refuse to make atonement?

The irony is that these slave-trading countries have been trotting around the globe today pontificating about the virtues of freedom and of democracy while their past is filled with historical skeletons. Their hands are still dripping with the blood of the sons and daughters of Mama Africa.

What about the demographic tragedy of Africa? The African continent had suffered an irreplaceable drain of human resources from first Arabs from the Middle East. They conducted the slave trade across the mighty Sahara Desert. Other Arab traders hauled slaves from East Africa through the ports of Mombassa, Pemba and Kilwa to the Arabian Peninsula. They must compensate Africa for the services of these slaves.

After the Muslims, then Christian Europeans came on their heels. Many people wanted to settle their problems in Africa and they ended up taking advantage of the African indigenes, destroying the continent and its civilization.

Of all the bizarre things the slave traders did, none was more shocking than how they made sure that they baptized every slave they'd removed from the continent. Was the practice an act of hypocrisy, blasphemy or a perverted sense of missionary zeal? What sort of curse did that bring to their ancestors?

How the gun makers of Birmingham, England dump more than a million guns a year on the African continent and repeated this for hundreds of years. Most of the conflicts in the African hinterland were the products of these guns. These gun dealers had used this gun diplomacy to push the back of the African chiefs against the wall and made it not only dangerous but also suicidal for these chiefs to refuse to remit their slave quotas?

The European scholars have admitted that their ancestors removed only ten million slaves out of the continent. This number was far lesser than the forty million slaves the African scholars had accepted. But are the European scholars not minimizing the numbers out of guilt? What about the truth that for each slave that was forced out of Africa to the New World another one died in the process?

Why the descendants of these Europeans have chosen to ignore this demographic onslaught on the economics, politics and culture of

Africa? The time has come for them to atone for the horrible crimes that their ancestors had committed in the so-called African Slave Coast and inside other parts of the continent.

Most of the youth had been hauled away; the industries in the land had been arrested and stalled. These were crippling blows to the burgeoning industries and agricultural developments in the sixteenth, seventeenth and eighteenth centuries. The African economy, which was vibrant before they'd encountered the Oburonis, became eclipsed almost completely. The culprits have denied this historical reality, though.

The European and American claims that they took the slaves gradually and did so over three hundred plus years didn't make the damage they had done to the African continent any lesser grotesque or any lesser dehumanizing. It simply meant that they had prolonged both the trauma and the agony of this unfortunate continent longer than any other oppression anywhere on the globe.

Their key strategy was to incite inter-group wars among the African groups for the purpose of rounding up prisoners of war in exchange for their guns? These were guns that generated more violence that translated into further destruction of life and the obliteration of the cultural ethos of the African people. The several centuries of suffering simply meant that the trauma had been prolonged, and had been much more debilitating to the continent.

As I said in a paper I presented years ago at a Third World Studies Conference at the University of Nebraska, Omaha, "If Africa had been a human being; it would have visited every psychiatric hospital in Europe and sought treatment in every ward in America and would still not have recovered from the lingering posttraumatic effects of the slave trade and the slavery past. The question is will the continent ever regain its sanity and economic vitality?"

Is it true then that Africa is unable to join the modern global economic network effectively today because "the slave brokers" had built into the system a mechanism which continues to provide justification for slavery and the slave trade. This prevents the continent from the kind of accelerated economic progress it needs. How can Africa polish its image, wash off the stigma of slave trade and plantation slavery to get enough respectability around the globe to attain economic viability like some Asian countries have recently done?

The fault is not totally with the African people. How does a car made in Africa sound to someone from Europe or America today? How can products made in Africa be accepted in the global community when the Europeans branded the people of Africa with the stigma of slavery, this gave the people a perpetual inferiority complex. Why can't African restaurants be on the same pedestal as a Chinese or Japanese restaurant anywhere in Europe or in America?

Maybe this was because the Europeans did not drag the Asians from their continent into America as slaves to build their country for free or sold them in the New World for labor and used the money to fuel the Industrial Revolution in Europe. They did not make them cultivate sugar in Brazil to feed the sweet tooth of the people of Europe.

If the Europeans would put their guilt aside and face the truth for just a moment, they would realize how much damage their ancestors did to Africa and to the people of African descent who live in the Diaspora. They have been so concerned about the economic bonanza that they have refused to pause to take inventory of the moral implications of their past enterprise of shame, especially the long term damage they'd done to the African continent materially and psychologically.

The Portuguese, the Dutch, the British, the French, the Danes, the Spanish, and the other European countries must admit the fact that their ancestors made tremendous amounts of wealth from the African slave trade—out of the misery of the African people. Their forebears gleefully confessed during the era that "the slave trade was the most lucrative trade they'd ever conceived and undertaken."

Their duplicity was horrible. These zealots earned substantial sums of wealth and used the money to finance the Industrial Revolution in Europe while preaching Christian socialism to their new coverts across the globe. They had been jubilant when the blood money from Africa filled the coffers of aristocrats, merchants, governments and even monarchs during the slave trade.

"Can one say that it was the raw greed of the Europeans and the American traders, and not the needs of the African chiefs, which spirited the slave trade and plantation slavery?" Trent asked. "Can we agree that the trade did not start from the needs of the African peoples?"

Africans had never sent any invitation letters to the Europeans, to the Portuguese, to the British, to the Danes, to the Spanish and to the Dutch to come to the continent and buy any slaves, or to abduct their kinfolk. If it were so, why did the Europeans have to use their cannons and their superior firepower to force the Africans to participate in the slave trade—the only way to survive the power game of the European guns?

The 'Tarzan strategy' of making Africans extremely backward, and therefore a people who ought to view slavery as a civilizing factor, no longer works. Were these pictures painted of Africa purposely to justify the slave trade and to lessen the guilt the Americans and Europeans slave traders felt?

Why do these critics constantly focus on civil conflicts and the so-called war lords in Africa to justify Africa's problems and not the root cause of the slave trade? The Americans and Europeans have never said anything positive about the collective image of Africa anyway; they have never done so, not to today.

The Western media refuses to show any kind of constructive pictures about Africa. On American and European television, for instance, the public is bamboozled with images of hungry, sick and unkempt Africans, or of an African warlord in civil conflict trying to iron out inter-group problems. But there have been no positive images of Africa in European and American media.

Recently, however, the face of Africa has become synonymous with the disease of AIDS as if other parts of the globe are untainted or are immune to the disease. But the undeniable truth is that initially when thousands had already died in the so-called developed areas in the eighties only a handful had even heard of the disease, let alone died of it in Africa.

The twisted fate of this unhappy continent continues even today.

The slave trade ended long ago. The last slaves left the shores of Africa more than two centuries ago. Some of the heavily fortified slave castles have been destroyed by the fury of the Atlantic Ocean. Some have been washed away into the bowels of the boisterous Atlantic

Ocean; they'd perished as edifices of shame and horrible symbols of European greed.

Nevertheless, the havoc, the shame and the degradation they had brought with them, had remained behind, had persisted and had continued to hold the continent back from making progress.

The Africans had rehabilitated some of these castles, the canons and the slave ships as tourist attractions, but the hurt, the havoc, the shame, the brutality and the degradation which they have symbolized are still as fresh today in the minds of Africans as if the trade had ended only yesterday.

Today, because of the legacy of the slave trade, Africans are somewhat reluctant to allow Europeans and the people of European descent a free access to African resources.

As for the African chiefs, they'd held the mirror for themselves and have found out where their ancestors went wrong. They have readily admitted that their ancestors were guilty of participating in the slave trade. In a sense, though their ancestors had been forced, cajoled or coaxed into doing so, the fact remains that they'd participated in the degrading trade.

As the horrible tragedy started from the coasts and spread to the hinterland, the African leaders saw the bloodshed and the cataclysmic destructions in the land. Subjects fought against kings, groups against groups and blood against blood as the cancer that spread to the entire continent, filled the land everywhere.

The reality, the truth, however, has been swept under the rug of history—all the opposition. The truth is that the Africans were forced into the slave trade with muskets, bayonets of guns and deadly cannons. Indeed, it was mainly the superior weapons of the Europeans that forced many of the African chiefs to participate in the slave trade, to supply the slave quotas, because failure to do so resulted in the slave master enslaving these leaders.

The Africans had no choice but to cooperate and collaborate with the Portuguese and British demands—more prisoners of war—exchange for more defective and impotent guns. They are still not glad that they'd participated in the slave trade, but what other options did they have? If they didn't want to suffer the impending genocide, they had to find the slave quotas for the Oburonis,

Not every chief took part in the slave trade, by no means.

Obviously, the Europeans wrote the historical accounts of the slave trade, so they'd left out the African opposition to the trade. All the wars of survival and self-preservation have been muted or completely ignored in their accounts. Instead, these Eurocentric scholars have blamed the slave trade on the victims, on the inter-group wars and on overzealous African leaders trying to trade slaves, despite the fact that many of them did so in the interest of self-preservation. They also left out the heroic struggles of the chiefs against the slave traders. Instead, they have painted a picture of African chiefs gleefully selling their own to the Oburoni traders for flimsy trinkets, guns and rum.

If you look at the size of the walls of the slave castles on the African Slave Coast today, those majestic-edifices of greed that had defined the worst aspects of the profane past, you would realize that these Europeans who resided inside them had something to hide. Some of the walls are thicker than four to six feet—impressive and imposing, yet these were fortresses of shame. They were places where people who were afraid of being attacked because of their immoral slave trading activities had barricaded themselves to escape the anger of the chiefs and their irate people.

The most troubling aspects of these castles were the chapels in these castles. These were the places where the Portuguese, the British or the Dutch, baptized the slaves before they shipped them out under the cover of darkness, at night. These chapels were symbols of unbridled hypocrisy by the Europeans. Why baptize a slave if you have decided to ship the one out, to deprive him of his freedom?

These castles still testify eloquently today about the horrible nature of the European assault on the continent. These were the places they hid to commit their heinous crimes against the African people, iniquities that have since been unsurpassed in global history. They remain the pinnacle of the humiliation the African people had to endure.

It did not matter that he got the charge to start the mission. Brandon felt as if he was paddling his boat against the swift currents of the Mississippi River. He had friends on both sides of the racial divide, but that did not break the stalemate for him.

Imagine having to address a subject that was like discussing religion or sex openly. Atonement and reconciliation were like taboo subjects in the land. He tried to get his message across to the people to make peace and become optimistic about the future, but he'd run into a series of roadblocks.

Though he knew it was still a taboo subject in several circles in Europe and in America, he was resolved not to give up on it. He thought both sides of the racial divide must be willing to let go of the guilt from the past eventually, but he knew that the rude reality was that this was easier said than done.

The truth about the past was still hurtful to many. Brandon knew that they were opposed to his mission. He also knew that they did not want to let go of their heritage, of the slavery past, or ignore their ancestors' heroic struggle to defend the region during the bloody Civil War. At best, these folks wanted the past to be left alone and not raked or tampered with.

Brandon agreed that it was a good idea on the part of these critics to preserve the good part of their heritage, but he wanted to help them to get rid of the heavy burden they still carried in their hearts as a result of the horrors of history. But the problem was that some would not let go of any part of it, not even the brutal past. They preferred to continue to carry this heavy burden of guilt in their hearts forever and did not mind even if they passed it on to their grandchildren, to the next generations.

"Well, why do you say this is not the time to let go of the hate from the past?" Brandon shocked the gathering with his bold and realistic style. "If this is not the time to let go of the guilt from the past, then when is the right time?"

"Why are you asking us to turn away from our own heritage?" the former cotton farmer asked Brandon, bluntly. His voice was drowned in a sea of protests and a loud cadence of boos. "We cannot continue to feel guilty because of the deeds of our ancestors."

"Well, let us proceed. If you would work with me, we'll march on to a better future," Brandon said. He marched toward the sanctuary, pointing toward the vault. "We need the falcon to guide the mission."

Brandon heard an eerie sound near the wooded area next to the shrine and got elated, because he knew that it was the falcon. He whistled the code word at the top of his voice, but was disappointed when his friend the falcon did not appear flapping its wings happily as usual.

So, he sat on the wooden bench in front of the shrine disappointed thinking about the next move. Was this the mission the ancestors had revealed to him in his dreams? Maybe the promises of the gods, the inscriptions on the tablets, were not real, or maybe the time for the mission has not come.

"Wherever you are, my friend the falcon, I still need you more than ever before," he said to himself, reassuringly. He felt it was time for the truth. He wanted to know the cost to him and the sacrifices he had to make. But he knew that he wouldn't start until the falcon makes an appearance to signal the commencement of the mission.

Meanwhile, in the woods around the shrine, you could hear the ominous voices of the spirits, the groaning of the ghosts and the hooting of the owls. You could hear their movements, the bitter complaints, the crazy and eerie yelling, though these were forces invisible to everyone.

"This is a scary place. It is haunted. This place is a challenge to human safety. You hear all types of sounds here, but you don't see anything," Trent said, prone to signs from the occult world.

"Do you think that maybe the threats he'd received the day before have begun to scare him?" Zora, the fundraiser for the movement, inquired calmly. Then she took a mixture of Egyptian musk and basil leaves and lit the fire to cleanse the compound. "I hope your friend does not give up, because things would certainly get better in the end. We need to be patient for him to get his message across to the hard-hearted folks on both sides of the divide."

"They'd crossed the line when they started burning crosses in front of people's yards in rural Mississippi, Tennessee and Alabama," Trent said without fear. Naturally, they knew of the problems from the past still rearing their ugly heads sporadically. "But why are they still acting out all the hatred they'd inherited from the past?"

"Don't forget at any time to use the command your grandfather taught you, if you are in danger," Steve shouted to Brandon, who was shocked by the opposition, and yet he was very much determined to continue with the mission.

"Calm down, calm down, calm down, Steven," Brandon told Steven. "Nothing is going to happen to me, not in the abode of the ancestors and certainly not in today's world of progress and tolerance."

"Oh! No. I am not afraid. We are in this together; we are solidly behind you all the way," Steve said.

Trent shook his head in disbelief. The biggest concern was how he would tell the other side to change without being viewed as racist himself. "The falcon has actually left you alone for a whole week? Your relationship with this strange bird gets deeper and deeper by the day, and you know it is getting even more and more ridiculous every passing day. But something tells me that the falcon is not going to abandon you; it would be around forever."

For a week, Brandon felt as if he was standing on the edge of a mighty river, but was pondering whether to take the deep plunge into the currents of the rushing river. As someone who believes in the ancestors, he knew that the disasters, the tornadoes, the storms, the floods, and the earthquakes in the land were harbingers from the past.

But he knew that he must level the playing fields for everyone, if he could. He wanted the time to be known as "a season of apotheosis" or "a time for atonement." It was a time of redemption from a horrible and shameful past and a time of ending the burden for all. In theory, all who heeded the call must finally lay down their heavy burdens of guilt and wash their conscience from the profane past in the mighty river of innocence and purity, but in practice, very few were ready to do that.

Though there were a lot of forces brewing inside him, he waited on the pier for more than two hours for the renowned Memphis Queen Riverboat to dock, to let out the passengers and make room for him and his small group of friends to go on a brief cruise on the Mississippi, to ride downstream toward New Orleans, to exhale their woes and inhale a breath of fresh air, and imbibe new paradigms.

The venue for this sacred ritual was the outskirts of the city. It was a sentimental journey of the spirit from the sacred banks of the old Mississippi River, the griot for all the rivers in America pointed to the legendary Nile River, the mother of all the rivers. As for Brandon and his team, they couldn't wait for the soul to soul experience to transpire.

There was the consecrated shrine that secretly controlled the affairs of many of the citizens in the region. The Native-American priests have known about this cult for more than seventeen generations. And they have known what good it could do and what havoc it could also cause among the people. That is, if the call of the ancestors for atonement goes unanswered.

The new generations of Native-American priests have retained the ancient name Chucalisa, but they must battle with the new radical groups who sought to change the old name Chucalisa into the new name "the Tomb of Doom." They want it that way because they feel that the new name defines them better than the old name.

The spirit of the ancestors, their desires, regrets in history and their plans for the future generation were all represented in the shrine. The gods, who had inhabited the shrine from time immemorial, have worked closely with Mother Nature. They'd sent their harbingers, their messages in tornadoes, hurricanes, earthquakes, fire, drought and even flood—these special and urgent messages.

The gods that dwelt and operated the Chucalisa Shrine, the restless souls of many who had perished in the land centuries ago, mixed with the souls of former slaves who died in cold blood, on the whipping posts, in the cotton fields, in the privacy of the plantations, or those who had perished on the high seas in the middle of the Atlantic Ocean during the notorious Middle Passage were still restless, still roaming the land like zombies.

So, the ancestors were in the storms, in the rains, in the hurricanes, in the tornadoes and in the floods. And they'd chosen to arrive in as violent a manner as the forces that had destroyed them. They had become tired of waiting for the apotheosis, so as angry spirits they haunted the land, tore down everything in their path and sent dark clouds of vengeance twirling in the fields. "Were these the pangs of retributive justice in the land that the ancestors had spoken about?" Trent shook his head.

These yeasty mixtures of forces had been roaming in the land seething for vengeance for years. But the ancient trees that'd witnessed these atrocities in the past failed to speak up on behalf of the innocent victims they'd spared. So did they ride the swift currents of the Mississippi River with the muddy waters to protest the deep dark secrets of horror? What did this legendary river has in its bosom, but refuses to spill these deadly secret toxins out in the open?

Why the mid-south and some other regions have become tornado alleys is difficult to understand. The restless souls of the natives in the land, those who still abide in Mother Earth, had banded together with Mother Nature to unleash their fury in the whirling, twirling and twisting winds. Brandon was disgusted with the number of disasters in the land and he felt like disappearing to somewhere so remote nobody would ever find his whereabouts.

Maybe the answers are locked up in the bosom of Mother Nature.

The people knew that these angry souls have not rested, but have marched across the land spewing their anger in all directions, destroying everything in their path and turning every structure they'd come across into piles of debris.

These forces are the Demon Deacons of the land, because when the restless souls got together to remember their history, to recall the events from the past, they acted as if they'd been possessed with demons from the past. They roamed the land acting out their anger and resentment against everybody and against everything in their path, but still it did not calm down their anger.

Did the ancestors have anything to do with the turmoil?

When the bright flashes of lightening lit the sky and all the children in the vicinity began to run for cover, just before the deafening thunder exploded and rocked the land, terrorizing the youth and badgering the grown ups, he knew he was completely in the dark about these parts of the mission. And those who had inherited the burden of guilt from the profane past, from their testimonies, have begun to hear voices at night, experienced ominous alarms.

The dark funnel clouds turned into tornadoes that ravaged the land with fury. They'd destroyed the farms, stores, huts, ranches, dwellings, churches and offices. They'd left a lot of devastation, but also horrible trails of blood.

Bubba watched the turmoil in anger. "How could this be? We need to put all these behind us once and for all," he told the wife.

Sixteen

I T TOOK A LOT OF persuasion to get the group to make the decision, to accept the proposition. Many refused to give in to the demand because it meant they would have to censor the past, criticize their ancestral heritage . . . though they knew they had to let go the guilt. The decision was a radical one, because they did not follow the same old practice of hiding everything about the past.

They kept working on the farms and on the fishing boats as the debate raged on across the region. It came to if agreeing to atone for the past implied disrespecting their ancestors or disgracing their heritage, then many of them were finally prepared to go that route. And so though many of them were still passionate about their past, they felt that it was time to go against their heritage and do the right thing anyway.

It was a difficult dilemma for many. But once they made the decision, they felt it was perhaps the best decision they'd ever made. Resolving the past, coming to terms with the good and the bad in their heritage was something that was long overdue anyway. There was no need to keep fighting the past.

"We need to dramatize the decision for the average person to know what we were about to do," Reverend Peterson emphasized; his hands blasted away a mixture of guilt, sorrows and concerns on his new modern piano of white ivory and ebony black keys. "They need to understand why this change has to come at this dramatic moment in history and not later."

"Who said we need the change anyway?" Jim McSwain in his typical Southern drawl shot back, blinking his eyes erratically. "You are alone in your foolish dreams. Do you realize that you are building sand castles on the banks of the Mississippi River?"

"Of course we are not," Reverend Peterson told him in softer voice.

Reverend Peterson knew better to complain about the youths not showing up in their costumes that evening when the weather was so terrible that it deteriorated into a tornado watch was being unreasonable. His hope of getting the members of the play to come an hour earlier for an additional rehearsal before the actual performance took place did not materialize because of the inclement weather. He was excited to see a dozen or so of the cast who made it on time, but he waited impatiently for the other two dozen to trickle in one after the other. He did not scream at them when they finally entered because just showing up took a lot of guts for several of them.

Nevertheless, there he stood in the parking lot next to the gym, expecting a miracle. He was hoping to have a full house for the play.

The audience had not seen the play "Let Go the Guilt" before, because thrice they tried to get the youths to act the play and thrice the inclement weather dashed their hopes. Maybe the ancestors refused to cooperate; indeed, they refused to let them prepare the public for the train of reconciliation with their dramatic depiction of the impending harsh realities.

Brandon knew they had minds to change, hearts to persuade and consciences to purge to let go of the past. It was a quest not only to get people to apologize for the past, but also to go beyond that to some sort of atonement. He thought the play would dramatize the virtues of accountability, admission of wrongdoing and apologizing for the past, or even going beyond this to remorse, to atonement and to reconciliation.

"Where are the rest of the cast members?" Reverend Peterson finally asked the half a dozen who had made it to the rehearsal. "These young folks are never reliable. You can never trust them."

He looked at the sky and was glad that the blue and gray funnel clouds of the storm had begun to dissipate. He knew that torrential rains, with possibly another deadly tornado would arrive that evening. So, he sat on the broken desk, pondering and waiting for the rest of the cast to show up for the show.

"The region has experienced several devastations in recent years," he told the deacons. "What do you think is the solution? What do we have to do to stop the strings of disasters from disrupting our lives, and destroying our businesses."

"It has been rough and scary," Deacon Branch said. "I don't want to admit where all these are coming from. Maybe the past has something to do with the turmoil, but I doubt it very seriously."

"You are probably right. Never a year had gone by without either powerful tornadoes tearing miles of pathways across the heartland or the mighty Mississippi River sending rushing floodwaters to inundate our crops, drowning some victims in the process," Reverend Peterson said hesitantly.

"And these disasters are as spontaneous as they are nerve-racking," the deacon said. "They thrive on their surprising elements."

"The sight of these powerful forces overwhelming the city, tearing neighboring homes in the country apart and destroying some lives is becoming much harder for many of us to bear," Reverend Peterson said. "If Mother Nature is responding to forces deeply buried in the past, where does that leave us?"

"Maybe, it is the present that is doing battle with the past," the Deacon shrugged repeatedly.

"The droughts should not destroy our crops; the corn, the soy bean and the cotton are withering in the soil from the blistering heat from the banks of the Mississippi River all the way to the Delta. The farms on the Ozarks in Arkansas have been shattered, a humbling sight," the deacon said.

He hid inside the storeroom during the tornado pleading, "Please, spare my life once more. And please, spare my people from another round of misery and pain."

When he came out and saw the devastation and the rubble scattered all over, the pain he felt was excruciating and his sorrow was as deep as the raging Mississippi River.

"The tornado has become much more frequent and also much more dangerous—they are like the killer bees from far away, from the African Coast—the other side of the Atlantic Ocean," the deacon told him sadly. "How long shall we continue to go against the wrath of Mother Nature?"

It was daylight when Deacon Branch returned to search for some of the valuables of the church, but what he discovered was absolutely horrifying and gut-wrenching. The church materials had been blown away. They were scattered everywhere, most of it was reduced to trails of devastation and piles of debris. Even the pulpit, from which comforting words oozed like honey from the tongue of the preacher, was completely torn to wooden planks. It was demolished and gone.

"Mother Nature has interfered in the affairs of the region once more. I thought this was supposed to be a dialogue between humans?" The preacher asked. "Why has Mother Nature taken over whatever this problem is, and has decided to wreck havoc in the land?"

He'd seen another deadly tornado creating a three-mile wide path deep into northern Mississippi, taking some lives and destroying several businesses and leveling several houses in its trails.

The tornado destroyed several antebellum mansions, reduced them to fragments of a decayed past, and this horror caught many people's attention, shuddering almost out of their wits.

"We are losing these valuable legacies," Bubba told the preacher when the sirens were silenced.

"I am not so sure how valuable they are, Bubba," the preacher remarked. "But we don't need to be losing anything."

When he came to the judges office, only the warped debris of rafters and bent sheetrock mixed with broken dreams and inadequate legal representation were scattered all over the basement and had spilled into the old, half-demolished parking lot.

Bubba got out of his vehicle, stopped sipping his iced tea and lemonade, as he stood in the center of the small city looking at the devastation, the work of the wrath of Mother Nature. His mind was working overtime to find the reasons for the disaster. Several houses had been ripped apart.

Whether a miracle or not, the old post office survived intact. Maybe it did so because it was the only strong and untainted building in the area? But is this succumbing to superstition, but he knew this was not based on any scientific facts.

As much as he cherished the aged artifacts from the mansions, he wanted them to be swept into historical oblivion. The picture of his great grandfather towering over his slaves in the cotton field, the picture his own father cherished most, had been blown away in the eye of the ravaging tornado, but he refused to go find it.

He'd bragged about his great grandfather's accomplishments to many of his friends on several occasions. He'd shown his pictures to his friends and colleagues several times before. And his heart swelled with pride whenever he told people that the man in the picture was his great grandfather, one of the wealthiest men that ever lived in the state of Mississippi. But he'd hid the fact that his great grandfather was a colonel in the confederate army and fought gallantly for the losing cause. But he was torn between putting a distance between him and his beloved relative— Great Grandpa Joe and still bragging about his role in defending the South under siege . . .

The problem was the wealth from King Cotton—human misery—the hard labor of African slaves. He knew they'd left a lot of hurt—maybe his Great Grandpa Joe could not be such a great role model after all. His great grandfather had no other choice except to make the best of what they had inherited from the previous generation—slavery— plantations—horse-drawn carriages and lots of guilt from the past.

He admired how his ancestors fought hard to preserve the heritage so they could pass it on to them intact. And yet, in the end, they'd lost almost everything, including their way of life, he mused. They fought so hard in the losing battle, defending a cause that was filled with contradictions, anachronisms and an unsustainable lifestyle that was no longer tenable in a changing world of technology and new ideas.

But there he stood like a man confronted with dilemmas. Maybe it was the agonizing end of the horrible stories from the plantations, with all the legacies of horror from the past, and the wealth they'd made at the expense of the African slaves.

Surprisingly, however, the old jail where a lot of justice and injustice had been done, including the abode of torment for several African slaves, stood intact. It was amazing how that jailhouse, the vortex of the travesty of justice in the district for many African slaves, had survived. He was surprised that it was still sitting arrogantly over the square, next to the old Post Office. Some were abducted at night, lynched and found hanging by the neck from the tallest oak trees on the outskirts of town the next morning for crimes ranging from rape, running away or even insolence to white people.

It wasn't the most infamous institution in the county, but the jail had a notoriety of its own. The annex to the aged courthouse was standing intact, reaching into the blue sky and arrogantly dwarfed everything in all directions in the small city. The old flag was still flapping noisily and defiantly on the one hundred year old flagpole, a symbolism that the past has not disappeared completely, not very much at all.

In their dreams and in their daily activities, they wondered where their loyalties belonged. Should these impressive structures from the past be demolished or should they be preserved for the verdict of the next generation? He didn't know what to do with the grey Civil War uniform of his great grandfather—Colonel Bridges—maybe he would donate it either to the Goodwill in Memphis or to the archive in Oxford, Mississippi.

If his mind was playing tricks on him, he knew it was no fluke when he heard strange noises coming from the Montross, the majestic three—storied antebellum home not far from the local hospital. It had built its notoriety on being the most actively haunted antebellum mansion in the county. The inhabitants nearby once woke up in the middle of the night to the voice of a slave pleading for mercy just before the planters got ready to lynch him from the tallest oak tree in the small city. They heard the slave pleading for his life rather frantically, "Please, I am innocent, spare my life. Please, please I am innocent, please I beg you, please don't hang me. I am innocent. I didn't do it." He heard the slave pleading fervently and frantically. "You go pay for . . . some day, somewhere," the voice said and finally became silent.

He made his way past the Montross to the meeting hall behind the old, antiquated post office. On the way, he got the chance to rehearse what he wanted to tell the group. That was because he knew that the lives of everyone in the region depended on this very meeting. No matter how much he loved his heritage or what affection he felt toward the region, it was obvious that the wheels of change had definitely arrived. The horse-drawn-carriages had disappeared and the bales of cotton had lost their critical importance. The royal days of King Cotton, its days of hegemony, had gone up in a fiery inferno during the Civil war to make room for new car assembly plants, for modern appliance factories, for refrigeration plants and for shoe manufacturing plants—the modern wheels of progress.

The African-American postal agent knew he should have been a slave if he had been born two hundred years earlier. He knew that he would have been a very stubborn and vociferous field hand; he had no doubt about that. He would have been certainly stubborn, uncompromising in his principles, but smart enough to stay alive to fight against his slave masters the next day.

His life expectancy would have been very limited; he had no illusions about that. There were so many ways he could lose his life in those difficult days of shame.

He used to visit the old cemetery not far from midtown. It was fascinating how on one side of the open field were buried the Caucasians, and on the other side were the African slaves. He would place flowers on the badly damaged graves on his side. He would walk quickly past the European side and wouldn't want to even read anything on the tombstones, things that would remind him of the blasphemous past. At the back of his mind, he could still see the former slave masters still riding their horse-drawn carriages, still chasing their slaves.

It surprised him to realize that it was necessary to separate the dead by race even in the cemeteries. It had been perhaps the stupidest practice in the region. Maybe the separation was absolute—partitioned in life and even in death.

The dynamic Bill was glad he was born after those horrifying days in the region, after those dreadful days of separation in everything including even burial plots. He was glad that he didn't have to live in those days of institutionalized racism, fraught with suspicion, brutality and unadulterated oppression.

"This crusader Brandon has the courage to tell us to end our guilt," Bubba told his wife as he stood next to the podium in the courthouse wracking his brain still grappling with the impending changes. "I wonder why he was so determined to bring this change about. Who does he think he is?"

"Maybe he is the only one with the gut to face the past without fearing for his life," Louise gestured with the small purse in her hand.

"The opportune moment to make atonement and seek reconciliation for the profane past has come and we must not let this opportunity slip away. We must do the right thing," Brandon told them. He saw the look of doubt and ambivalence on their faces, there was anger in their hearts, but they tried to hide them under the dry smiles and exaggerated warmth they showed.

"Would he succeed in convincing the majority to finally let go of the dark past and seek a future filled with peace, security, progress, prosperity, forgiveness and reconciliation?" Trent asked. "And would they receive the forgiveness that they so badly want?"

"This has to be a two way street of give and take, which involves sacrifices," Bubba nodded repeatedly.

"Well, though many of us don't say it publicly, our hearts are still clogged with guilt from the past," Louise confessed. "You don't feel it all the time, but every now and then the horrors from the past creep up on you and begin to gnaw at your soul like a leach on a bad leg."

"Well, speak for yourself," Bubba told his wife. "I have learned to come to terms with the past long ago, though I still struggle with it sometimes. My conscience is getting better today; it does not bother me as much as it did twenty years ago."

"What brought about this drastic change in you?" Louise asked Bubba.

"Well, let us say, I have made a conscious decision to work with Reverend Peterson to put the past behind me once and for all," Bubba confessed. He held Louise and kissed her gently, still holding her hand warmly. "I mean we've got to do whatever it takes to put it behind us."

"Let us listen to Brandon. He is telling us to lay down the heavy burden of guilt, make peace and get forgiveness for the things in our past that we are not so proud of," Louise told Bubba. "I hope he knows what he is saying and how not to embarrass us too much."

"Well, though these are changing times, I still fear for his life, very much so," Bubba told her. "Someone could easily hurt him. But we have to support him to see how he can help."

"Well, Bubba. These words coming from your mouth, trying to get away from racial separatism are fascinating and very encouraging for the future too," she told him. "I am proud of you and the children are proud of you too."

"If the atonement would set our children free from the heavy burden we still carry from the past, why don't we lend him our support?" he asked her, rubbing his hand on her back gently. "We are not doing it for ourselves; we have to do this for our children, and for the next generation."

"You are right," Louise said. "Our grandchildren and their children deserve better . . . they must live without this guilt hanging around their neck like a corroded brass necklace."

Brandon held an old slave shackle, which he had kept from his grandfather's collections in his hand. This was supposed to be a visual symbol of the horrible past. He wanted the audience to have a fresh glimpse into how atrocious the past really was. "Just look at this, just imagine what went on in this land in the past . . . who can say that this was right, and who would not feel some remorse for doing such a thing?" he asked the audience.

"What our ancestors did was legal then, so what is all the recent fuss about?" the old cotton merchant, who operated a store on Front Street, near Cotton Row and Beale in Memphis, said quickly. "We need to leave the past alone. Stop raking the old dirt from the past."

Bubba's mouth twitched slightly and his lips trembled as if he was ready to make his move—personal atonement. He held the old plantation records of his grandfather's estate in a handbag and thought about burning them in order to keep them from getting into the hands of the victims. He must keep them out of the hands of those who have been searching for their ancestry in the archives, ransacking the antebellum plantation records to find their former slave owners, and are looking through microfilms, court records, old census ledgers, tax records, birth and death records, for their ancestry, looking for more than that—looking for trouble.

"I think we need to make atonement now before the victims begin confronting the descendants of the former owners for explanations over the past," he told them. "Who knows where all these are heading?"

"Are you sure the Africans will not run the delegation out of the continent and send them back home in anger?" Louise joked.

"No, I don't think that will happen," he declared. "They are ready to find some closure for the slave trade for themselves as well."

"Some are still very angry, but if they are, you can't blame them, not after what had happened to them in their own land, they ought to be angry," Bubba remarked forcefully.

"Well, I guess they have every reason to be angry with us for what our ancestors did to them," Louise admitted, straightening up her pocket book.

"Do you think the Africans would greet the missionaries with hostility and anger?" the senior pastor asked. "The pain from the past of slavery and the slave trade have begun to emerge from the ashes of history, and it has recently made its way to the frontlines in many places including Africa."

"What exactly are we going to do about this?" Louise asked, gesturing with both hands repeatedly.

"It has created some animosity between the Europeans and Americans on one side and the African people on the other," Reverend Peterson continued. "The past of the slave trade has destroyed whatever goodwill the missionaries have developed on the continent."

Bubba was a deacon in his church. He was also the mouthpiece of the church group that was debating the atonement. His life was that of a paradox. His conscience tormented him for being too critical of his heritage, and yet his heart secretly pushed him to convince the four hundred plus member audience that it was time for them to put the past behind them, make atonement, so they could lay down the heavy burden of guilt they'd inherited.

"Bubba, not you of all people," McSwain said. "I don't believe the great grandson of Colonel Noble would turn his back on his great grandfather and be telling the people this nonsense about atonement."

"Well, Bubba is a changed man," Louise told him.

"Well, I think we must go to Africa with red roses in hand, as Reverend Peterson suggested, atoning for what our ancestors did to the continent during the slave trade. We cannot continue to postpone the inevitable. The time to do it is now," he told them in a heavy baritone voice, which ricocheted against the walls and reverberated on the cobblestones outside resounding in the nearby cotton fields.

"You have taken the high road, Bubba," Reverend Peterson commented.

Seven days later, a committee of twenty met in the church basement to finalize the strategy to help them to finally decide to let go the guilt from the past. It all came down to a final critical vote on the matter. The majority realized that time was no longer on their side. They knew that they should hurry up and do the right thing since the age of technology has begun to expose the details about the dreadful past.

The room was very quiet. The solitary ceiling fan could be heard even from the back of the room spinning noisily. The guilt from the past and the urge to do the right thing collided violently in the conscience of those who sought to preserve their heritage and those who wanted to change the status quo. Thoughts of goodwill, which inundated many minds and the quest for a better future for their children, battled against the quest to preserve a decayed past which was predicated on an old lost cause.

Reverend Peterson heaved a deep sigh of relief after the last critical vote ended and he said to his friends, "I am glad we can finally get this behind us once and for all and give our children a clean slate in the future."

"Well, we cannot keep hiding our heads in the sand forever. We must come to terms with this reality at some point in our history," Bertha Robinson, the local leader of the Women Christian Temperance Union said. "I have campaigned personally, though secretly, for this particular cause for years. I have been worried about all the plantation records out there with several family names from this area that have recently found their way into the archives. I worry about my own family name and the legacy of slavery it represents."

"You saw the records as well?" Bubba asked her pointedly. "I was embarrassed when I read some of what my ancestors did to their slaves . . . they have the family names in bold prints too. I couldn't believe it."

"Well, I have come to the conclusion that if we don't do something sooner or later, someone would come after a family and try to even scores for the brutalities their ancestors had suffered at the hands of former slave-holding families," Bertha admitted regrettably, though she was reluctant to get these words out.

"That is my fear as well," Louise told Bertha Robinson. "The past, what happened in our history, is no longer hidden. It is everywhere. With the coming of the computer revolution, it is simply a click of a mouse away."

Of course, the decision to make amends did not come easily. There were voices of people yelling like bears that opposed the plan. Several people did not see the need for the action they'd voted for. "Why should we send a delegation to Africa to atone for the slave trade or for plantation slavery in the past? Their chiefs sold their people to our ancestors," Jim McSwain remarked angrily. Jim McSwain had been a missionary in Africa and had been to three African countries. Though he was a devout preacher and had done a lot of philanthropic activities in Africa, he has never believed that the slave traders and the slave holders did anything wrong during the antebellum slavery period. "The decision to make this atonement is as ridiculous as it is mind-boggling."

"Well, we need to bite the bullet and make this atonement once and for all," Bertha said. "Times have changed."

"It is like we come from two different worlds; we have two different points of view," Jim McSwain said. "It is as if you don't have anything better to do with your time and money."

"Oh, well, I believe we don't have a choice," Reverend Peterson told him bluntly. Rising to his feet and moving to the microphone quickly to avoid a backlash, he tried to explain why it was necessary to make atonement for the slave trade at this point in history. "Time is not on our side. There are several people who can try to even scores with those that had enslaved their people in the past; some have the ability and capacity to do so. With the computer revolution, the records are floating all over the world."

Time was running out. The reform group must put some pressure on the extreme conservative wing to come to terms with the past. They must deal with the guilt in their hearts and reconsider their stand. They must cross the bridge and bite the bullet to make peace.

Though the movement was not popular with some people, Reverend Peterson knew that they were traveling down the right road. They had been working on this project for the last fifteen years, because the past had left such dark clouds hanging over their heritage, over the future of their children, over the schools, over governments, over everything and even over the entire country. "Indeed, if the aged oak trees could speak, they would tell tales of incredible horror, of incredible toe chopping offs, castrations, beatings till the flesh fell off the backs of the slaves, and the whipping of pregnant women who tried to run away to the North to have their children in freedom," Reverend Peterson told the audience, raking the sordid past. He sat on an oak chair.

"What of the hand that fed, sheltered and clothed these slaves for centuries? Who is talking about them?" Jim McSwain asked, playing with the suspenders on his overalls and stumping his alligator cowboy boots on the concrete floor repeatedly as if he was demanding answers to his questions. "How convenient that you don't ever mention what our ancestors did for these slaves?"

"Maybe what we did for them was to keep them alive so we could get the labor out of them," Bubba answered him. "They probably didn't do those things for them because of love."

The decision to send a group of missionaries to the heart of Africa, to sit before the chiefs and the African people and to atone for the past, though was the right thing to do, was very unsettling to several folks to the point that they decided to quit a church their families had attended for several centuries. They did not understand why the atonement for the slave trade, or giving something in recompense for the free labor that their ancestors had enjoyed for more than three centuries at the expense of their African slaves became so controversial.

While the decision to go on the mission was a difficult one for some people, the group had no idea even which country they would go to make the atonement. That was even if the majority of the members agreed on sending a delegation to Africa. Since almost every country on the African continent suffered some losses, some damages directly or indirectly, the group must address an entire continent that'd been plagued with psychological insecurities.

It was impossible to visit every country, not all twenty or more, so the committee of twenty debated which country to visit. The interesting thing was that each of the members selected different countries, though they were located on what used to be the former West African Slave Coast.

Naturally, they wanted a country that still harbored visible legacies of the slave trade, a country with slave castles, remnant boats and lighthouses. The choice, they decided, was among the following locations: Senegal's Gore Island, Benin's Slave Castles, Nigeria's Port Harcourt-Calabar area and Ghana's Cape Coast Castle.

The location, they agreed upon, was Cape Coast Castle in the country of Ghana, a country that the Portuguese formerly named the Gold Coast. The venue was the Cape Coast Castle, a majestic-looking and yet notorious structure that became the headquarters of the British slave trade to the African continent at the height of the European slave trade to Africa.

If the delegation had a problem visiting the scene of their ancestors' crimes, imagine what the visit might do for the African people. Not getting any apologies for centuries, the fear was that it would reopen the old wounds of the shameful and bloody commercial enterprise that their ancestors had to endure on their own shores. That was the sort of feelings they wanted to avoid at all costs, if they could.

Ghana was located on the western coast of the continent. Its southern tip kissed the Atlantic Ocean. The beaches were filled with several slave castles, though Ghana was by no means the leading slave trading country during those tumultuous days. It, however, ranked very high as the port of departure for many slaves, especially the preferred port for British slave traders in those dark and shameful days. It featured prominently also in Portuguese, Dutch and Danish slave trading activities.

The inhabitants didn't know whether it was the gold or the slaves that led the British to make Cape Coast Castle the headquarters of the British slave trade to Africa, serving as the hub for the Royal African Trading Society for many years. Of course, they came into conflict with the African people on the coast. They refused to surrender their sovereignty to these Oburoni aliens, no matter how powerful they had been.

The Africans didn't realize that the European slave traders had built more slave castles on the then Gold Coast than inside any other country. Of course the local leaders fought and opposed them many times, but they were forced to act as middlemen for the gun trade along the Slave Coast.

It was mere coincidence for Ghana; we have to repeat this fact. It was not because Ghanaians were more interested in the slave trade than other countries. It was mainly because of the gold in the area. Many cities and villages are named for the gold mining activities in the area.

The delegation selecting Ghana as the country from which they would render apology to the continent of Africa, to the descendants of the victims of the greatest crime in global history, was the right one. Thus, from the Cape Coast Castle, from the former Gold Coast, which had been renamed Ghana when the land attained independence from the British colonial masters under the legendary leadership of President Kwame Nkrumah, definitely the greatest African politician that ever lived, the Europeans decided to seek atonement.

For centuries the descendants of both the European and American slave traders did not realize how much the world wanted amends from them for the deadly calamity their ancestors had imposed on the African continent. Or, to be more specific, how the slave trade had not allowed these countries to regain their self-confidence because of the prolonged trauma the slave traders had caused.

But there was the still small voice among them, which wondered how in the world their ancestors got away with not apologizing and making atonement for so long, given the magnitude, the scope and the horror of the slave trade. Though they tried to camouflage the crime with missionary zeal, altruistic projects and political development, marked with years of colonialism and subjugation, they had never directly apologized and made amends for the slave trade or plantation slavery.

Of course, they had used all kinds of subterfuge, shibboleths and all sorts of hypocritical posturing to avoid making amends for it. Not many Africans were bold enough to grab the bull by the horns and demand from them directly that they pay for the past crimes of their ancestors until recently. The time has finally come for the African people to make that demand from the descendants of countries that participated in the dehumanizing and shameful trade.

When the members of the delegation arrived on the former Slave Coast, you could imagine their fears and anxieties; they considered themselves peacemakers, those who would make the past right. Some were anxious to show their remorse and unveil the terms of atonement they'd carried with them. But some were overwhelmed by the unbridled guilt, plagued by the embarrassment because their ancestors had committed such enormous atrocities against the African people.

There was refuge waiting for them on the African shores. That is if they were serious to purge their souls, free their conscience, which had continued to nag them like a disease. They would have mercy and forgiveness in their hearts for any remorseful group of Oburonis who have made a trip to seek it.

Ask and you shall receive forgiveness, but only after you make the long-overdue atonement.

The trip sounded better than any missionary work that the Europeans had ever performed on the African continent. It was the best thing they could do to address the lingering questions, animosities and distrust form the slave trade past. Some of them, though others violently disagreed with their countrymen and women, believed that their ancestors, wherever they were, could look down on this particular journey of atonement and be very proud of them. They felt the ritual could help the victims of the past to get some rest. They could also get the very relief and solace that they had been craving.

On the other hand, the trip to Africa triggered a firestorm among the more conservative descendants. They did not agree with the apology, or let alone endorse the idea of atonement for the slavery past. As far as they were concerned, there was nothing in their past for which they had to make any apology or atonement. "Our ancestors, those who fought gallantly and died in the Civil War, would turn in their graves if they see us making any atonement," Marybeth Causley shrugged her shoulders.

Initially Jim McSwain regarded the trip as the ventilation of a guilty minority, the work of people with too much time on their hands, a stupid venture and emotional ejaculation of a renegade few. But later on, he realized that it was not an exercise in nihilism and that the movement had gathered momentum.

But he laughed and drank some whiskey. He was sure that the African people would not even receive, let alone entertain the delegation. "The delegation would certainly face the wrath of the African people and abuse from their leaders. They would face their own music down there," the self-righteous man said.

"Well, though the direct victims of the slave trade, which ended centuries ago, are no longer alive, it does not mean that the African people have forgotten the tragedy," Bubba reminded him. "The impact of the trade still lingers among them. And some of them have some deep-seated anger inside their hearts."

"The African people have probably tried to come to terms with the impact of the slave trade, but from what the chiefs are reported to have said, the scars are so deep that they cannot easily forget the tragedy," Reverend Peterson interjected.

"Do you think the Africans might try to retaliate against us because of the slave trade?" McSwain asked.

"Well, who knows? That is one of the possibilities," Bubba declared. "I hope I am exaggerating this."

"What do the people of Portugal, Spain, Holland, Britain, France, Belgium and Denmark, the other European countries that conceived and masterminded the slave trade and carried it out so unabashedly for so long, ought to do to calm down the anger of the African people?" McSwain asked.

"Well, what the Yankees from the Northeast, from Delaware, Rhode Island and other Northeastern states that heavily financed and participated in the slave trade did, someone needs to address," McSwain noted, looking at Bubba and the preacher.

"The members of the delegation would contact these people to make atonement for their share in the slave trade." Reverend Peterson told Jim McSwain. "In fact, they must get actively involved. The Portuguese, the country that started this tragic trade, followed by a host of other European countries—those who are still busy trying to hide their guilt from the profane past under some thin veneers of philanthropy, must step up to the table of accountability."

Bubba could only think about innocent Africans crammed in slave boats in a stormy weather. He had dreams about infants that had been shot and killed because they were too young to be enslaved and also about aged men and women who'd been executed because they were too old and weak to be worth anything on the slave market. Then, he heard "the blues". These were the wailings and groaning of the captured victims expressed in sentimental songs. These were youths usually ranging from the ages of thirteen to thirty-five. In his dreams, he saw them still struggling to get out of their shackles, battling their captors hysterically to free themselves from the bondage. These have continued to prick his conscience like a bouquet of thorns.

Bubba could also still smell burning gunpowder in the air from the cannons their ancestors had used against the Africans during the slave trade, shedding oceans of blood. He could hear the roar of these cannons reverberated against the castle walls and echoed through the forests, across the land, crisscrossing the valleys, spreading fear and desperation among the African people.

Bubba hoped that the spirits of the victims would hear the plea of the delegation for forgiveness from the Cape Coast Castle in Ghana. Maybe they would make a stopover on the Gore Island in Senegal to discuss the terms of atonement. He also hoped that the spirits of the departed ancestors, Africans and Europeans, would let go of their anger and sorrow from the past and finally find some eternal rest.

As for those who had died during the slave raids or had perished inside the dungeons or had drowned during the notorious Middle

Passage on their way to the New World, the delegation hoped to ask them humbly to find some solace and rest in peace.

What McSwain and his group were afraid of were a series of potential lawsuits from the descendants of the victims asking for damages. Though the statute of limitation might not support some of these suits, how could his region deal with the several suits that might arise from the descendants of the victims who could claim that their ancestors had been stolen from Africa, brutalized, murdered and forced to work for free over several centuries?

"Would the new DNA evidence prove that there'd been contact between their ancestors in the past and the accused families?" McSwain asked. "It could cause anxious moments for some families that had owned slaves in the past, but that should not intimidate us into making any rush decisions."

Nevertheless, haunted in his dreams, encountering ghosts in his mansions, the conservative Bubba personally wanted the opportunity to be part of the delegation, to pour out his heart, to let the Africans hear the sincerity in his voice, to let them feel his pain and to see the authenticity of the remorse on his face. He wanted to release the guilt, to let go of the heavy burden that he'd personally inherited from his ancestors.

For centuries the Africans had endured. For hundreds of years they had been silent over the pain and for endless years they had refused to demand compensation. That, in itself, was very wrong on our part or from their end. Though the slave trade had receded into historical subconscious mind, the pain still lingers on and the degradation has never ended. He had no doubt in his mind that his ancestors had been wrong in what they did. If they were wrong, it was about time for his generation to do something about this wrong.

Bubba's dream, above everything else, was to stand on the shore of the African slave coast, battling the rays of the blistering tropical sun, enjoying the soothing breeze from the Atlantic Ocean as he read out the terms of atonement on behalf of his ancestors to the African leaders, to the victims, to the new generation of Africans in their efforts to save the future generation from the guilt—from the wrath—of the ancestors. His goal is to free his children, and give his children's children a free, unencumbered future.

SEVENTEEN

T HEY WERE THE VICTIMS OF the slave trade. Their ancestors had been forcibly hauled out of the continent of Africa years ago. They live in the Diaspora, but they have special ties to their roots. They have to make the pilgrimage back to the mother land at least once in their lifetime, if they could afford it. They actually bet on it how much welcome they would get whenever they step on the sacred soil of Africa for the first time.

Many, however, always expect a red-carpet treatment whenever they arrived. Some want to be treated like V.I.P's, maybe some even act as if they expect nothing short of a twenty-one gun salute to announce their visit.

They would be pleased with the warmth. The African governments have gone to great lengths to give these "returnees" as the Africans call them, the warmest of welcomes. Some are given rituals reserved for heads of states and extraordinary celebrities only.

Whatever the Africans give, they never get satisfied. A few complain about certain things. Some even expect the continent to remain "uncultivated" just the way it was when their ancestors were snatched away.

Nevertheless, the Africans have always been glad to see their brothers and sisters return home. They usually give them the warmest of embraces and the friendliest of welcome. They congratulate them for making the journey back home to reunite with their ancestors. The idea of returning to the motherland has been of high appeal to many. They are glad that they have come back to visit Mama Africa, a land they had heard so much, but only dreamed about. The event would go on to become a major hallmark in their lives and a small victory over the ontology of history.

The returnees usually enjoy the warmth of the "akwaba welcome mat." But it is always amazing how their hearts are filled with reservations, concerns and even open resentment for what they've learned from the "white man's history books" about the role the African chiefs had played in the slave trade. How and why their ancestors were sold and ended up in the Diaspora, why they sojourn on the other side of the Atlantic Ocean, do become major concern for them.

"Welcome home. Akwabaa—you are most welcome to the sweet bosom of Mama Africa," they read from the huge signs at the airport.

Jacqueline saw the sign, but her mind was filled with ambivalence, resentment and regret over the past. Her heart was also filled with sorrow, and genuine pain. She was obsessed with only one question: "Did the African chiefs really sell their own people to the white folks for guns and for some cheap rum?"

"I have the same question on my mind," Sherri said with some bitterness as well, as she dragged her tote bag along the route outside the airport, and showed the tattoo of Yaa Asantewa clearly visible on her back.

"And she has the nerve to tell me welcome home. I wonder what the truth is," Jacqueline Dukes asked herself. Though she heard the past was not that simple, she had to say that to calm down the anger burning inside her soul.

Jacqueline knew that the African chiefs had to comply with the demands of the cannon-wielding Oburoni traders, if they wanted to remain free and not become slaves themselves. She also knew that the Africans never invited the Oburoni over to their shores to buy any slaves. She agreed that these Oburoni aliens just showed up one morning with guns in hand, greed in their hearts and armed with their coldhearted consciences and started abducting the African youths, impressing them into slavery.

To the likes of Jacqueline, some Africans have even gone to the extent of rendering private apologies to their blood relatives. To most of the returnees, they'd apologize for what happened to their ancestors in the past. Others, who heard the truth from the griot, quickly learned that the past was not only complicated, but also very difficult for our African ancestors. And it was because the kings and chiefs of the area, their African forebears, couldn't withstand the firepower of the cannons the Oburoni people used during the slave trade, though the fight was on African shores.

The rumor, more or less propaganda, the returnees have ingrained in them has been how the Africans hate their brothers and sisters who live in the Diaspora, especially the returnees. This is simply a fabrication designed to separate people of the same bloodline that had been divided by the wheels of history.

In fact, some governments on the so-called West African Slave Coast have gone out of their way to ease up visa restrictions to make it easier for the Africans who live in the Diaspora to return home easily or to visit the motherland. Some of the returnees have made Africa their permanent residence, or some even have the paths to citizenship made easier for them. The idea is to facilitate their return home. That is if they themselves decide to return to their continent of origin for any reason, but the choice is strictly theirs—no compulsion and no coercion.

The irony is that within the last decade, several have quietly and successfully returned to visit the continent. Many have actually resettled their families in the land they still passionately call "the motherland". No one can really tell how many have done so, but many have quietly returned to live on the African continent.

With the debate over atonement still raging on at home and abroad like bamboo fire, the African people have continued to apologize to their kinsfolk for the role their ancestors played in the slave trade, That is even though a more critical analysis now reveals that the masterminds behind the slave trade were not the African leaders. Secondly, that the slave trade did not rise out of the needs of Africa, but from the labor needs, but more importantly, from the greed of the Oburoni people.

"Why should we feel guilty about anything?" the chief asked the linguist. "It was the fault of the Europeans. It was their ancestors that brought this form of slave trade to the continent. What they brought with them was so different from the domestic awoba slavery in which you used your daughter as collateral to borrow money from a richer person. When you paid the loan back, then your daughter returned home to you safely, all happening in the same village, and it was without the brutalities."

"What they brought in their trail was not a trade, it was an abomination," Elder Buamah told the chief. "It was a greedy Oburoni plot to live off the blood and flesh of their fellow human beings. I wonder why the God of love they speak so fervently of in their faith did not caution them that trading in human flesh and blood was an immoral thing."

The past brought thousands from the Diaspora, the likes of Jacqueline from the Diaspora for the Panfest. Some came from Europe and from other African countries. The assortment of people all over the globe descended on Cape Coast in droves. They came by the planeloads, truckloads, and by car for the festival. They came with the intention of searching for their identity. So, they came with several questions, and wanted some solid answers.

Many come to the Panfest to join their souls with that of the ancestors. Thus, the thousands who come to the Panfest spend a lot of time visiting the notorious legacies of the slave trade on the African shores. They ask several pertinent questions about what really transpired during the profane past. Most importantly, however, many, if not most, simply want a spiritual connection with the part of them which has been lost under the wheels of history.

They drink the water from the well, from the fountain of life and taste the milk of Mama Africa. They look at the rising sun as a new gift of life, a new beginning for the rest of their remaining years. They regard the connection as a blessing, indeed, a fulfillment of deeper spiritual needs, of all that had been missing in all their years in the Diaspora.

Zakiya Homers went to Mankessim, a small village about ten miles from Cape Coast Castle, where she thought her ancestors originated. The twenty-six year old lady, the identity seeking freak, went to experience spiritual satisfaction with a villager just to merge her soul with her bloodline.

She did what she did in order to fulfill some deep psychological yearnings she thought she needed.

The returnees endlessly crisscrossed the dungeons of the Cape Coast Castle and frequented the door of no return, meditative and reflective on all occasions. Most of them captured every detail of the tour. They retraced their steps from the dungeons below to the notorious and legendary door of no return, which led to the boats on the shore. Wherever they traced it from, many of them admitted that they'd felt the presence of the ancestors, an experience no amount of money could buy, they agreed.

"No question that the thickness of the walls of the slave castles speaks volumes as to what really happened on the African shores during the infamous slave trade," Jacqueline told herself. "If the Africans sold their brothers and sisters willingly, I mean without any pressure from the European slave traders, then why did the slave traders need so many castles and with so many fortified walls?"

The castles and their thick walls revealed the truth of what actually happened in the past to them.

Jacqueline found out that a lot of what she had read was completely the direct opposite of what actually happened. She agreed that the Africans did not gladly sell their kinsfolk to the Europeans. She agreed that it was the insatiable greed of the Europeans that was behind the slave trade. And she agreed that the slave trade was not because of any pressing needs of the African people. She also saw the rusty cannons sitting next to the chapel, and the guns that were facing the pirates who came from the ocean to steal "the stolen loot" of the Oburonis. And she saw those cannons facing the inhabitants on the other side, which were ready to take down the African Asafo soldiers whenever they charged at the castle.

As for their African hosts, they were not too enthusiastic about explaining the past to the returnees. They were very reticent because they felt that the visitors should discover the truth and find out the reality of the past for themselves.

"What happened on these shores ages ago was something even the gods could not adequately explain to anyone," the griots finally told Jacqueline. "It was as if the Oburonis held the heads of our ancestors, the way you hold the head of a cobra—incapacitated completely—then they looted, abducted and destroyed them."

King Zendo stood on the beach looking at the majestic Cape Coast Castle. "I don't care how majestic the structure was meant to be, but for me, it has always been an eyesore on this pristine beach. It is obstructing the beauty of the deep blue sky, but most importantly, it reminds us of the shame of the past, a symbol of man's cruelty to his fellow man."

"Speak to us King Zendo!" Dokuwa shouted loudly interrupting the king. "You couldn't have described the ordeal better."

"Well, if you listen carefully, you can still hear the silent voices of the departed from the dungeons beneath the castle," he said. He shook his head and stumped his feet on the ground angrily as he remembered the millions of people who died during the shameful commercial nightmare the Oburonis had masterminded.

King Zendo knew that his ancestors, in the interest of self-preservation, had been forced to betray their people. Many had to exchange prisoners of war for European guns and muskets, if they wanted to defend their families, villages and kingdoms and live in freedom. "Our ancestors could not withstand the relentless pressure to sell slaves in exchange for guns. Some chiefs gave in to the pressure, because that was the only way for them to remain free," King Zendo told the visitors at the Panfest Festival at Victoria Park in Cape Coast, Ghana. "They'd pushed our ancestors backs against the walls with their cannons and with bayonets."

"But why didn't our ancestors fight back more than what they did?" Jim Jacobs, a visitor from Jamaica, asked, bluntly. "This is our land, why didn't our folks fight to death, I mean till the very last person dropped dead?"

"They'd the latest guns. Our chiefs had very little firepower, in fact, they had only the inferior Danish muskets the Danes, the British or the Dutch were willing to exchange for slaves. So they had no choice but to comply with their demands, or become victims of genocide," King Zendo said disconcerted. "Their greed knew no moral boundaries during the slave trade; they would have gladly wiped our people off the surface of the earth."

"The fact still remains that some of the chiefs cooperated with these Oburonis to round up our ancestors," Jim Jacobs continued, his voice much more sentimental and his mood was more restless.

"Well, the European slave traders manipulated our people, fanned several inter-group differences, started warfare among the groups mainly to get the prisoners of war they needed as cargoes to haul to the New World to work on sugarcane, cotton and tobacco fields. They'd created a fierce power struggle that set one African group against the other, a chief against a king and an elder against a chief. They manipulated our ancestors into trading their own people into slavery," the king told the gathering. "If you refused to exchange your prisoners of war for guns, you became vulnerable to the slave traders and your neighbors were sent to attack you."

"Weren't some criminals sold as slaves?" Jim Jacobs asked without mincing words.

"Yes, but only very few suffered that fate. The number was less than one out of every ten thousand," the king explained. "We are talking about cases involving murder or treason. And of course, if you slept with the king's wife, he sent you on the longest of journeys . . . the severest of penalties—a journey to the land of no return."

"What kind of serious crimes are we talking about?" he asked, anxiously.

"Africans who committed murder or became traitors to the cause, and those criminals that faced execution were sent into slavery, maybe to give them a second chance," King Zendo emphasized. "The chiefs did not enjoy selling their own to the slave traders. They did so in order to get weapons to defend their kingdoms and their families from the slave raiders."

"Well, the king is right," the linguist said, drinking the last bit of palm wine in his calabash. "It was a case of the survival of the fittest—those with weapons survived the chaos."

"You either got the Oburonis the quota of slaves they wanted for their guns or they withheld their weapons and left your kingdom a weak target for your neighbors," Mankrado asserted, playing with the old rusty rifle. "You were prone to attack and enslavement. It was an era of a European-created gun politics."

"These European traders were too greedy," the king said. "It was like the more slaves they got from the chiefs, the more they demanded from them the next time around.

"Well, their greed was deeper than the bottom of the Atlantic Ocean," the linguist joked.

"How our ancestors managed to survive the slave trade to this day is still a mystery," Jim Jacobs reflected. "I am just wondering how they managed to . . . if the Oburonis were so insatiable, and yet so powerful, how did they manage to remain alive?"

"Well, my son, those were the dark, horrible days. Indeed, those were the bitter days of agony, days of difficult dilemmas, and there were plenty of shame to go around," King Zendo pointed out. "It was a long struggle for survival. It was one obstacle after the other, one confrontation after the next," He pointed to the labyrinth of secret dungeons beneath the Cape Coast Castle.

"How could the Oburonis do this to our ancestors, people in their own land?" Zakiya asked angrily. Maybe it was simply a misfortune or a wicked, twisted fate."

"Why the gods let this abomination come to pass in the land, nobody knows," Jim Jacobs lamented, straightening up the new kente cloth he wore for the first time. "I still don't know why Jah allowed his people to meet such a cruel fate."

"What really took place on these shores had been incredible," Zakiya moaned. "It is like half the story has not yet been told to those of us who live in the Diaspora—the opposition of the chiefs to the slave trade—the chiefs' struggle for self-preservation."

"My son, we feel exactly what you feel right now," the queen mother moaned sadly. She moved restlessly in her chair as she wiped her eyes gently with a brown handkerchief. "If you didn't do anything to protect your people, you quickly ended up as slaves, and if you did, you more than likely betrayed your people."

"The suffering of our ancestors in the cotton fields or on the sugarcane plantations on the other side of the Atlantic Ocean had been more gruesome," Jim Jacobs declared before the elders. "You know nothing about plantation slavery, picking cotton, tending tobacco or harvesting sugarcane." He held out a bottle of rum, the product of molasses.

"The Oburoni said very little about what happened to the slaves after they'd left our shores," the linguist told Jim Jacobs. "They only talked about civilizing and converting them."

"Are you bitter toward the Oburoni slave traders from Europe and their allies from America?" Jim Jacobs asked pointedly.

"There is peace and quiet now, that is centuries after the tragedy. But there was nothing peaceful and quiet during those chaotic and hectic days of slave raids, abductions and torture in the dungeons, and the malicious fate of the victims. It was a struggle for survival and a fight for self-preservation for everyone," the king explained.

"I just don't wish this on anyone anywhere, and not at any time," the linguist watched the priest burned some incense.

"Obviously, it was a contest between iniquity and innocence, insatiability and self-preservation," Jim Jacobs said and took a few steps toward the beach, looked at the ocean and turned around.

"Even the African ancestors," the linguist chewed the kola nut angrily, "did not protect our people against the invaders. They did nothing to stop the greed. Instead, they let them have their way and they took advantage of my people."

"Were the African chiefs cowards during the slave trade?" Jim Jacobs asked.

"No, it was a race for survival . . . self-preservation . . . not a lot of open offensive?" Mankrado got him some palm wine and sat down to enjoy it.

"Our ancestors were anything but cowards. How much could they do in the face of the cannons the Oburonis freely used to mow them down like grasses?" the king remarked.

"It was a pity they were outgunned and overwhelmed," Jim Jacob said.

"The Oburoni traders and their agents destroyed any chief who refused to participate in the slave trade," Linguist Ohene told the crowd.

"They quickly supplied the enemies of those chiefs with the necessary weapons and encouraged them to go after them, or remove any leader who had the courage to oppose the slave trade from power," Mankrado heaved a deep sigh.

Though the king didn't want to go down memory lane, he opened up about his family too. "Some of my family members became victims in this vicious cycle of slaves for guns," the king remarked. "It wasn't as if the chiefs folded their arms or sat down idly like cowards and watched the slave traders to have their way. In fact, they tried their best to disrupt, to ambush and even to fight off the slave dealers, but because of the cannons, the Oburonis had the upper hand in most of the battles."

"Well, except during guerilla assaults, our ancestor's efforts were almost always not successful," he said.

"My great grandfather was one of the chiefs who was removed from power and was taken into slavery for not cooperating with the Europeans during the slave trade," the linguist said. "He refused to allow any more slaves from his village to end up in the land of no return in exchange for guns. So the Oburonis removed him from power, enslaved him and made an example of him for the other chiefs."

"That was the event the griot sang about earlier on, the tragedy in his family history," the king reminded Jim Jacobs, as he sat down.

"I remember he came close to him, rang the small bell next to his ears and sang the history into his ears," he said excitedly. "I did not know what that was all about, but I just saw that his head was swollen with pride."

"Since we could not write down the history, the griot recorded these heroic acts in songs, proverbs and adages for posterity. The chiefs were confronted with such a difficult dilemma, but nobody had the ability to record their heroism or ordeal in any history books," Nana Kamkam da Costa said. "It was like a bag of porcupine for them; you were damned if you put it on and doomed if you didn't."

"My grandfather refused to betray his subjects, so he closed the slave trade routes that passed through his kingdom. He did so on more than a dozen occasions," the linguist recalled. "The British governor at the Cape Coast Castle finally got so angry that he ordered his arrest. Why the history books have been silent on the roles of such opposing African chiefs, no one really knows."

"Their books are like propaganda to cover up their guilt . . . they had to be a self-righteous group of people in their accounts," Jim Jacobs said. "Then they tried to clean up the greed and brutality out of the history."

"Well, the chief was supposed to be a traitor if he traded his people as slaves to the European people for guns, but then the Oburonis used their stooges to remove him from power, if he failed to trade the slaves in to them," the chief said.

"It was a horrible dilemma. It was indeed an era of shame and centuries of difficult dilemmas for all the African leaders," the king sat on his mahogany stool.

"As the ordeal unfolded, the Oburoni traders drank heavily to contain their guilt," the linguist revealed.

"I heard they drank gallons of rum each night to mask their guilt," Jim Jacob said angrily, staring at the Portuguese chapel in front of him. "And they drowned their conscience in oceans of booze, maybe after they'd prayed over their iniquities."

"They were either chasing after the females in the dungeons, holding one of those endless drinking parties just to avoid the pangs of homesickness, or trying to combat the fear of dying from malaria or the slave raids," the king said.

"Obviously, the Africans did not just sell their own. The Europeans say that to avoid the guilt and shift it to the African leaders, reality that was too embarrassing for their conscience to bear," Jim Jacobs sympathized with the African chiefs.

"Well, we have very little guilt because our ancestors fought gallantly against the European intruders who showed up uninvited and started fomenting trouble," King Zendo said irritated.

"What a shameful chapter they'd created in our history?" the linguist lit his pipe.

"Well, every African lowers the head in shame whenever this subject comes up," Kamkam da Costa remarked. "This is the part of our history that we prefer not to talk about, because it is not only very embarrassing to us, but also stirs lots of bitter memories."

"You speak for everybody, Africa could never forget how chaotic things were in those days," Linguist Ohene moaned, clearly unhappy about the past. "You didn't hear anyone talking about how their grandparents were comfortable during the slave raids. They usually talked about their quest for survival and the guerrilla plots they came out with to sabotage the efforts of the slave raiders in those fateful years."

"What I have heard from you has been enlightening," Jim Jacob nodded, surprised and concerned. "My heart is somehow relieved; I can even forgive the chiefs for the role they played, though not completely."

"Just look at what the Oburoni Christian people did and draw your own conclusions," the king reminded him, holding his staff in his right hand.

"Well, you have heard the reality," Kamkam Da Costa, the historian asserted. "The slave traders and the gun dealers refused to accept even gold for their guns. They wanted nothing but slaves, human flesh and blood for these guns. Our ancestors who wanted the guns to protect their families, their villages, their groups and even their kingdoms, had no option but to procure the slaves and exchange them for the guns, not unless they wanted to end up as slaves themselves!"

"Why don't you ever tell your side of the history to the outside world?" Jacqueline asked, making several notes in her red notebook. "Why have these facts been suppressed in the history books?"

"Many Africans know the truth. Our grandfathers and great-grandfathers did not sell their own. They did so to survive, though this fact is still troubling to many of us," Kamkam said. "It is hard to admit that the African chiefs gave in to the pressure from the European slave dealers and their agents to sell their own for guns. But many did so at the threat of bodily harm or the loss of their own freedom or the overwhelming need for weapons to defend their families."

"No matter how much coercion took place, we must admit that our ancestors played a role in the forcible exodus of over forty million of our own out of the continent to the New World," the linguist reported. "That is something that we cannot change."

"But our ancestors had their backs pushed against the walls, and they had guns pointed at their heads," Mankrado explained quickly, listening to the fontomfrom drumbeat.

"Many Africans are still not willing to talk about the tragedy because it stirs such deep emotions within them," King Zendo said as he suddenly became emotional and asked for more "akpeteshie" or the home brew corn whiskey.

"One thing is clear, even the African children know that the traders used their big cannons," Linguist Ohene said quickly. "The remnants of these cannons, though rusty and idle for centuries, are still stockpiled in front of the Cape Coast Castle and scattered around other castles in Ghana, Togo, Benin, Cameroon, Nigeria and several countries in Upper Guinea region, Mali, Senegal, Gambia, Sierra Leone and the Ivory Coast, to mention just some of them. And these cannons killed over fifty people or more with every single discharge. This happened whenever the Africans charged angrily at these slave castles along the coast."

"We find it very difficult to accept, let alone defend all what our ancestors did in the past," the queen mother said. "But some of these things they did just to survive the Oburoni onslaught. These European Oburonis were like pests that refused to go away, sucking the sap out of the continent."

"Every griot tells the youths about what really happened during the slave trade era. But they only do so after drinking some palm wine, or akpeteshie moonshine whiskey," interjected Lady Salo Lagoke, the queen from Ogbomosho. "Well, after a few calabashes of palm wine, the griot gets the courage to loosen his tongue to tell the children the bitter truth. They are then able to reveal the difficult dilemma our ancestors faced and then point out it was all self-preservation."

"This was an era of human injustice, of terrible feeling," Jim Jacobs said.

"Well, in one sense, we have this collective guilt that our ancestors had let our people down at the time when they needed to protect them most. In another sense, they did what they had to do to avoid a complete genocide in order to protect their families, villages or even their empires in order to pass these on to their children, and to the next generation, to the perennial progeny of the African continent."

Then it happened that in those days our ancestors had a very narrow view of what constituted group society. So, it was easy for the Europeans to pitch Ibos against Yorubas, or even Yorubas against Yorubas in a bitter civil war, or Fons against Anechos, Krobos against Gas, Ewes against Akwamus, Mandinkas against Wolofs and Akyem against Asantes. These groups thought of other groups as aliens who had to be feared and subjugated; otherwise, they might defeat and force the weaker groups into slavery.

"Our people, by these inter or intra group rivalries, played directly into the hands of the Oburoni slave traders. This allowed the traders to pick our ancestors by the millions and shipped them off to the land of no return," Chief Zendo confessed sadly.

"We need to blame the European Oburonis for the terrible calamities of the continent today," Elder Amina said, straightening up her headgear more firmly. "I wished these Oburoni aliens had never landed on our shores, let alone introduced this brand of slave trade to our land. This was a vicious cycle of guns for slaves, bloody slave raids, man stealing and going to war to subjugate one's neighbors, or even going against one's bloodline for prisoners, a practice which brought so much havoc and pain in the land."

"Women could not even go to fetch water or get foodstuff from the farms to cook for their children, it was a time of shame," the queen mother lamented. "The women could not give birth to the children fast enough for the Europeans to abduct and carry away to the land of no return."

"Another complicated mix was how they used their religion to soften our people to give them more slaves?" the chief remarked. "Why did their God allow that?"

"Maybe the use of their religion to facilitate the slave trade was the lowest these slave traders had stooped to get the labor force they needed," Jim Jacobs declared. "How in the world did Jah allow these Oburonis to use his name to brutalize the African people?"

"Well, many people have believed what the slave traders had told the world. Their scholars have sanitized the accounts, minimized their guilt and exaggerated the role the African chiefs played in the transactions. They have blamed the trade on the chiefs," King Zendo regretted.

"Some day, however, they would begin to accept responsibility and accountability for the slave trade. They would finally agree that they were wrong," Mankrado said.

"I think when this happened, they would trace their way back to our shores to make atonement for the past," the queen mother breathed heavily, tears in her eyes.

Meanwhile, the African people, must continue to cope with these lingering feelings of anger, frustration and guilt from the slave trade past, a mixture of feelings that never go away even to today.

When you weigh the predicament, the abductions, slave raids, pain and suffering from the uninvited guests from Europe, one would learn to temper criticism of the role the African chiefs played in the trade with some sort of mercy or understanding. Who can forget the old African proverb, which says that the one who has inflicted a wound on another person easily forgets the tragedy, but the victim does not forget because the scar serves as a constant reminder of that wound.

Where was their morality when they shot and killed thousands of Africans who invaded the castles to rescue and reclaim dozens of elders or chiefs who had been abducted from the forests and housed in these dungeons? What of all the blood they shed on the green savannah grasses or splattered on the white pristine beaches, or how they blasted their victims with cannons in the tropical virgin forests?

For a people who love to talk about morality, who love to show their zeal to plant the seeds of the gospel in Africa, these Europeans fell shamefully short of the same principles that they were trying to plant among the so-called heathens.

Don Pedro, the most notorious slave dealer in the history of the slave trade waited for the setting sun to hide some of the miseries of the slaves in the dungeons below the slave castle. Not only did it increase the level of drunkenness among the slave traders and government officials. Don Pedro, the most dreaded slave trader that ever stepped on the shores of Africa, must have his favorite entertainment—nearly three gallons of rum each day. He had to do so, just to stay sane and free from the unbridled feelings of guilt that he felt. He had to numb his conscience, program himself not to feel any compassion toward his victims.

"We have to go on the next raid," he told Fred Slowball, chewing some tobacco furiously, as he marched his victims on the slave rout through the forest toward the coast. "We need to get the cargo for the next shipment in a matter of days; we couldn't wait for weeks and certainly not for months."

"Well, what's the rush, we need some rest anyway." Benson told him.

"We need to hurry up and get the cargo, so that we can get the hell out of this malaria infested coast," Don Pedro told Fred Slowball.

Because they felt the trade winds had changed, the crew must leave immediately or encounter deadly storms and hurricane force gales on the journey to the New World. The possibility of delay angered Don Pedro, so he decided to take his dissatisfaction for the next two nights on two African slave women he'd forcibly removed from the dungeons. He went against standing orders, which did not allow him to take slave women to the sleeping quarters, but he'd washed them clean in the courtyard and got them ready for sexual activity. That was the nightmare that the female slaves dreaded most.

Five other slave dealers followed his example those nights.

Though he pretended that he did not have any qualms about buying and selling Africans, he needed all that rum to numb the heavy guilt he had within his conscience. If he was not heavily drank, he had sleepless nights during which he often saw ghosts chasing him in his sleep.

Though he was passionless, he was afraid of dying. He dreaded the pandemic malaria on the African Coast. The mosquito bites on his arms and face made him very frightened. He was secretly afraid of dying. He realized that those bites might turn out to be his doom. They might give him malaria. So he'd been drinking heavily to get his mind off this particular threat.

He had an earlier experience two weeks into his sojourn on the African Coast. So he was only sober long enough to go to baptize the slaves before he shipped them out to the land of no return. It was not a religious ritual; it was rather, for lack of better expression, a sacrament intended to enslave souls for their maker. The souls they claimed they saved, indeed, they'd enslaved. And those they claimed they civilized, they'd abused. Such was the miserable plight of the inhabitants of this unfortunate continent.

Their scholars still try to justify the slave trade as a humanitarian mission—to spread civilization to an unfortunate group of people—while masking their ethical decadence, and their conflicted conscience.

We may jump to hasty conclusions that the Africans had practiced slavery long before the Europeans arrived. We may subscribe erroneously to the idea that the Europeans did not teach Africans anything they did not already know. It is obvious that these arguments are meant to ease the conscience of a troubled European and American group of traders and their descendants. But the harsh truth is that the Africans practiced a benign form of slavery, "awoba system" based on maids and house servant relationship, and this was what prevailed before the Europeans brought the brutal commercial enterprise of man stealing and hauling of slaves in droves to the New World.

Today, many people are still demanding answers and accountability for this sordid past. The forceful arguments of civilizing and humanizing the Africans might help alleviate, if not purge, some of the heavy burden of guilt in the conscience of the descendants of the European and American slave traders, but they must return to deal with the horrible crimes their ancestors had committed . . .

The domestic slavery Africans practiced in the villages and in the kingdoms before the Europeans arrived was not the brutal type that they'd brought on their heels. How can the benign African domestic slavery be compared to the brutalities the slaves suffered during the raids, in the dungeons, during the Middle Passage and on the plantations in Mississippi, Tennessee, Virginia, Alabama, Jamaica and in Brazil?

Is it not a distortion of history to say that because the Africans practiced some sort of benign domestic slavery before the Europeans arrived and introduced the trans-Atlantic slave trade that the Africans ought to bear the primary responsibility for a slave trade during which the Africans received no tangible benefits.

To these Oburoni aliens, their victims were faceless, nameless. They were just numbers. They represented only money, and a labor force.

EIGHTEEN

F ROM THE BALCONY OF HIS palace, King Gizenga stared pensively
into the amber glow of the sunset. The sun had dipped itself,
extinguished its blistering rays as it marched into the darkness. The
king was still civil to the Oburoni visitors even though they had defied
his orders not to photograph any naked African fishermen and women
for adverse publicity when they returned home. He was not against
forgiveness, but he just could not continue to ignore the dark deeds
from the profane past?

In the countries along the former African Slave Coast, the people
continued to struggle for medicine for the ailing, to feed the hungry,
to build school buildings for the children that were attending school
under trees, and to recover from the lingering catastrophic blows from
the slave trade—the chaos, the brutalities and the depopulation. The
harder the leaders tried to recover from the long, protracted ordeal, the
more they discovered the depth of the negative forces that the slave
traders had left behind. But the king knew that they as the leaders they
just had to do their best to lift their kingdoms from the ashes of the
past calamity.

The most difficult part was telling the youths about how their
ancestors were forced to collaborate with the slave traders, to help

find the slave cargoes for the Europeans to haul away in their caravel boats. This was not only a very difficult conversation; it was also a very shameful and degrading subject.

Our ancestors, led by the kings and the chiefs, had spent their lives evading the slave traders, fighting against the Oburoni encroachment on the land, on their villages and on their empires just to capture the slave cargoes they so badly needed.

Then looking back on the scenes, the king wondered why several of the leaders that opposed the traders vehemently and gallantly had been left out of the historical accounts. No one hears anything about the opposition of the chiefs and their gallant efforts at self-preservation.

"Tell the young people about the inability of our ancestors to shake off the plague, to get rid of the European pests in the land," the queen mother told the griot.

"In those days of shame, the Oburonis pushed the backs of our ancestors against the walls. They pointed their guns at their heads and demanded slaves. They were the victims of European and American yearning to exchange slaves for guns and rum. These slave dealers were ruthless, but the leaders remember them more for their insatiable appetite for slaves. It seemed as if they were dying to take the youths to the land of no return, so they worked around the clock to round up their cargoes," the griot explained.

"But why did they write in their books that our leaders sold their people to them?" Ofori Cooma demanded to know.

"That is not the whole truth," the griot responded. "They forced these leaders to sell their own, because if they refused to do so, the slave traders simply turned on the chiefs and the elders and enslaved them soon afterwards, if not immediately."

"So, they didn't give them much of a choice?" Ofori Cooma said, chuckling and shaking his head.

"Huh" the griot said, after a deep sigh and a short pause. "It was a difficult dilemma for the African leaders—the bitterness of betrayal or the shame of enslavement. This was such a sad era for our ancestors."

The charge that Africans sold their own people into slavery, probably one of the most controversial issues in African or African-American histories has not gone away. For anyone to make the charge without critically examining the circumstances under which the African ancestors participated in the selling of their own people is to be very naïve, unfair and essentially amateurish.

The European scholars can continue the propaganda that the African leaders were itching to get rid of their kinfolks, but the truth is that the Africans had never invited the Oburonis to the continent to trade in slaves or to buy their blood relatives. The slave trade rose from the labor needs of Europe and from their economic dreams and aspirations in the New World—plantation laborers—led to the ugly drama of slave trading, fueled by the intense greed they brought with them. The truth is that the African leaders had never been the primary culprits in the slave trade, and they did not mastermind this trade, the greatest tragedy in human history.

Our African ancestors were reacting to the critical labor demands the heavily armed European traders demanded from them. It wasn't as if they had to sell slaves because of any particular need or needs of the African people at the time. The African leaders were merely reacting to the powerful guns that these heavily armed Oburoni traders, missionaries and government officials, had unleashed on the continent, particularly on the so-called West African Slave Coast.

"It was like a bag of porcupine for the chiefs. To hang it around your side is painful and not to hang it around your side is also not self-preserving," as the African griot aptly described the sort of role our ancestors played by using this old African proverb.

Our ancestors resisted the pressure to provide the slaves for years, but when the Oburonis confronted them with death and destruction, that was if they refused to sell the slaves to them, they chose the path of self-preservation. It was only when they wanted to stay alive, or to survive in the deadly power game of exchanging guns for slaves that the European and American Oburoni slave traders made them to reluctantly participate in the trade.

The Africans had witnessed the abduction of their people, had seen their loved ones disappeared and had seen their leaders deposed from power, or even gunned down in cold blood in the tropical heat. These traders abducted these victims and hauled them away in their slave boats, and the practice started even before any African participated in the slave trade.

The shame of it was, of course, these Oburonis who bragged about being moral people, hid in the bushes around the slave castles and secretly abducted the African people, dragging them away kicking and screaming, then warehousing them in the dungeons for long periods, and then hauling them out of the continent in droves, doing so under the cover of darkness—as if the slaves were not human and were destined to only serve their needs.

The earliest victims had been the people who lived along the coastal regions. Never had they seen such tragic cases of human stealing before, so when they became aware and resisted the dragnets of the slave traders, the Oburonis shifted their attention to the hinterland, into the forests, into the river beds and beyond the grasslands to find their victims. When those victims were still not sufficient, they organized the notorious slave raids into the hinterland. They did so with the help of dozens of African traitors, renegades who had axes to grind against the leaders of their communities.

The slave trade, the bloodshed, the intrusions and the raids were like a sweltering Harmattan heat, which overwhelmed the continent and burned everything it came into contact with. The blow was so demoralizing that Africa had not recovered from it for centuries, and is still battling the lingering effects even to today. The land was devastated, the people were hurt and the means of agricultural production became sluggish. The continent has essentially remained the same in many places even to today.

In addition to the insecurity and the psychological fear of death, the disruption in the continent's agriculture and the disappearance of the cream of the labor force from the land, had been crippling blows to this once a very proud continent. The constant removal of the youths did a lot of damage to the labor force. The goal was to get the entire Slave coast to supply their labor needs, so any leaders who stood in the way, whether it was in Calabar, Abeokuta, Whydah, Senegambia, Anecho, Wolof, Keta, Ho or Sokoto, the Oburonis quickly mowed down these rebel leaders with their cannons as if they were tall elephant grasses.

How did the Africans deal with an alien religion planted to soften their hearts and to facilitate the slave trade? Those who were converted quickly lived in a web of confusion as the same missionaries who tried to save their souls also wore the hats of slave dealers.

The converts could sing some hymns, recite passages, tasted some of the sacraments, and mastered the rudiments of the religion, after a while. Unfortunately, however, when there was an acute need for slave cargo, hell broke loose and the converts became targets and some ended as slaves in the land of no return.

On the other hand, the Oburonis fanned the flames of inter-group wars among the African people along the Slave Coast. Then they waited anxiously on the sideline for the prisoners of war. In the end, they had left not only a continent devastated but also an indelible distrust between the Oburonis and the African people.

The records left at the slave castles, long after the departure of these Europeans, indicate that the African Slave Coast was inundated with guns and cannons. The Africans knew that the Oburonis brought in a steady supply of guns, which included heavy cannons to crush any resistance from the chiefs and the elders, but the leaders did not know that they brought in several millions of guns each year and repeated this for many centuries.

Though it was not easy to convince all the chiefs, the other leaders and King Gizenga to send emissaries to the United States to apologize for the role their ancestors played or were forced to play in the ugly European slave trade to Africa, it was more out of respect for tradition rather than any compelling feelings of guilt. They did not do so because the Africans conceived the idea or that they needed to start the trade to fulfill a particular need on the continent, but they did so because their ancestors were forced to participate in the trade for reasons of self-preservation. How could you rest in peace when you knew that the Europeans forced your ancestors to trade slaves for guns or face enslavement themselves, or were even confronted with death?

So, that was why they succumbed to the Oburoni threats?

King Gizenga rose to his feet and made a passionate appeal to the gathering. "For the role our ancestors played during the slave trade era, my brothers and sisters, we have sent emissaries to our blood relatives, those who live in the Diaspora to offer apologies on behalf of the African continent and to make ritual atonement to the ancestors," the king told the Panfest audience. "Though most of the actions our ancestors took in the past were acts of self-preservation."

"Why do we need to apologize to our own blood relatives in the Diaspora?" the queen mother pulled her eye brows in disgust. "I don't understand why we have to do that. I need to know why that is necessary."

"Well, though we don't really have to apologize to our own for the past, we have agreed to do so simply because we want to appease the gods and ease our conscience in the process," Togbe Kwasiga Abliza, the tall seven foot paramount chief said bluntly, as he stood like a monument of hope in front of the thousands of visitors to the Panfest at Victoria Park, in Cape Coast, Ghana.

"You are okay with us," Natakyi, the sister from Ackerman in Northern Mississippi, shouted. "We understand that your ancestors had to do what they did to survive the carnage the Oburoni folks brought to the motherland."

The audience nodded and agreed with the chief's proposition and the comments from Sister Natakyi. But the king's oldest daughter did not endorse the idea of sending people to America to offer apologies to our own blood relatives . . . but, she did not want to be openly disrespectful to her father, the king, especially not when there were visitors from overseas and from the neighboring African countries at the festival.

"Why do we need to slaughter cows, pour libation with both palm wine and Kantamanto Dry Gin and ask for forgiveness for something that the Oburonis had forced upon our ancestors?" Princess Samiah asked the king. "Tell me why we need to apologize for the slave trade, instead of asking the Oburonis to apologize to us and follow the apology with atonement?"

"You have a very valid point, Sister Samia," Kamkam, the historian, said. "On the other hand, history does not follow the path of logic. Whether our leaders were forced into the trade in the past or the Europeans created a predatory "dog eat dog environment" that forced them to act in self-defense and took some of these actions against their better judgment, just to survive the exigencies of the time, the fact still remains that our ancestors participated in the "separation of our bloodline" and they'd contributed directly or indirectly to the hauling away and the scattering of the sons and daughters of Mama Africa across the globe, with millions ending up in the American Diaspora."

"It was the greed and "the sweet tooth" syndrome of these Europeans, which propelled them to bring the trans-Atlantic slave trade to our shores," the princess said. "It was their love of leisure, their laziness and their sweet palate for sugar, which propelled them to come up with the idea of the trans-Atlantic slave trade."

"It was all because of the raw greed in their hearts. That was the key to the slave trade," Kamkam pulled his eyebrows and winked at Samia. "They exploited our miseries to become wealthy, and they ruined the Africans as a people in this sinister quest."

Some of the women hated the idea of apology. "When the Oburonis arrived on our shores, of course, they came uninvited. They came to brutalize our ancestors, why then should we the descendants of the same victims of their greed, who are still experiencing the effects of this onslaught on our lands today, turn around and ask for forgiveness from our kinsfolk in the Diaspora?" Samia, the princess, continued to make her point. And she did so much more aggressively this time around.

"She is right. The whole thing does not make any sense to some of us," Dokuwa, the female leader exploded, wielding a cutlass in the air. "Their scholars have never remembered how hard our ancestors fought against the invasion of their Oburoni ancestors, the slave traders, in their accounts."

"No one can say that the Oburonis did not start the slave trade. They conceived the idea, brought the guns and conducted the slave trade on our shores," the queen mother said.

"Why do we have to send our chiefs to America to slaughter cows and ask for forgiveness in New York or in Washington D. C," Samiah asked. "By doing this, we are accepting the lion's share of the blame for the slave trade; because, this was something their ancestors brought to our shores, and violated our people. We must never accept the lion's share of the blame."

"You are a strong lady and you have driven home your point with zeal and conviction. You drive a hard bargain indeed," Kamkam broke into a hearty laughter. "You are a born leader with royal blood in your veins."

"I have followed the slave trade keenly, and I have not seen how our folks are guilty of anything, except their efforts to survive the chaos. But sending our leaders to the Americas to apologize to our own sounds ridiculous to me," she sat down dejected as the debate played through her mind for hours.

At the festival, the returnees were filled with ambivalence. Their faces were lit with sorrow as they began to view the legacies of the European slave trade, the degradation these traders had caused in the motherland.

"No more apologies from us to anybody anywhere, home or abroad. It is the descendants of the European culprits who must return to our shores to make atonement," the queen mother kept her hands on her hips repeating.

"They must make atonement for "the mfecane" they'd unleashed in the land. And they must do so immediately if they want to avoid the wrath of the ancestors," Dokuwa warned.

"If they think that the few churches and schools that their ancestors had set up after the slave trade have softened our sorrow and pain they'd inflicted on our ancestors, then they'd better think again," King Gizenga said. "In fact, the agony, the distrust and the trauma, especially the destruction of our self-esteem have continued even to today."

"You are absolutely right," Linguist Gorka said. "Well, no number of apologies to the people of Africa would calm down the angry ancestors. Only time could heal the wounds and calm them down."

"Well, the damage they'd done to our civilization, the bloodshed, the loss of population and the psychological insecurity they'd caused cannot be rectified. We are still dealing with all of them," Kamkam told the group."

"But how do we as Africans march forward into a glorious future with this stamp of inferiority on our chests?" Samia asked bluntly. "It is like tying our hands behind our backs and sending us into the global arena to compete for wealth, prosperity and to create a future filled with progress for our children."

The irony is that about ninety percent of the African people on the continent, sad to say, did not know that the African slaves who'd left the African shores had been severely brutalized and dehumanized in the New World to the extent that their owners did. They had no idea that most of the African slaves had been tortured, beaten, starved, castrated, raped, dismembered, slaughtered, lynched and even killed on some of the plantations in the New World.

Most Africans had the impression that the African concept of domestic slavery, the benign "housemaid or houseboy prototypes in Africa" was what prevailed in the Americas as well. They did not know about what awaited the slaves or what actually happened to them once they departed the shores of Africa.

"The physical pain of slavery had somehow stopped since the slave trade ended two centuries ago, but many of us are still dealing with the psychological scar, which had been inflicted on our ancestors, and on the descendants of the victims in the Diaspora," King Gizenga declared. "This has been passed down from generation to generation, and what is it going to take for us as a people to heal from these scars?"

"Time has destroyed many of the guns and several of the empires, but the agony they'd caused in the land has not ended," Kamkam said.

"There is still the pain of the past in the hearts of the chiefs," the priest declared as he poured libation to the ancestors. "The sorrow was clearly visible. You could hear the emotion in his voice and see the deep sorrow on his face during the ritual."

"We cannot defend the roles some of the chiefs played in this evil trade," Mankrado stood up like a bamboo pole. "We do not maintain that these chiefs were innocent, but we know that they were trading the prisoners of war for weapons to defend their families, to protect their villages and to save their kingdoms."

"Even if they'd opposed the Oburoni traders more aggressively, they would have been no match for the cannons the slave dealers used anyway," the queen mother lamented. "When it came to destruction,

the Oburoni slave traders had been more destructive than the wrath of
the god of thunder."

"Militarily, our ancestors were no match for the Oburoni invaders.
These Europeans simply used their cannons to mow down our ancestors
like weeds in the dry season," the king said. "The blood flow was like
river falls, which spilled down from the top of the mountains of despair
and ended up in the oceans of sorrow."

"Though many Africans would want to leave the past alone, how
can we ever forget the unfortunate victims, the lost sons and daughters
of the continent?" Togbe Abliza reflected, speaking to the gathering
after some soul searching.

"Never in a million years," the queen mother assured the gathering
pointedly. "We would never forget them, certainly not to the end of
time."

"Though our ancestors were by no means cowards, the cannons
the Europeans introduced into the slave trade immobilized and
overwhelmed many of them," Togbe Abliza said. "We would never run
out of apologies for whatever our ancestors did wrong."

"We in Africa today, have the deepest sorrow and regret when it
comes to the slave trade. Since our ancestors did not fight the slave
traders till the very last soldier died or had been gunned down, we
render our sincere apologies for that," Kamkam told the audience. "But
we didn't want to be written out of history as a result of European
atrocities."

"You must understand the pain of our ancestors, what they had to
go through in the past," Togbe Abliza told the group. "Their role was a
difficult balancing act of survival and self-preservation."

"Maybe if our ancestors had known that the Oburoni concept of
slavery was far different from our relatively benign domestic slavery in
Africa, a system which the Africans practiced on the continent before
the Oburoni people's arrival, perhaps things might have been different,"
Mankrado said.

"Well, the Africans have accepted their share of the blame, what
they'd done wrong or had been forced to do during the slave trade.
But what is taking the descendants of the Europeans and Americans so

long to come forward to show remorse and do the right thing, no one really knows."

"The griots have recorded these deeds in the oral traditions. They tell about the old invoices of shipments and the records of the guns the Oburonis had exported to the African Coast. These weapons came from Birmingham, Lisbon or Madrid," the queen mother revealed.

"How can the descendants of the gun manufacturers of Birmingham, England live with themselves today knowing that the role their ancestors played in the slave trade to the African continent in the past?" Mankrado inquired. "How could they deny that their ancestors exported millions of guns every year to the African Slave Coast and did so during the entire time that the slave trade lasted?"

"How can those shipbuilders in Liverpool, England, deny the colossal profits their ancestors had made from the making and selling of slave boats to slave dealers, boats that gained notoriety as the infamous workhorses of the slave trade?" the king asked.

They ended the slave trade when they finally realized the harm they were doing to the continent. But it took a lot of fight to end the addiction of the notorious slave dealers to African blood and flesh. In fact, it took gunboats and coastal patrols to enforce the decrees banning these.

The guilt cannot disappear into thin air overnight. They don't need to keep harboring this burden in their hearts. There is definitely a way to let go the guilt. Though essentially without adequate remorse and restitution, there had been some gestures of apology in the recent past already. But they are yet to muster the courage to make atonement for the past.

If it is peace and harmony they want for the future generation, how can they hesitate to make atonement for these crimes of history?

"We gave those Oburonis several centuries to think over this tragedy, but time is running out," the queen mother gestured and walked to the center of the gathering as she sighed deeply and shook her head sadly. "The only way they can let go the heavy burden of guilt that they still carry in their hearts is when they make the atonement."

NINETEEN

I T WAS ODD FOR AN assorted group of Oburonis from America and Europe to show up at Cape Coast Castle unannounced with red roses in hand, warm smiles on their faces and a package of atonement in their bags. The African chiefs did not believe their eyes, though they had known all along that the descendants of the Oburoni slave traders would return one day to our shores to show their remorse and make atonement for the past. They weren't sure when the trip would happen, but the kings and chiefs knew that the time for the atonement was getting nearer and nearer.

Maybe the string of disasters and the raging currents of the Mississippi River, the dozens of twirling tornadoes that'd leveled many antebellum homes, and the sighting of the ghosts of slaves from the past had shocked many people to rethink the past. The land was flooded much more intensely; it became the "flood of the century" in some areas along the legendary Mississippi River. Racial bickering was also on the rise as modern technology has revealed many of the deep, dark secrets of shame from the past to the world.

"What do they want from us again?" the queen mother inquired from the elders. Maybe they finally had a change of heart."

"Well, whatever forced them to cross the Atlantic Ocean again and return to our shores, into the midst of thousands of Panfest participants, it better be something worth the while," Dokuwa remarked.

"Do you blame those who did not want to welcome them to the festival because of what their ancestors had done to us in the past?" Mankrado asked.

"We don't know what brought them or what they would do this time around," Chief Ledo said.

The linguist, the assistant to the king, gave them the calabash of water, the symbolic African gesture of 'akwaba' welcome, though he still was not sure what their mission was really about or who sent them to our mist, or who invited them back to the continent.

"And wasn't their visit wrapped up in secrecy?" the queen mother walked back to her seat.

"Maybe they have returned to haul the rest of us away to the land of no return like they did our ancestors," the linguist joked, and the gathering roared with laughter.

"I'd hate to have them nursing their guilt for many more years. They must atone for the damage they'd done to our land in the past, because that is the only way their descendants can finally have some inner peace," the priest told the queen mother and the elders. "That is the voice of the ancestors."

"Their guilty conscience is killing them," the queen mother said. "All that pain and suffering that their ancestors had caused by hauling out of the bosom of Mama Africa so many millions of youths, and crippling the continent has begun to haunt them."

"They got some nerves to come back to face the descendants of the victims of their ancestor's greed," Dokuwa said. "I know the ancestors have made it impossible for them to sleep in peace in their land till they make atonement for the past."

"That is why they have arrived on our shores to show their remorse and make the necessary atonement so they could escape the wrath of the ancestors. We know that the ancestors are getting angrier and angrier with every passing day," the queen mother poured the water on the ground.

"When you do evil to others, the consequences follow you like a dark shadow, forcing you to eventually drown in a pool of guilt," the priest revealed.

"Since they have always denied their role in the slave trade and try to blame the tragic event on the victims, why should we even accept their delegation back to the continent?" the linguist asked.

"Hmm, it is because we need the atonement to find some closure to the long ordeal from the past," the linguist told the gathering.

"But why did it take them fifty years to make good on their promise to return?" the queen mother asked.

"Because of the shame of what their ancestors did, do you think coming back would be an easy decision for them?" Dokuwa asked the queen mother. "They ought to be a very nervous group, perhaps they are shaking in their shoes."

Everyone was stunned when the Oburoni delegation finally arrived on hallowed African ground, olive branch in hand, bouquets of red roses in their bags and atonement on their mind. The chiefs wondered how much atonement they would be willing to make, or whether they would throw dust into their eyes once again as they'd done several times in the past.

Admittedly, though their arrival was a surprise to the people of Cape Coast, the former headquarters of the British slave trade to Africa, the chiefs had somehow known that the Oburonis would somehow, in some moment in time, show up out of the blues on our shores penitent. They would come knocking on our doors to make atonement for the profane past and seek forgiveness. In fact, they'd expected the descendants to show up sooner than they did, maybe decades ago, to render an apology and show remorse considering the scope of the horror and the depth of the degradation.

Since they did not inform the chiefs ahead of time about the date of their arrival, there was very little fanfare for them at the airport when they finally landed on the hallowed grounds of Mama Africa. That was the only reason that Mama Africa and her offspring were not at the airport in massive numbers waiting for them with torrential tears on their faces and grief in their hearts.

The chiefs did not know exactly what to say to them or how to treat them, but most importantly how to deal with the request they'd brought with them. Naturally, the king and the elders were still nursing remnants of grief and anger over how their ancestors had completely destroyed the continent, shattering Africa's dreams of prosperity, and disrupting the way of life of the inhabitants with the wicked slave trade.

But somehow the elders knew that they were restless, tormented by the wrath of the ancestors, bombarded with torment from the spirits of the departed, and haunted by the ghosts of the victims.

"I suspect they finally had a change of heart to make the atonement, which is long overdue," the queen mother whispered into the linguist's ears. She was excited and smiled broadly as if her daughter had delivered a set of twins. The arrival of the delegation and the possibility of atonement forced her to be civil toward the Oburoni visitors, though she did not intend to forget about the tragedy.

"Well, if inflicting injury on defenseless and innocent people demands apology and atonement, then the descendants of the Oburonis have plenty of atonement to make," the linguist told the gathering.

"Their closets are filled with the skeletons of dead African slaves and battalions of ghosts from the past marching for redemption," Mankrado nodded his head, even as he was reaching for another calabash of palm wine.

"You have a lot of courage to show your face up here once more with your insidious demands," the king said to himself quietly.

"We need to seize them, we need to enslave them or teach them a lesson similar to what they did to our people," the linguist joked.

"I still can't believe my eyes. I am still in a daze over whether this is actually happening, whether the descendants of the Oburoni slave traders, the human thieves, have actually returned to our shores to admit wrongdoing, have returned to our shore to apologize for the past," Zogan, the priest, remarked to the elders and the queen mother.

"I see that the king is equally surprised, though he is not showing it openly in front of the delegation," the queen mother said.

Though their visit meant some sort of closure for the inhabitants of this unfortunate and unhappy continent, their arrival had caught the African leaders off guard.

"The Oburonis are laboring under the guilt, tormented and rattled with what they'd inherited from their ancestors' enterprise of shame centuries ago," the griot moaned. "The voices they hear in the dark and the ghosts they see in the night have all been haunting them."

"I think it is about time for them to appease the departed sons and daughters of Africa anyway," the queen mother smiled broadly, content that history was about to be made. She was seated next to the king and in between the king and the linguist. "They need to pacify the angry spirits, which are still roaring with vengeance, looking for the chance to do all sorts of havoc."

"Those who had been kings before me would jump up and down in their graves, if they see or hear about what is happening in the kingdom this afternoon," the king said quietly to the elders, whispering under his breath. He was downcast in his demeanor, and yet he was very happy inside his soul that the Oburonis had finally returned to do the right thing, to perform the long awaited ritual, to make the atonement for the past as they'd promised years ago.

The advent of the delegation to the kingdom gave the king the right to dream about greatness, to dream about immortality, as the most remarkable leader of the kingdom ever.

The gods of Africa were also watching the Oburoni people with amusement as the visitors entered the king's palace, one after the other, on their way to the Panfest Festival to begin the process of atonement. The gods never forgot how the Oburonis violated the sons and daughters of the land, how they killed some of the youths and finished off the aged in cold blood, and all the atrocities in the past.

The ravages to the so-called African Slave Coast in particular had been horrible. Millions were dead in the process. Empires were destroyed. Kings were removed from power and enslaved. The devastation the Oburonis caused on the African continent and the damage to its institutions had never been surpassed in global history. Though some of these facts have only recently come to light before the rest of the world, through the workings of modern informational technology, these deeds have been at the back of the minds of many.

How does it feel to be victims of the slave trade, which was not only the worst tragedy in global history, but also the most horrible crime ever committed in the world? How much accountability for these horrendous deeds do the African leaders expect?

"We need to hear whatever message they'd brought with them," the priest said quietly. "The suspense appears to be killing some of the Oburoni visitors."

"Well, their ancestors forced our people across the ocean to the land of no return. Their descendants must face the music of the voices from yesterday. They must step up and make atonement for the tragic event," the linguist said quietly. "He who sows evil must reap evil," so the saying goes.

"Let us hear what they have to say first," the king whispered into the ears of the linguist, partially covering his mouth so that the visitors could not hear him.

"Let us make them wait a few more hours," the linguist replied.

"Just let us hear their amanie; they might surprise us," the king advised him. They have been coming individually to show their remorse. Church groups came and then some students followed.

The king rose up to the podium to welcome the delegation members to the festival. He asked for the linguist to give them some water and the celebrated Kantamanto Gin for libation to the ancestors, to appease the gods so they would smile on the event. The gesture warmed the hearts of the Oburoni visitors, made them relaxed and eased their fears. To the group leader, this was a very good sign, perhaps a promising sign for the mission, maybe a prelude to greater cooperation to come.

Except the youths who'd come from far and near, those from the Diaspora that had gathered for the Panfest, most of them were first timers. There were thousands of the local people who were anxious to hear the "amanie" the Oburoni delegation brought with them.

Some of the Panfest visitors from the Diaspora were still too angry over the past to even want to listen to what the Oburoni delegation had to say. As far as this group was concerned, the members of the delegation had nothing but crocodile tears for their plight because they did not believe that they were capable of genuine remorse.

"They don't want to make any atonement," Lillian, the visitor from Trinidad, said loudly, a statement that nearly destroyed the fragile goodwill in the forum. "They are not genuinely sorry for the past. Look at them standing there laughing at our ancestors. They are definitely shedding nothing but crocodile tears!"

"Well, don't be rude to our guests," the linguist warned her, reminding her to be patient. "They are the guests of the king and we require that you treat them with respect."

"I wish you had been rude to them three hundred years ago, we would not have been returning from across the Atlantic Ocean to all these horror and degradation, I would have been standing among you here," the visitor said angrily.

"The king must ignore the Oburoni delegation and send them back home with the impunity they deserve," Dokuwa said to the other women. "Their ancestors had done enough to traumatize our people, and so why should we even talk to them this time around?"

"Tell Dokuwa to be quiet," the linguist said quietly. "This is not the time for clever words. It is time to find closures."

"Well, before you even open your mouth and tell them what our mission is all about, looking at all the hostility in the air, why don't we just get up and go back to the airport, get on the plane and leave, if they are going to be this rude and hostile to us?" Bubba asked Reverend Peterson, the leader of the delegation. "We can't force them to listen to the terms of atonement that we brought."

"Well, be patient, we've got to kill them with kindness," he told Bubba. "They have strong reasons to be very angry. Just think about it."

"Well, I am not sure if they will be a bit nicer later on or continue to be so angry that we would have to walk away, suspend or postpone the meeting," Bubba debated.

"Don't worry about that part; because we are about to find out," Shelley, the designated secretary, said quickly.

"It is gracious of you to extend such a warm hand of welcome to us. We hope you would like the message we have from our people," Reverend Peterson muttered, ignoring the angry outpour of the gentleman from Trinidad, and the angry looks from the queen's assistant, Dokuwa. He was uncomfortable in the presence of the king and his elders. His secret fear was that the king and his elders might not allow them to do anything about the past. They might not even accept the terms of atonement they'd brought.

"We are glad you are here, but we have tons of questions for you," the linguist informed the members of the delegation. "It took longer than expected, but we were sure that you would one day return to our shores, like you have just done, to show your remorse."

"Well, we have some answers. If the king would permit us to do so, we can proceed and place the atonement on the table," Reverend Peterson said. He sat down and started to study the expressions on the faces of the king and the elders for clues about their chances.

They are doing the right thing. The delegation members reminded themselves. Their worry was that they might run into an arrogant and stubborn king, who was still so angry over the past, that he would be unwilling to even listen to them. That thought lingered in their minds during the flight and worried them on arrival as well.

They were also worried about what the ancestors of Africa might do to them since they had heard rumors about how the gods might try to pay the Oburonis back in their own coins.

"What sort of retaliation would you call it if the gods decide to let the thunder god destroy the Oburoni visitors in one powerful blast? Would that be poetic justice or a senseless act of murder, or killing people without adequate provocation?" Reverend Peterson joked, though he was very serious.

The slave trade ended long ago. Its toll on Africa had been tremendous. But though it ended centuries ago, the effects of the slave trade have not ended. They are still as real and as fresh as the tropical lemons in the virgin forests. At times, from all the legacies lingering around, it appears as if the slave trade ended only yesterday.

"It is our custom to make all visitors feel at ease in our land," the linguist said, after the chief spoke his words of welcome.

"The moment of atonement, which the African people expected for centuries, has finally arrived, though it was delayed for centuries, till the dawn of the twenty-first century . . . the dawn of the age of advanced technology . . . the dawn of the power of DNA . . . and the dawn of the era of reconciliation," Mankrado said.

"The moment of atonement and reconciliation, which has been looming in the air for centuries, is finally on our doorstep," King Gizenga said, after clearing his throat. He was still angry, but not too bitter over what his great grandfather had experienced during the slavery era, and not too disturbed by what had happened to his family centuries ago.

"Don't start celebrating yet," the queen mother said. "You can't predict what these Oburoni people have in mind."

"Are you sure they are not going to boo us when we render the public apology and announce our terms of atonement?" Bubba asked Reverend Peterson, the leader of the delegation for the third time. He felt quite awkward and didn't know exactly what they would say to pacify the people of Africa, after all these years of silence. He was particularly concerned about what it will take to make peace.

"What would it take to settle the huge debt that we owe not only to the African people, but also to those who live in the Diaspora?" Reverend Peterson asked. "Even if we can make atonement, I don't see us making anything close to the debt we owe the victims."

"Just be yourself," Brandon, the peacemaker told Reverend Peterson, Bubba and the other members of the delegation quietly. He was not sure if the preacher would say the wrong things to the African leaders and ruin the mission, making it impossible to dialogue with the leaders. "Just try to be yourself . . . no need to exaggerate your grief or fake the remorse."

"Some of the African leaders are still very angry over the past, still bitter over things that had happened centuries ago," the reverend told Brandon. "Many have still not come to terms with the slave trade, not after all these years, though some of us have begun to deal with it openly from our end."

"But how can you blame them? Just be ready for a barrage of questions from the audience," Brandon warned his colleagues.

"What a shame, what a shame?" Bubba said. "Where was God before all these were happening?" He squeezed the small holy book in his hand firmly trying to get some answers and draw some comfort from a higher power.

"Your majesty, make sure no one attacks any member of the delegation, we expect you and your elders to protect us while we are your gusts," Reverend Peterson requested nervously. Brandon, who was acting as the intermediary simply laughed.

"We hope that will not be necessary, since the reception we have received so far has been quite warm," Brandon said.

"But the rage on the faces of the Asafo soldiers was like a deadly storm waiting to explode," Bubba said. "They looked as if they were in ambush ready to foil another slave raid."

"Well, perhaps you've a reason to be afraid and worried about the past," Brandon said deliberately trying to tease Bubba. "Perhaps you know what your ancestors did in the past and how much they owe the African people."

"But we are worried about the heavy burden we still carry around our necks," Bubba explained. "This mission is like stepping into a lion's den and opening up some deep, old wounds, instead of just simply letting go the guilt."

"I hope not," Brandon reassured them. He secretly felt that an attack from the African people could destroy the mission. That would worsen an already tense situation, even defeating the mission altogether, so he went to great lengths to make sure that the mission succeeded.

"What about the atonement, should we promise them more money, programs or what?" Reverend Peterson inquired from Brandon, whispering into his ears and feeling quite uneasy. He was so nervous that he did not remember the terms of atonement that the committee back home had decided to present to the leaders. "How could we forget the package of atonement that the executive members gave to the delegation to bring to the table?"

Brandon paused and sighed briefly. He thought a big bag full of money might pacify the African people or soothe their wounds from the past or appease the spirits. But he knew that though the money was enticing, it was not the most important thing in the resolution, in the reconciliation. "First and foremost, it has to do with a change of heart. Then the need to find a way to pacify the gods, to stop Mother Nature from unleashing its wrath on others," he told himself. "Then y'all need to put Africa back on the road of progress, whatever it takes to get that done."

"How exactly do we present this package?" Bubba looked for answers from Reverend Peterson a fifth time. "I am getting nervous about the mission, about the package."

"Just build the most modern university—African University—a complex of Olympic Training Facilities for all sports—a modern Hospital Complex—a Food Complex and Food Bank—and a Hall of Remorse for the continent," Trent said.

"You must do just what the leaders back home asked the members of the delegation to do before you began the trip to the continent," Brandon told Reverend Peterson. He did not want to alienate the group, or make it look as if they were under siege from the African leaders to cough out resources they did not have. "I thought the groups back home you are representing here have already decided on what they wanted you to do on their behalf when it comes to the atonement package."

"Yes, they have, but will that be enough to appease the king, his elders, the people and the ancestors, judging from the angry look on some of their faces?" he asked Brandon as he studied the demeanor of the king and the elders.

"I am hoping that they won't reject whatever you offer."

"Well, if that is all they gave you, then you must tell the leaders what atonement you have brought," he told him. "At least you have something on the table, unlike when you had nothing in the past."

"We certainly do. Some cash and lots of programs for the victims on the continent and in the Diaspora," he told Brandon.

The Reverend Peterson and the other members of the delegation stood in front of the massive crowd at the Panfest Festival, in front of the chiefs and wondered how the chiefs were going to receive their terms of atonement. The audience at the festival came from all across the globe, many came from over fifty African countries and several others also came from the African Diaspora.

As the dark clouds of remorse silhouetted against the deep blue sky in Victoria Park, a greenish park overlooking the Cape Coast Castle in the Central Region of Ghana, the falcon reappeared again once more unexpectedly from behind the amber clouds, perched on Brandon's hands. It circled the pristine beach quickly at an incredible speed and landed on a nearby coconut tree, right next to the notorious coconut grove, the spot where thousands of European slave traders who had died from the wrath of the African killer mosquitoes had been hurriedly laid to rest without any fanfare.

Brandon smiled and nodded his head repeatedly and then patted Reverend Peterson on the back gently. His heart was beaming with joy, though he was secretly concerned about the success of the mission, they were so close to the atonement and yet so far away. He knew the appearance of the falcon was a symbolism for good things to follow.

"Was this justice delayed or simply poetic justice in the making?" Brandon joked with Reverend Peterson, but in his heart of hearts, he believed the event was finally poetic justice for an unhappy continent.

"You tell me which one it is, Brandon," he replied. "You can make this the final settlement for the mother of all wrongs, crimes committed in the past amidst racial ignorance and limited global enlightenment, forces that are still active from a dead past."

Bubba's mood was somber. He was not talking very much. He was trying to put his words together to express exactly what he felt. "We don't care what you call it, we just want to get it over, so we can put this heavy burden of guilt in our past behind us once and for all," Bubba nodded his head repeatedly. "You can't continue to hold our feet to the fire for ever."

"Indeed, so we can move on with our lives and for our children to grow up free from this ancient plague and tainted history. And our grandchildren and their children will be free from this forever," Reverend Peterson added to what Bubba had already said, though he was still feeling uneasy about the reaction of the king and his people.

TWENTY

S O THEY CAME FOR SEVERAL reasons. But the main reason they came from all across the globe, from the Diaspora was to make the pilgrimage to their beloved motherland to find closure to their identity crises. The group from the Diaspora would get the chance to mix their blood with their kinsfok on the continent, to break bread with them and to discover the final rout of their roots.

Jacqueline, Davi Santos and Jim Jacobs had the wrong impressions about what the leaders on the African continent did during the slave trade, but the encounter gave them the opportunity to find out the facts behind the exodus, the bare truths of the global tragedy to change their perspective on the slave trade and the forcible exodus of their ancestors.

For those from the African Diaspora, the climax of the Panfest Festival, which was the Grand Tour of the Cape Coast Castle, couldn't come soon enough. To the thousands of brothers and sisters who came from the Diaspora to seek closure to their identity crisis, the time to break bread and merge their souls with those of the ancestors had finally arrived.

When the tour of the slave castle was announced, many became extremely emotional, as they followed the tour guides into the courtyard.

The deafening silence was not only eerie but also moving as many of them clasped their arms behind their backs meditating over the past, feeling the spirits in the dungeons and even communicating with the ancestors as they marched along in the creepy silence.

To them, this was a sacred moment—a rendezvous with the spirits of the ancestors—the hallowed grounds of history. Tears were streaming down several cheeks as they walked along the route that many of their ancestors had once taken in chains and in shackles. As they walked down the same consecrated paths in the profane past, paths that meant a lot of pain and hopelessness to their ancestors, many broke down in tears.

Many of them spent a lot of time in the dungeons and wondered why the lights kept flickering on and cutting off. They walked in the darkness toward the labyrinth of stone crafted tunnels which ended in a maze. When the lights finally worked, many of them saw the ebony black dirt on the ground, perhaps the old dirt that the footprints of their ancestors had left behind centuries ago.

"I smell a mixture of urine, human excrement and body odor," Jim Jacob said softly to Jacqueline. "I feel chills down my spine."

"It is very musty down here," she told him. "I have an eerie feeling inside me, though I cannot put into words what I really feel down here."

"You are right, the feeling is indescribable," he sighed deeply.

Besides the members of the delegation, there were some of the descendants of the former European slave traders, dozens of representatives from the descendants of the American Northeastern commercial slave trading network and dozens from states of the former Old South. Though the slave trade had ended centuries ago, they'd been extremely embarrassed by what their ancestors did, since some were saddened by the way their ancestors had destroyed Mama Africa and her offspring, and especially the way the slave trade had arrested the development of the African continent in general, they chose to make the pilgrimage.

But the unkindest impact was how the chaos had set the continent centuries behind other continents and how it had placed an eternal stigma on the people.

"The stigma of inferiority on the people of Africa has derailed the confidence and dreams of an entire continent," Reverend Peterson confessed, watching carefully, how the queen mother and Dokuwa were watching him for clues to find out whether he was genuinely remorseful or if he was simply putting up a front. "I am one of those who have drifted in and out of guilt, genuinely troubled by what our ancestors did to the Africans and the manner in which our ancestors had stigmatized the continent. Why we have put the label of inferiority on the African people forever with the slave trade."

"You came with gifts, you have flowers in your hand, an olive branch inside your hats, but most importantly, you have remorse in your hearts and not to forget, you are here to make atonement," Brandon reminded the delegation. "If you recall, it was your ancestors who started this calamity on the African continent. It was the Portuguese, followed by the Spaniards, the Dutch and the British and the others who traded guns for slaves in those dark days of sorrow."

"Well, we are extremely sorry for what our ancestors did years ago," Pieter Ritz emoted as his face crumbled with sadness when he said those words. He didn't think that he could say those words loud enough, firmly enough, and sincerely enough to satisfy the African chiefs, their elders and the descendants of the victims from the Diaspora who were present at the festival. "All I can say is that we are truly sorry for this ugly and inhumane past in our past and in your history."

"To hell with you, stop lying, you don't look that sorry!" the Jamaican visitor retorted quickly. "Jah will make you suffer and the next generations would suffer for what you and your ancestors did to my people. I mean for taking advantage of the continent for so long and in such a brutal manner."

"Order! Let us come to order," Quansa, the tour guide said firmly. "This is history, so please avoid personal attacks and don't get too upset over it to the point of getting personal with anybody."

"I hate these legacies, because they are nothing but abominations from the decadent past," Joseph Sellers from Trinidad said firmly. "I can see the hypocrisy written all over their faces, again. They are pretending that they are sorry. No one should believe them. Why should we believe them this time around?"

"I believe they have something up their sleeves again," Davi Santos from Rio de Janeiro said.

The African-Americans from the United States were anxious to catch a glimpse of the inside of the Portuguese chapel, the aged old notorious place of worship in a slave castle, which had been the scene of many baptisms of shame and rituals that were repeated millions of times. The chapel was notorious for the place where the slaves were baptized before they were shipped out to the New World. They came to see for themselves this symbolism, this pinnacle of European hypocrisy. They wanted to concretize how low the slave traders stooped during the slave trade. They came to see the chapel of abomination, which is a church used for baptizing slaves before they were shipped out to the land of no return, degraded and brutalized.

"Those who once worshipped inside this chapel, who had the ridiculous boldness to baptize our captured ancestors in this chapel should twirl in their graves," Crystal, the librarian from Byhalia, Mississippi, said loudly as she sat on a pile of rusty cannons next to the entrance of the chapel humming an African-American spiritual song.

The group was on the final leg of the Grand Tour of the Cape Coast Castle when they reached the notorious "Door of No Return", a heavy iron gate that led directly to several waiting slave boats on the beach, the final steps into the boats used to haul away the slave cargoes to the land of no return, the final destination of the "black cargoes of labor from the African shores."

"The experience was spiritual," Kena Gemares from Brazil said. "The idea of threading the same hallowed grounds the ancestors once walked hundreds of years ago has been quite spiritual. Walking the last few steps which their ancestors took before they were deprived of Mama Africa's nurturing bosom was too sentimental for me to put in words."

Jacqueline and several of the visitors broke down in tears and cried like babies. It was tearful, but it was also revealing. As a result, it was defining as well and clarified some of the identity crises, which several of us the returnees wanted to resolve.

"We must bring every African-American child to this place to see the past for themselves," Jacqueline asserted. "It would give them a perspective no classroom could ever give them"

"My personal apologies to you young lady, I understand where those tears are coming from," Bubba told Jacqueline.

"Coming from someone like you, this means a lot to me. I truly forgive you Mr. Bubba," Jacqueline told Bubba.

The silent thought on the minds of the more than five thousand tourists at that point and on that day was how many African slaves had once taken those same final steps of destiny, or had once passed through the same fateful door and strode reluctantly, walking obviously with heavy legs, crying their hearts out, pleading on top of their lungs for their freedom, as they took those final steps away from the protective bosom of their beloved continent?

At that stage of the tour, most of the tourists had a mixture of anger, sorrow and pain. Millions of eyes, millions of hands seemed to grip them as they walked with heavy legs and tears in their eyes. The salty breeze from the Atlantic Ocean greeted them in the face and the blazing African tropical sun blinded them like lightening flashes, but it was the invisible hands of the ancestors which touched their souls—every step deepened their sorrow as everyone argued with themselves as to why the horror took place.

The vociferous and screeching calls from the white seagulls and the dozens of dirty crows competing for hegemony over the once deadly seashore was no comic relief, but a symbolism of the tragic historical drama that once unfolded on these pristine shores of Africa, though all these happened centuries ago.

Though the trade ended long ago, the guilt and sorrow were everywhere still written in tears and in blood. It was as if the event happened only yesterday. You could feel the sorrow and the pain in the air. You could even hear the cries for freedom of the slaves from inside the labyrinths of dungeons underneath the slave castle. You could feel their pain, see their tears, hear their agonizing pleas for freedom, smell their combative bodies and sense their desperation.

Visibly remorseful, the members of the delegation, the squad officially representing the people of America and Europe, threw seven bouquets of flowers into the Atlantic Ocean from one of the boats, from the Liberty Express in memory of the departed souls of Africa. In the emotional outpour, the delegation knew the historical horror their ancestors had made on the African shores centuries ago, and they were somewhat relieved that they'd come to atone for the past, though centuries later.

Some of the returned brothers and sisters from the Diaspora took a long time to get over what they'd seen in the dungeons. They still have not been healed; they were more devastated than the Oburoni delegation. It was harder for them to deal with the reality of what they had just seen with their eyes. Though they had read, heard or imagined how it had been, nothing could compare with the sentimental realities they'd seen. They were still shocked by what they had personally seen, felt or experienced.

"It all boils down to human greed and racism. I wonder which of these passions was uppermost on their minds," Tunisia sat on a pile of old, rusty cannon balls. She came from Little Rock, Arkansas, and she continued to wipe repeatedly the silent tears that were streaming down her cheeks freely. When she finally was able to speak, she said: "I hope no one anywhere has to ever go through the same brutality that our ancestors had to go through for years. Never! Ever!"

"It was the pure evil on the part of the Oburoni people," Dokuwa said bluntly. "It was the guns, which the Europeans brought that created all this misery. They caused the bloodshed and chaos in the land."

"Of course, it was greed on the part of a few of the African traitors who collaborated with the Oburoni traders to round up their own kinfolks. But we can argue that it was the Europeans who'd bribed or pushed them into this pernicious line of trade," Zakiya said, emoting profusely and breathing heavily. "These African traitors made the wrong choices as well."

"The Oburoni slave traders bribed some of them with guns and rum," Tunisia said, shaking her head from side to side and chuckling loudly. "For rum and guns, these stooges were convinced to put a price on the heads of their own people?"

"Well, it was not that simple. But you seem very much disturbed by what you'd seen," the queen mother remarked. "Just gather yourself;

remember these were events that happened in the past, several centuries ago, that was definitely before we were even born."

"I am a product of that past, can you bear with me?" Tunisia asked angrily, wiping her face. "What your ancestors did was never excusable."

"Yes, my sweetheart! I don't know what else to say, or how best to say it, but we are very sorry for all these," She told her, putting her arms around her affectionately. "The slave trade past was a very difficult period in our history. The chiefs were completely at the mercy of the Oburoni slave traders."

"Damn it! I have seen it all—the dungeons, the Palaver Hall and the Door of no return—evidence of the ultimate brutality in this world, but I still can't believe my eyes," Zakiya said quietly. "I can't believe that they actually did these things to fellow human beings, to our ancestors. It is just impossible to believe that people could be that cruel anywhere in the world."

"Well, what bothered me most was that I could still smell the mixture of human sweat, excrement and the salty tears of our ancestors in the dungeons. And I could still hear their moans and groans in the darkness, hear the sad dirges from their tongue and see their bodies shimmering in the darkness" Martel Parks from Detroit, told his girlfriend Marisa. "It was so dark inside the dungeons, but with the help of my flashlight, though it kept cutting on and off very strangely, we could see the dirt the soles of the feet of our ancestors had left behind many centuries ago."

"What a sad day this has been for me. But what a shame the past had been? It was nothing but shame, and absolute shame for that matter," Tunisia said loudly. She couldn't express her disgust adequately over these sordid legacies. "She had the nerve to laugh when the tour guard was talking about how they kept the rabble raising slaves under lockdown in supine position for days. I got really angry then."

"I understand where you are coming from," Jacqueline said. "I experienced several emotions—sadness—anger—regret—vengeance during the tour. No doubt in my mind that the slave trade was the worst tragedy in the world. The visit had been the saddest event in my life."

"Incredible," Zakiya said in a sad and somber voice. "I came all the way from Castalia Heights in Memphis to seek personal closure, but the irony is that I am leaving here with more questions than answers to my identity crisis."

"Don't let any of these upset you too much. As bitter as the scenes were, these are pieces of ancient history," Deh Deh from North Carolina warned Zakiya, as the two made their way toward Victoria Park, a large park that was within a walking distance from the Cape Coast Castle. They were still inhaling the putrid air around the castle as they walked along, too devastated, too confused, too shocked and too sentimental to wake themselves from the tearful journey into the profane past, making personal rendezvous with the horrors of man's cruelty to man.

The European and American tourists simply lowered their heads in silence, obviously too embarrassed as they continued to tour the legacies. They pondered over the items sometimes in shame. Some were still in denial of some of the legacies that their ancestors had left behind. They were careful not to say anything that the African-American returnees from the Diaspora might construe as them adding insult to the injury their ancestors had inflicted on them.

Kwasi Blessing, the African-American activist from Westwood, Memphis was too stunned to say anything. His reaction was incredible. "In the castle I'd found the truth. In the dungeons I'd received another special call. And in the air, I'd felt liberation. To my life, I have been given a new sense of direction," he said smiling quietly. "It's all a blessing in disguise that I have seen all these for myself and with my own eyes."

He simply clasped both hands on top of his head, walking in a daze like a zombie, shaking his head repeatedly as he silently continued to express his anger over what he'd seen, stumping his feet especially over the final agony of his ancestors, we are talking about the scenes just before they got inside the slave boats for the notorious Middle Passage, the detestable journey from Africa to the land of no return.

"Why do we have to pay for this tour anyway," one of the Diaspora returnees asked. "I don't have to pay a penny to see the agony of my own ancestors."

"Well, it is a tour, though a very special and unique one. However, it is run just like any other museum anywhere," Quansa, one of the tour guides explained to her patiently.

"You are making money off the misery of our ancestors. Yes you are," she said angrily. "Do you know how all these have touched and offended some of us?"

"Well, we are sorry, but we need the resources to preserve the castle for the living. We also want to save it for the unborn, indeed, for posterity to see and learn from this horrible tragedy," he told her passionately but politely. "Please remember these departed souls are our own flesh and blood, you know that very well."

The MC for the occasion was the Minister of Tourism. She gave a brief speech reminding everybody that the government has preserved the castle not because it wants to make money off the misery of our departed brothers and sisters, but because we want to create a positive link between those who live outside the continent and want to reconnect with the motherland. She reminded the new generation to be vigilant and make sure that such a tragedy is never repeated in the annals of any history anywhere.

Tunisia let out a long and heavy sigh. "You sold your own! Why did you sell your own brothers and sisters to the white man? Tell me why?"

Before the minister could even answer her, Edmund Washington finally broke his long silence and said, "How could you do that to your own people? Tell me why our own ancestors did what they did to their own?"

"Well, as I said a million times, the Oburoni traders pushed the backs of our leaders against the wall, threatened and forced them sometimes at gunpoint. They had to find the slaves for them or they became slaves themselves. It was as simple as that," Dokuwa confessed. "It was very chaotic. It was a life of desperation, a time for self-preservation. The various groups tried desperately to survive the ordeal one day at a time. The European slave traders created "a lion eat lion world" on the African continent.

"But your ancestors were guilty of helping the white folks too," Deh-Deh continued. "Why did they not stand together as one to face the slave traders?"

"It is not as simple as that, my sister and my brother. Remember we never invited these Oburoni Europeans to our shores. They just showed up with guns and shackles. Some of them said they had itching feet. You have seen the cannons at the castle; the Oburonis had one set of cannons overlooking the Ocean aimed at their fellow pirates and the other set at the gate aimed at our ancestors. The Europeans did not hesitate to use these cannons whenever our ancestors went to the castle to free some of the victims. The deciding factor in the ugly slave trade drama was simply the huge cannons the Oburoni slave traders brought with them and how they used them to quickly crush any opposition to the slave trade."

Zakiya chuckled and wanted to make a sarcastic comment about what the minister said, but she decided to swallow her words.

"I know our ancestors didn't have the guns," Zakiya finally broke her silence. "But they should have fought harder, perhaps continued the struggle to the very last person."

King Twumasi, Togbe Abliza and Ohenba Samia were seated next to the guests on the podium. They were quiet and they said very few words after the emotional tour and the sentimental outpour of grief from the returnees. They had already performed their brand of ritual atonement. They'd sent people to appease those in the Diaspora.

"If we can go back into the past to redo everything, many things will definitely be different," Samia, the beautiful princess with royal ancestry said politely, as she tried to comfort the devastated and distraught brothers and sisters from the Diaspora.

After a brief libation to the ancestors, the European and American guests were asked to step forward to address the gathering and state their terms of atonement. They proceeded to render an apology to the people and then a major apology to the ancestors, to the gods. They admitted that, though it was immoral their ancestors thought that they had found what they needed to make their dreams in the New World come true. "The African continent gave our ancestors the help they needed to emerge as economic giants today. And for that, we would always be grateful to Africa and the people," he told the chiefs.

"Speak from your heart, preacher," Bubba said softly, speaking under his breath. "Let them know that we are truly remorseful, so we can put down the guilt."

"They had no right to force the Africans out of their land, ship them out to the New World like chattel and then used them for free labor for centuries," Reverend Peterson said. "For these and all the other brutalities, we are deeply sorry and remorseful."

More than seven thousand guests came from across the United States and Europe and more than seven hundred from the Caribbean and several dozens came from South America, especially from Brazil to the Panfest. Most of them were very quiet and reserved in their demeanor, though several were also sentimental in their identity and soul-searching needs.

Those from European descent huddled together to keep their guilty consciences from stepping over the edge. Though some remained stoic throughout, you could see sadness and remorse on some faces as well. There were no smiles or senseless jokes during the tour. It was as somber as the moment of apotheosis the world had been expecting.

The new and young Mankrado, the war chief of Oguaa, thought that the members of the delegation were shedding crocodile tears just so they could put the past behind them and get on with their lives in peace.

"They want to make atonement to end the wrath of Mother Nature," he said. "They are afraid of the continued wrath of Mother Nature."

"What they have brought must better be something substantial to pacify the gods and the spirits of the departed sons and daughters of the continent," the queen mother said. "It has been such a long agony for the inhabitants of the continent, especially for those of us who live along the former Slave Coast.

Kena Guimares, the tall Portuguese lady from Sao Paulo, was the second to speak. "My Portuguese ancestors started the slave trade because they wanted labor on their plantations. But the trade quickly got out of hand and this development came to impose unimaginable hardships on the African people and the people of African descent all over the world. I am here to express my heartfelt sorrow over what my people had done and for how much pain and suffering the African people had endured over so many centuries. I hope you can find it within your hearts to forgive us and the descendants of the other European nations for starting, masterminding and heavily participating in the European slave trade to Africa."

Jose Garcia from Mexico started to say how sorry he was for the participation of his Spanish descendants in the trans-Atlantic slave trade. "No number of apologies we offer here today would be enough for what our ancestors did to your ancestors," Jose Garcia told the quiet and subdued African audience. "We are extremely sorry and we ask for nothing but your forgiveness. We are ready to spell out the terms of atonement for this sordid past."

"Nothing we do today can bring back the dead, the lost loved ones or comfort anybody for the horrible past, but we are on the road to a national apotheosis," Bubba said in a whiskey voice. "We have decided to make atonement for the past and in turn receive reconciliation."

The representative from Brazil was next to say that he was sorry and remorseful over the past deeds of his Portuguese ancestors. "Our people needed labor on the sugar plantations and we are grateful that the African people, though they were forcibly brought over to the plantations in Brazil, rose to the occasion to provide the much needed labor," he told the audience and got a rousing round of applause from them. "How can we not be thankful for the help your ancestors had given us? We apologize for whatever hardships they had to endure in the course of this valuable contribution that made the economic dreams of our ancestors a reality."

Reverend Peterson followed Jose Garcia and spoke on behalf of the people of his region rather fervently, determined to show how sorry his region and country were for the slave trade and its effects on the continent. He was especially remorseful over what the people of the Slave Coast suffered.

"For the millions that were forcibly uprooted out of Africa and hauled to the New World, hauled to Mississippi, or hauled to Alabama and were forced to grow tobacco in the Carolinas, sent to Maine to fish and pushed into Missouri, we can never thank Africa enough," he stopped to take a sip of a bottle of water. "For all the degradations and abuses our ancestors had heaped on the African people, we say that we are truly sorry for this profane chapter in our histories."

"Atonement! Atonement! Atonement!" the audience repeated loudly. "We want the terms of atonement!"

"Let me finish, please. Try to imagine how shocked your ancestors were when they arrived in the New World," Reverend Peterson continued. "The slaves were treated no better than the beasts of burden—just like cattle. Words could never express how sorry we are for the slave trade and for the plantation slavery which took place in our lands, though your chiefs did not know much about this at the time. But for all that came to pass on the other side of the Atlantic Ocean, we ask for forgiveness."

"Atonement!" the audience shouted once again.

"Well we have generous terms of atonement for the pain and suffering of the African continent. My country has pledged a large sum of money to put the continent back on its feet and had earmarked some money for the people who live in the Diaspora for businesses and for the education which was denied their ancestors during the slavery period on the plantations. Europeans have also pledged equal amounts of money for the same causes. Above all, we are determined that this sort of blatant abuse of human dignity and the degradation of an entire race of people must never happen in any part of the world again."

"How soon do you think your people would make the atonement available to the African people?" Brandon asked Reverend Peterson. Brandon was trying to find out for himself and spoke on behalf of the African people as well.

The other six members of the atonement delegation listened to the question and reacted to it in their heads differently while Reverend Peterson tried to provide his answer.

Trent and Steve had stormed out of the meeting before it even ended. They were unhappy and disappointed that the members of the apology team said nothing about giving the Africans any immediate monetary compensation and did not want to witness the descendants of the slave traders throwing dust into the eyes of the African people once more.

They did not want to see them add insult to the injury.

King Batazinga and his Chucalissa priests were equally disappointed and did not hesitate to show their disappointment by abandoning the meeting unceremoniously. They might return to the negotiating table again to accept whatever specific amount the European and American members of the delegation decided to offer them.

"These sounds like empty promises," the visitor from Haiti pointed out. "Don't fall for these "empty promises" and don't allow your continent to be taken for a ride once more. Let the zombies and the ghosts deal with them, let them send some more hurricanes and tornadoes their way, then they would come running back here with better terms of atonement," Marie Pierre said.

"The ancestors would turn in their graves, if you sell out once more, settling for a paltry sum in the end for the pain and suffering they had endured for several centuries," Trent warned.

The group named the Daughters of Mama Africa wanted one hundred billion dollars after their efforts to sabotage the Panfest Festival ended in a fiasco. They wanted to stop the festival, because they did not want to revisit the horrible crimes the Europeans and their American counterparts had committed against their ancestors, even though they wouldn't mind settling for the one hundred billion dollars, which they had suggested to the chiefs.

"One hundred billion dollars seemed an inadequate compensation for the tragedy, but no amount of money can make up for what the victims had actually suffered years ago," King Gizenga insisted. "Nothing can make up with the huge losses which we have suffered on the continent and continue to suffer even today, especially those who live in the Diaspora."

"Absolutely," Brandon supported his stand quickly. He was scared the meeting might become too sentimental and too violent,

"No matter how hard you try, you can never let go of this burden of guilt, no matter how much money you are wiling to offer," the reggae singer from Jamaica, Peter Chuncey, told the members of the delegation. "The curse from this trade would live on in notoriety, and would continue down your perennial progeny till the end of humanity."

"We are here today as a delegation to ask for forgiveness for all that," Reverend Peterson said quietly and politely. "We want to make atonement and get this notorious past behind us, not only because of the guilt that we have, but because of the sake of the next generations."

"There has been great efforts of atonement in the past, but what you are offering us now, even the damages for the losses of the Ibo group alone will be double what you have offered the entire continent and to the people in the Diaspora," Chukwu Emeka said, he was the resident pastor in Enugu. "I am ashamed of the role my church had played in the entire slave trade tragedy."

"Well, finally, the descendants of the European and American slave traders have come to their senses," the Nfantsiman Ohene said scornfully, shaking his head in disgust. He was still as angry as if the slave trade had ended the week before. "What amount could be deemed a fair compensation for three and half centuries of free labor, for the loss of freedom and for the lives of millions of Africans?" he asked and sucked hard into his long mahogany pipe. "What of the forty million who died in the process and the forty million that your ancestors had hauled away?"

"You have forgotten the pain and suffering of the continent," the queen mother shouted. "They have to know that they owe the continent a lot of debt, an amount they could never repay to the people."

"Aha, it is your guilty conscience that has brought you down here to do what you have come here to do," the spokesperson for King Gizenga said. "We can never accept only empty words for what your ancestors did to the continent. He pointed his sword of state at the sky to emphasize his point. The dead and the abducted victims among my people alone would exceed the one hundred billion dollars. So you need to come again."

"Get ready to give us billions more than what you are offering our people," the representative of the Alafin of Oyo said, pointing his fingers at the head of the delegation. "Either you pay for the crime right now or pay for it later in the wrath of the ancestors, in tragic disasters that you will live to regret forever."

"Of course, you have not told us what you will do with our blood sisters and brothers who still live in the Diaspora, who continue to experience the direct effects of the past brutalities," the spokesperson for the Oba of Benin asked the members of the delegation. "So you will need to come up with a bigger package than what you are offering the continent for the pain, suffering and the perpetual stigma you have inflicted on the African continent."

"One hundred billion dollars in today's money is such a small amount, it is like adding insult to the tragic crime your ancestors committed centuries ago," Trent said sarcastically, staring at the members of the delegation angrily as if he wanted to settle scores right there.

The members of the delegation sat down and pondered over what they'd been hearing from the African leaders for the past one hour.

They were down and were sorry for what their ancestors did. It was hard to admit it, but they had no choice but to admit guilt and seek forgiveness. To sit in the presence of the people who could forgive their ancestors for the profane past of slavery, and to see how angry and adamant their leaders were, it made the task of atonement much more frustrating.

The euphoria the festival generated started to wear off as the participants began to depart to their hotels and lodging places. The salty breeze from the Atlantic Ocean took over and dried out the tears of some of the visitors and washed their feet and hands. Those of them who expected to break bread with the elders on the hallowed grounds, where their distant ancestors once walked and breathed the air of freedom, could do so because they'd already washed their hands and could eat with the elders, according to the African proverb.

In spite of the tense atmosphere, Reverend Peterson saw a picture of leaders who wanted to help them let go of the guilt, leaders who were willing to work to put the past behind them and people who wanted to join the modern economic system in a much more positive manner, but they were very much afraid of being duped a second time.

"Very important," the most senior leader, the king of kings, the pride of Africa, and the one and only legendary king of kings of the Oyoko clan, told the delegation members. "The single most important problem facing Africa today is how to get the continent to join the community of progressive continents, to do business without the stigma of slavery from our history interfering with our ability to do so."

This personable and brilliant king, told the members of the delegation. "We need the billons of atonement money, which ought to be far higher than what you are putting on the table. That is considering the scope, duration and impact of the slave trade on our land.

But, most importantly, your governments must help the continent to join the global economy in terms of industries, manufacturing plants and modern banking systems, this you must do for Africa through the instrumentality of your leaders."

The ancestors have made their decision. They have spoken their minds. Helping this unhappy continent to get back on its feet is your responsibility.

EPILOGUE

---ooo≫◉≪ooo---

T HE ARCHBISHOP OF CANTERBURY, HEAD of the Church of England,
boldly apologized for the role his church played in the European
slave trade to Africa, and also regretted the embarrassing blemish
of this tragedy on his country. England participated heavily in the
trans-Atlantic slave trade, and so did the Anglican Church. Though
the European slave trade to Africa ended some two hundred plus years
ago, and the guns, the cannons, the groans and the tears are all silent
now, the victims have not recovered from it, and those whose ancestors
conducted the trade to the continent also continue to labor under the
heavy burden of guilt from the slave trade.

The Archbishop didn't blame the slave trade on the victims. He
didn't make up any excuses for why or how it happened. In fact, he was
very remorseful for the tragedy and asked for forgiveness for his church
and his country. He spoke for his country when he uttered the words
of apology, particularly for all those who continue to feel this heavy
burden of guilt still lingering in their conscience. Thus, he tried to help
his nation to end the conflict in its conscience.

He recalled how England was the kingpin in the sordid enterprise,
and the use of English caravel vessels as the workhorses of the shameful
trade. And for decades, England controlled the lion's share of the slave
trade, hauling millions of African youths out of the continent in droves,
and did so perhaps more than any other nation.

Obviously, he knew about the forces that propelled his country
men and women to embark on enslaving the Africans on their own
continent and then hauling them across the Atlantic Ocean to the New
World to perform free labor on their plantations. He knew the extent
to which his country was involved in the trade and how it had touched
many fabrics of society.

He'd admitted wrongdoing in his apology, but why didn't he
mention anything about atonement for the profane past? Maybe the

idea was too radical, too embarrassing or maybe he didn't know whom to make the atonement to?

The so-called African Slave Coast suffered the brunt of the pain, the vortex of the slave raids, the backdrop of bloodshed and the theater of cannon thunder. So, for any atonement for the ugly tragedy, there should be no debate about the area of Africa that gets most of the atonement.

Why did he choose to express his remorse openly over the deeds of his countrymen and women, transactions which took place centuries ago? Why did he choose this time in global history to render the apology? Maybe it was the advent of the bicentennial of the end of the slave trade at the time, or perhaps it was the general feeling of apotheosis on the part of the descendants of those who had committed these atrocities against Africa?

He didn't say that those who'd committed these atrocities had been dead and gone centuries ago and so why bother to apologize to the modern generation? He probably felt, I could be exaggerating, that the hands of his country men and women are still dripping with the blood of the innocent African slaves, inherited from the past.

How many of his country men and women still stagger under the burden of guilt didn't matter to him. He didn't care whether slavery was legal or illegal at the time of the slave trade. He just wanted to do his moral duty as the leader of his faith, to show remorse and to put a shameful past behind his church and his country forever.

What twists of forces propelled him across time to speak those noble and dramatic words of apology—genuinely sincere—pleading for forgiveness for his church and his country? How would his ancestors view his apology statement? Some of them would turn in their graves for the event, but most of them would breathe sighs of relief.

He was saying, though he might not have been cognizant of it at the time, exactly what the descendants of the victims truly wanted to hear at the time and even today. Many had not healed; we know the trauma lingers on. During visits to the slave castles, these shrines, you could still see the pain in their faces, hear the grief in their voices and notice the trauma in their lives.

The Archbishop sounded very erudite and compassionate in his apology speech. If only men of such character, of such kindness and conviction had been alive during the era of the slave trade, we probably would have been talking about a different kind of history today. Unfortunately, he lived three to four centuries too late. But one could not but admire the forces that goaded him on to utter those noble and memorable words.

He realized the collective guilt of his country, and was tired of dragging this heavy burden of guilt from the past from one generation to the next. He wanted to put to rest forever the stain in the history of his church from the slave trade past.

"Well, we have finally arrived at the historic moment—or the time which the Africans have anxiously waited for—though some people have continued to still go down the old path of denial of wrongdoing—the time for some sort of apotheosis," King Gizenga said.

"The time has come for the descendants of those who'd wronged the sons and daughters of Mama Africa to step up to the table of accountability and redeem the memory of the ancestors and purge their own conscience in the process," the African griot remarked.

"For all the enormous injustices against our people in the past, the African ancestors expect more than verbal apology, no matter how sentimental or how much soul-searching has gone into it," the king told his subjects. "They must follow these soothing sugar-coated words of apology with some concrete deeds."

"Why several people are rendering apologies on behalf of their countries, churches or organizations and pouring their souls over the sordid past of the slave trade and plantation slavery, no one can adequately explain," the griot remarked pointedly. "Why are they doing this at this point in history?"

"At least it is a step in the right direction, wouldn't you agree with me on that?" the queen mother asked.

"They have, however, failed to mention what the African people really want to hear—atonement—put Africa and the people of African descent back on the road of prosperity," the king said. "It would help the healing process of the people, particularly the so-called former African Slave Coast and the entire African continent in general."

Africans might forgive the slave trade, even grant the reconciliation, but they would never ever forget the tragedy.

It would have been logical for him to go beyond the sweet words of apology and start a movement for some form of atonement for the victims, measures that will be atonement for the role his people had played in the ugly, historical drama.

Hasn't it been established in history that, beside the coal, the technology and resources that the British had, that they'd used some of the proceeds from the slave trade to spark off the Industrial Revolution, which, among other things, catapulted Britain into the forefront of prosperous nations that spread to other European nations later.

How many people remember that for several centuries, the economies of English cities such as Birmingham, Liverpool, Bristol, Manchester and even London were heavily predicated on the European slave trade to Africa, therefore, on the miseries and sufferings of the people inside an unhappy and unfortunate continent.

The records attest to the fact that in the British parliamentary debates, constituents lobbied some parliamentarians to ensure the continuity of the European slave trade to Africa. They asked their members to derail efforts to abolish the slave trade in order to prevent the total economic collapse of those English cities that based their economies heavily on gun-making, boat-building and commercial-banking activities.

The noble clergyman chose the path of reconciliation through dialogue between his faith and the ill-feelings among the African people over the sordid past. We have to reiterate that it would have been easy for him to choose the path of denial, or the path of blaming the victims as has been the case for centuries. But he chose the path of righteousness and magnanimity, the mark of a true visionary leadership in these changing times.

As for Africans, he has become an icon, and in the eyes of several progressive peoples across the globe a role model. He has chosen to confront the dark pain in his nation's history and to ask for forgiveness on behalf of his church, his country and his continent in general.

The people of Africa and the people of African descent who live in the Diaspora must respond to his pleas favorably and positively. His legacy to the future generation must be etched in magnanimity and altruism.

The same sort of guilt that the Archbishop of Canterbury felt had plagued the descendants of the Old South in America for centuries. Some of the descendants have felt the heavy burden of guilt that they still harbor over the past as well. They were tired of the profane in their past, a burden they'd inherited from generation to generation, and so they want to be free from this heavy burden.

We must recall the equally noble utterances of the members of the powerful Southern Baptist Convention a decade ago. It would have been easy for the members of this vital church to continue defending slavery, which was the historic role of the church for centuries. They played this role fervently in the annals of Southern history. They provided the religious ammunition to defend an institution, which was the bedrock of the lost cause of the region.

In the late nineteen nineties, however, the leadership of the Southern Baptists apologized for slavery on behalf of the Old and the New South at their convention. This was a dramatic reversal of role for one of the most powerful institutions in the South that vigorously defended and strengthened the institution of slavery in the past.

Maybe, the church leaders know the slave trade and slavery legacies were troubling. They could hear the voices of the slaves from the slave ships singing the Blues, and hear the slaves pleading for mercy on the plantations. They could hear the cracking of the whip coming down mercilessly. And they could see the whip tearing off the flesh from the backs of some slaves. Maybe, they could hear the dogs chasing runaway slaves deeper and deeper into the marshes. They could also see the North intruding on their hallowed grounds telling them how to run their lives, a request that forced the region to explode in a tragic cataclysmic inferno.

Though the apology sounded well intentioned, it stopped short of any mention of atonement for the profane past. How could the sons and daughters of Mama Africa die in vain without any atonement for their labor and for the lives lost? Though these Southern Baptist Churches had opened their doors to several people of African descent in an admirable way, can we say, with conviction, that this church is truly remorseful for the slavery past? But without any mention of atonement for the pain and suffering of the victims, how can we be doubly sure of the genuineness of the remorse?

Furthermore, how could the slave traders who had wrecked so much havoc on Africa in the past, those who had destroyed an entire civilization over the span of nearly four centuries, ask for forgiveness without any atonement to the descendants of the victims, the Africans of the so-called former Slave Coast?

It was the African blood and sweat that helped them in the New World. But this help has led to the continued suffering of the continent and this has been over many centuries.

It is not necessary to ask other bodies to intercede on behalf of Africa. Or could the church do something for the continent and for those Africans who live in the Diaspora as a result of the European slave trade to Africa?

Should these become legal issues for third parties to arbitrate?

An expedition to the continent, a goodwill gesture, with red roses showing remorse and packages of atonement would be the right thing to do. If the delegation land on the continent, the two sides would dialogue over the past—the delegation would offer the terms of atonement, talk about helping the people to rise out of the ashes of the profane past.

The Africans would hear the apologies. They would see the sincerity in their eyes and feel their remorse. But if they have no intention of making atonement, then the mission would more than likely end on a sour note—the inability to accept liability—lack of sincerity—no reconciliation.

For all the youths that'd perished in the tragedy and did so for centuries, now you would be appeased and atoned for.

Though the United States Congress gave its verbal apology, it made no mention of atonement. The world admired, though centuries belated, how the US House of Representatives and the United States Senate, on different occasions, passed apology resolutions for slavery. The words were noble and the intentions were magnanimous. Who would not admire these noble gestures from these two most powerful and august bodies in the world?

Admittedly, these measures had been impossible a few decades ago. Those were the years of modern Jim Crow laws. That was the time when some powerful voices were still singing tunes of eternal segregation if not in the whole country, at least in some parts of the South.

This fact makes the resolutions of apology even much more dramatic, and much more epochal, if not earth shattering.

The words of apology by these two august bodies, however, had been very carefully selected and meticulously framed to avoid any acceptance of wrongdoing, or any semblance of culpability, liability or responsibility for damages stemming from the slavery past.

Though the apology gesture was a step in the right direction, how do these empty words appease the departed ancestors? How do we appease Mother Nature and prevent her from displaying her wrath, or vengeance on behalf of the victims?

They knew their ancestors were wrong. They knew they caused slaves to die on the cotton fields or to drown at the bottom of the Atlantic Ocean. How could the Oburonis and their descendants stop the wrath of the African ancestors or the angry African gods from going on the offensive?

Doubtlessly, the centuries of slave trading and plantation labor yielded huge lucrative profits for the slave holders and the slave dealers. The proceeds had sustained businesses, supported national economies and sustained even royal dynasties. It had also impacted global economies; perhaps it did so more than any other single venture in global history.

Bubba confronted the dark fears he'd inherited in his heritage—blood on his hands, old antebellum mansions swarming with and haunted by evil spirits, He cherished his heritage. He took pride in its past, and he especially cherished the Protestant fundamentalist mores of his region. But his fears and guilty conscience constantly tormented him till he decided to meet these forces head-on.

Reverend Peterson felt the same forces, but he became several pounds lighter when he offered the words of apology and then spelled out the terms of atonement before the king and the rest of the chiefs.

It was an unforgettable moment, standing on those hallowed grounds and doing the right thing.

None of the delegation members denied that it was African sweat and blood that created the foundation on which the European and then American ascendancy to material greatness stood or continues to stand today.

But the five hundred billion dollar question has always been why if you have apologized for slavery and admitted wrongdoing or responsibility for this profane part of your history, why have you stopped at the apology level? Why have you not done anything to help the continent which had once helped you to become the envy of the world?

Why can't you help Africa rise up from the ashes of slavery? Or why won't you appease the ancestors in order to avoid the wrath of the angry ancestors of Africa?

As for the Africans on the continent and those who live in the Diaspora, though the slave trade and plantation slavery were in the past, the wounds from the past are still visible today. They are scars that have never healed nor disappeared. The pain, suffering, chaos and insecurity continue to today.

How could you turn your backs on the inhabitants of this unfortunate continent that once helped you achieve your economic dreams of greatness? Or who enjoys watching the offspring of Mama Africa, who were forced to live in the Diaspora to continue to suffer and to live in abject poverty even though they live in some of the richest countries in the world today?

Then, the truth is that the angry spirits of the departed victims are still roaming in the doldrums, still looking for their reward. They have run out of time and have started down the warpath of vengeance. Could atonement for the past calm down the wrath of Mother Nature, as the Africans believe? Recent events have left some signs of what Mother Nature is capable of doing, but the opportunity to end her wrath and bring peace still exists. At this dramatic moment in history, the chance for peace still exists across America and the rest of the world. The good thing is that many people are revisiting old relationships and making changes to past paradigms. How long this window of opportunity would remain open, no one knows. The past cannot continue to be swept under the rug anymore, the forward looking people told the audience, wondering if . . . probably the spirits behind these disasters could be appeased and calmed down.

If it is peace and quiet in the land that you wanted, why have you not done the right thing to bring these about? Why have you not tried to soothe the angry spirits on the high seas, in the forests, on the shores and on the plantations?

The past continues to follow all those involved like a dark shadow. Like all dark forces, it brings all sorts of havoc in its trail. Your guilty conscience would continue to trouble you and your descendants from generation to generation, and at every turn in history.

Africa is still suffering from the wounds of the past. For this unfortunate continent, the history of the profane is indelible and forever fresh in the memories of its perennial progeny. But you can change that trend. You can reverse all that with atonement.

The lingering stigma of inferiority complex that the slave traders had created inside our psyche still exists today. Do you also realize how much the slave trade and slavery have tainted the image of the African continent globally?

The habit of shifting the blame for the tragic slave trade onto the shoulders of the African victims, the old strategy that you have used for centuries, has done nothing but simply postponed the inevitable, delaying the day of reckoning for this horrible tragedy.

The empty words of apology have done nothing to appease the ancestors of Africa. These are mere perfunctory words that contain no actionable plans for helping Africa and its victims to heal. They have done nothing to calm down the spirits of the African victims.

The descendants of Mama Africa, those who have been victimized and traumatized for centuries and still bear the scars of the past, have heard nothing but carefully chosen sarcastic rhetoric masked with thin veneers of remorse. They have no plans for atonement.

How could the African people begin to heal, if you do not help to set us on the path to do so?

Though you have forgotten and might never remember what your ancestors did, the past continues to follow the descendants of the victims everywhere they go. Whether in Africa or in the Diaspora, in Canada, across the Old South in the United States, in Europe, in the Caribbean or even all the way in Brazil, the past has been obstructive and degrading.

There has been some gradual progress in the New American South. But even in this New South, in many southern cities, the past is still holding the present a hostage. The issues from the past are still as fresh today as if some of them had happened only yesterday.

It is not enough that Dr. Martin Luther King's blood was shed in a city like Memphis some decades ago. His sacred blood has still not cleansed the city of the evils of the profane past. The history lives on, the anger of the ancestors continues. The guilt from the past still lingers on in notoriety. What are the descendants of the former slaveholders going to do to end the heavy burden of guilt still dangling around their necks?

Racial matters continue to plague Memphis and many other cities. These issues dominate many facets of life. Whether it is housing, jobs and even education, race becomes the deciding factor in many issues. What the parties involved must do to unite the races and wipe away the vestiges of the profane past, which still hang like a dark cloud in the sky of this legendary, fun-loving and musical city, is still up in the air today.

These are problems with no easy solutions, though we have several capable hands on both sides of the divide applying their political ingenuity to battle these problems. Maybe they could come up with some more holistic solutions to these problems.

Though the regions are undergoing rapid changes, the race issue is still like a taboo subject that hangs over several cities and in many countries. It is like a huge, dark curtain that people make conscious efforts to pretend that they don't see, but all across the nation people know that race is a factor.

But how could you become oblivious to the racial tension in the air, the chaos in the streets and to the confusion in the schools when it is so obvious and so glaring? How could you not hear the political dialogues that are clothed in garments of racism, coming from all sides of the divide?

It is paradoxical that the racism has not destroyed the city or the region completely, though we can say that it is impeding meaningful progress in many areas. Whether white, yellow, brown and African, all those who continue to live in this historic city, do experience some racism.

But all the parties can take advantage of the dawning of a new day in history and make some sort of atonement for this tragedy and end the heavy burden of guilt from this sordid past.

This generation must decide to address the unresolved past in a concrete manner. They must do something special for Africa, especially for those who still inhabit the former so-called African Slave Coast, where the bulk of the Africans who live in the Diaspora came from. We are talking about countries such as Nigeria, Cameroon, Gabon, Congo, Benin, Togo, Ghana, Ivory Coast, Liberia, Guinea, Mali, Gambia, Senegal Sierra Leone and the others.

Overwhelmed and overpowered by cannons, several technologically superior muskets, the inhabitants of Africa, especially those who lived on the former Slave Coast tried for years to rise up from the ashes of slavery and from the state of near annihilation. As for the perpetual stigma of slavery, who can remove that badge if not those who imposed it on the continent?

Definitely, some forms of compensation oozing out of the pockets of the descendants of the former slave traders would go a long way to ease Africa's problems. It might stop the pain and end the stagnation.

These descendants must rise to the occasion and do the right thing for the descendants of the Africans in the Diaspora and then do something to appease the people of Africa who still live on the continent in the aftermath of the past.

Remember the gods of Africa are still angry. Remember that the ancestors are watching you closely. But the good news is that they are still open for reconciliation—atonement.

Finally, if you want to live in peace, if you want to let go of this heavy burden of guilt, why wouldn't you pacify the angry gods of Africa?